BETWEEN TERROR AND TOURISM

AN OVERLAND JOURNEY ACROSS NORTH AFRICA

MICHAEL MEWSHAW

COUNTERPOINT
BERKELEY

Library of Congress Cataloging-in-Publication Data

Mewshaw, Michael, 1943-

Between terror and tourism : an overland journey across North Africa / by Michael Mewshaw.

p. cm.

ISBN 978-1-58243-434-6

1. Africa, North—Description and travel. 2. Mewshaw, Michael, 1943—-Travel—Africa, North. 3. Africa, North—Social conditions. 4. Africa, North—Politics and government. 5. Social conflict—Africa, North. 6. Islam—Social aspects—Africa, North. I. Title.

DT165.2.M49 2010

916.104'5—dc22

2009042027

Cover design by Black Eye Design

Interior design by Tabitha Lahr

Printed in the United States of America

COUNTERPOINT

2117 Fourth Street

Suite D

Berkeley, CA 94710

www.counterpointpress.com

Distributed by Publishers Group West

10 9 8 7 6 5 4 3 2 1

This book is dedicated to James Dyke and Helen Porter, who have been generous with help and hospitality over many years.

CONTENTS

Many Egyptian cities may you visit

that you may learn, and go on learning, from their sages.

Always in your mind keep Ithaca.

To arrive there is your destiny.

But do not hurry your trip in any way.

Better that it last for many years;

that you drop anchor at the island an old man,

rich with all you've gotten along the way,

not expecting Ithaca to make you rich.

—From "Ithaca," by C.P. Cavafy

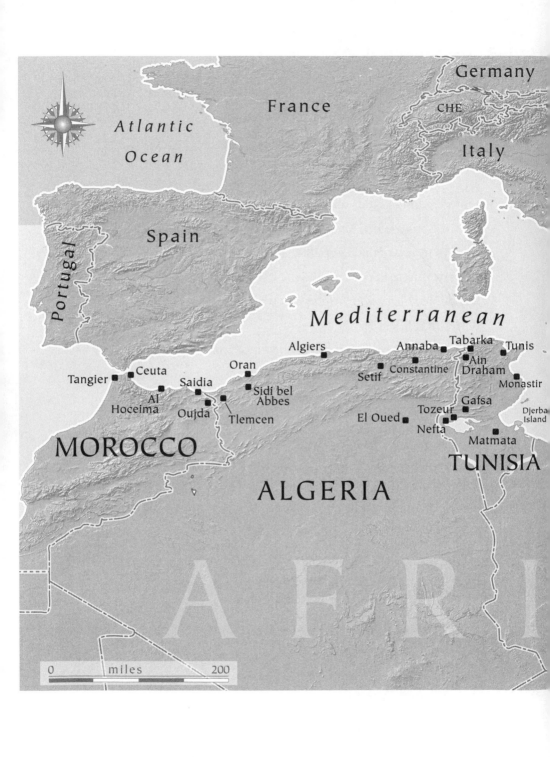

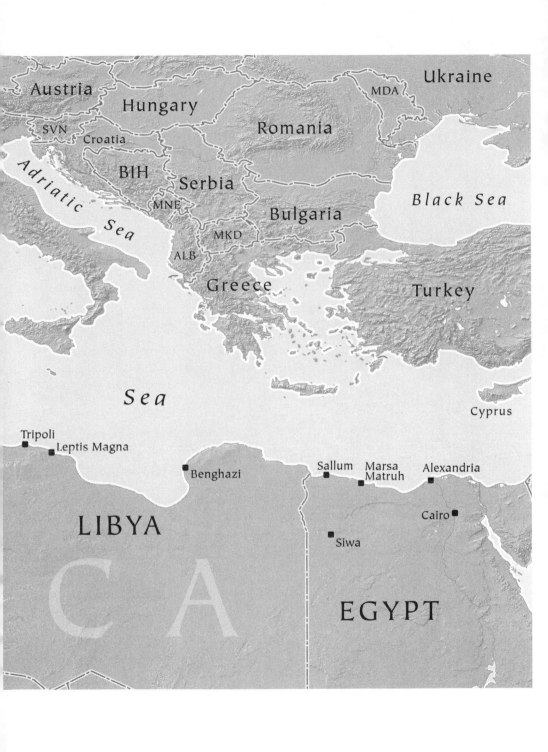

PREFACE

When my family and friends learned that I intended to travel overland from Alexandria, Egypt, to Tangier, Morocco, they reacted with incredulity. My wife, Linda, and adult sons, Sean, 33, and Marc, 28, seemed to think that I was suffering from senile dementia. A three-month, twenty-one-hundred-mile trip that would take me through Libya, Tunisia and Algeria struck them as too difficult and too dangerous.

Even casual acquaintances expressed deep concern and offered advice about U.S. Embassy contacts, armed bodyguards and Global Positioning Systems. Suddenly everyone was an expert. People who had never set foot in North Africa—especially those who had no firsthand knowledge of North Africa—regarded the entire southern tier of the Mediterranean as one long, turbulent strip of radical Islamicism, and they quoted news accounts about Egyptian terrorists having attacked tour groups in Luxor and Sharm El Sheikh, killing dozens.

Libya, ruled by Moamar Qaddafi—"the mad dog of the Middle East," in Ronald Reagan's words—was still infamous for a litany of atrocities, the bombing of Pan Am 103 over Lockerbie, Scotland, primary among them. Although the country had just emerged from two decades of UN, U.S. and European sanctions, it sometimes reverted to the behavior of a rogue state: flouting international law, abusing its own citizens and expelling and occasionally imprisoning foreigners. While it courted tourists, it wouldn't permit them to travel anywhere in the country without an official guide and a preapproved itinerary.

Pictured in brochures as an Eden of peace and beauty, tiny Tunisia had had troubles too. In 2002, on its resort island of Djerba, a truck bomb killed nineteen people at one of the country's last functioning synagogues. More recently, Tunisian troops had had a shootout with a regional branch of Al Qaeda, and a terrorist band had kidnapped two Austrian tourists and held them for ransom.

As for Algeria, the country had become synonymous with Islamic fundamentalism and sectarian violence. Over the past fifteen years, two hundred thousand people had died in an undeclared civil war between an autocratic government and a shifting cast of insurgent groups. Vast tracts of the country had degenerated into killing fields, and foreign diplomats and businessmen huddled in fortified bunkers. Paris, London and Rome were only a couple of hours away by plane, but conditions in the country remained largely unknown, particularly in the United States, because Algerian terrorists targeted journalists.

Morocco boasted friendly relations with America and promoted itself as Europe's winter playground. Luxury hotels, condominium developments and golf courses had cropped up in remote oases, along ancient caravan routes. Yet here, too, there had been riots and suicide bombings. Terrorist cells had killed dozens in Casablanca during coordinated attacks in 2004, and a band of Moroccan immigrants in Spain had planted the bombs that killed almost two hundred that year on Madrid's commuter trains.

While the geopolitical background to my trip was chaotic, even the basic facts about border crossings and road conditions seemed uncertain. U.S. Embassy officials in Egypt advised me that the frontier with Libya was theoretically open, but nobody knew of any American or European who had tried to cross it. State Department employees had had personal experience of driving west into Tunisia, but they could tell me nothing of the five-hundred-mile stretch between the Egyptian border and the Libyan capital of Tripoli.

The U.S. public affairs officer in Tunis urged me to submit a precise itinerary and to alert her by cell phone as soon as I entered the country. Yet I had no precise itinerary and no intention of bringing a cell phone or a BlackBerry. This was a practical, not a philosophical, decision. I'm computer illiterate and don't like traveling with any device, even a camera, that comes between me and direct contact with my whereabouts. Then, too, I knew from previous trips that nothing marks you as a tourist and target in Africa more than carrying expensive equipment.

Algeria was the country that caused the greatest consternation. U.S. Embassy personnel warned me that the northeast region was unsafe and that overland travel from the Tunisian border to the capital, Algiers, should be avoided at all costs.

Through contacts in Rome, I hired an Algerian fixer who promised to meet me at the frontier and drive me to Algiers. These same contacts said that the fixer was rumored to work for the Algerian secret service. This seemed plausible when the fixer sent word before I arrived that he had read a review of a book about Algeria I had written in *The Washington Post*. If I didn't take greater care with the views I expressed, he added, I could expect to be followed throughout the country. On balance, being followed seemed to me no bad thing, and I assumed that anyone I hired would probably be forced to file some kind of report.

An executive with a nongovernmental organization based in Oran told me that although he had never traveled in the northeastern part of the country, he routinely drove back and forth to Algiers, through what had been dubbed the Triangle of Death in the darkest days of the Islamic insurrection. He thought I'd be safe on my own in the northwestern provinces. But he warned that the border with Morocco was closed and uncrossable by anybody except smugglers.

I processed this contradictory information and conjecture as little more than elevator music: inescapable, slightly annoying but of no consequence. I meant to go ahead with my plan. Nothing could dissuade me. To those who asked "Why?" I replied, "Why not?" To those who demanded "a real answer," I replied that I didn't understand why anyone would *not* want to travel across North Africa on a grand, sweeping passage through legendary cities, each with its deep historic and literary associations. I looked forward to Lawrence Durrell's and E.M. Forster's and C.P. Cavafy's Alexandria; André Gide's Tunisia and Algeria; Albert Camus' Algiers and Oran; and Paul Bowles's Tangier. From the Nile delta to the Pillars of Hercules, where the Mediterranean empties into the Atlantic, my itinerary would pass through alluvial swamps teeming with wild birds; battlegrounds dating from antiquity to World War II and contemporary border skirmishes; ruins of Roman and Greek empires, preserved in desert sand; pilgrimage sites revered by Jews, Christians and Muslims; vertiginous mountain ranges inhabited by bellicose tribes; and vast, unspoiled expanses of the Mediterranean, once celebrated by Homer and now by hyperventilating travel agents.

I didn't argue with those who insisted that North Africa was a Petri dish of dictatorial regimes, angry impoverished peoples and hostile religious fanatics. I simply observed that if Islamic terrorism is the most pressing international problem facing the West, if the world truly suffers from a clash of civilizations, what writer wouldn't want to witness and record events firsthand?

I wasn't a war junkie; I didn't have a death wish. I wasn't going to Iraq or Afghanistan. I was traveling to a region where I had a grasp of the countries' second languages, French, Italian and Spanish. In addition to my U.S. passport, I had an Irish one, through my maternal grandmother, and I assumed this would ease my way in spots where Americans weren't so welcome.

For the past decade, I have rented a winter house on Key West, an island that refers to itself as Paradise. But however heavenly it may be, a two-by-four-mile scrap of land can get boring, and while I had no desire to forsake it forever or trade it in for hell, I was ready for something edgier, a challenge. At the end of the day, I suppose my trip to North Africa had to do with . . . the end of the day. Having started my career with a coming-of-age novel, I was dealing with a different coming of age. I had just turned sixty-five and was a senior citizen, a card-carrying member of Social Security and Medicare. Much as I didn't like to dwell on it, the issue was unavoidable: If I didn't make the trip now, I might not get another chance. And there was no denying that I felt I had something to prove—to myself if nobody else.

When I was younger, I needed no such excuse. I just went. I moved to be moving, for the pleasures of "merely circulating," as poet Wallace Stevens wrote. I hit the road at seventeen and haven't stopped since. If anything, I've grown more restless with age and still don't own a home or have a permanent address. For me and for my work, travel is a need as urgent as oxygen.

Before I left Key West on a series of flights to Atlanta, then Rome, Athens and Alexandria, my sister Karen phoned to say good-bye. She mentioned that she had seen a movie, *Into the Wild*, that reminded her of me. She suggested that I see it.

I already had. I'd read the book, too—the story of a fellow in his twenties who, spurred by ecstasy and neurosis, abandoned his home and family and surrendered himself to an incessant quest. He ended up in the Alaskan wilderness, marooned in a wrecked school bus, slowly starving to death on a diet of roots and berries.

"Age aside," Karen said, "are you that guy? Don't get me wrong, Mike, but are you really ready for this trip?"

"I'm headed for North Africa, not the Arctic. There are plenty of hotels and food and doctors where I'm going."

"That's not the question. Do you know what you're getting into?"

"Absolutely."

But her call gave me pause. While I didn't see myself falling apart or going haywire, I knew I might blunder off course into a sick-bed. Over the decades, I've sometimes had to be hospitalized while traveling. In 1968, on the Paris Metro, I flung out a hand to stop a door from shutting and wound up with twenty-six stitches in my wrist. I then suffered a feverish reaction to French tetanus serum, and my scar oozed glass splinters for the next month.

Years later, in Paris again, I was knocked flat by an infection and spent a week in the American Hospital. Then, during a 2001 rail trip through South Africa, I suffered such severe nausea and breath-lessness that I had to be removed from the Blue Train and rushed to a clinic in Johannesburg. I thought I had food poisoning, but to my shock, I was confined to an intensive care cardiac unit, with a resting pulse rate of 138 and a heart wracked by atrial fibrillation.

Doctors prescribed medication that managed the condition until 2003 when on a trip to San Antonio, Texas, I slipped into arrhythmia again. An alert cardiologist attached jumper cables—actually, a defibrillator—to my chest and jolted my heart back into a regular beat. But a month later, in Miami, I had to undergo a catheter ablation, a procedure in which an electrical charge zapped the arrhythmic areas of my heart. This, along with beta blockers, had kept me on an even keel for the past five years.

My most disturbing episode of ill health occurred in Laos dur-ing a boat ride down the Mekong River. On the advice of a doctor in the States, I had dosed myself with the anti-malarial medication Lar-ium. Too late I learned that the drug's possible side effects include severe depression, suicidal ideation and psychosis. For hours I lay stunned on the boat's throbbing deck. The odd foray ashore did little to relieve the despair that alternated with my panic. At every village Hmong tribesmen dashed out of the jungle, selling jars of pickled snakes and scorpions.

Among the other passengers there was, providentially, an American woman who recognized my symptoms and told me to throw away the Larium. A psychologist, she kindly listened to my gibberish for the next two days, and by the time we disembarked, I was as normal as I've ever been.

So as I packed for North Africa, I made space in my two small bags for Lomotil for diarrhea and Phenergan for vomiting; a statin to regulate my cholesterol; an anti-inflammatory in case my aching back flared up; Atenolol for my heart; and Prozac for my depression. All these and an extra pair of glasses, and I was set.

In early April, on the flight to Rome, I read Shirley Hazzard's novel *The Transit of Venus*, and several of its sentences found their way into my notebook. "Men go through life telling themselves a moment must come when they will show what they're made of. And the moment comes, and they do show. And they spend the rest of their days explaining that it was neither the moment nor the true self."

This was my moment. I was convinced of that. But was I the man?

ALEXANDRIA

The Chinese sage Lao Tzu remarked centuries ago that the longest journey commences with a single step. But on this particular trip, I'd be hard-pressed to pinpoint when my foot first hit the pavement. I had been thinking about the project for years and arranging visas, travel permissions and transportation for six months. Yet these were mere preludes, stumbles toward the starting block: Alexandria.

Arriving in Athens at 10:30 PM, I learned that the flight to Alexandria had been postponed until 2:30 AM. If we had no further delays, I'd reach my hotel at daybreak; not the most propitious start, but good practice for the vagaries of North Africa.

My fellow passengers all appeared to be Egyptians, returning from Europe with curios and souvenirs in string bags and cardboard boxes. Like me, they seemed frazzled and exhausted as they shuffled through the gauntlet of metal detectors, passport controls and X-ray machines, juggling hand luggage, boarding cards, tickets, loose change and shoes. The security guards in Athens were an officious bunch, testy to a man and contemptuous of the Egyptians, whom they frisked and interrogated, shoved and assaulted with sword-length electronic wands.

I'll concede that in the squinty eyes of a prejudiced airport profiler, this might look like a planeload of terrorists. Most men were turbaned and bearded, their foreheads darkened by *zebibahs*, or prayer bumps, from pressing their brows to the ground five times a day. The guards treated the women as if their ample burnooses and veils were designed to conceal a machine gun or belt of Semtex. While it was true that the passengers displayed a bewilderment that might have been mistaken for truculence, and they had names that must have set the computerized watch list shrilling, the guards overdid it with their rough hands and sneering disdain.

Then it was my turn to be patted down, chided for not having removed my watch and grilled about my destination. As the conveyor belt trundled my carry-on through the X-ray machine, a guard ordered me to open the bag and empty every zippered compartment. No point in protesting that I had already done this three times today. I showed him my transparent sack of liquid containers, then waited while he pawed through my shaving kit.

"What's this?" he demanded in English.

"A nail clipper."

He fingered the tip of the tiny file and said, "Knife."

He was about to chuck it into the discard bin when I stopped him and snapped off the file. "Okay?" I asked.

His brow furrowed in disappointment. He dropped the nail clipper into my shaving kit, resumed pawing, then broke into a smile and again said, "Knife." Now he held up a pair of scissors with plastic handles and flimsy blades less than an inch long. I had bought them expressly because they met international security standards. They had passed screenings in the U.S., Europe, Africa and Asia. They had passed Italian security in Rome just hours ago. But the man insisted they violated European Union regulations and had to be confiscated.

Was it the late hour? The long flights and the delay? The abuse I had watched him heap on the Egyptians? I knew I should have shrugged and let the man have his bumptious way. But I also knew I was right and he was wrong. And I imagined that dozens of cowed passengers were watching and waiting to see whether petty tyranny or the rule of law would prevail.

"I'd like to speak to a supervisor," I said.

The supervisor was a schoolmarmish lady with a name tag on her bosom and a bun in her hair. She stood by her man, supporting him 110 percent. While she conceded that the scissors didn't violate EU regulations, she maintained that Athens airport followed a stricter code. I was free to take it or leave it. That is, take my scissors and leave the airport. Or leave my scissors and take the plane to Alexandria. I left the scissors, but before moving on, I leaned close, scribbling her name and employee number on my ticket.

As I proceeded down the chute that funneled us onto the plane, somebody shouted, "Meester, meester, one minute."

It was the supervisor, her heels hammering the metal floor. For an instant I thought she meant to apologize and give me back my scissors. Then I noticed a guard at her side, armed with a rifle.

"I need your name and passport number," she said.

"Why?"

"When there's an incident, we take the passenger's name."

"What incident?"

"The argument about the scissors. You took my name. Now I take yours."

"There was no argument. No incident." Abjectly, I surrendered my passport. "What does this mean? I'll be on a no-fly list?"

"That's not my decision. I just keep the records." She jabbed the passport back into my hand and clattered up the chute in her high heels.

After that, I'd like to say that my flight to Alexandria went smoothly. But even in the absence of air turbulence, I had a bumpy ride. I made the mistake of reading the *Lonely Planet* guide to Egypt, and it began with a discouraging general assessment of the national situation. After twenty-five years of President Hosni Mubarak's rule, the guidebook declared, "Egypt is in a pretty bad state. Unemployment is rife (some analysts put it as high as 25 percent, the government bandies around the figure of 9.9 percent), the economy is of the basket-case variety and terrorist attacks are starting to occur with worrying regularity."

As for Mubarak's "lousy human rights record," *Lonely Planet* noted that Amnesty International and Human Rights Watch "excoriate Egypt year after year, asserting that the media and judiciary are allowed no real independence and that police regularly abuse their legislative right to unlimited powers of search and arrest . . . Egyptian police regularly torture and ill-treat prisoners in detention . . . and scores of members of Islamist opposition groups are regularly imprisoned without charge or trial."

The guidebook added that Mubarak, in defense of his regime, had pointed out that the United States held hundreds of Islamic detainees at Guantanamo and at secret prisons or black sites in compliant countries around the world. While not acknowledging that his country was one of those black sites and that his security forces were alleged to have tortured suspected terrorists at the behest of the Americans, Mubarak said, "We were right from the beginning in using all means, including military tribunals, to combat terrorism."

Mubarak demanded whether Egyptians would prefer that their "moderate democracy" (*sic* on both scores) go the way of Lebanon, Gaza or, God forbid, Algeria. In this region, Algeria was everybody's bogeyman.

Under U.S. pressure to open up the political process, Mubarak allowed a slightly fairer election in 2005. But when eighty-eight members of the Muslim Brotherhood won seats in Parliament, America ratcheted back its rhetoric about the virtues of democracy. As critics remarked, the United States tended to lose interest in free elections when the "wrong" candidates prevailed.

Switching from the *Lonely Planet* to that day's *New York Times*, I read an article headlined "Day of Angry Protests Stuns Egypt." It described a country in turmoil—abandoned roads, shuttered businesses and brigades of riot police mobilized to stamp out a nationwide strike. Many Egyptians had stayed away from work and school to protest the rising price of bread and basic foodstuffs. Hardly limited to the working class, this movement had spread to doctors, lawyers, journalists. According to reports, the protests had nothing to do with religious fanaticism or regime change. Egyptians didn't demand democracy or human rights. They had had little experience of either. They were simply desperate for economic survival in a society where professionals with twenty years of experience earned 80 U.S. dollars a month.

My plane smacked down at 4 AM, and as it taxied at high speed across the runway, passengers bounded to their feet and fumbled their belongings from the overhead racks. Nothing the flight attendant or the pilot said could persuade them to sit down and buckle up. It was something I would witness again and again—the indomitable spirit of Egyptians, their cheerful disregard for any authority figure not carrying a gun. I admired their exuberance but didn't have the energy to emulate it. Sleepwalking, I collected my luggage, collapsed into a taxi and headed through the inky desert night toward town.

A sprawling conurbation with a population estimated at five million, Alexandria seemed to be under a wartime blackout. Cars blundered along with low beams or none at all. There were lampposts but no bulbs, neon signs but no fizz. Amid the blur of dun-colored apartment buildings, no window shined. I wondered if the cabbie had followed a fast track through a neighborhood that had been evacuated. Chunks of concrete and piles of debris dotted the streets, as if they were under construction. Or were they being demolished?

We swept to a stop at the celebrated Cecil Hotel on Midan Saad Zaghloul, a main square, the epicenter of Durrell's literary depiction of the city, *The Alexandria Quartet*. The hotel lobby and its potted palms lay beyond a metal detector, unmanned at this hour, perhaps on the assumption that terrorists sleep too. The snoozing desk clerk raised his head from the counter only long enough for me to register.

I was in my room unpacking when day broke, the *muezzin* called faithful Muslims to prayer and sunlight fell like a gold bar through the window onto a table topped by a paper arrow angled toward Mecca. I was soon lulled to sleep by the tide surging against rocks four stories below. Durrell had written that the sea with its "dim momentum in the mind is the fugue upon which this writing is made." For me the Mediterranean was amniotic fluid—no, a mild narcotic—that I trusted to sedate me for hours.

But all too early, the phone rang, and a perky voice asked, "Did I wake you?" It was a secretary at the American Center reminding me that I was scheduled to give a lecture tomorrow. "I also thought you might be interested in today's program at the Bibliotheca Alexandrina. Ibrahim Abdel Meguid—I'm sure you know his novels—is speaking to a group from the States. If you'd like to attend, please feel free."

I told her I'd be there and tried to get back to sleep. But the lullaby of the sea had been supplanted by the hotel's grumbling to life, groaning and creaking as guests flushed toilets, showered and rode the lumbering caged elevators down to breakfast. I didn't join them at the buffet. I was eager to explore the city.

Durrell had poetically evoked it, preserved it so lovingly in the sweet aspic of his purple prose, that droves of undergraduates still prowled the streets toting the *Quartet* as their guide. As a twenty-year-old I had read the four novels—*Justine, Balthazar, Mountolive* and *Clea*—and liberally cadged lines for letters I sent to impressionable coeds. Rereading *Justine* recently, I was stunned by the number of paragraphs that had remained lodged in my memory after forty-five years:

"Capitally, what is this city of ours? What is resumed in the word Alexandria? Five races, five languages, a dozen creeds: five fleets turning through their greasy reflections behind the harbor bar. But there are more than five sexes and only demotic Greek seems to distinguish among them. The sexual provender which lies to hand is staggering in its variety and profusion . . . Alexandria was the great winepress of love.

"Long sequences of tempura. Light filtered through the essence of lemons. An air full of brick-dust—sweet-smelling brick-dust and the odor of hot pavements slaked with water."

Passing through the hotel's metal detector and out the revolving door, I had no illusion that a winepress of love awaited me. Durrell's Alexandria didn't exist even in his day. As he described the place in a letter to his friend Henry Miller, it was a "steaming humid flatness—not a hill or mound anywhere—choking to the bursting point with bones and the crummy deposits of wiped out cultures. Then this smashed up broken down shabby Neapolitan town with its Levantine mounds of houses peeling in the sun . . . no music, no art, no real gaiety. A saturated middle European boredom laced with drink and Packards and beach cabins. No Subject of Conversation Except Money."

Three decades earlier, E.M. Forster had written even more dismissively of the contemporary city. In a preface to the 1922 edition of his *Alexandria: A History and a Guide*, he characterized the thousand years of the Arab Period as "of no importance." As for his own day, "the 'sights' of Alexandria are in themselves not interesting, but they fascinate when we approach them through the past. Alas! The modern city calls for no enthusiastic comment."

This made me want to defend Alexandria, to love it as a cockroach loves its ugly offspring. Seediness, shabbiness, loud crowds and pandemonium can have their appeal. The world would be poorer if every corner of the globe aped the orderliness of the United States and Europe. So what if the city's legendary past had disappeared under asphalt and broken bricks? You had to admire its survival instincts. Didn't you?

I was too preoccupied with my own survival to consider the question. On the Corniche, the coastal road and its waterfront walkway, I confronted eight lanes of hurtling, horn-blowing traffic. Billboards proclaimed Alexandria the CULTURAL CAPITAL OF THE ARAB WORLD IN 2008, and Durrell had written of "horse-drawn cabs ('carriages of love') which dawdled up and down the sea." But these days dawdling lovers would be crushed or asphyxiated by carbon monoxide.

According to urban legend four people are killed every day on this curving east-west drag strip. I could believe it. Crowds lined the curb in both directions, poised like hurdlers prepared to dart out and leap over fenders and bumpers whenever the cars and trucks and buses and taxis choked to a stop.

I made it to the median strip, bucked up my courage, then plunged on to the far side. The walkway was thick with pedestrians happy, like me, to have pulled through alive. But we had to watch where we stepped. The pavement had disintegrated into a checkerboard of cracked tiles, gravel pits, drains without grills and open ditches snaking with wires and pipes.

The wind and sea that Forster wrote were "as pure as when Menelaus . . . landed here 3,000 years ago," smelled now of sewers and rotting fish. Out in the harbor, under the gentle chocolate waves, lay the ruins of a metropolis designed by Alexander the Great and nourished to full glory by the Ptolemaic kings and queens. But seismic cataclysms had consigned that city to the deep in AD 365. This coast, like the rest of the littoral between Alexandria and Tangier, had always been a geological shatter zone, a landscape riven by fault lines and grinding tectonic plates. Over the millennia, earthquakes and tsunamis destroyed entire civilizations—and the remaking and unmaking of the region has continued to this day. Every so often, Atlas shrugged, mountains moved, and the sea reestablished itself where it pleased.

The Pharos, a lighthouse more than four hundred feet high and one of the Seven Wonders of the World, had served for seventeen centuries as the symbol of Alexandria and as a beacon for ships approaching the treacherous shores of Africa. It, too, had crumbled in stages, and now existed as shards on the seabed and as building blocks incorporated into the fifteenth-century Qait Bey fortress.

Two French archeologists, Jean-Yves Empereur and Franck Goddio, had vied in mapping and photographing a great trove of underwater treasures. Busts, statues, sphinxes and obelisks were dredged up and displayed. Entrepreneurial fishermen offered boat trips and diving expeditions to this ancient royal quarter and to what some scholars claim was Cleopatra's castle. But I wasn't tempted. I stayed on land and watched a team of brown fishermen in brown underpants drag empty nets out of the brown water. From what I'd read, harbor divers have to be disinfected to ward off skin diseases.

Braving the Corniche stampede again, I roved through neighborhoods where the clocks appeared to have stopped decades ago and the residents had regressed to village life in the dense mesh of the vast metropolis. In cafés, men without women smoked *sheesha* and played dominoes. In back lane shops women without men went about their daily rounds dressed in *hijabs*, or headscarves. Some wore the *niqab*, a veil that covered the face except for slits at the eyes. Children, dogs, cats and blowing plastic bags eddied around their feet.

On every corner a heap of rubble as high as a man's head blocked the street. I had my choice of scrambling over it or crawling across the hoods of parked cars. Usually I climbed the rubble. The cars were blisteringly hot and scalded my palms. Also, I found the piles fascinating as archeological middens, layered with stucco and filigree, bits of balustrades and iron balconies that had snapped off of buildings. It was a rare facade that hadn't shed its fretwork or patches of masonry, exposing raw bricks and spider webs of wiring. I now understood why Hollywood's version of *Justine* had been filmed In Tunis.

Alexandria differs from Italy, where the view generally improves the higher you raise your eyes. Looking up in Rome, for example, you'll catch glimpses of campaniles, graceful domes and palazzo ceilings that blaze with gold leaf angels gliding over famous mosaics. But in Alexandria, it was dangerous not to watch where you were going. You never knew when the sidewalk would yawn wide and swallow your shoe in a pothole or an uncovered sewer. Smart Egyptians sauntered down the center of the street where the footing was safer and there was nothing to dodge but traffic. I soon followed their example.

The unwritten rule—well, sometimes it's written prescriptively by book reviewers—is that travel writers must never sound disappointed. They must remain resolutely upbeat. Negativity, any hint of whininess, must be suppressed. Unless, of course, the Bad Trip is presented humorously. The British are best at this. Lose a leg to an alligator, stagger through the jungle bled white by leeches, starve to the brink of death in the desert, and all is well as long as you leave everybody laughing.

Yet I'll be honest. My first brush with Alexandria left me depressed. While I never expected to discover the sensual dream Durrell described, I had resisted the cynicism of a journalist friend who spoke of it as "strictly a twenty-four-hour town." Now I wondered how I'd last there for the week I had reserved at the Cecil. Maybe longer if the Libyans didn't hurry and grant me a visa.

At noon, men unscrolled carpets on the sidewalk, crouched and murmured their midday prayers. Careful not to step on their fingers, I backtracked to Midan Saad Zaghloul and traipsed past exhaust-spewing buses, taxis and trolleys to Café Trianon. A landmark in the city when it was a multicultural melting pot, not a poor Egyptian outpost, the Trianon had been one of C.P. Cavafy's favorite haunts. I had come here less for lunch than for a lift to my spirits and a connection to literary history.

Cavafy was a member of the Greek diaspora, a poet who was born and died in Alexandria (1863–1933) and whose career spanned much of the Cosmopolitan Era from the mid–nineteenth to the mid–twentieth century. A deeply learned man in classical Greek, he integrated the demotic language of the streets into his verses. His themes were loneliness, the vertiginous passage of time, the quicksilver nature of love and the spiraling history of Alex, as its citizens affectionately called it, from its ancient gods to the young boys he brought home to his bed. In a city where the past was ever present and also an augur of the future, Cavafy had, in the words of critic and translator Daniel Mendelsohn, a perspective that "allowed him to see history with a lover's eye, and desire with a historian's eye."

The Trianon today had a faded Art Deco interior, beige and brown walls, a stained wooden ceiling, four cobwebby chandeliers and a floor of scuffed grey linoleum. On the PA system, Louis Armstrong sang "What a Wonderful World." But I felt more in sync with Cavafy, who spent three decades of dreary employment in the Office of Public Works, plugging along in the Third Circle of Irrigation like a condemned soul out of Dante. Much as he might have yearned to travel to some other land, some other sea, he had no illusions of escaping. As one of his best known poems, "The City," concluded: "Don't bother to hope / for a ship, a route, to take you somewhere else; they don't exist. / Just as you've destroyed your life, here in this / small corner, so you've wasted it through all the world."

Then the waitress brought my food and the soundtrack switched to Jim Morrison's "Light My Fire." The coffee was strong, the yoghurt and honey delicious, the chicken sandwich fortifying. My blood sugar and spirits soared. When the bill arrived, with each item an Egyptian pound or two more expensive than listed on the menu, I didn't protest. Grateful to be feeling better, I paid at the cash register, where one fellow dug my change out of the drawer and a second handed it to me. In Egypt, there were never enough jobs to go around, yet everybody has a role to play.

Reinvigorated, I went in search of Cavafy's apartment. Like his drab professional life, it offered little indication of its owner's lyrical intelligence. Located on rue Lepsius, it used to have a brothel beneath it, prompting Cavafy to joke, "Where could I live better? Under me is a house of ill-repute, which caters to the needs of the flesh. Over there is a church, where sins are forgiven. And beyond is the hospital, where we die."

Though I always visit writers' houses, they strike me as melancholy places. They're like locust shells. The fragile shape endures, but the guts are gone, along with any sense of the singing, the cyclical sleep and joyous flight, the long underground burial followed by a short burst of brilliance. Now a museum, Cavafy's flat was spacious and bright, with two rooms decorated as he had left them. A friend of Cavafy's wrote that the place "reminded me of a secondhand furniture store," a hodgepodge of overstuffed chairs, Bokhara carpets and "tasteless turn-of-the-century vases." The other rooms were filled with random memorabilia, photos and portraits of the author, two death masks and photocopies of his manuscripts and editions of his books in glass display cases. On a nonstop tape, a husky female voice recited his poems in Greek.

All that appeared to be missing was . . . everything. Still, Cavafy's apartment had none of the bogusness of Karen Blixen's house in Nairobi, which is decorated with stage dressings and posters from the film version of *Out of Africa*. Nor was it thick with tourists and docents chatting about six-toed cats as is the Hemingway house in Key West. A guard let me in, locked the door behind me, and sagged into an upright chair in the hallway. After listening to Cavafy's verses day after day, he might have learned them by heart, but they no longer kept him awake. He nodded off and I had the museum to myself for an hour.

Much of that time I spent at a window surveying the ochre-colored neighborhood, the ant colony of activity on the street below and in the car park across the way. The car park's corrugated roof might have been a postmodern installation, a puckish exhibition of urban debris—broken plates, bald tires and cardboard boxes spattered with seagull shit.

I didn't need to wrack my mind for a suitable quote to mark the end of my visit. Cavafy's work lay under glass all around me, and a translation of "The God Abandons Anthony" provided today's text:

> Turn to the open window and look down
> To drink past all deceiving
> Your last dark rapture from the mystical throng
> And say farewell, farewell to Alexandria leaving.

Late that afternoon I made my way to the Bibliotheca Alexandrina for the lecture by Ibrahim Abdel Meguid, one of Egypt's foremost novelists. The setting struck me as fitting for a writer of his stature, and I welcomed the chance to meet him and visit this contemporary riff on Alexandria's "Mother" Library, built by Ptolemy I in the third century BC.

The original library contained a vast compendium of the world's—that is, the Greek world's—corpus of knowledge. With more than three quarters of a million volumes, it had been the greatest center of classical learning of its time. Under the auspices

of the Mouseion, its umbrella institution, the library supplied resources to Archimedes and Euclid, who dedicated themselves to
geometry and physics; Aristarchus, who discovered that the earth
revolved around the sun; and Eratosthenes, who calculated the circumference of the globe.

But in literature, as Forster fumed, "The palace provided the
funds and called the tune . . . Victory odes, Funeral dirges, Marriage
hymns, jokes, genealogical trees, medical prescriptions, mechani-
cal toys, maps, engines of war: whatever the Palace required it had
only to inform the Mouseion, and the subsidized staff set to work at
once. The poets and scientists there did nothing that would annoy
the Royal family and not much that would puzzle it, for they knew
that if they failed to give satisfaction they would be expelled from the
enchanted area, and have to find another patron or starve."

Gradually, the glory that was Greek classicism dwindled in Alexandria to work that Forster judged "had no lofty aims. It was not
interested in ultimate problems nor even in problems of behavior,
and it attempted none of the higher problems of art. To be graceful or pathetic or learned or amusing or indecent, and in any case
loyal—this sufficed."

The decline continued into the fourth century AD, when Christians began to shove the Pagans aside. Appalled by what they
considered to be the library's licentious contents, the Christians
destroyed the building, burned its books and constructed a monastery on the site.

It was doubtful that these cautionary events dimly occurred
to the UNESCO fundraisers and Egyptian cultural mavens who in
1987 decided to reincarnate the "Mother" Library. They viewed their

project as a move to put Alexandria back on the cultural map, with the Bibliotheca as "the world's window on Egypt and Egypt's window on the world." An impressive structure of glass and metal, it was shaped to resemble a radiant half-sun shimmering behind an infinity pool. As I approached, a team of men sidestepped up its slanted facade, pushing floor polishers that buffed the library to a handsome gleam.

Inside, the brilliance dimmed, the air was chill and the stacks had curiously few books. It opened in 2002 with shelf space for eight million volumes, but it held just 540,000, most of them in Arabic or English. Only 10 percent were in other languages and none in Hebrew. There were, however, plenty of computer terminals. One local expatriate characterized the Bibliotheca as "just a big Internet café, bloody elitist and too expensive for locals to get in."[1]

The conference room reserved for Ibrahim Abdel Meguid's lecture looked out through blue-tinted glass to the greasy harbor and a crumble of biscuit-colored islands. It occurred to me that the metaphor about the library's being a window on the world and vice versa was unfortunate. Whether you turned outward or inward, there wasn't much to see.

Justin Siberell, the U.S. consul and director of the American Center, welcomed me to Alex and introduced me to Dr. Sahar Hamouda, deputy director of the Alexandria Mediterranean Center. She invited me to return to the library in two days to talk with her about the city's Cosmopolitan Era. Then I joined a dozen people sitting at a varnished table, all of them Americans in Egypt on a

---

1. In August 2009, the London *Guardian* reported protests in Alexandria at the news that the Bibliotheca had licensed six firms to open food outlets in the library. People were particularly incensed by rumors that a branch of McDonald's was among the franchises to sign deals. This sparked criticism of the growing "ties between capitalists and politicians and the ensuing corruption scandals." In a country of pervasive poverty, it was bad enough to spend more than $250 million on a library that had few books. To install a food court at the heart of it prompted calls for "cultural resistance."

lightning-like junket sponsored by a cultural initiative called the Big Read Program. Representing the South Dakota Council on World Affairs, Arts Midwest and similar not-for-profit organizations, they had landed in Cairo last Saturday, were spending thirty-six hours in Alexandria and would fly home this weekend.

Apologizing for my ignorance, I asked Regina G. Cooper of Alabama's Huntsville-Madison County Public Library to explain the Big Read Program.

"We take a book each year," she said, "and have everybody in the community read it and talk about it. We started off in Huntsville with *The Great Gatsby*. We figured it helped that Zelda Fitzgerald came from just up the road in Montgomery, Alabama. Second year we read *To Kill a Mockingbird*. It's set in Alabama, and Harper Lee lives nearby."

"So you keep things local."

"Not at all. Last year we read *The Maltese Falcon*. There's no Alabama connection. We thought a mystery might be more popular with men. Next year we're doing Naguib Mahfouz, the Egyptian Nobel Prize winner."

"Why Mahfouz?"

"I don't know. The National Endowment for the Arts chose the book, not us. That's why we're in Egypt."

When Ibrahim Abdel Meguid entered the room, he didn't stand on ceremony nor at a dais. He seated himself at the table with the rest of us. Big and fleshy, with curly silver hair, gold-rimmed glasses and an engaging smile, he was a man in his sixties, confident of his ability to win over strangers. Though his English was far from perfect, he never appeared frustrated not to be speaking his own language in his hometown. Friendly himself, he counted on the friendly attention of his audience.

He talked a bit about his best-known novel, *No One Sleeps in Alexandria*, and recited lines from the Federico García Lorca poem that was the source of its title. "No one sleeps in heaven/ No one sleeps in the world. / No one sleeps/ No one / No one." Then he named the foreign writers who had influenced him. Among them he mentioned Durrell, which surprised me.

Set during roughly the same period as the *Quartet*, Meguid's novel is generally regarded as a gritty corrective to Durrell's lush, romantic vision of the city. Narrated from the point of view of poor Egyptians, *No One Sleeps in Alexandria* mixes realism and magic, religion and profanity, the folklore of northern and southern Egypt, rural and urban myths, Christian and Muslim theology. It quotes the Koran, the Bible, Durrell, Cavafy and Tagore, and in the style of John Dos Passos, it grounds the action in historical context by reprinting snippets from contemporary newspapers.

Inevitably, Meguid discussed the Cosmopolitan Era, which ended when Nasser seized power in 1956, nationalized the Suez Canal and expelled most foreigners. "The city was clean back then," Meguid said, "and women wore Western fashions and there was café life and jazz music in the nightclubs. Now everything has changed. People come today and don't find Alex; they don't find a mythical city like Samarkand. It's crowded with peasants from rural villages and people who return after working in the Persian Gulf and bring with them Wahhabi ideas. The city has lost its tolerance."

When Justin Siberell announced that Meguid would answer questions, my instinct was to sink down in my seat. In my experience, Q&A sessions in North Africa can be skin-crawling embarrassments. Once, in Tunis, after I had lectured on Hemingway, a prim young woman in a headscarf stood up in front of a large audience of students and professors, and asked me, "Is it true in the United States, as I have read, that when a black woman has an orgasm she screams, 'Jesus, Jesus, Jesus!'?"

I didn't know what to say. I didn't know where to look. No Tunisian professor or U.S. Embassy official offered the mercy of intervention. I weakly muttered, "Where did you read that?"

"In a novel called *Trailer Camp Women*."

"I'm not familiar with the book. Let's talk about this later."

At the Bibliotheca Alexandrina, however, the Big Read group tossed nothing but softball questions at Meguid, and once he grooved his swing, he could have gone on for hours had Justin Siberell not interrupted to say that a bus was waiting to take the Big Readers to the airport and back to Cairo. Profuse in their gratitude, they each gave Meguid a business card. This was a ritual popular throughout North Africa. Everybody handed out cards and expected them in return. When I apologized that I didn't have a card, people looked at me as if I must be an imposter.

I invited Meguid to join me for tea and more talk about Egypt and literature. He suggested that we meet at the Cecil Hotel, and I assumed he was staying there too. But as we settled at a table in the lobby, he made it clear that he was registered at the Hilton in the Green Plaza Mall. "This place has good tradition," he said of the Cecil. "But Green Plaza has more life."

The city's center of gravity was shifting in that direction, he said, out to the suburbs and the malls and gated communities. Although Meguid's fiction has always been identified with Alexandria, he hasn't lived there in decades. "When I publish my first short story," he said, "I move right away to Cairo. I want to be at the center. I worked thirty years in the Culture Ministry because it gave me time to write." Like many Egyptian artists, he had been a state employee until his retirement.

Did it rankle him, I asked, that Westerners, when they thought of Alexandria at all, knew the city through non-Arabic writers—Cavafy, Forster and Durrell.

"No, no." His scorched cheeks creased in a smile. "The tradition here is to be open and tolerant to different views. You can find resentment, especially from the fundamentalists, about colonialism and foreign authors. But most writers appreciate other writers. I always look back to the era of Durrell and the other Europeans as a good time."

"Better than now, when you have your own literature and identity as a nation?"

"In some ways, yes." The waiter brought a plate of salted peanuts, and Meguid helped himself and poured more tea. "We had good schools back then. Small classes. Fifteen students. Now it's seventy students. They taught English. They took us to the cinema. I saw *Moby Dick* and *Gone With the Wind*. Cinema was my guide. I read the novels afterward. I read *Moby Dick* as a Koran. The language is very deep. It has the taste of a religious book. I admire many American writers—Walt Whitman, Faulkner, Steinbeck. I read *Tortilla Flat* and it changed my life."

Words spilled out of him, not wistfully, not ruefully, but with genuine pleasure at recollecting his youth and what, surprisingly, he regarded as the city's golden age. His fondness for American and European mass culture, for even the kitschiest manifestations of colonial occupation, astonished me.

"Three magic things we had in Alex when I was a boy," he said. "Cinema. Nightclubs for foreigners. And sailors coming into port. Gregory Peck, Kirk Douglas and Robert Mitchum were our heroes."

"What about Nasser? What about Sayyid Qutb?" I asked about the godfather of modern Islamic radicalism.

Meguid gave a weary flick of the hand. "Nasser had Sayyid Qutb hanged in 1966 for subversion. That's politics, not heroes. I used to be a good socialist. I was in the Communist Party. But when I went to Russia I saw it was a lie. This wasn't the Soviet Union we dreamed of. It was corrupt. You couldn't even find a photocopy machine. They thought it was a machine for spying.

"Then I lived eleven months in Saudi Arabia. I wrote a novel about it, *The Other Place*. I look on Saudi as a kind of hell. You can't live in a city without music or art."

"Do other Egyptians agree with that?"

"Some. The educated ones. In private they say what I do."

"And the rest of the people?"

"We're in crisis. We changed from socialism to capitalism. The government says they encourage capitalism, but it doesn't want to accept capitalist practices like strikes and other freedoms. Our leaders don't really believe in competition. They give one guy, a friend in politics, the import business. They give another friend the export business."

A loud buzzer sounded. It might have been an alarm warning us that we were discussing forbidden topics. But no, it was Meguid's cell phone. He pried it open and spoke in Arabic. He stood up and paced, listening and nodding. Then he shut it and said, "My wife. Where were we? I hope my ideas about Egypt don't discourage you on your trip. There are good things all across North Africa. I even like Libya. I don't feel like a stranger there. I like Morocco—Casablanca, Marrakech, Fez. I went there and it seemed like an open society."

Out of courtesy I asked about his current writing projects, and his comments about our profession sounded sadly familiar. Does there exist a writer in the world who, regardless of his fame or fortune, doesn't feel he's been fucked over by editors, writers and reviewers?

"My publisher in Beirut steals from me," Meguid said. "Every year he reprints my books, but says they're still in the first printing. The American University in Cairo makes translations into English, but it has bad distribution."

"I'm sorry. I admire your work and hope you have better luck with it."

This elicited a chuckle. "You know what Hemingway said? He said, 'If I was born in Africa, I would not be Hemingway.' He had a big powerful country behind him. It's hard when you don't have that. It's hard when you write in Arabic. But we go on, don't we?"

He signed my copy of *No One Sleeps in Alexandria* and urged me to send him copies of my books. "I can't buy them, I don't have the money."

The Cecil Hotel boasted a Chinese restaurant on its roof, but I had no appetite for anything quite so exotic as Alexandrine-Cantonese cuisine. I wanted . . . not home cooking, but something vaguely familiar. I asked the concierge about the Greek Club, which was reputed to have excellent *mezzes* and seafood and exhilarating views of the harbor. Since Greeks had once formed a sizable minority in the city—they had numbered almost one hundred thousand—I imagined some expats had lingered on, congregating each night at the Club for ouzo, *rembetike* music and nostalgic conversation.

But the concierge discouraged me. He claimed the Greek Club was far away and overcrowded. "You'll need a reservation and a taxi."

"I thought it was on the Corniche."

"Yes, but at the end, near the fort. You shouldn't walk. After dark, the streets aren't safe. I'll call and book a table, and reserve a taxi to take you and bring you back."

The price he quoted, fifty Egyptian pounds, about $10, was a princely sum in a country where half the population earned less than $2 a day. It occurred to me that the concierge might be hustling for his cab-driving brother. Still, I figured it was worth ten bucks not to get lost or mugged.

The taxi proved to be a rattletrap Lada left over from the '60s, when the Russians made common cause with their Pan-Arabic socialist brothers and bestowed battalions of technical and military advisers on Egypt. A hole in the Lada's floor allowed me to look down at the racing Corniche. It also allowed toxic gusts of carbon monoxide into the car. Coughing and spluttering, I groped for the window. The handle was missing. The driver noticed my distress and dug a window roller from the glove compartment and handed it back to me.

While I hung my head out for air, he bombed along as if in a demolition derby. Only when he spotted a traffic cop did he slow down and loosely drape the seat belt across his shoulder. For a couple of blocks we crept along at twenty mph. Then he discarded the belt and stomped on the gas. Nothing I said could slow him again. Cyclists, pedestrians, horse cart drivers all panicked as he zipped past. Even other cabbies were alarmed.

We barreled on through Anfushi, a poor neighborhood that Durrell had described as a nest of streets with a "tattered rotten supercargo of houses, breathing into each other's mouths, keeling over. Shuttered balconies swarming with rats, and old women whose hair is full of the blood of ticks."

A hammer-headed peninsula separated the eastern harbor from the western harbor, and at its point where the lighthouse once stood, Fort Qait Bey looked like a freshly baked pastry topped with towers of meringue. There the cabbie had no choice but to stop.

"Greek Club," he declared.

"Where?"

He indicated a dilapidated building. "Upstairs," he said. "I wait here."

"Don't bother." Head swimming with exhaust fumes, I paid him in full and sent him off, figuring I'd rather risk walking than asphyxiation.

Nothing identified the building—no number, no sign. Through an open door, a room was visible, along with several men who lounged on folding chairs, fingering worry beads, mesmerized by a television. Wearing striped *galabiyyas*, long, loose robes, they might have been in pajamas, settling down for the night. Much as I hated to invade their privacy, I asked, "Restaurant?"

One fellow cocked his thumb toward some stairs. I started climbing, though I had little faith that I'd find food. But then on the third floor, the walls brightened with murals of islands and blue skies and whitewashed villages, and I arrived at a reasonable facsimile of a Greek taverna. Not a lively establishment—there were very few customers and none who appeared to be Greek—but at least it was open for business.

I took a table on the terrace, caressed by a breeze. Lanterns necklaced the harbor, and painted boats floated like confetti. Through a long lens and in flattering light, this was the optimal view of Alexandria's charms. I might have been gazing at an aging movie star filmed through gauze. I marveled, as I would many times in the next few months, at how, depending on the hour or the air density, the North African light changed and in the process altered your very understanding of light and how it could scramble a landscape and your head.

I ordered hummus, tahini, tabouli and grilled calamari, and washed it all down with cold Omar Khayyam white wine. Say what you will about the quality of Egyptian vintages, but the exotic labels—not just Omar Khayyam but Obelisk and Sheharazad—were wonderfully evocative. After a few sips, the day's glum start was forgotten, and I veered toward full-blown, manic sentimentality. When the waiter brought a honeyed wedge of baklava for dessert and said that he loved America and would like to live there, I exclaimed, "But it's so beautiful in Alexandria!"

This wasn't what he wanted to hear. I suppose he was hoping for help with a visa.

Though well fed and fortified by Omar Khayyam, I left the restaurant feeling skittish. This wasn't Baghdad or Beirut; it wasn't even East London or Brooklyn. But it was Egypt at night, a Muslim city, and I was a white-haired, white-faced American walking the crowded streets alone.

From two previous trips to Egypt, I recalled hordes of hotel touts, scheming shopkeepers, anti-Israeli agitators and boys who professed to be students but offered their services as guides, pimps or sexual partners. But this night was blessedly free of that hands-on, full-court press. Nobody badgered me to buy. No one called out, "Hello, America," or cursed me as a *khawaga*, a foreigner, or as a *nasrani*, a Christian.

Along the stone waterfront of the eastern harbor, boys played soccer under street lamps. On the seawall, young couples—girls in *hijabs* and boys in blue jeans—sat watching them. At the western harbor, whole families from infants to grandfathers luxuriated in the bracing April air. Cafés had set out tables where people drank tea and smoked hubbly-bubblies. A waiter invited me to have a seat, but nobody else noticed my presence. Kids whooshed by on scooters and bikes. Laughing teenagers dared one another to dart to the end of the quay where waves crashed over the jetty in a frigid spray. Middle-aged married folks lugged plastic chairs from the cafés out to protected coves and watched the stars.

Heading back toward the center of town, I walked on and on, telling myself I'd catch a cab at the first sign of trouble, the first time anyone got too friendly. Or too hostile. But block after block, I felt nothing from the crowd except benign indifference.

On the Corniche my late-night ramble turned into a contact sport, a kind of body surfing, as Egyptians flowed around me, into me, over me. To a claustrophobe, this might seem menacing, but I didn't mind, and gradually the realization came to me that within the chaos of an Arab mob there was an intrinsic order, within the apparent irrationality there was a logic.

Still, I thought my good luck couldn't last. If not in Egypt, then in Libya or Algeria, I'd be assailed on all sides by a boisterousness indistinguishable from mayhem or misdemeanor. There'd be murderous anti-Americanism, palpable danger, places I dared not go.

But for the moment I gloried in a feeling that American author Eleanor Clark best expressed when she wrote that Mediterranean streets constitute a great warm "withinness," an inclusion that permits people to believe that to go out into a city is to go home.

The next day, I reviewed my notes for the lecture on travel, travel writing and travel literature that I had agreed to give at the American Center. Justin Siberell had read a similar paper I'd presented four years ago at a Modern Language Association meeting in New Orleans, and he assured me it was appropriate to the audience he expected in Alexandria. Typically, he said, such talks attracted a large turnout of Egyptians and a smattering of expats. Since there would be a simultaneous translation, his only warning was to speak slowly and distinctly so that the interpreter could keep pace.

Yet I felt a growing uneasiness, not so much premature stage fright as topic regret. In the context of Egypt and the Muslim world, in view of the life-and-death conflict within Arab countries, and between them and the West, it struck me as lightweight and elitist for an American to breeze into Alexandria and discuss his personal hobbyhorse. Okay, I could argue that travel is crucial to political and religious understanding. I could quote the eleventh-century Sufi Imam Qushayri, who declared that the objective of travel was "to discover inner ethical values." I could cite Robert Byron, widely regarded as the best travel writer in English, who blamed the failure of British colonialism on "insufficient, or insufficiently imaginative, travel." Still, I feared I'd sound like another self-indulgent foreigner larking around North Africa, another Orientalist presuming to lecture the natives.

Siberell swung by the Cecil to pick me up in a tanklike American SUV whose door shut with the solid *thunk* of a safe deposit box. It sounded armor-plated. A chauffeur steered us through the evening rush hour, and a powerful AC system screened out the heat, grit and smells of Alexandria. Yet Siberell seemed as tense as I was—and with much better reason. His assignment here was drawing to a close, and within days he would depart for Baghdad. He'd done a previous tour in the Green Zone. Now he was married and had kids, and he would be away from his family for a year.

"Shows you how smart I was to study Arabic," he joked. It was a lament that I would hear from Foreign Service officers all across North Africa. Their hard-won fluency had sentenced them to the worst posting in the world. Sooner or later they would have to serve in Iraq, and while no American diplomat I met openly criticized the war, none defended it, either.

The American Center occupied the former private mansion of a wealthy Alexandrian family. In 1967, during the Six Day War, Egyptians had overrun and ransacked the building, and it had remained shut until Egypt and the United States resumed diplomatic relations, in 1974. Now it was surrounded by walls and wrought iron fences and flanked by armed guards. At the front gate, eyed by U.S. Marines, I stepped through a metal detector, traded my passport for a clip-on badge and crossed through a garden, following Siberell to a side entrance. There another squad of security guards scrutinized us.

From the American Center's foyer we climbed a marble staircase to a loggia where locked doors of bulletproof Mylar lined the hall. Behind them, offices were accessible by computer code. Egyptians crouched on the carpet, as though begging for admission. They were reciting their evening prayers.

After they finished, we proceeded into a conference room where a crowd of seventy or so was divided between those in Western and Egyptian garb. But even men wearing suits and ties had prayer bumps on their foreheads, and all the women wore headscarves. One was in full *niqab*, staring out through slits. Lacy black gloves covered her hands and arms up to her elbows. Not a centimeter of her skin was visible. Beside her a man in a knit cap combed his fingers through a beard as broad as a broom.

Siberell introduced me in Arabic. The only words I understood were "Sharon Stone." She had starred in a movie made from *Year of the Gun*, a novel I had written about terrorism in Italy. Mention of her name drew scattered laughs.

There were one or two American or European faces in the crowd, but I didn't focus on them. As I spoke I tried to maintain friendly eye contact with the Egyptians, who listened through earphones. I couldn't read anything from their reactions, and it disconcerted me to stare out at a sea of beards and prayer bumps and dark eyes with no idea how the lecture was going. Just one line prompted smiles and a brief outburst of applause—I criticized George Bush for having lumped together Iraq, Iran and North Korea as an Axis of Evil.

The Q&A session lasted longer than the lecture. Each questioner stood up, introduced himself or herself by name and profession, gave a formal ritual greeting, welcomed me to Alexandria, praised my past accomplishments, expressed fascination for my current project, then lashed me for a multitude of intellectual shortcomings and cultural misapprehensions.

One gentleman complained that he had looked me up online and read the same lecture I had just inflicted on the audience: "It's four years old. Have you learned nothing since you first gave this talk?"

Siberell interrupted, explaining that he had invited me to give this particular address.

"*Shukran, shukran,*" said my interrogator. "Thank you, thank you," said the interpreter. The man sat down and a lady in a floral headscarf stood up and repeated the ritual greeting and gratitude and fulsome praise, then laid into me. "How can you come to our country and expect to understand anything when you don't speak Arabic?"

With deep apologies for my ignorance, I attempted to make a case, just as I had in my lecture, that language was not the lone means of understanding and that words weren't always the best links between people. Human beings had other means of perception, and sometimes words got in the way. For me, I said, one of the delights of travel was that it brought my dormant senses alive. Suddenly in foreign surroundings, I could see and hear and smell again. And afterward, if I was lucky, I could write. Blank pages, I pointed out, were like blank spaces on a map. In both cases I was eager to fill them up.

"Egypt is not a blank space," someone shouted.

"Of course not," I apologized. "A poor figure of speech. I realize I'm bound to make mistakes and misunderstand your history and religion. But I'm traveling in good faith to see things for myself and to learn. I've read the Koran and I . . ."

"You read it in English. That's not the Koran. Only in Arabic is it the Koran."

For more than an hour, their cavils crashed over me. Though nobody asked about orgasms and black women, I almost wished someone had. That would have been preferable to their accusations that travel was a species of colonialism, an exploitation of poor countries by privileged people like me. Wasn't I aware that Egypt had been invaded in 1798 by Napoleon and subjected to cruel dissection by squadrons of French scientists? Had I never heard that the British bombarded Alexandria in 1882 and ruled the country afterward like a royal fiefdom?

To my astonishment, this rough and tumble Q&A ended with the audience surging forward for an up-close-and-personal rapprochement that made me suspect that their harsh questions had been as formulaic as their greetings. Like other academics I would meet, they seemed to believe that giving a speaker a severe going-over was a sign of respect. But now there came a laying on of hands, a kind of benediction, heartfelt invitations to tea, promises of hospitality, requests for my e-mail address.

Although they had listened to me in translation and posed their public challenges in Arabic, they spoke to me privately in excellent English. A bespectacled young woman in a *hijab* asked, "Are you a feminist?" and when I said I supported equal rights for women, she exclaimed, "So do I. Everything I do is for feminism." To her, she said, the *hijab* was a symbol of female empowerment.

A pale man in a dark suit, starched white shirt and black tie patiently waited his turn and introduced himself as a professor of literature at a university in the Nile delta. He had read online that forty years ago I had lived in France on a Fulbright Fellowship. He was in contention for a teaching Fulbright to the United States, and it appeared that he would have his pick between a college in St. Paul, Minnesota, and one in Walla Walla, Washington. "Which city is most like Alexandria?" he asked.

"I'm afraid there's nothing in America like Alexandria."

"Okay, but which one is warmer? I've never seen snow."

"They both have snowy winters."

"Okay, but where won't I need a car?"

"I think you'll have to drive wherever you go."

"Yes, America is so big," he fretted. "My field is science fiction, but they want me to teach Arabic and comparative literature. What I would like to do is work on my own novel. Do you think I'll be permitted to take a creative writing course?"

"I'm sure you can arrange that."

"What I'd really like is to write for the movies," he said.

"Sorry, that's not my field." Someone gripped my elbow and steered me toward the exit. I assumed it was Siberell rescuing me.

"But one of your books became a movie."

"I wasn't involved. Good luck to you."

On the carpeted loggia that had served as a prayer rug, a caterer had set out sweets and soft drinks. I noticed then that it was a young man, not Siberell, who'd been clutching my arm.

"Unless you want to be stuck answering questions all night, I'd suggest getting out of here," he said.

His name was Michael Nevadomski, and he was an undergraduate from Middlebury College in Vermont, spending a year in Alexandria to improve his Arabic. He was already quite fluent and had translated some of Durrell into Arabic. The son of a Polish-American father and a mother from the island of Guam, he had been raised in Florida and looked like a preppy New Englander in his tweed jacket. But he was completely at home in Egypt.

At Michael's suggestion, we went to Pastroudis, another Art Deco relic from the Cosmopolitan Era. Although we had the paneled dining room to ourselves, waiters scurried around as if we had arrived with an entourage. Mineral water and a bottle of Obelisk wine promptly appeared on the table. A booklike menu came inscribed with a quote in English from Durrell about "Alexandria, the Capital of memory" and paragraphs of commentary about Cavafy and Mahfouz and King Farouk, Egypt's deposed monarch, whose immense girth might have qualified him as a food critic. All the dishes had French names and were described at length in that language—which was strange since none of the waiters spoke a word of it. Michael ordered for us in Arabic.

In the adjacent bar, a radio played Lionel Richie. "He's the most popular singer in the Arab world," Michael said. "A lot of people don't know any English except for his songs."

From pop culture, he moved to local lore and arcana. Michael seemed to have read every book and to know every bit of minutiae about Alexandria, Egypt and Islam. He discussed sects and sub-sects. Not just Sunnis and Shiites, but Sufis and Salafi'ists.

When I mentioned that I was headed for Libya, he warned me that the border was littered with mines—some left over from World War II, others from more recent conflicts. He hadn't crossed the frontier and didn't know anybody who had tried to. But he had traveled by bus throughout the western desert and he urged me not to miss the oasis at Siwa, where Alexander the Great had consulted the oracle and discovered that he was divine.

While I wondered when my Libyan visa might come through, Michael went on to say that he'd take me to a mosque this Friday where worshippers chanted *Dhihr*—a repetition of the ninety-nine names of God, or the repetition of one of his names ninety-nine times. Then, on Sunday, since we were both Catholics, we could attend a Sudanese Mass, with drumming, at Sacré Coeur cathedral.

I liked his eagerness and energy, his curiosity and intelligence, his sense of adventure. It occurred to me he might have friends who were fundamentalists, maybe members of the Muslim Brotherhood. If so, I wanted to meet them. Because I didn't care to put him in danger, I didn't mention that I actually wanted to interview a terrorist. Why travel all this distance and not meet the Beast everybody raved about?

"I know a few hard-core believers," Michael said. "Let me ask around and get back to you."

After dinner, he strolled with me toward the hotel. Actually, "strolled" is the wrong verb. We "vaulted" ditches. "Traversed" construction sites. "Clambered" up and down slag heaps. "Tiptoed" over a sidewalk inexplicably flooded with water. "Dodged" cars and trolleys. "Picked" our way past café tables where men smoked *sheesha* and played dominoes in the glaring light that splashed from open doors. And "swam" against the tide of pedestrians until we achieved the relative sanctuary of the Corniche.

Young couples perched on the seawall. The daring held hands. The brazen embraced and kissed. Not unnaturally, we wound up talking about women and love, but since we were both bookish guys, we thrashed out the subject through literature. Michael asked what I thought of Durrell's Justine. Not the novel but the sexually predatory title character, the inscrutable beauty who leaves half the men of Alexandria panting in her fragrant wake.

World-weary and wise, I observed that I accepted Justine's assessment of herself as "a tiresome hysterical Jewess." But at his age Michael was alive to the mysteries of sexual allure. What impressed me, though, was the allure he exercised over young Egyptian girls, who gave him sidelong glances as they glided by.

Michael whispered, "The girls behind us are talking about us. They wonder whether you're my father."

This flattered me. I was closer to his grandfather's age.

Arms linked, a trio of girls speeded up and pulled level with us. They wore tight jeans and tight sweaters, and although they had on headscarves, they didn't hide their smiles. Surging ahead, they darted kohl-rimmed eyes over their shoulders at Michael, flirting outrageously.

Hands in pockets, wind tousling his hair, he called out to them in Arabic. I expected that to send them scampering. But the girls didn't suddenly go silly and goosey. They stopped, and one of them, the cutest, told him in English, "You are very handsome."

"*Shukran*," he replied.

The three young buds showed no interest in me. So much for the respect Egyptians supposedly accord their elders. With eyes and ears for Michael alone, they were willing to linger there in the parade of pedestrians as long as he stayed too.

They were university students, they said. The prettiest one majored in geography and was about to take her end-of-term exams. She had finished cramming and needed a break tonight. What was Michael doing, she asked. Why was he in Alexandria? Did he like Egypt? Where did he learn Arabic?

It looked to me like Michael was about to get very lucky. All he needed to do was take his choice of Charlie's Angels—or, what the hell, invite the three of them to a café. But a minute later, he blew them off. He did it suavely, with flourishes of Arabic as decorative as the fretwork on a harem screen. Still, there was no mistaking that he had sent them packing.

"What was that?" I asked.

"It happens to me all the time," he said.

"Bullshit."

"No, seriously, it does. Because I'm blond."

"You're not blond. You have brown hair."

"Well, by comparison to an Arab I'm fair."

"Why didn't you ask them to have something to eat or drink? At least, ask for a phone number."

He shook his head at my ignorance. "That's not done here."

"It looked to me like they were up for anything."

"Ready for a marriage proposal, maybe," Michael said. "But not a date. They were wearing *hijabs*. That's what gave them away."

"Gave what away? They couldn't have come on any stronger."

Slightly pedantic, yet never condescending, Michael attempted to educate me in the complexities and paradoxes of the headscarf. According to him, the University of Alexandria had almost eighty thousand female students, most of them enrolled in the College of Arts, which was disparaged as the College of High Heels. Girls were reputed to enroll there to pick up a degree and, at the same time, an educated husband with good job prospects.

"What's that got to do with headscarves?" I broke in.

"I'm getting to that. For a lot of girls the *hijab* is a badge that says they don't want to be bothered by boys. But it's also a license to flirt because it's clear they don't intend to do anything."

If I found this confusing, it was no fault of Michael's. And no failure of my grey matter. Throughout the Mediterranean basin the issue of *hijabs* had provoked debate, anger, violence, even killing. In France, which had seven million Muslim immigrants, the controversy raged from schoolyards all the way to the Elysée Palace. Turkey had banned headscarves for decades to preserve itself as a secular society, yet it was confronted by a segment of the female population that persisted in wearing them. Nobel Prize-winning Turkish author Orhan Pamuk's finest novel, *Snow*, centered on the question of whether a headscarf is a symbol of liberation or repression. Of resistance to the government and its masculine hegemony? Or of submission to Islam and its masculine hegemony? In the end, the *hijab* seemed to mean whatever the individual woman said it did.

During the Cosmopolitan Era many Jewish families in Alexandria were wealthy, and in a city thronged with expatriates and displaced persons, they held positions of social prominence. Yet they had reason to feel insecure. In *Out of Egypt,* his beautifully evocative memoir about Jewish life, André Aciman looks back from exile in America and recalls a household of eccentric relatives who longed to escape Alex's provinciality, then regretted it once they'd been banished by President Nasser. Although they viewed themselves as citizens of the world, they were attached to local customs. Like their Egyptian neighbors, they ate *foul*, a refried bean paste, for breakfast, and along with the rest of the privileged classes, they migrated with the seasons, moving to beach houses in summer. To Aciman's shame, he discovered that his elderly grandmother treated the home bathroom as Muslims do, planting her feet on the porcelain bowl and squatting down. Aciman's picaresque Uncle Vili complained, "It's because of Jews like them that they hate Jews like us."

But when Nasser confiscated their property, it was less from racial or religious prejudice than political expediency. Nasser needed an enemy, and he found one ready-made.

Now the synagogue in Alexandria didn't even have ten men to make a *minyan*, the minimum number required by Jewish law to conduct a communal religious service. Constructed more than a century ago on Nabi Daniel Street, and renovated after the Germans bombed it during World War II, it stood forlornly behind locked gates guarded by Egyptian soldiers. With curt hand gestures, they directed me to a side entrance. It was difficult to guess whom they were protecting or guarding against. Terrorists? Tourists? Jews?

By telephone I had spoken earlier to Ben Yusuf Guon and arranged a tour of the synagogue. I pictured him as an ancient rabbi, a patriarchal figure with a long white beard. Instead I met a middle-aged man in designer jeans and a burgundy shirt, with a fashionable four-day growth of whiskers.

Ben Yusuf Guon identified himself as the vice-president of Alexandria's Jewish community and as its youngest member. "I'm the baby," he joked. "I'm fifty-three."

Crossing a courtyard planted with palms and ficus trees, he told me there were twenty-three Jews left in the community, mostly women. "We have eighteen very poor ladies and two very rich ones. Cairo has thirty Jews, all women, no men."

Among the buildings in the compound that still belonged to the synagogue, one had been a Yeshiva. Now the state rented it as an Egyptian girls' school. "We have no rabbi," he said. "One comes from Israel for Passover and stays until Yom Kippur. When he's not here, we don't have services. I light a candle for my mother and father. That's all."

Under the portico, well-fed dogs napped on the stairs. They didn't stir as we stepped over them. Arabs consider dogs unclean, little better than vermin, and chase them away from mosques. But Ben Yusuf Guon laughingly referred to these as "Jewish dogs."

"For security?" I asked.

"The Egyptians take care of that. No problems. We have good relations. All the police are very correct."

"Now that Egypt and Israel have diplomatic relations is there any chance Jews will come back to Alexandria?"

We were in the rear of the synagogue putting on paper yarmulkes. "They return to visit," Ben Yusuf said. "A woman was here today. A lady in her fifties, like me. She found her family pew and was happy."

"I mean is there a chance Jews will resettle?"

He shook his head, saying, "There's always a good smell here. It's very clean."

It was an olfactory theory of religious distinctions that I had first encountered in Beirut in 1969, and had heard since in a dozen countries and would hear again throughout North Africa. Arabs, Christians and Jews believed their own neighborhoods smelled sweet and other ethnic groups stank.

Ben Yusuf explained that the synagogue had been designed by an Italian architect in 1890. He invited me to admire the Corinthian columns that supported a gallery where women had once worshipped. Then he called to the custodian, an old black man, and had him unveil the Ten Commandments, chiseled in Hebrew.

Ben Yusuf's cell phone cut him off in mid-sentence; its ring tone was "Dance with Me" by Dean Martin.

While Ben Yusuf spoke in French, the custodian introduced himself as Abdel Naby, which he said meant "Servant of the Prophet." He came from Aswan, in the far south, and he saw nothing exceptional about a Muslim being employed in a synagogue. He said the Jews treated him well and had even taught him a little Hebrew.

Ben Yusuf snapped his phone shut and appeared eager to finish the tour. He had little interest in discussing why he had stayed on in Alexandria and how he had managed to do so. Only when pressed did he reveal that his father had been Nasser's tailor. "Nasser used to send a car to bring my father to his villa for fittings."

"So it was a personal relationship?"

"No. Professional."

"And that's why your family wasn't expelled?"

"No. It was because we didn't have dealings with Israel. The people who were expelled were in contact with Israel."

I didn't argue. The absurdity of the statement was its own re-buttal. Alexandria's fifteen thousand Jews hadn't been uniformly Zionist. Still, all except for a handful had had their property seized and been exiled.

We returned our paper yarmulkes to the table and stepped out over the dogs on the portico. I asked what would happen after the last Jew died. Ben Yusuf Guon chuckled. "When I die, it's finished. They'll turn the synagogue into a museum."

In the eighteenth and nineteenth centuries, when Christians were forbidden to ride horses in Egypt, Europeans reached Pompey's Pillar on donkeyback. I doubt, though, that their buttock-bruising expeditions were any more unsettling than my taxi trip to one of the few monuments in Alexandria that have remained intact since antiquity. We hadn't gone three blocks before the cabbie picked up a second passenger. "My brother-in-law," he said.

"I assume we'll be splitting the bill?"

The cabbie pretended I had exceeded his fluency. "I speak small English." He held his thumb and index finger a millimeter apart.

"I am journalist," the brother-in-law spoke up, "making pictures on tourism." He swiveled around in the front seat and handed me his card. When I didn't exchange the courtesy, he demanded his card back. He carried a camera and from time to time he told the driver to stop while he snapped shots through the windshield. He didn't bother to climb out for a clearer view. But it wasn't laziness that kept him in the car.

"My brother-in-law is a bad man," the cabbie said. "He makes pictures of trash and other things the government doesn't like to show. He has to hide."

The guy did have a splendid eye for ugliness—and often the city appeared to be nothing but ugliness and oddities. Inch by inch the car advanced through a bazaar of intimate apparel. Brassieres were stacked shoulder high, smaller cups nestled in larger ones, like Russian dolls. Sherbet-colored panties fluttered in a breeze that kicked up dust and spicy odors. Then, on a street of furniture stores, there were sidewalk displays of brocade chairs as grand as pharaohs' thrones. Chickens and cats roosted on them.

The brother-in-law clicked away, then clucked with delight when he spotted a herd of goats gnawing weeds from the wall around Pompey's Pillar. Leaving him to his antic amusement—I couldn't imagine that his was a real job—I paid admission at a wooden shack. Beyond it, the pillar and a pair of sphinxes dominated a mound of potsherds and crushed bricks, crumbling walls and tunnels. A wooden staircase zigzagged uphill, punctuated by newel posts without hand railings. Yellow plastic tape, the kind that police string up at crime scenes, connected the posts.

A uniformed man bolted from the ticket shack and raced after me. He didn't bother with the stairs. He chugged straight up the rubble heap, setting off explosions of sand. He wore an armband stenciled in English: TOURISM & ANTIQUITIES POLICE, which suggested that his job was to protect the site and its visitors. But he viewed his mission as that of cheerleader. "America! Number one!" he panted. "Pillar of Pompey, twenty-seven meters tall."

From between the sphinxes, I surveyed the whelming desolation that stretched from the pillar to a Stonehenge of bleak modern apartment towers, with carpets flapping from balconies and TV antennas trembling on rooftops. A spring wind, the *khamseen*, swept the city, blowing cinders between my teeth and grating my nasal membranes.

"Pillar of Pompey, twenty-seven meters tall," the man repeated. "Now we see library-temple Roman."

Whatever he expected in the way of *baksheesh*, I would have paid double if he would have left me alone. But he urged me over footpaths and splintered bridges, down into a gopher hole whose sandstone walls had been hewn into shelves.

"Books all gone," he said, "to Cairo Museum."

I felt in my pockets, but found no change, only bills, frayed as old handkerchiefs. I was reluctant to drag out a wad of Egyptian pounds and inflame the man's avarice. But he turned the tables and produced a sheaf of American dollars. Far from angling for a tip, he wanted to do a quick currency exchange. I was glad to oblige.

Back at the cab, the driver and his brother-in-law had their heads drooped in a catnap. But the instant I opened the door, they were good to go. "Where now?" the driver asked. "Kom es Chogafa catacombs?"

Forster declared that the catacombs were "odd rather than beautiful" and he cautioned "not [to] read too much into them." I didn't read anything into them at all; I simply let my eyes slide over the scene and catalogue the miscellany of chipped columns, shattered friezes, decapitated sphinxes, Corinthian capitals, mastabas and sarcophagi. On my first visit to the Cairo Museum decades ago, my initial impression of Egypt was of a pack rat's paradise. People saved everything, all of it preserved for eternity by the arid climate. The whole country was a kind of reliquary of mummified remains—human, animal, mineral, emotional.

The catacombs' ramp corkscrewed into the earth, down to cooler, humid layers of air, then to dim grottos. Stone banquettes lined alcoves where ancient mourners had reclined and eaten ritual meals after funerals. Glass cases, not unlike those at Cavafy's apartment, displayed bones instead of poetry. Some of the bones weren't from humans; the sadistic Roman emperor Caracalla had slaughtered horses here along with their riders.

Dozens of guides hectored tourists in a Babel of languages. Amid French, English, Italian and unknown tongues I recognized the names Cerebus and Anubis, Medusa, Isis and Osiris. Along with folks in sensible shoes and drip-dry safari suits, I squeezed into a burial chamber and attempted to make sense of the bearded serpents and ox heads and lion-shaped biers. A British woman read aloud from her guidebook that a married couple had been interred here. Her husband observed that there were three tombs in the chamber. "There must have been three in the marriage. Remember the trouble that caused Princess Di?"

That was my exit cue. I trudged up the ramp into the blisteringly dry air, glad to get back into the taxi with the cabbie and his shutterbug brother-in-law. On the way to the Cecil, it dawned on me that what I liked best about Alexandria wasn't its mythic past or its literary associations. It was the tumultuous present and its good-natured citizens. Joining in the spirit of his enterprise, I pointed the brother-in-law to photo ops that he had overlooked—bloody carcasses dangling from chains in butcher's shops, toilet fixtures for sale on the sidewalk, freelance grease monkeys repairing broken-down cars at intersections, burlap bags lying on the curb, plump with cotton.

On Friday Michael Nevadomski showed up at the Cecil to take me to a mosque. He dismissed the taxi drivers in front of the hotel as "rip-off artists" and flagged down a cab on the Corniche. We piled in with four other passengers. "It costs a pound—twenty cents—to go anywhere in the city," he said.

Michael explained that he had chosen the mosque of Abou el Abbas Moursi with me in mind. Built by Algerians in 1766, it commemorated a thirteenth-century Andalusian saint and had become a pilgrimage site for those traveling to or from the Maghreb, generally the Atlas Mountain regions of Tunisia, Algeria and Morocco. "Since that's where you're headed," Michael said, "you qualify for spiritual protection."

The mosque was an imposing structure of snow-white marble, a modern interpretation of the Islamic architectural idiom, with a minaret two hundred and fifty feet tall. Yet, as always, Alexandrians showed an unfailing talent for reducing such intimidating edifices to human dimensions. On its front steps, street merchants had spread their wares—underpants, socks, plastic toys and stuffed animals.

We removed our shoes and carried them with the soles pressed together. "Shoe soles, like the bottom of your feet, are considered impure," Michael said.

In some Islamic countries, nonbelievers are banned from mosques. Here, we were free to roam around under the domed ceiling with its great waterfalls of faience and alphabet rivers of Kufic script. The carpeted floor was itself carpeted by Egyptians, some bent double in prayer, some supine in repose. "Mosque literally means 'a place of prostration,'" Michael said. "The Prophet was all for naps, and people come for that reason, among others."

Men hung together, companionably chatting. A few hovered at a filigree screen, gazing in at the women and children who prayed separately. Some young fellows cupped cell phones to their ears and whispered. But the bulk of the congregation was lost in incantatory chanting, clustered at the tomb of Abou el Abbas. For a moment, I stood with them, a Catholic muttering a prayer for a safe trip.

A smiling man—he may have been a bit mad—cozied up and asked if I was Michael's father. Then he asked for money. Michael chastised him in Arabic, and we left.

Across the square in a smaller mosque, we pried off our shoes again and entered a courtyard where a fountain quietly splashed. In the Mosque of Sidi Daoud, a center of Sufism, we heard men chanting the *Burda*, a song of praise whose aim was the annihilation of self in the presence of God.

The smiling man had followed us and Michael gave him money—which prompted another beggar to try his luck. I let Michael deal with them, while I cooled off under a slow ceiling fan. An old man on the carpet extended a hand to me. I thought that he, too, was begging, but he needed help standing up. "*Shukran*," he said, then kissed his fingertips and touched his heart.

In the courtyard, a young woman smiled at Michael. In nunlike black robes that hung to her ankles and a *hijab* that cinched her face into a tight oval, she wasn't another of his flirtatious admirers. She was from the University of Manchester and, like Michael, was in Alexandria to study Arabic for the year. They lived in the same housing complex.

He introduced her as Fidehla. No last name. With her caramel complexion, she could have passed for an Egyptian. But her parents had migrated to England from India, and she had a British accent.

When Michael suggested we go to a café for orange juice, Fidehla readily agreed, and I began to suspect that this might not have been a coincidental meeting. Maybe she was one of his "hard-core" Muslim friends, a fundamentalist with radical leanings. But that was difficult to believe as she joshed and giggled.

We sat under an arcade thick with flies drawn by the aromas of a cooking brazier. A waiter waved sticks of incense to cut the smell and the smoke, but that didn't disturb the flies that landed on our lips and eyelids. A blind man, hand in hand with his daughter, waited wordlessly at our table until I pulled a bill at random from my pocket. The daughter grabbed it and hurried her father away, and Fidehla and Michael broke into laughter. "You gave the guy six bucks," said Michael, howling. "He can afford to retire."

Suddenly, the café convulsed in frenzy; everybody shoved a palm out for *baksheesh*. The waiter rattled a sheet of paper claiming that he had serious medical ailments and needed money for an operation. I promised a big tip, which mollified him. He refolded the document and fetched our orange juice.

With minimal prompting, Fidehla recounted that she had been born into a devout Muslim family; all the women wore headscarves. She didn't consider this extremist. To the contrary, she believed in dialogue between Christians and Muslims and planned to return to England to bridge the gap between communities.

I mentioned Martin Amis, one of England's most prominent novelists and essayists, who currently taught at the University of Manchester. Fidehla had never heard of him or the controversy over his supposedly anti-Islamic sentiments. This was surprising, since some of the most strident accusations against Amis had been leveled by a fellow faculty member at the university.

I knew Martin Amis and considered him a friend. He was no racist or right-wing rabble-rouser. But he had made some ill-judged comments about Islam. In 2006, he told the London *Times*: "There's a definite urge—don't you have it?—to say, 'The Muslim community will have to suffer until it gets its house in order.' What sort of suffering? Not letting them travel. Deportation—further down the road. Curtailing of freedoms. Strip searching people who look like they're from the Middle East or Pakistan . . . Discriminatory stuff, until it hurts the whole community and they start getting tough with their children."

Fidehla promised to look up Amis online but said she thought she already understood his position: "Probably he wanted to provoke discussion." She saw his comments in the context of the July 7, 2005, suicide bombings in London. The English referred to the attacks, which killed more than fifty commuters on the Underground and on a bus, as 7/7, a date that resonates in the UK as 9/11 does in the US. Fidehla said she understood why people were scared and why they lumped together everybody who appeared to be a Muslim. She had been scared herself, twice over because she was in jeopardy both from random terrorism and from indiscriminate reprisals against Asians.

I had been living in London at the time of the Tube bombings and remembered the tension—the sense that a lethal virus had invaded the city and might sicken and kill anybody, everybody. In the newly flat world, it wasn't just goods and services, trade and opportunity, that circulated freely. Personal grievances and ideological conflicts festered in obscure corners and then insinuated themselves throughout the globe. Everyone with a gun, anybody with a bomb and a willingness to die for an idea, had the opportunity to make his point—even a point nobody could comprehend.

I confessed to Fidehla and Michael that in the aftermath of 7/7, I had eyed every Middle Easterner with suspicion. "I'd catch a bus with my wife and notice a brown person with a backpack and wonder whether it was racist of me to be afraid—and whether it would be worse, a terrible insult and sign of cowardice, if I got off the bus."

"Well," Fidehla said, "at least you didn't force them to get off. I'm all for tolerance. I don't support any type of prejudice or violence. Killing innocent people violates the Koran. So does suicide. You know, those men with bombs on their belts, that's not Islam."

The small circle of Fidehla's face showed lively eyes, a prominent nose, a generous mouth without lipstick. She had a disarming smile and a warm, extroverted manner. She stressed that she didn't subscribe to the concept of *takfir*, the conviction among *jihadis* that immoral acts, such as the killing of innocents, were permissible in defense of Islam. "I believe in being strict on myself, not on other people."

She and Michael suggested that we get together again, with Muslims from their student residence. Fidehla had a roommate named Helima who was more devout than she. A Salafi'ist, the girl was part of a group dedicated to reestablishing the radical practices of early Islam. She had forsaken all idle amusement. No music, no movies, no videos, no photographs.

"Where shall we meet?" I asked.

"At a restaurant," Michael suggested.

"Brilliant," Fidehla said. "I haven't had a good meal since I went to Fuddruckers at the Green Plaza Mall and got sick on a cheeseburger."

Fuddruckers! The word, the concept, the image of an Anglo-Indian Muslim girl in a *hijab* eating fast food at an Egyptian mall was enough to give me the bends.

Later that day, with hours to kill, I toured the final resting place of thousands of foreigners who had died in what they regarded as *Europa ad Aegyptum*. In the neighborhood of Chatby, a series of graves, segregated according to national origin (British, Greek, Armenian) and religious affiliation (Orthodox Greek, Protestant, Jewish, Coptic Orthodox), lay in separate cemeteries along rue Anubis. While the street, named after the jackal-headed Egyptian god of the afterlife, might suggest that in death we're all equal, the subdivided tombs showed how varied in life were the citizens of colonial Alexandria.

The Greek Orthodox graveyard was half botanical garden, half sculpture park, and a gardener-cum-guardian insisted on guiding me to its highlights. If he hadn't, I might have overlooked the flat stone inscribed with Cavafy's name, the date of his death (but not of his birth) and a single word, POET.

Nearby, nobody with a capacity for wonder could have missed the marble extravaganza commemorating la Famille Nader Chikkani. Rhapsodically described in Lucien Basch's study *Les Jardins des Morts*, the tomb featured a cascade of roses swirling around a beautiful couple who embraced "for eternity in a spiral without end; Eros and Thanatos forever inseparable."

By comparison the grave of Victor Khouri was a monument of restraint. Khouri's widow expressed her lapidary sorrow in French: *"Mes larmes retombent en rosée rafraichissante sur ton âme, chéri"* ("My tears fall down like refreshing dew on your soul, my darling").

The Old British Protestant Cemetery also had an attendant. It was hard to guess, though, when he had last done any gardening much less any guarding. The entrance was a trash-strewn staircase leading to a desolation of brown grass and desiccated palms. Most gravestones had been leveled like a forest cross-cut by a giant scythe. Was this the work of vandals or of marble thieves?

Still one tomb stood tall, that of Knight Bachelor Henry Edward Barker, commander of the Orders of St. George and St. Michael, who was born in Alexandria in 1872 and died in 1942. Its English inscription sounded slightly hollow in these circumstances: "Proud of his country and a staunch believer in her destiny of service to the world, he spared no effort to bring to Egypt and specially to his birthplace, Alexandria, some measure of the blessings Great Britain herself enjoyed."

The Coptic Christian cemetery offered no such grand sentiments. Nor did it have a gardener/guardian. Copts, who numbered more than eight million in Egypt, played important roles in the nation's financial sector and Hosni Mubarak's wife was said to be sympathetic to them. When Coptic pope Shenuda III was made to pass like a peon through security at Heathrow Airport, Mubarak's government declared that all British officials, regardless of diplomatic rank, would henceforth be searched when entering Egyptian territory. But the power and wealth of the Copts were nowhere apparent here.

A pyramid of discarded bottles and wadded up plastic bags marked the entrance to a slum cemetery. Chairs, tables and benches barricaded the paths between tombs, and families lounged under shade trees eating a late lunch. Egyptians were on easy terms with the dead.

One mausoleum—or was it a gravedigger's hut?—had a stove and a TV. At other mausoleums doors hung loose from their hinges, and buckets and wheelbarrows, picks and shovels, were tossed inside. A crude wooden ladder led to a cruder cinder block addition to a high-rise tomb. At the bottom of the ladder, as if outside a mosque, shoes and sandals lay scattered.

A parked motorcycle blocked my way. Did it belong to a grave-digger? Or was it a grave marker? And what about the rusty engine in front of the adjoining tomb?

A grizzled old man carrying groceries in a string bag called out, "What's your name?" Before I could answer, he shouted his: "Nabil."

I kicked at the rusty engine. "What do you suppose this is?"

The old man, wearing a woolly sweater on this sweltering day, regarded me as if I were the one suffering from heatstroke. "It's a car motor." What else? "You Amriki?" he asked, again not awaiting an answer. "I have brothers in Houston and Albany. One city hot, one city cold."

"Where do you live?"

He motioned up the dusty path. "Once this road was big. Now small because of more dead."

"You live in the cemetery?"

His face contorted in a bemused expression. Now he knew I was nuts. "No, no. I take shortcut to house." Warily, he backed away, leaving me to the enigma of the engine.

As I returned to rue Anubis, I spotted a billboard rearing above the necropolis, another of the improbable sights that the city always seemed to drop in my path. Spilling over with photos of smiling babies, the sign advertised a fertility clinic.

I n a packed communal minibus, I headed east on the Corniche from Chatby toward Montazah Palace. From the rear-view mirror swung an eclectic collection of sacred and profane objects—a miniature soccer ball, wooden rosary beads, a tiny striped soccer jersey and a Coptic holy card. To further confuse matters, the radio blasted Koranic chants and the dashboard was upholstered with what looked to be a wolf pelt. My fellow passengers helpfully passed my money to the driver, then returned the change hand to hand.

The Corniche curved along for miles, lined on one side by beaches and cabanas, and on the other by condos and hotels, including a Four Seasons with a Starbucks on its terrace. In the summer, before Nasser took over, in the '50s, the king and his court and thousands of government officials used to decamp here to escape Cairo's brutal heat, and Alex had served as the country's seasonal capital. Today the city still swells by a million or more during the months when the coast is twenty or thirty degrees cooler than inland. But on this April afternoon, the beach season had yet to start, and lounge chairs were chained to the pavement outside boarded-up cafés.

During World War I, Forster had worked as a volunteer at Montazah Palace when the Spanish-style Mudejar castle had served as a military convalescent center. Its gardens were still a healing refuge, its trees and shrubs thoughtfully labeled—casuaria, oleander, date palm, tamarisk. On the quiet streets, husbands taught their wives and daughters to drive, safe from the maelstrom outside the wall. Everywhere on the grass, girls in *hijabs* paired off with boys. But the young here were definitely not in one another's arms. They sat at a demure distance, separated by the leftovers of picnic lunches.

Then an extraordinary phenomenon electrified the air and focused all eyes. As a young European woman walked by, a prurient hush fell over paradise. Although she wore a modest shirtwaist dress, she radiated the erotic charge of a G-stringed pole dancer. Her hair was uncovered and hung in lustrous ringlets. A week in Alexandria had redefined my notions of sensuality. Like those red-eyed Biblical elders leering at Susannah in her bath, I felt my thin blood pulse.

On Sunday, a workday in Egypt, I returned to the Bibliotheca Alexandrina to see Sahar Hamouda, the Mediterranean Center's deputy director. On the esplanade out front, university students milled around a pair of glinting sculptures. One was *Prometheus Bearing Fire: Symbol of Knowledge. Synonymous with Creativity and Imagination.* The other was a brushed aluminum bust of Alexander the Great. Over the door for paying customers, a sign proclaimed the current exhibition, "Bio-Vision Alexandria: New Life Sciences, From Promise to Practice."

At Hamouda's office, I discovered that we wouldn't be having a one-on-one conversation about the Cosmopolitan Era. Seated on a couch, I confronted a panel of three that reminded me of my PhD oral exams. Along with the sweet, plump Hamouda, there was a middle-aged woman with melodramatic hair, highlighted by henna. She introduced herself as Mona Khlat, and said she was a writer and former teacher.

The third party, a man in a swivel chair, volunteered nothing about himself, not even his name. But when Hamouda referred to him as Professor Awad, I divined that this august eminence in slacks, open collar shirt and Top-Siders was Mohammed Awad. An architect educated in Alexandria and London, he was the center's director and the founder of the city's Preservation Trust. Awad embodied Alexandrian cosmopolitanism and was a ruling authority on the subject.

As I had with Ibrahim Abdel Meguid, I asked whether it bothered them that Alexandria was best known through European writers. Durrell, for instance.

Awad cut me off. Like the two women, he spoke English with a British accent: "Durrell writes badly of Alexandria. He's not popular here. When I read Durrell I don't think it's about Alex. I don't think he's truthful."

"Too romantic," I suggested.

"No, romanticism isn't the problem. The problem is factual accuracy. Not even the names in Durrell exist. I don't know any Nessims or Justines. Only Clea means something to me because I knew the real Clea—Clea Bardero, the artist she was based on."

I brought up André Aciman and his memoir, *Out of Egypt*, but Professor Awad wasn't one to grant extra credit to a hometown boy. "Aciman is not very accurate. His own experience as an expelled Jew overwhelms his book. His was a quite particular experience at a time of crisis."

"Particular?" I asked. "Certainly the crisis was personal and deeply felt. But Aciman's family weren't the only Jews expelled from Egypt."

"I don't know how much of a victim he was," Awad said. "He talks about cruelty to him at school. I went to Victoria College with Aciman. The teacher he complains about was cruel to everybody. So it wasn't because he was a Jew. Nobody knew or cared that he was Jewish."

"We are a very open society," Mona Khlat piped up.

"During the Cosmopolitan Era, Alex was like Shanghai or Thessalonika—multicultural, multilingual, multiracial," the professor said. "Much more refined than New York City. We didn't have discrimination against blacks and Jews and foreigners."

"In many ways that's still the case," Khlat said, while Hamouda kept silent.

"You should attend my lecture tomorrow," Awad told me. "It's in French. Do you speak French?"

"Yes, I—"

"Three things contributed to our cosmopolitanism," he powered forward, counting on his fingers. "The stock exchange, the port and our legal system. As early as 1870 we had institutionalized international law. What other country had that? Egyptians are quite civilized because they have had contact with other civilizations."

"That remains the case," Khlat insisted. "I'm a Christian. I'm married to a Muslim. My husband lived in the United States and became more and more Islamic. He went through various phases of fanaticism. But I wear a bikini."

Awad reached over to a desk and retrieved some papers. They were old bordello licenses. "I'm looking for a license for a homosexual bordello. I know it exists, but I can't find it."

Khlat contributed another example of what she considered Egyptian tolerance. "Prostitutes used to sing a song when they came back clean from their medical checkups: 'Safe I went. Safe I come.' That's a popular song we sing now whenever we return from a journey."

Timidly, I asked how they reconciled Egyptian tolerance with the treatment of women who remained second-class citizens and more and more often wore headscarves.

"The *hijab* is a passport for women to do what they want," Hamouda said. "When we were in school, nobody wore the *hijab* or the *niqab*. But you never saw couples holding hands. Now you see students at the university lying on top of each other. I ask what they're doing and they say 'Nothing.'"

"Youngsters are quite loose compared to our generation," Awad agreed. "Women are in the streets at odd hours of the night. The veil is a mask. It's no indication of moral attitudes. For some it's to attract attention."

"Mores have changed," Khlat added, sweeping her hair out of her face with both hands. "My husband makes the *hadj* to Mecca. I go to the beach in a bikini."

Awad smiled indulgently. "You're not typical. It's part of your exotic charm and appeal. But our young people are not integrated with the rest of the world. They go to Europe but—"

"The culture has become impoverished," Khlat said.

"Students smoke *sheesha*, fool around on computers and watch videos, not the news," Hamouda joined in.

"The quality in my time was different," Awad said. "Even poor students at the university were interested in learning."

"They were more cultured," Hamouda suggested.

"Those were the people I mixed with," Khlat said. "The intellectuals."

"I remember going to Cairo to the book fair," Professor Awad said, "just to buy one French architecture magazine."

"The new rich—" Khlat started off, but Awad interrupted her. "It's always the same. There's no model to follow. My grandfather worked his ass, as they say, and made a small fortune. But he had models. Now there are no models. Society today doesn't promote this kind of thing."

I had the horrible, itchy, post-haircut feeling that I was trapped in Cavafy's poem "Waiting for the Barbarians." Trampling on one another's lines, the trio continued to kvetch that the world had gone to hell in a handbasket, and that far worse was imminent. Snug in this glass and chrome office, sheltered by the Bibliotheca, surrounded by every known communications device, they nevertheless felt cut off and frightened. Some menace, some rough beast, some unimaginable horror advanced over the horizon. Or had it already done its damage and withdrawn into the desert?

They might have rattled on and on had a strange shape not lurched into the room. No, not a barbarian. It was a benighted one-legged man in a wheelchair. "Oh, god," Khlat groaned. "He's here for money, and I don't have a penny."

I dug a few bills from my pocket, and the man grabbed them and rolled away to the next office.

"Poor fellow," Awad said.

"You know him?" I asked.

"Of course. He worked here for years. Then he developed diabetes and lost his leg."

"Now he comes to the library to beg?"

"Where else? He knows us. We know him."

I waited for one of them to say more. When nobody did, I asked whether they saw any significance in the incident. They shook their heads.

To me it seemed a caricature of conditions in Alexandria. While we sat in the Bibliotheca, bloviating about literary matters and deteriorating mores, people in the streets lived and died without basic medical care and social services. It was almost tragic. Almost grotesquely humorous. Almost worth mentioning. But what could I have said that wouldn't sound judgmental and intolerant?

Awad broke the silence. He was having guests to his home tonight, and he invited me to join them and continue our conversation. But I begged off, and thanked him and the two women for their hospitality.

Before leaving the library, I toured the Awad Collection. Much of it had been drawn from the professor's family's heirlooms— maps, historical papers, paintings and photographs of Alexandria as generations of foreigners had seen it. Or at least as they had conceived it. From the instant the first colonialists arrived, there had always been this parallax between the factual place and the fanciful vision of it. Now, it seemed to me, even its own citizens couldn't see it clearly.

That night I roamed the back lanes of Anfushi, where a street market thrummed until the late hours. It smelled of seafood and eastern spices, fresh meat and deliquescing vegetables. The stalls had radios tuned to a chaos of stations—classical Arabic, Koranic chanting, old albums of the long-dead popular singer Oum Kalthum, new covers of Lionel Richie hits. Lionel aside, the rest of the music sent up strange reverberations. To borrow from Saul Bellow, there were "winding, nasal, insinuating songs to the sounds of wire coat hangers moved back and forth, and drums, tambourines and mandolins and bagpipes."

Some shops and all the cafés had TVs blasting soccer from Spain, South America and England. Despite the profusion of goods and the frenetic hawkers, few people bought anything. Like me, they were here for company, not commerce. School kids, *niqab*ed women, married couples and oldsters on crutches congregated to see and be seen. Only I was out of place and unnoticed, able to watch without being looked at or spoken to. A definite advantage for a traveler, but one that was beginning to make me question whether I actually existed.

The next morning I slept through the alarm clock. Or rather, I heard it and incorporated it into a dream. A hurricane had smashed into Key West, and the emergency siren was shrieking. Frozen with fear I lay in bed in Florida, listening to shutters bang and the front door split into kindling.

I woke to find a mustachioed man in a blue smock beaming down at me: "Good morning. Ready to clean your room, sir." He had started showing up earlier each day, inquiring whether I was happy with his services.

I dressed and went downstairs to the breakfast buffet. It was good food and plentiful—freshly squeezed fruit juices, cereals, eggs any style, beef sausage patties, croissants and sticky buns. But every mouthful reminded me that I was stuck in Alexandria another day waiting for my visa. I had been here a week now and was ready to hit the road.

When I phoned my contact in Libya, he counseled patience, he had things under control. He or one of his minions would meet me at the Egyptian border, and drive me along the coast, stopping at the battlefield in Tobruk and the Greek ruins at Cyrenaica, a region that he referred to as the Libyan Alps. He stressed that I had to accept the caprices of the Leader Moamar Qaddafi and his Great Socialist Peoples' Libyan Arab Jamahiriya.

I reminded him that in prepayment for hotels and meals and a mandatory guide, I had already shelled out $3,000—and still my visa hadn't cleared bureaucratic channels. But he promised me it was a dead-solid certainty. Soon he would fax a copy of my visa. Then, at the border, he or his man would produce the original.

The pressure of these contingencies—or was it the high calorie breakfast?—caused a queasiness in my stomach. My health had been fine so far. I hadn't touched my stash of medications except for a daily antidepressant and a beta blocker three times a week to keep my heartbeat regular. But at the back of my mind—okay, occasionally at the forefront—there was a needling disquiet.

To counter it, I made myself move, setting off for an appointment with the curator of the Alexandrian Contemporary Arts Forum (ACAF), Bassim Baroni, whom Justin Siberell had urged me to contact. At an intersection, I climbed the usual slag heap and had started my cautious descent when the ground gave way beneath my feet and I tumbled into the street, like a turtle flipped on its shell. I realized then that Alexandrians are indeed a people of remarkable urbanity. To save me from embarrassment, they passed by without so much as a backward glance.

I made it to the forum on time, but Baroni had visitors and asked me to wait. Shaking sand out of my shirtsleeves and pant legs, I sat in the hall, where I overheard a conference on "Art, Shelter, Visibility and Love?" The moderator explained that ACAF's mission was to encourage "contemporary arts practices that have social implications. We hope to refresh the arts in Alexandria. A new generation is coming."

This sounded all too much like the Bibliotheca's boosterism. I had had a bellyful of that. But I didn't leave, and once Baroni was free to talk, I was glad I hadn't, because at last here was somebody with a sharp eye and a fresh take on the city.

"Whenever Alex is praised for its cultural renewal," Baroni said, "the talk is always about the past, never the present. Every new idea is really an old idea about dredging antiquities out of the harbor or excavating ruins from under the modern city or recreating a library that burned down thousands of years ago. If you can believe it, there's a proposal to rebuild the Pharos. I can't change this tendency on a general level. But maybe ACAF can help break the constant habit of looking backward.

"The image of Alexandria is almost entirely literary," he continued, in excellent English. "It's not based on factual research. It's based on novels and poetry, so there's the illusion that the city can develop an economy around culture. But this effort is distorted by power struggles in the government and because of empty branding. The Bibliotheca is just another attempt to brand Alex as important for its heritage. The intention is good. How it functions is something else. The Bibliotheca attracts tourists, then has nothing to show them. They visit for a day, look at the library, maybe look at the city for an hour, eat fish in a restaurant, then jump on the bus to Cairo."

I asked him to back up and explain how the problem reflected power struggles in the government.

"I work a lot with university students," Baroni said. "On the surface they seem like students everywhere—the way they dress and watch MTV and use the Internet. But embedded in the educational system is a total lack of critical thinking. From the early grades on, schools fear analysis and criticism. Everything in Egypt—the government, the police—survives on this lack of criticism. Religious fundamentalism is another negative," he added. "But it's been caused by failed nationalism, by the whole baggage of untruthful socialism that started in 1952. As a result some students see fundamentalism as the only option. Islam gives them a magic potion—a way to express their criticism and dissatisfaction."

Baroni swore he wasn't naive. He had no messianic belief that he and ACAF could solve all of Egypt's problems. Still he thought they had a role to play. "All hope is for the future," he said. "Not the past. Not the present we have today. I do what I do because I believe that art helps and can offer an alternative education to the uncritical one they get at school."

Back at the Cecil Hotel, the concierge passed me a note. I prayed it was news of my Libyan visa. Instead, it was a reminder from Michael Nevadomski that I had agreed to buy dinner tonight for

Fidehla and a few friends. All part of my effort to touch base with Islamic terrorism.

Michael said we'd have to eat after the girls finished their evening prayers. They had chosen the old-fashioned supper club Santa Lucia, which had waiters in bow ties and bolero jackets and a menu heavy on Italian dishes. It had good wine, but Michael cautioned me not to drink alcohol, out of respect for the girls' faith. What's more, since Helima was a Salafi'ist, I shouldn't touch her, not even to shake her hand.

I had to laugh at myself. In *The Daily News Egypt*, Riccardo Fabiani, from Exclusive Analysis, a British strategic intelligence firm, had warned that "worsening social and economic conditions in Egypt could fuel a reprisal of terrorist attacks on a large scale." In his opinion the country was at risk for a "new kind of terrorism." At the same time, a BBC World Service poll of more than 100 countries had revealed that Egypt was one of only two nations that didn't have a negative impression of Al Qaeda. Yet here I was in this Muslim hotbed and the best I could manage was a rendezvous at a stuffy restaurant with an American undergrad and a few English girls in *hijabs* from the University of Manchester.

Despite Michael's warning, I decided that I'd better arrive early at Santa Lucia and sneak a stiff drink. Our table was in a wood-paneled, beam-ceilinged nook. The place settings sported bone china, silverware, crystal goblets and starched napkins folded like origami birds. It seemed a shame to shake one out and plop it on my lap.

The restaurant had the aura of a men's club on Ladies' Nite. The scent of Shalimar overlay the tang of testosterone. Sedate yet seductive, the Santa Lucia was the kind of joint where a gent my age might wine and dine his much younger mistress. At nearby tables, grey-haired, brick-faced fellows appeared to be doing just that, and the soundtrack—Sade crooning "No Ordinary Love"—did what it could to help them get lucky.

Furtive as a relapsed alcoholic, I let the waiter spirit away my glass before the girls made an entrance with Michael. They created quite a stir. Fidehla and Helima, swaddled in black robes and *hijabs*, had brought along their roommate, Sarah. Born in Bahrain to a British father and a Filipina mother, she wore designer jeans and a pink Empire-line blouse that might have been a shortie pajama top.

I presided at the head of the table, like long-in-the-tooth King Lear among his three fractious daughters. Never have I wished so fervently for a second drink. I remembered not to shake hands with Helima. It required greater effort not to settle her onto my knee and cuddle her like a doll. Small and fine-boned, she had a lovely face— or sliver of a face—whose eyes appeared kohl-rimmed even without makeup. She handed me a brochure explaining Salafi'ism.

I said I'd read it later. Then I added, "Sorry about the music."

She smiled sweetly. "It's not your fault."

The recorded soundtrack stopped and a live piano player struck up a medley of old torch songs—"September in the Rain," "Stardust," "The Summer Wind."

"This is nice," Sarah said. It was unclear whether she meant the music or the menu. The three girls ordered soft drinks, and Michael and I asked for fizzy mineral water.

"I Googled Martin Amis," Fidehla told me. "I was wrong. He *is* a racist."

"No," I said. "He shot off his mouth and I'm sure he regrets it."

"Who's Martin Amis?" Sarah asked.

She and Helima, like Fidehla, hadn't heard of him or the controversy he had sparked. And when Fidehla filled them in, they showed little enthusiasm for the subject. Food held far more interest. They were tired of cooking for themselves, they said, and were delighted to be eating out. But they weren't very adventurous: They all ordered chicken.

I asked Helima about her family, and she said her parents had emigrated from Bangladesh. She had six sisters; all of them wore the *hijab*.

"How have you girls gotten along together as roommates?" I asked.

"Absolutely fantastic," Fidehla spoke for the three of them.

"Will you room together back in Manchester?"

After an awkward pause, Helima said, "I'll live with my family."

"I'll have my own apartment," Sarah said.

"It never causes problems that Sarah doesn't wear the *hijab*?" I asked.

"She's not a Muslim," Fidehla said. "But she respects our beliefs and we respect hers."

"What if she were a Muslim and didn't wear a headscarf?"

"You can be a good Muslim and not wear the *hijab*," Helima insisted. But personally neither she nor Fidehla could conceive of doing that. It didn't accord with their idea of Islam. They believed there would never come a time in their lives when they'd go without headscarves. Just as earnestly, they maintained that this didn't mean they were intolerant of people who disagreed with them.

"I have a twenty-eight-year-old son," I said. "Would you like to meet him? We can arrange a marriage."

"That depends on what he looks like." Fidehla caught the teasing tone in my voice and matched it.

I showed them a wallet snapshot of my younger boy, Marc.

"He'll do fine," Fidehla said. Helima giggled and agreed.

But when I reminded them that he wasn't Muslim, Fidehla and Helima turned serious and said they wouldn't marry a nonbeliever.

"Oh, he's a believer," Michael said. "He's Catholic. Like his father. Like me."

The two girls reiterated that their husbands had to be Muslims. In Helima's case, he also had to be a Salafi'ist. For Fidehla it wasn't an issue of a particular sect, but of sharing the same values. Sarah supported this sentiment. She wanted to move back to Bahrain and marry an Arab, because, "I like the values of Arab men."

"Would you accept an arranged marriage?"

"No, no." Sarah laughed. "I wouldn't accept his having more than one wife either."

Fidehla and Helima rejected polygamy, too, but had no compunctions about arranged marriages. "You can learn to love anybody," Helima contended. "My sisters had arranged marriages, and they're happy."

"I don't want to sound jaded," I said. "But it's been my experience that you can learn to hate someone you once loved."

"How many times have you been married?" Fidehla asked.

"I've been married to the same woman for forty-one years."

"That's longer than my mother's been alive," Michael crowed.

But the girls were enchanted and asked how I'd met my wife, how old we had been and what our parents had thought. They listened intently to a PG-rated version of my first blind date with Linda when I was twenty-two and she twenty-one. Her parents hadn't been thrilled that I was a grad student and planned to become a writer. But we married a year and a half later.

"That's so romantic," Sarah sighed.

"You were so poor and young," Helima marveled. "You were brave and lucky."

"And the way you met," Fidehla said, "it wasn't much different from an arranged marriage."

"Sure it was," I said. "Our families didn't bring us together. We were free to choose."

"We're free too," Helima said. "We don't have to marry a man just because our parents introduce us."

"But you don't go out on dates and get to know each other in different situations. What possible basis," I asked, "could you have for accepting or refusing a proposal?"

Helima giggled again. "The man has to be good looking."

"To me," Sarah said, "it's more important to marry an Arab who has a British passport."

Fidehla and Helima agreed that a British passport was crucial. Helima planned to move to Saudi Arabia after graduation and teach women or children. But she wouldn't marry a Saudi unless he had U.K. citizenship.

After dinner the three girls moved over near the pianist to listen to the music. I stayed at the table with Michael, who was as surprised as I was that Helima had joined in this idle pleasure.

I liked all three girls, but the two Believers filled me with the kind of anxiety and sadness with which fatherhood had acquainted me. They seemed so naive, so unformed. During my teaching stints,

I'd sometimes had the same reaction to American students. But with them, change and growth were inevitable. I could picture Michael, for instance, going in a dozen different directions. He might become a spy or a priest, a professor or a writer.

But Helima and Fidehla appeared forever fixed. Everything in their family history, everything in their psychological makeup suggested that they were now what they would always be. Maybe they'd claim that that was the point. In a world where whirl was king, they intended to follow the path their religious upbringing had laid for them. And who knew? They might be happier for that.

An hour later, as we filed out of Santa Lucia, past the doorman in gold livery, Sarah exclaimed, "Isn't it amazing? Here we are still in Egypt."

On my walk to the hotel, her words rang like a bell clapper in my skull. *Still in Egypt. Still in Egypt.* But then it struck me that I needn't stay in Alexandria. The Libyan border lay four hundred miles to the west, a faint scribble in the sand near the town of Sallum. I could cover the distance in stages, stopping along the coast or at the oasis of Siwa. I could check in by telephone with my contact in Tripoli, then rush to meet him at the frontier once my visa was ready.

At the Cecil, digesting my meal and the evening's religious discussion, I switched on the TV. CNN reporters were grilling Hillary Clinton and Barack Obama, the 2008 Democratic front-runners for president, about their Christian faith and the role it played in their lives and political beliefs. As they vied to replace George W. Bush, a born-again Christian whose favorite philosopher was Jesus Christ, they sounded less like citizens of a secular society based on the separation of church and state than like . . . well, like Fidehla and Helima and hundreds of other fervent Muslims I would meet.

THE DESERT

From Alexandria, a long-distance cabbie, Anwar, drove me west, destination unknown. I hadn't made up my mind whether to stop on the coast at Marsa Matruh or press on to Siwa. In either case, the charge was $100, about the same as a taxi ride from Heathrow to downtown London.

Anwar was a tall, sturdy man. He spoke English, but never played tour guide or insisted on telling me what I could see for myself. He wore a splashy sport shirt and sunglasses, as if for a day at the beach. Yet he had a prominent purplish prayer bump on his forehead that suggested he spent a lot of time at the mosque. He opened the door for me, and although I felt uncomfortable in a chauffeur-master relationship, I appreciated the space in back—and the added protection.

As we sped down a four-lane divided highway, many motorists regarded the median strip as a trivial imposition. Eastbound drivers bumped across to the westbound lane and cut against the grain of traffic. A few idiots relished playing chicken. Saner souls sailing along in the wrong direction veered onto the shoulder of the road, though that was no guarantee of safety since it swarmed with donkey carts and pedestrians.

Unflustered, Anwar handled the wheel with aplomb. He didn't curse or cry out. He left that to me. He seldom sounded his horn. He left that to other drivers. He cruised along at a steady clip, pausing only at roadblocks, where he chatted amiably with the soldiers as if they were in this together, keeping Egypt safe from terrorists and ignoring the terror of the traffic. Beside the road, the husks of wrecked cars, trucks and buses were sandblasted down to bare metal.

Mile after mile out of Alex, I made notes about the landscape. It was soothing to scribble, as many a dying explorer has discovered as he recorded his last impressions.

Durrell described the "sand-beaches off Bourg El Arab, glittering in the mauve-lemon light of the fast-fading afternoon. Here the open sea boomed upon the carpets of fresh sand the color of oxidized mercury; its deep melodious percussion was the background to such conversation as we had."

But the background to such conversations as Anwar and I had featured no "mauve-lemon light," no "carpets of fresh sand," no "deep melodious percussion." The coastline was crushed by the unbroken weight of tacky resorts, busy with workers polishing signs in English for The Riviera, Porto Marina, Charm Life, Long Beach, Diamond Beach and the Mubarak Military Resort.

This wasn't what I had expected. Having witnessed in my lifetime the despoliation of the Mediterranean's European shore, I had hoped to find better in North Africa. Better, that is, than the urban blight that extended a hundred miles from Alexandria to El Alamein.

The site of a famous World War II battle, El Alamein means "two flags." But in the bloody back-and-forth between the Germans and the Allies, many more flags had flown here, each for a short time. Then, just when it looked like German general Erwin Rommel might overrun the town and rumble on into Alexandria, the British made a stand. The landscape favored the Allies. El Alamein occupied a bottleneck between the sea and the desert, and this prevented Rommel from mounting one of his vaunted flanking maneuvers. The victory allowed the British to advance and join the Americans in Tunisia, pincering the Axis army between them.

Now the town was a patchwork of English, Italian, German and American cemeteries and grandiose memorials. Anwar asked if I wanted to stop. But I had seen enough graves in Alexandria. As we raced past row after row of white tombstones stenciled with dates and names, the melancholy of this mineral wasteland made me wonder whether my sons might one day drive through Iraq and question whether the war had been worth it.

Anwar opened the throttle, doing eighty through the desert. Mud houses and dovecotes like big bread ovens replaced the battlefields and burial grounds. Camels grazed on scrub brush, and tumbleweeds of trash blew across the road. The sea was close by, and high combers appeared to crash over the beach. But what I took to be salt spray proved to be clouds of sand scudding along the coast, scalding any sun worshipper foolish enough to stop for a dip.

At the outskirts of Marsa Matruh, a mirage welled up out of the sun-warped landscape. I thought I saw flamingoes arching their necks over a rippling pond. But the illusion gave way to an even more bizarre reality—a vast, empty parking lot with bird-shaped streetlights.

Anwar lifted his foot from the accelerator and gestured right, then left. He was asking, Marsa Matruh on the sea? Or Siwa in the desert? I pointed south toward the Siwa oasis. It felt terrific to be moving. Why quit now? Why not go someplace new—and very, very old.

Forster described Alexander the Great following this route ages ago, and the last traces of civilization disappearing in an immensity of limestone hills: "Around him little flat pebbles shimmered and danced in the heat, gazelles stared and pieces of sky slopped into the sand. Over him was the pale blue dome of heaven, darkened, if we are to believe his historian, by flocks of obsequious birds, who sheltered the King with their shadows and screamed when he rode in the wrong way. Alexander rode, remembering how, two hundred years before him, the Persians had ridden to loot the temple, and how on them as they were eating in the desert a sandstorm had descended, burying diners and dinner in company. Herein lay the magic of Siwa. It was difficult to reach. He, being the greatest man of his epoch, had of course succeeded. He, the Philhellene, had come. His age was twenty-five. Then took place that celebrated and extraordinary episode. According to the official account the Priest came out of the temple and saluted the tourist as Son of God."

On my journey to Siwa no gazelles stared—although camels did hunker on the roadside and squint at me through luxuriant eyelashes. No obsequious birds shaded my path, but Anwar did thumb the AC setting higher. No one would greet me as the Son of

God when we reached the oasis, but after six hours on the road, an extraordinary episode did transpire at our arrival. Hundreds of miles separated me from that reception, however, and Anwar and I had to traverse an enormous emptiness.

Straight as a die, the road deteriorated from a dual-lane highway into a torn ribbon of asphalt. Our route was littered with the remnants of blown tires, coiled anacondas of black rubber. Off to both sides, unpaved tracks led to numbered oil fields and rigs, invisible amid the heat convection. There were no other cars, just stray camels and sheep, and the odd shepherd and the odder concrete picnic table, canopied by palm fronds. Instead of picnickers, prostrate Egyptians napped on the tables that must have been hot as griddles.

We stopped at a ghastly hovel to fill up with gasoline and buy something to drink. The place was, to borrow a phrase from the French poet Charles Baudelaire, "an oasis of horror in a desert of boredom." There was no bottled water, and even Anwar wasn't willing to trust the dark dribble from the spigot. We ordered Turkish coffee, muddy and turbid as the Nile. I gagged mine down like medicine against sleeping sickness. Men loitering around the hovel looked diseased. They curled against the wall in the shade and cracked open their rheumy eyes only to check their cell phones for messages.

Who could be texting them? And why? Saying what? In such a grim spot, SOS seemed the only imaginable message. And yet I wasn't unhappy here. The pleasure of being where I had never been before, doing what I had never done, bound for who knew what—I found it all thrilling. I always have.

A few miles farther along we found bottled water. Better than that, refrigerated bottled water, at an establishment called Cleopatra

Beatch. Had the owner misspelled "beach"? Or had the name come from hip-hop, the joint rendering the word as rappers pronounce "bitch"?

Near Siwa the earth began to buckle, and the crust of the desert broke into hillocks that resembled ziggurats. It was as if the Step Pyramid at Saqqara had been duplicated dozens of times and surrounded by pebbles piled into burial cairns. Then the arid countryside turned abruptly verdant; lush fields poured through palm groves. And lodged at the center of the oasis, like a brown pit inside a luscious fruit, was a mud village.

Flatbed carts rolled along silently on recycled car tires through streets smothered in heat, dust and somnolence. The ruins of a thirteenth-century fortress dominated Siwa's low skyline. Constructed of *kershef*, a compound of clay, gravel and chunks of salt from a nearby lake, the battlements had once been five stories tall, but a freak rainstorm in 1926 had reduced them to nubs.

After Anwar succeeded in locating the Shali Lodge, he shook my hand ceremoniously and said it had been a pleasure. He was heading straight back to Alex.

To loosen the kinks in my legs, I strolled around the town, crossing paths with an albino man. In other parts of Africa—Tanzania, for instance—albinos are hunted down and killed, and witch doctors sell their bones, skin and organs as folk remedies. While this fellow didn't have that to contend with, the sun had cruelly scarred his skin and baked his white hair yellow.

Nearby, a shop rented snowboards. In the window, snapshots showed grinning tourists *shooshing* down mountainous dunes. I was convinced I'd see nothing stranger this day, but then a turbaned man sauntered out of a palm grove and said, "Hello, Mr. Mike. You have a message from your wife." Ali went on to explain, in serviceable English, that Linda had phoned to say that Libya had granted me a visa. A faxed copy of it was waiting for me at the hotel.

The Shali Lodge resembled a mud daubers' nest, shaded by soaring bamboo. Beams jutted from the exterior walls like cannon barrels. It had a rooftop restaurant teeming with flies, and a courtyard swimming pool empty except for ankle-deep sand. Blessedly cool, my room was furnished with folkloric handicrafts that I couldn't properly appreciate because of the poor lighting. Only the bathroom had bulbs bright enough for reading, so I hauled a chair into the shower stall.

The Shali Lodge, I'd read in a brochure, was one of three establishments in Siwa owned by Mounir Neamatallah, a Coptic Egyptian environmentalist dedicated to preserving the oasis in its natural state. His hotels promoted sustainable resources, organic gardening and low-impact tourism—a kind of Spartan chic. While my room cost $40 a night, a double at the Adrère Amellal set back rock stars and royalty—Prince Charles and Camilla had stayed there—$400 for an un-air-conditioned suite lit by lanterns and furnished with hunks of hewn rock salt. Adrère Amellal did, however, have an amenity that convinced me I should visit: It was the one establishment in this devout Muslim oasis that served alcohol.

I hiked back to the center of town over a road that had been milled to talcum powder. The third of Mounir Neamatallah's projects, the Heritage Hotel, was situated among restored sections of the fortress. No booze there, though: I slaked my thirst with mint tea on a terrace above the main square and watched the citizens of Siwa, groggy from the day's heat, emerge for the evening.

Once the air had cooled I climbed from the hotel into the ruins of the thirteenth-century battlements. What had at a distance looked like a mouthful of rotten teeth now suggested the fantastic shapes of those celebrated Gaudi houses in Barcelona. Mica chips glittered in mud bricks. The summit opened onto a view of the white Great Sand Sea in one direction, a blue salt lake in the other and between them the green splurge of palm trees that sprouted from Siwa's three hundred freshwater springs.

The descent offered less exalting panoramas. At every turn, I bumped into a pile of crushed rock or shattered bone. One path was blocked by white porcelain shards. Someone had dragged a bathtub, a sink, a toilet and a bidet up here and sledge-hammered them into smithereens.

I ate dinner at an open-air pizzeria pestered by feral cats. They didn't slink around and rub seductively against my legs. They demanded to be fed, and when I didn't do it, the fiercest among them sank a claw into my hand, drawing blood. I yowled, but no one gave me a second glance. Like the spill I took from that trash heap in Alexandria, a cat attack didn't strike anybody as noteworthy.

At a pharmacy, I bought gauze to staunch the bleeding and alcohol to clean the scratch. Then I stopped in a cubbyhole where a fellow wearing a G-Star Raw T-shirt presided over an international phone cabin. Dialing my wife in Key West, I thanked her for the news about the Libyan visa. I missed Linda and we wound up talking for twenty minutes about the boys, about a rendezvous in Tunis, about her tireless detective work in tracking me to the Shali Lodge. In the background we could hear the *muezzin* calling the faithful to the last prayer. The guy in the G-Star Raw T-shirt cut us short. He had to shut the shop and hurry to the mosque.

In the morning, my goal was the Temple of the Oracle, where Alexander the Great had received word of his divinity. Under a canopy of palms, it was pleasantly cool and frogs trilled in the irrigation ditches. Cultivated fields flourished wherever water moistened the sand, and thousands of olive and fruit trees sheltered mint and clover, tomatoes and onions. Layer on layer, the oasis was a perpetual motion machine of chlorophyll, an ingenious self-contained system that permitted survival in this otherwise inhospitable environment.

Siwa's Berber population had remained culturally and linguistically distinct from the rest of Egypt's. Christianity had never made inroads here, and Islam prevailed only after several centuries of punishing military campaigns. But once the Koran took root, the people committed themselves to a conservative brand of the religion. Guidebooks warned that it was unwise for women to walk alone in the palm groves, and those who traveled in groups were urged to dress modestly, covering their arms and legs.

I noticed no women, no tourists at all. It occurred to me as the day heated up that they had probably come here earlier. By the time I reached Bridal Spring, an oval of water as beautifully blue as the grotto on Capri, I was drenched in sweat and tempted to take the plunge. A sign in English warned: TO SWIM HERE YOU HAVE TO BE A GOOD

SWIMMER. But that's not what kept me from jumping in: I didn't have my bathing suit, and skinny-dipping was out of the question given local attitudes.

At the Temple of the Oracle, I circled the ruins, ducking from one patch of shade to the next, much as I would dart from tree to tree during a rainstorm. Still, I was bedraggled and sun-dazzled and in no doubt at all about my mortality. It would have taken a god, or a mountain goat, to clamber to the top of the temple's shattered walls.

I pushed on to the Temple of Umm Ubayd, which was in a terminal state of disrepair. An Ottoman governor had blown it up in 1896 and carted off the rubble as building material. One fragment was still standing, and I made for its shade. But somebody had beaten me to it. A nattily dressed Arab flattened himself against the rocks like a lizard and was thumbing a text message. If he had any sense, he was calling a taxi.

I reeled on through the heat following the hoofprints and droppings of a donkey. Then I caught sight of the animal up ahead, and was thunderstruck when it collapsed to the ground as if felled by lightning. It hadn't died of the heat. It rolled and kicked its heels and heehawed in a frenzy of flea-scratching.

Farther along, Cleopatra's Bath, a basin in the middle of a dirt road, didn't look half as inviting as the donkey's dust bath. A man with a net scooped algae out of water that smelled of rotten eggs. I trudged on and on, and when I made it back to the Shali Lodge, I belatedly checked a map of the oasis, calculated the distance, and realized I had covered almost seven miles in hundred-degree heat.

That afternoon, I arranged to visit Adrère Amellal. A boy in a pickup truck drove me out to it, through fields that had a marvelous vividness. Green patches alternated with bare red earth. The salt lake of Birket Siwa was cobalt blue, its shores fringed in yellow rime. The closer we came, the more the White Mountain and the hotel in its limestone lee grew in monumentality.

"Don't use mobile phone," the boy said.

"I don't have one."

"Good. Against rules."

There was a gate and a charade of security. There was a swimming pool. There were horse stables and a paddock. There was a preening bellboy who escorted me around, admiring his turban in each room's mirror. The hotel was stylishly stark, innovative in its use of handicrafts, wall hangings, camel halters, cedar doors and banisters fashioned out of gnarled olive branches. The bare stone floors were polished as smooth as soap.

But all this was a tedious prelude to the main event. I was raring to get to the bar, and once I got there I couldn't be bothered admiring the romantic alcoves cut into rock or the cocktail tables made from millstones. I tried to wheedle a drink from the bartender. But my entreaties fell on deaf ears. He refused to sell alcohol to a nonguest.

Back at the Shali Lodge, sober as a judge, I ate dinner on the rooftop with Ali, the turbaned man who had given me the news about Linda and the Libyan visa. He urged me to let him set up a trip to the desert tomorrow. Two Frenchwomen at a nearby table cocked their heads, eavesdropping on our conversation. The price of a three-hour excursion was $150. An immense sum in Egypt. I told Ali that I'd have to think about it.

The next morning at breakfast, the Frenchwomen tarried over glasses of mint tea. "So you go to the desert today?" one said in English. I answered in French, *"Peut-être"* ("Maybe").

It was difficult to estimate their ages. They might have been as old as I was. But with their trim figures and sporty clothes, they possessed that plausible attractiveness that Parisian women seem to maintain until death. *Bien dans leur peau.* Comfortable in their skin, as the saying goes. They offered to split the cost of a driver and a four-wheel-drive vehicle to the Great Sand Sea. Fifty bucks a person.

I went to make plans with Ali, who told me that desert treks required special permission and he needed our passports. I returned to the roof to inform the women, but they had gone to their room. Ali, of course, knew the number, as he knew everything. So I knocked on their door, and from inside a mellow voice trilled, *"Qui est là?"*

We hadn't exchanged names. We never would. *"L'américain,"* I said.

The door swung open, and one of the women greeted me wearing a big smile and a small towel that couldn't quite hide all that she pretended to want to keep private.

"I'll come back later," I said.

"Pas du tout. What do you need?"

"Your passport and your friend's."

"Of course." She turned her tanned back and pale butt to me, swanned over to a suitcase and fetched their papers. "Anything else?" she asked.

"Not a thing. See you this afternoon."

I didn't presume that the woman had sex on the brain, nor would I ever be so egotistical as to imagine she was interested in sex with me. But it wasn't farfetched to imagine that travelers of any age or nationality might yearn to spice up their itinerary with erotic encounters.

In fact, some of the greatest literary figures of the past few centuries have been relentless explorers (in some cases exploiters) of the world's flesh. With his landmark work of scholarship, *Orientalism*, Edward Said, the noted American academic of Palestinian origin, discussed dozens of illustrious authors who roamed the globe, ostensibly seeking inspiration and creative material, but settling for sex. For these men (and a few women, too, such as Isabelle Eberhardt), adventurous journeys were a way of joining a "community of thought and feeling described by Mario Praz in *The Romantic Agony*, a community for which the imagery of exotic places, the cultivation of sadomasochistic tastes (what Praz calls *algolagnia*), a fascination with the macabre, with the notion of a Fatal Woman, with secrecy and occultism, all combined to enable literary work."

Analyzing the political and psychological implications of this sort of travel, Said argued that it replicated in the personal realm the colonializing impulse that dominated the public domain. Whatever their stated reasons—spreading freedom, civilization or religion—Europeans, and later Americans, actually came to the Middle East and North Africa to conquer, occupy, penetrate and possess. The place remained for them a "private fantasy, even if that fantasy was of a very high order indeed, aesthetically speaking."

For examples of Said's thesis, one could do no better than consider Alexandria's famous triad of foreign writers—Cavafy, Forster and Durrell. The first two were obsessed with the Fatal Fellow, not the Fatal Woman, yet the result was much the same—a whole city and years of experience and thought filtered through the alembic of sexual intimacy. The parade of boys passing through Cavafy's room, the streetcar conductor who electrified Forster's life, the many women who, Durrell told Henry Miller, had been conflated into Justine—all these are twentieth-century incarnations of what had intrigued earlier travelers.

French novelist Gustave Flaubert, for instance, arrived in Egypt in 1849 on a bogus mission from the Ministry of Public Instruction in Paris. He and a male companion were supposed to be photographing inscriptions from pharaonic monuments. But a large part of the trip consisted of committing to memory and to paper sexual escapades that Flaubert never intended to share with the Ministry of Public Instruction. After a close personal inspection of an impressive number of prostitutes, Flaubert noted in his journal: "Their shaved cunts made a strange effect—the flesh is hard as bronze." He also visited the syphilitic ward at Kasr el-'Aini Hospital. "At a sign from the doctor [the patients] stood up on their beds, undid their trouserbelts (it was like an army drill) and opened their anuses with their fingers to show their chancres."

There was, I decided, a learned dissertation to be done on the connection—the interpenetration, if you will—of travel, sex and literature. André Gide, Henri de Montherlant, Paul Bowles, Brion Gysin and William Burroughs are just a few more of the authors whose sensibilities were shaped by their sexual marauding in North Africa, and whose books then shaped public perceptions of the region, often prejudicially.

I won't be doing that book. I will admit, though, that seeing a Frenchwoman's bare ass set me to thinking and free-associating.

I thought about Linda again and how much I missed her. I thought about the story she had told me of her college classmate who, while on a junior year abroad, took a vacation to Cairo and within a week married an Egyptian waiter. The girl's horrified parents promptly flew over, hired lawyers, had the marriage annulled and bundled their daughter back to the States. What was it about the air or food or water here that set foreigners' hormones aflame?

The excursion to the Great Sand Sea required preparation. I brought along sunblock and bottled water, and since we'd be visiting a couple of desert springs—one hot, one cold—I also brought my swimming trunks. The women were advised that if they cared to take a dip, they'd have to do so fully dressed. They regarded this as ridiculous and demanded to know why.

The driver spoke little English and no French, and couldn't answer this or any other question. When at the edge of the Great Sand Sea he paused to let air out of the Toyota Landcruiser's tires, the Frenchwomen babbled, "*Pourquoi, pourquoi?*" And they weren't mollified when I explained that lower tire pressure would improve our traction in the dunes.

As we progressed onto the undulating sand, their interrogation soon gave way to gushing. "*Magnifique! Extraordinaire! Charmant!*" they cried out. It was, to be honest, pretty *fantastique*. Castles of rock reared up like coral reefs, tortured by wind into flamboyant shapes and marbled by bright mineral deposits. A few palms had survived the encroaching desert, their trunks buried in sand up to the fronds.

The women fell dead silent when the daredevil driver chugged up a tall dune and teetered there, fiddling with the gearshift. As on a black diamond ski slope, we could see the bottom of the dune, but nothing in between. Gunning the engine, the driver plunged into the abyss, and after a gut-churning free fall, we jolted over a few moguls and sluiced onto flat ground. Then, barely slowing down, he soared up the next dune, down it and up another and another. My ears popped and the French ladies whooped in joy.

Eventually, we arrived at what appeared to be an antimacassar spread over the desert. That got the women going again. *"Qu'est-ce que c'est que ça?"* they wanted to know, and could not believe that it was a fossil bed littered with bleached seashells and starfish and the spiny carapaces of primordial crabs. Along with the rest of Egypt, the area once lay beneath the ocean. I would have thought this paleological zone would be off limits. At the very least, I expected the driver to warn us not to walk on the fossils. But he did no such thing, and the Frenchwomen raced around plundering sand dollars.

At Bir Wahed, we stopped first at the hot spring, a sulphurous pool the size of a Jacuzzi. After jouncing around for hours in the desert, I was eager for a therapeutic soak. The pond's surface floated a skin of algae, and the bottom felt like wet fur. Cavorting fully clothed, the Frenchwomen didn't mind the smell or the slime. But I slipped in over my head and swallowed a mouthful of awful water that sent me scrambling back to dry land.

When the ladies finally climbed out, they chortled at something I was too polite to mention. Their slacks and blouses had turned transparent in the hot spring, and since they weren't wearing bras or panties, they might as well have been naked.

It was a short ride to the cold spring, and en route we passed a pride of teenage boys snowboarding on a sand dune. When they caught sight of the Frenchwomen in their dishabille, they slalomed downhill with loud, yodeling shouts and jumped into the water with us. I paddled far out, away from the reed-fringed shore and flipped onto my back. Floating blissfully in the icy pond, I gazed up at sun-scorched hills on all sides. It was an experience to treasure—swimming in one of the most arid spots on earth, glorying in the immense blue sky and the Great Sand Sea and, most remarkable, being tenderly nibbled by minnows. How in Allah's name had fish gotten in here?

Rejuvenated, I swam ashore and changed clothes behind the Landcruiser. Then the Frenchwomen asked me to stand guard while they stripped off their wet duds and put on dry ones. Meanwhile, the driver and the snowboarders smoked cigarettes and whispered with what seemed a mixture of adolescent anxiety and age-old contempt. In a country where women hid their faces and hair, what were they to make of this?

The drive back to Siwa was a sensory delirium. In the heat, my hair dried in minutes. No one spoke. None of us needed words to recognize that the moment was *incroyable*. As the sun sank behind us and the moon rose ahead, the driver parked at the crest of a dune and stretched out full length in the sand, like that Henri Rousseau painting of the Sleeping Arab. Only a lion and a lyre were missing.

The ladies, too, reclined on the sand, and one of them swept out a snow angel with her arms and legs. The temperature was perfect, the air clear and still. I felt at peace, and at the same time believed I was changing, cracking open, realigning my relationship to the world. Was this what explorers in the Sahara had described as the Baptism of Solitude? This crystallizing sensation of cosmic harmony?

The driver sat up and crouched, straining to capture the last sliver of the golden disk of sun as it slid behind the horizon. Then he stood up, readjusted his robes and kicked a little sand behind him, as a cat would do.

One of the Frenchwomen shrieked. The other moaned, "*Ça, c'est dégeulasse!*" ("That's disgusting!")

The driver didn't react, simply climbed into the Landcruiser and revved the engine. On the ground where he had crouched lay a steaming turd.

B ack at the Shali Lodge, the women brushed past Ali and stalked off to their room. I paid him, and Ali paid the driver, who said something in Arabic that made Ali laugh. Then Ali told me, "You are invited to dinner at Adrère Amellal."

This struck me as a heartless joke. Last night I had complained to him about my abortive attempt to persuade the barkeep to serve me alcohol. But Ali insisted he was serious. Yolande, the PR woman at Adrère Amellal, had phoned to say the owner, Mounir Neamatal-lah, wanted to meet me.

"He doesn't know I'm alive," I said.

"No. The bellboy told him he saw you writing in a little book. He thinks you might write something about the hotel."

Well, I would have done that anyway. It could hardly compromise my integrity—it was basic politeness—to accept a dinner invitation and perhaps a glass of wine from a prominent citizen.

Neamatallah dispatched a car, and as it approached the White Mountain, moonlight softened the hard-edged geometry of the hotel. Yolande gave me a tour that retraced the one I'd had yesterday. But now, lighted by candles, the rooms looked less severe. We sat outside at one of the millstone tables, and a waiter brought a bottle of Château des Rêves. Had it not been for the pesky mosquitoes that spawned in the nearby lake, the moment would have been bliss.

I asked Yolande how she liked living here, and she responded with a candor rare in public relations: "I leave during the hottest months of summer and the coldest part of winter. Without electricity, we don't have heat or air conditioning."

Spring and fall were the best seasons, she said. But on this April night, the Adrère Amellal had just three paying guests. While the hotel had won high praise from the press, its message of environmentally sensitive tourism apparently hadn't caught on.

We were joined by a Belgian filmmaker, a histrionic fellow with baggy drawstring trousers and a red-checked *kaffiyeh* on his shaved skull. The three of us talked until ten o'clock, and I was lightheaded from hunger when Yolande led us to Dr. Neamatallah's private residence on the far side of the mountain. Bellboys with torches lit an *allée* of neatly spaced and meticulously pruned palm trees. At the end of the *allée* was a cubistic building constructed, like the hotel, from *kershef*, an amalgam of clay, gravel and rock salt.

In a courtyard, around a fire pit that contained heaped ashes, no flames, five people chatted in French. Neamatallah bounded to his feet and pumped my hand. A short, compact man, he wore an olive green shirt and wire-rimmed glasses that lent him an air of wizard-like wisdom. His manners were impeccable, his English as flawless as his French, and the elaborateness of his welcome made me wonder who he imagined I was. "Please, call me Mounir," he said.

There was a French couple, Patrice, a spry businessman, and his attractive wife who took me aback by saying, "I'm Bob."

"Barb?" I asked, sure I had misheard.

"No, Bob. Pronounced the same as the word for 'gate' in Arabic."

The other couple came from Beirut. Gianni, with hair as white and curly as lamb's wool, wore glasses reminiscent of the heavy-gauge tortoise shell shades favored by Aristotle Onassis. His wife was an American of Chinese descent, and while she was as attractive as Bob, she had on a pair of large white-rimmed spectacles that would have been better suited to a circus clown.

The conversation reverted to French, with the enthusiastic participation of Yolande and the Belgian filmmaker. Gianni, an old friend of Mounir's, held forth on the hellacious condition of Egypt's Mediterranean coast, its squalor, the over-development, the extortionate cost. "They tell me villas sell for $1,000 a square meter. But who'd buy at that price?" he asked. "You could get something in Beirut for that kind of money. Beirut's the place with potential for someone prepared to take risks."

Patrice and Bob hoped that what had happened to the Egyptian coast would never happen to Siwa. Desert oases were fragile environments, easily destroyed. The French couple had traveled to Tozeur, in Tunisia, and complained that it was overrun with tourists and ruined by luxury hotels.

Since Tozeur was on my itinerary, I would have liked to have known more. But Patrice and Bob started to talk about the bed and breakfast they ran back in Aurillac. "We operate on the same principles at Adrère Amellal. We raise our own food and serve nothing except organic products."

At this, Mounir Neamatallah, exercising *droit de seigneur*, assumed charge of the conversation. Despite his diminutive stature, he was a magisterial figure and a mesmerizing speaker. Sounding more philosophical than your average entrepreneur, he recounted his education in the United States—how he had earned an undergraduate degree in chemical engineering somewhere in the Midwest, then enrolled in the PhD program at Columbia University. After completing his coursework, but before finishing a dissertation, he switched to environmental studies, started over, and got a doctorate in urban planning. He spoke of himself as a dreamy visionary, content to leave the number crunching to the accountants.

When dinner was ready, Mounir ushered us into an oval dining room, like a beautiful Fabergé egg cracked open at the top for a view of the stars. He continued talking, mostly in French, but with English buzz phrases thrown in for punctuation: "sustainable resources," "carbon offsets," "reduced ecological footprints."

"These places," he said, alluding to the Shali Lodge and the Heritage Hotel along with Adrère Amellal, "can be a model for tourism throughout the Third World."

Just one thing jeopardized his dream. People in Cairo, powerful men in political and military positions who had influence with President Mubarak, were determined to build a commercial airport in Siwa. They wanted to bring in package tours by the planeload and transform the oasis into an international resort.

"Well," Gianni urbanely remarked, "the drive to Siwa is very long. If you come by the desert road from Cairo, it's boring. And if you come by the coast from Alex, it's ugly. An airport might not be a bad idea."

"No, no, no," Mounir protested. "The trip to Siwa must be long and hard, just as it has been ever since the time of Alexander the Great. People appreciate it more when they have to deal with the desert. They understand better what we are doing here."

As his guests, the eaters of his organic food, the drinkers of his Château des Rêves, what could we do except applaud his spirit and urge him to keep fighting the good fight? We raised our glasses and toasted Mounir Neamatallah and declared that Siwa should remain forever ecologically pure.

The Belgian filmmaker left before dessert, departing on the nine-hour trip to Cairo. Though he seemed dressed for a camel ride, he was being chauffeured in a minivan. Then Gianni and his wife wished us good night and walked off with a torchbearer. Patrice and Bob came in the car with me, and as we rounded the White Mountain to the hotel, Patrice explained that they were in Egypt to celebrate their thirty-fifth wedding anniversary.

"We wanted to do something special," he said. "Bob researched on the Internet, and that's how we learned about Adrère Amellal. Since we're in the tourist business ourselves, we always try to find a place that's new and different before it's ruined. Of course Dr. Neamatallah's dream is praiseworthy. But it's hopeless. Sooner rather than later, the airport will be built and Siwa will be destroyed. That's how things are. And that's why we're here now."

I woke with a headache, the result not just of the wine and a long night of speaking French, but of the hangover that sometimes attends the promiscuity of travel. The hunger, if not the energy, is boundless. Yet you're no sooner satisfied with one place than you're on to the next destination. I hated to think that Patrice was right and I couldn't come back to Siwa without finding it (or did I mean myself?) changed.

That afternoon I caught a ride to the coast, to Marsa Matruh, where I would spend the night, then travel tomorrow to meet my Libyan contact at the border. In summer, Marsa Matruh was a popular resort for Egyptian vacationers. Now it was in hibernation, abandoned except for stray dogs. At the Hotel Beau Site, situated on a translucent turquoise bay, pooches took the sun like Florida retirees. The clerk at the reception desk quoted me a room rate of $35 a night. But his boss promptly corrected him and said the price for foreigners was $56.

"Why should I pay more than an Egyptian?" I asked.

"That's the rule. Foreigners don't get the same rate as legal residents."

I checked in and walked down the windblown beach, then out onto residential streets, where every house was closed, every window shuttered, every door locked and every dog deep in sleep. The sea air was thirty degrees cooler than it had been in the desert. I might have changed seasons as well as locations: I actually shivered. Marsa Matruh had the haunted look of a town struck by a neutron bomb that had killed off the population, but left the buildings intact.

Although spanking new, the marina, like so many spots in Egypt, was steeped in history. A sign advertised boat service to a pool where Cleopatra and Marc Antony supposedly swam. Legend had it that the lovers committed suicide in Marsa, but there was no historical proof, just as there's no proof Cleopatra killed herself by clasping a venomous snake to her breast. Scholars theorize that the Romans might have captured and executed her. At any rate, she didn't die until after Marc Antony killed himself, and archeologists have started digging for her tomb not here but on a hillside west of Alexandria, under the ruins of the temple of Taposiris Magna.

That evening, at the Beau Site Restaurant, I ordered fish. It looked like a "square grouper." In Key West, that's what we call jettisoned marijuana that's been hauled out of the ocean. The breadcrumb-encrusted cod on my plate was as brown and indigestible as a brick of hash.

At the table next to me, a man in a polo shirt sported a gold Rolex watch. His wife wore the *niqab*. Somehow she managed to finish a bowl of soup without once revealing her face or staining her veil.

Up in the room I repacked my bags, two small carry-ons with shoulder straps. Their combined weight was thirty-five pounds. I knew I had to cross the frontier on foot. I had no idea how far I'd be walking—a few hundred yards, half a mile at most, I figured—and I wasn't worried, not after all the hiking I'd done in Siwa. I felt primed, excited, convinced that the exodus from Egypt heralded the true start of my trip.

By 9 AM I was in a long-distance cab hurtling toward the border, about two hundred miles west. On one side of the road, a sandy beach ended at the Mediterranean. On the other side sand stretched a thousand miles into the immensity of the Sahara. It was already hot and getting hotter by the minute. I had chosen to travel in spring to avoid the worst of the heat. Now I wondered whether winter wouldn't have been better.

Sidi Barami slid past, a Bedouin settlement with what the guidebook referred to as "a few unsanitary places to eat." Then there was a village whose name was spelled three different ways on three different signs: BAKBAK. BAQBAQ. BUQBUQ. In three hours we reached Sallum, the last town in Egypt, and the driver asked whether I wanted to change money. It seemed sensible to have some Libyan cash. So we stopped in a marketplace.

The driver steered me into a candy store, not a bank, and I handed him a $100 bill. He said he'd be right back and disappeared into the rear of the shop. A stock boy was unpacking candy bars, stacking them haphazardly on shelves and heaving empty boxes out into the street. The boxes bounced off passersby, but nobody appeared to mind. The boy tossed me a Mars bar and refused to let me pay for it. I wolfed it down, not knowing when I'd eat next or where.

The driver returned with a clump of Libyan dinars and counted them out. I hadn't any idea about the exchange rate and accepted his word. Trust, blind trust, was a key ingredient of the trip. I found myself filled with fatalistic calm. I felt my age, my solitude, and my ignorance were advantages.

From Sallum, we climbed toward Halfaya Pass. The car coughed and sputtered, and downhill traffic careened around hairpin curves, nearly sideswiping us. A tractor trailer had jackknifed into a ditch, crushing the driver's compartment. Gawkers gathered, waiting for a tow truck, an ambulance, a hearse. Where would help have to come from? Marsa Matruh? And where could the injured be evacuated? Alexandria was at the other end of the country.

I preferred not to think about Egyptian emergency care. I hefted my bags and told the driver to drop me as close to the border as possible. At the customs booth, a soldier flashed a big smile. "*Amriki?*" he asked in astonishment, and couldn't contain himself when I produced an American passport. It delighted him to meet somebody from the States and, more remarkable, somebody on foot.

"Now where?" I said.

He jabbed a thumb toward a gate that was far away in the heat haze.

"Libya?" I said.

He jabbed his thumb again.

"Taxi?" I asked.

He scissored his fingers, imitating two scurrying legs.

I started walking. No problem, not even in hundred-degree heat. I did wish I had worn a hat. But I peeled off my coat and rolled my shirtsleeves and covered a kilometer or so with more than enough breath to ask at the next gate. "Libya?"

This soldier wasn't smiling. "Egypt," he said, and searched my bags. Then he presented me with papers printed in Arabic. A fellow who spoke a bit of English helped me fill them out and kept repeating "*Amriki? Amriki?*" while shaking his head in wonderment. Maybe that was why he led me up a flight of stairs to what smelled like a latrine, but proved to be an office. Maybe he just wanted to show off the white-haired, now pink-faced American to his superior.

Then he shepherded me downstairs, through a turnstile, to the head of a long line. There must have been a hundred people stoically waiting to have their papers stamped. They accepted it as an inexorable aspect of their fate to step aside for a foreigner. I wanted to apologize to them individually, but my English-speaking savior shoved me out the door toward the next gate, another kilometer up the road.

By now my ears burned. My hair was on fire. The asphalt, blistering with tar bubbles, burned my feet through my shoes. I dabbed sunblock, SPF 100, on my forehead and cheeks until I was as pale as a kabuki dancer. It was the heat, not the distance, I decided. The heat and the dryness and the fact that I hadn't worn a hat or carried a water bottle.

At the third gate I recognized the uniforms and didn't waste energy asking, "Libya?" This was an Egyptian outpost, a currency control. Libya was still lost in a mirage down the road.

There were no taxis. No buses. A few private vehicles bubbled past. I tried to flag one down, but they overflowed with passengers. Plenty of people on foot plodded along beside me, all of them burdened with cardboard boxes and black garbage bags stuffed with cotton shirts and pants, underwear and socks that they had bought cheaply in Egypt and intended to sell dear in Libya.

Something gave way with a jolt, and I felt a stab of pain. My first fear was for my back or that my shoulder had popped out of its socket. The bag on that side splatted to the soft tar. The strap had broken, not my bones or tendons. I picked it up and staggered on.

At the fourth gate, the soldiers wore smart blue uniforms. Libyans! They were no less shocked than the Egyptians to see a white man; they, too, guessed "Amriki." But I switched to my Irish passport, the one that would supposedly make my entry smoother.

These troops were more of a greeting committee than final arbiters. They sent me marching on. Cars splashed through a trough of brown suds that I would gladly have swum across to cool down. I trudged around this trench of disinfectant to a blazing concrete plaza snarled with trucks, buses, cars and rambunctious pedestrians. Among them, a small, handsome man with a shock of black hair and a megawatt smile waved a sign with my name on it.

Struggling to be seen above the maelstrom, Khalil had been waiting for hours. He grabbed my bags and my Irish passport and tucked the original visa and photocopy into it. Then we elbowed through the crowd. I knew that I didn't have the stamina to stand in the sun and wait my turn in line, and again no one questioned my rightness, my whiteness, to go to the front of the line. I also knew now what the ancient Egyptian general Amir had meant when, on his deathbed, he whispered, "I feel as if heaven lay close upon the earth, and I between the two, breathing through the eye of a needle."

Khalil and I squeezed into a room not much bigger than the desk it contained. The officer behind the desk must have had to shimmy across it to his chair. While Khalil passed him my documents, and they spoke in Arabic, I fantasized about a cool drink of water, a shower, clean clothes, a hotel room with AC.

"Problem," Khalil interrupted my reverie. "Your passport isn't translated."

"And?"

"And you cannot enter Libya unless your passport is translated into Arabic."

"Fine. Let's do it." I was eager to snuggle back into my daydream.

"It has to be translated and stamped by the Irish Embassy."

"What? Where?"

"Maybe Alexandria."

My blood went cold, then hot, then cold again. I turned weak at the knees and goose-pimply on the arms. We were more than nine hours by car from Alex. I couldn't afford to have an outburst like the "incident" at the Athens airport. I needed to stay calm and find a solution.

"Why don't you translate it?" I suggested.

"I'm not qualified," Khalil said.

"Sure, you are. You speak Arabic and English."

"An official has to do it." Khalil was gentling me outside.

"Then let's pay this good man to translate my passport." I pulled a $100 bill, plus some Libyan currency, from my pocket.

"Put that away," Khalil said. With shocking strength for his size—he couldn't have been more than five feet three—he manhandled me into the plaza.

"This is bullshit," I shouted. "I've already paid your company three thousand dollars. I'm not going back to Alexandria."

"Maybe Cairo," he said, as though that weren't worse. "You should have known. It's on our website—Arabic translation required."

"Nobody told me. I didn't know you had a website. I don't do the Internet. I've been dealing with your boss by telephone. Call him and tell him to fix things."

"There's no cell phone coverage here. And he can't do anything. The translation is the Leader's decision. You'll have to go back to Egypt."

"Go back how?"

"The same way you came."

"I walked. I walked five miles. I can't do it again." To my mortal shame I found myself whining, "I have a heart condition. Explain that this is a medical emergency."

No matter that I must have seemed the picture of ferocious health, more than capable of breaking this little guy across my knee, Khalil agreed to give it a shot. But first he persuaded a soldier to lead me to a hut, out of the sun, away from the crowd. The room was sweltering, airless, painted a chalky green. I asked for water, but there was none.

While Khalil went to plead my case, I showed the soldier my passport and said, "Make Arabic." I held out my $100 bill. "Translate."

He reacted as if I had exposed myself—which, in a sense, I had. More shameful than claiming to be sick, I had exposed myself as an imperialist pig, a bumptious foreigner attempting to bribe and bluster his way across North Africa. The soldier waved off the money and fled.

As the elaborately constructed artifice of my trip trembled on the verge of collapse, I thought of the wasted time and money, the days waiting for a visa, the nauseating prospect of retracing my route down the coast of Egypt. Then what? Somehow get my passport translated and double back to this godforsaken border station? Eighteen hours, going and coming, on the horror highway. What if I went to all that trouble, and Libya still refused to let me in?

It crossed my mind that I could hole up in Siwa and pretend that I had reached Tangier: invent some yarns, write them up and publish a bogus travelogue. I wouldn't be the first author in recent history to perpetrate a hoax.

But the sliminess of the impulse was a shock to my nervous system. Like the cardio-conversion I had undergone years ago in Texas, it jolted me into an almost normal rhythm, a sounder beat of reason. I had merely hit a bump in the road, the first hurdle. If I couldn't cope with this, I should have stayed home. What the hell: It was an opportunity more than a problem. Insight into what people in this part of the world contended with every day—physical hardship, disappointment, arbitrary rules and ham-fisted authority.

I decided I had to admire the Libyan soldier for his refusal to accept a bribe. Much as I might wish it were otherwise, the rule about translating passports into Arabic was no more absurd than the hoops that the United States made foreigners jump through.

When Khalil came back with bad news, we agreed that I would call him tomorrow or the next day from Alexandria. He clasped my arm in encouragement, murmuring in English and Arabic. Of the latter I understood two words, "Mektoub" ("fate") and "Inshallah" ("God willing"). Then I started walking, and what transpired in the next ten hours cannot be recounted in logical sequence. It can only be dredged up piecemeal from painfully repressed deeps. As the Prophet wrote: "Does there not pass over every man a space of time when his life is blank?"

I had advanced a mile toward Egypt when a Libyan policeman caught up with me and persuaded me to return to the customs office. They were reconsidering my case, he swore. He deposited me in a sliver of shade where a merciful woman poured me a glass of orange juice. The policeman never reappeared, and when after an hour I searched for him, a different cop informed me that I had been rejected again.

And so for a second time I set off walking. Desperately I searched for a white face, an English speaker, a fellow traveler who might help. But I was on my own.

As I staggered along, listing like a drunk, I was nearly side-swiped by a minivan. The driver stopped to apologize. He was a Libyan, deeply tanned, dressed in black slacks and shirt, and bearing an unnerving resemblance to the aging crooner Tony Bennett. Or was that a hallucination? Somehow, despite our ignorance of each other's languages, it became clear that I wanted a ride, and he wanted money—$40 of my Libyan dinars—to carry me across the frontier and back to Marsa Matruh.

I dragged my bags into the rear seat of the minivan where six stick-thin, thoroughly swaddled Chadian women made grudging space. They were wary of the slightest contact with me. Even my brushing against their billowing robes caused them to recoil. Up front with the driver sat two young Egyptians who had been guest workers in Libya. One was happy to be going home. The other was sad—he was returning for a glaucoma operation. Nobody seemed particularly curious about what misadventure had parachuted me into the van and into their lives.

Slowly, kilometer by kilometer, we renegotiated the police barriers and passport controls that I had slogged through a couple of hours ago. Back then the Egyptian officers had been amazed and amused by the "*Amriki.*" Now that the Libyans had rejected me, I was tainted. Or perhaps they recognized an easy target: One cop pointed out that I didn't have a visa to re-enter the country.

"But I never left it," I said.

"Pay me $10 and I let you back in."

I capitulated, believing a bribe would spring us from coils of red tape. It did no such thing. It just got us to the next gate, where we had to unload the minivan, shove our luggage through a metal detector and submit to a frisk.

Tony Bennett haggled for hours at the Traffic License Office to bring his vehicle across the border. The Egyptian boys lounged in the van, drinking water and tossing plastic bottles out the windows. The women climbed down, unfurled a carpet on the asphalt, bowed toward Mecca and prayed.

Recalling W.H. Auden's remark that prayer is also a matter of listening and paying attention, I strolled around and kept my eyes and ears open. I might have been wiser to have crouched beside the women on the carpet. A soldier warned me to stay away from the parking lot fence. Guards patrolling for smugglers were sometimes quick on the trigger.

It was pitch dark by the time the Traffic License Office approved us, and we sped toward Marsa Matruh through wind-borne sand. The van's high beams poured out ahead of us like quicksilver through a sieve. Animals, domestic and wild, scampered across the road, and traffic rushed at us in the wrong lane. The blinding flash of headlights and taillights, the glitter of animal eyes, the cacophony of horns and screeching tires turned the ride into a real-life video game, a kind of *Grand Theft Auto* in which every near miss made some future catastrophe seem unavoidable.

Tony Bennett stopped in Sidi Barami at one of those "unsanitary places" that the guidebook advised against. My fellow passengers ate a leisurely meal, then changed money with a Chinese man at the cash register. Bunches of their mysterious currency boiled down into a thin gruel of Egyptian pounds. Hoping to make it back to the Hotel Beau Site in time for dinner, I cooled my heels on the terrace until mosquitoes chased me into the van.

My eagerness to get underway again warred with my fear of being back on the highway. But the rest of the drive was at least slower. Repeatedly, soldiers rousted us out at checkpoints and demanded what an American was doing with this crew. Though it wasted time, Tony Bennett always produced a satisfactory explanation.

I stumbled into the Beau Site at eleven o'clock, headed straight to the restaurant and ordered a veal chop. It came as heavily breaded and as perfectly square as last night's cod. But having had nothing to eat since the candy bar this morning in Sallum, I didn't mind that it tasted like sawdust.

Afterward, in my room, I took a long look at myself in the mirror. My face was braised beef jerky; my hair had been blown into Medusan whorls. Sweat stained my shirt and pants with salt crystals so that I shimmered in the fluorescent light. I went to bed but couldn't sleep. I tried to form a plan but couldn't think. I never wanted to see the border crossing at Sallum again, but it was etched on the inside of my eyelids.

In the morning, dozens of things needed doing. I hired a car to drive me to Alexandria. I phoned the Cecil to reserve a room. I called Justin Siberell. He had departed for Baghdad, so I spoke to a secretary at the American Center who said she could "unofficially" translate my passport. She had no authority, however, to stamp it with a U.S. seal. America didn't do that. As a matter of diplomatic policy, it viewed a U.S. passport as sufficient in itself and it wouldn't sanction an Arabic translation.

When she learned that I meant to travel to Libya on my Irish passport, she said that would require some creative fiddling. There was no Irish consulate in Alexandria, but she had a friend at the British Consulate who might do us a favor.

On the trip back to Alex, I steamed with impatience, determined to resume my original itinerary as quickly as possible. But the driver had his own agenda. He stopped for coffee. Coffee dragged into lunch and lunch segued into an oil change. Late that afternoon, two hours behind schedule, we hit the suburbs of the city just as an apocalyptic rush hour erupted, and I nearly erupted, too.

But then as we sat stalled in a storm of pollution, I experienced a moment of clarity. I wasn't "behind schedule." There was no schedule. I had invented the rules and I could reinvent them. Yes, I preferred to cross North Africa overland. But I had already traveled twelve hundred miles of rough road and hadn't gotten out of Egypt. The sensible course was to catch a plane to Tripoli and then make up my mind how much of the Libyan coast I wished to cover.

I'd like to claim that after that, my path ran straight and true. But the Fates hadn't finished with me. I arrived at the Cecil to find all the hotel employees wearing green T-shirts for Earth Guest Day. A flyer in my room instructed me "to remember the following: Plant trees and not cut flowers, apply power saving and water saving plans at home and every were [sic], wastes should be sorted and recycled, take action against poverty, assist orphans, fight against child diseases, fight against AIDS, we should also take more care about our health and fitness and eat healthy food."

Daunting as the list was, I would have done my bit, if I hadn't had more pressing tasks to attend to. Since all direct flights from Alex to Tripoli and to Benghazi, Libya's second-largest city, were full, I bought a ticket on a plane from Cairo. A round trip, at that. The travel agent informed me that because so many foreigners got turned back from Libya, a return ticket was obligatory. But Egyptair guaranteed to refund half my fare as soon as I landed in Tripoli. Perhaps that's why it insisted on cash payment in local currency—so I'd get my money quicker than by a credit card voucher.

During the penitential process of having my passport translated, then stamped, many more bureaucratic and accounting accommodations became necessary. At the American Center, a kind woman translated the information from my Irish passport onto a separate piece of paper and dispatched me to her friend at the British Consulate—who put an official seal on the paper and sent me back to the American Center. There the kind woman, who refused payment, made some Arabic inscriptions in the Irish passport. Sighing, she conceded that all this seemed silly to her. The seal should have been on the passport, not the paper, and it should have been an Irish seal, not British. But maybe these shenanigans would work in Libya.

Two further points merit a mention. At the American Center and at the British Consulate, my taxi driver bribed the guards to let him park in a no-go zone while he waited for me. Had the cab been packed with explosives, it could have flattened the buildings and everybody in them. I would recall this whenever I heard Westerners brag about ironclad security in North Africa.

On the drive back to the Cecil through the normal hell-storm of traffic, I counted thirty-six mounted horses cantering down a main street. That the horses were headed north in a southbound lane struck me, after two weeks in Egypt, as unremarkable.

I received conflicting counsel about the best route to the Cairo airport. Some advised me to catch a train. Others suggested that a taxi would be quicker less than four hours—and more comfortable. I chose speed and comfort, and when the cabbie asked whether I preferred the desert road or the Nile delta, I said the delta. I had had enough of the sand.

Fields of cotton flanked the highway, and palms and banana plants shaded grazing cattle. The stink of fertilizer and irrigation canals overpowered Egypt's usual perfume of carbon monoxide. Where the delta was once given over completely to agriculture, it now had gated residential communities, gigantic shopping malls and international schools plunked down on flat expanses of land.

Predictably, the driver asked, "*Amriki?*"

"Yes," I replied, anticipating that he would exclaim, "Bush bad, USA number one." Instead he demanded, "Why Americans no like Arabs?"

In the rear-view mirror I made out the oblong of his face with a blue-black *zebibah* on his forehead and anger in his eyes.

"We don't dislike Arabs," I said.

"Yes, you do."

"Most Americans know nothing about Arabs."

"Nothing except they hate us, they hate all Muslims."

"Some Americans may be afraid of Muslims, but that's because they don't know them. And that's why I'm here—to learn."

"You journalist?"

"No. Just a traveler learning about Egypt."

"Egypt safe," he insisted. "All peoples safe here—Muslims, Christians, Jews."

I felt compelled to point out that only a few dozen Jews remained in the country.

"No, many, many more Jews." He met my eyes in the mirror. This unnerved me, not least because he wasn't watching the road. "In U.S. you have money, you get stole. In Egypt your money safe."

I didn't care to discuss my money. I wanted to change the subject.

"In America," he sputtered, "you have guns."

"Not me."

"Boy goes to school with gun and kills everybody. That's crazy. Not terror." On the chance that I didn't catch his drift, he added, "Crash into buildings with airplanes, that's crazy. Not terror."

"What terrifies me," I said, "is the traffic in Egypt."

"I drive safe. Journalists write bad about Arabs. They lie. They write we dirty."

I repeated that I wasn't a journalist. I was just anxious to get to the airport in one piece.

We drove in silence then. In silence and, for my part, in stomach-flipping traffic terror. A welt, a bruise, a monstrous brown prayer bump swelled on the horizon—the exurbs of the suburbs of the outskirts of the slums of the far periphery of Cairo. Estimates of the city's population had ballooned to eighteen million. Nobody knew the precise number.

How could they possibly calculate the communities that subsisted on rooftops, in tombs, on Nile River barges and in shantytowns?

Like its population, Cairo's pollution was beyond reckoning. The heat, the airborne grey-brown particulate matter, the musical backbeat on the car radio—everything called to mind Los Angeles. An adrenalized American DJ chirped, "Hey, it's a hot one today downtown. Ninety-nine degrees on Talaat Harb. Let's cool off with a Golden Oldie from the Beach Boys."

In the El Salam Industrial Area, within sight of the airport, the driver declared, "I have to visit one friend." As he thundered down an exit ramp, I yelped in alarm.

"Ten minutes only," he said. "For a friend."

"See your friend later."

"Now is best."

Swallowed into a maw of alleys, we squeezed past droves of animals and humans to a curious zoo of inanimate objects. Behind barbed wire and steel bars, automotive parts basked in the sun. Mufflers, pistons, engine blocks—everything, no matter how old, had been salvaged. No wrecked chassis was too damaged to go unredeemed. Hundreds of automobiles, including a snazzy red BMW, had been dismantled in these chop shops, and fenders and bumpers and hood ornaments were for sale.

"Where's your friend?" I shouted over the clangor of hammered metal.

"Not friend. He owes me money."

"Look, I'm going to be late."

The driver didn't deny it. His face glistened with sweat; his prayer bump glinted like a third eye. The thought hit me hard—this was how it had been for Daniel Pearl, the *Wall Street Journal* reporter. Not the same, but similar—kidnapped en route to an interview, in Pakistan, held ransom and decapitated.

I vowed to stay calm. Then I vowed not to stay calm. I'd fight. But how? And with what? On the floor at my feet was an empty plastic bottle—hardly a weapon to hold off Al Qaeda.

Suddenly we encountered an oncoming car; the two drivers collided at low speed. This was my chance to run for it. But before I could budge, my driver shouted what I'm sure was an unprintable oath, reversed onto a side street and halted at an apartment house constructed of secondhand cinder blocks and rusty scaffolding. A man on the front steps didn't look happy to see us.

The driver climbed out and accosted him. I got out, too, poised for flight. Poised also, I'll confess, to wet my pants. Not from fear. Or not just from fear. We'd been on the road for hours and I had drunk the whole bottle of water. I needed relief urgently. Looking around, I wondered whether to let go in the street. I decided not to add indignity to ignominy—even though the street wouldn't have been any filthier for my piss.

The men were arguing. Over a debt, I hoped. Not my worth as a hostage. Again, though tempted to run, I figured I wouldn't get far before my bladder burst. "Bathroom," I barked. That shut them up. "Bathroom," I barked again, and they understood the seriousness of the situation.

The driver stayed with the car. The second man led me into the apartment house, up an Escher-like staircase. The cement risers were deeply scalloped; thirty-watt bulbs dangled like dying birds in cages; the walls blazed with graffiti, then, astoundingly, with a hand-painted Coptic icon.

All this was as nothing, however, compared to the astonishments that awaited on the top floor. The man unlocked a steel-plated door, flicked on a battery of fluorescent lights, and there before me spread a storage room crammed with stolen antiques or artful knockoffs. There were candelabras, ceramic vases, blown glass lamps, amphorae and ormolu clocks. I followed him past Oriental screens and industrial-sized rolls of bubble wrap to a corner, where he indicated a hole in the floor and politely withdrew.

If they meant me harm, I had played into their hands. They could have locked the door and left me here until they decided whether to demand ransom or to lop off my head. But by the time I went downstairs and outside, the two men were chatting peaceably and chewing sunflower seeds, spitting the shells onto the ground.

In the end, I arrived at the airport and found that there would be no food and certainly no alcohol on the flight to Tripoli. Unlike its neighbors in North Africa, all of them fervently Muslim, Libya alone forbade the importation, sale and consumption of liquor by citizens and visitors alike. So I rushed to the bar for a drink and a sandwich.

Glad to be alive, I nattered away at an Australian Air steward standing next to me. He listened to my tale of temporary abduction with poorly disguised boredom. As travel anecdotes went, mine, he wanted me to know, was lukewarm beer measured against his flights from Dubai to Manila.

"The plane's packed with Flips flying home from the Gulf," he said. "A percentage of them are always pregnant. The Arabs are really"—*riley!*—"hard on their Filipino help. So as not to come back knocked up, the women abort during the flight. We've got special procedures for dealing with miscarriages and collecting bloody blankets after we land. Last week I found a live baby on the floor."

I nodded, sipped the last of my drink, and conceded that he had me beaten hands down.

LIBYA

At Tripoli airport a banner in English greeted arriving passengers with a quote from Qaddafi's *Green Book*: "Partners. Not Wage Workers." But this pretension to egalitarian cooperation was belied by thuggish men in dark suits and black shirts who herded us into separate queues. Libyans were directed to one desk. Foreign guest workers to another. White people to a third desk, which had the shortest line. I waited there alone until a Libyan matron bedizened with a gold Buccellati necklace broke in ahead of me. The customs guards welcomed her with great unctuousness.

With me, they were less lavish. They led me into an office, and I feared I'd be expelled on the next plane. Instead they produced the original of my visa and pasted it into my Irish passport, next to the Arabic scrawled by the woman at the American Center. The British seal on the separate paper didn't interest them. Thus I passed through the Looking Glass into the Land of Oz.

It was after midnight, but Khalil greeted me cheerily, with a grin and a handclasp. He carried my bags to the parking lot and piled them into his new Hyundai SUV. He asked me to guess how much the SUV cost, and when my estimate was way off the money, he quoted a price in Libyan dinars, then Egyptian pounds, then dollars. I was sure he could have translated the figure into euros or rubles if I'd asked.

Out of the airport, we advanced on broad, empty, brightly lit boulevards. After Egypt, Libya seemed cleaner, quieter, more orderly. And much less crowded. An immense country of 679,360 square miles, it had fewer people than the city of Alexandria. Yet the orderliness was also a reflection of the mental grid of the authoritarian ruler, Moamar Qaddafi. Citizens had little choice except to follow him in lockstep—although "lockstep" might imply that the Leader marched in a straight line when, in fact, he lurched between lunatic extremes, dragging the nation behind him like a dog by the tail.

For an avid traveler any country that's closed, any Forbidden Land, possesses totemic power. It may be dreadful. It may be dull. But it must be seen and experienced. So I only half listened to Khalil's gabble—he was discussing gas mileage now—and studied a place that had been off-limits to Americans for decades.

The United States broke diplomatic relations with Libya in 1981, accusing Qaddafi of sponsoring international terrorism and spreading subversion to neighboring states. In 1984, after a ten-day siege and shootout at the Libyan Embassy in London, Great Britain also declared Libya a pariah state, agreeing with President Ronald Reagan that Qaddafi was "the most dangerous man in the world."

As if set on proving Reagan right, the Leader praised the December 1985 terror attacks in Vienna and at the Rome Airport. Several friends of mine were shot in Rome, one of them fatally, a young girl who attended the same school as my sons. The assailants had traveled to Italy on Libyan passports.

In April 1986 a bomb exploded in a Berlin disco frequented by American GIs, killing two and wounding two hundred. The United States blamed Libya and fired missiles at Benghazi and Tripoli. The target in Tripoli was the Aziziyah barracks, Qaddafi's residence. The missiles killed a hundred people, and wounded two of Qaddafi's sons. Among the dead, the Leader lamented, was his adopted daughter, Hanna. Some whispered that Qaddafi had adopted Hanna only after her death.

Then, in 1988, in the most traumatic terrorist attack to that date, Pan Am Flight 103 exploded over Lockerbie, Scotland, killing everybody on board and a dozen people on the ground. The United States blamed Qaddafi, and ultimately a Libyan intelligence agent, Abdel Basset Ali al-Megrahi, was convicted of the crime and sentenced to life in prison.[2] But the atrocities continued. Libya bombed a French airliner over the Sahara, killing all passengers. In an especially gruesome move, Qadaffi televised the executions of political dissidents and personal enemies. And meanwhile, the Leader threatened to undermine Egypt, Algeria, Tunisia and Morocco, and financed terrorist groups in Ireland and in sub-Saharan Africa.

Khalil pointed to the Aziziyah barracks as we sped past the walled compound. "There's a memorial to the barbaric imperialist aggression," he told me. "We're at peace with America now, but we remember. Putin comes soon from Russia to pay his respects." (In addition to his respects, Putin would pay millions of rubles for access to Libyan oil and natural gas. He would also sign contracts for Russian high-tech companies to rebuild Libya's frazzled infrastructure.)

"Does Qaddafi live here?" I asked.

---

2. In August 2009, Scottish authorities released al-Megrahi on humanitarian grounds, explaining that he was terminally ill with prostate cancer. Rumors that al-Megrahi's release was tied to business deals guaranteeing Great Britain access to Libyan oil raised an international outcry. The outcry increased when al-Megrahi was welcomed in Tripoli by jubilant crowds.

Khalil shrugged. "His wife, yes. The Leader, who knows? He prefers a tent."

"How many wives does he have?"

"Just the one. He divorced his first wife and married again. That's all we know. The family is very private."

The Leader, however, was very public. His grinning or grimacing likeness was plastered on billboards beside the road, on banners fluttering from telephone poles and on gold leaf mosaics festooning buildings. Since Muslim culture discouraged representational art, this might have struck some Believers as blasphemous. But if it did, they kept their opinions to themselves. One man who had spoken up, a former provincial governor named Fathi al-Jahmi, had languished in a psychiatric hospital for four years after advocating democracy and a free press and joking about Colonel Qaddafi's cult of personality: "All that is left for him to do is hand us a prayer carpet and ask us to bow before his picture and worship him."

"Martyrs' Square. Now Green Square!" Khalil exclaimed as we approached it. "Here in colonial times the Italians executed hundreds of Libyan freedom fighters. A dark, dark day in human history. Italians visit now as tourists. We don't bear a grudge, but we don't forget. The Italians, they remember nothing."

Khalil had it right about Italian amnesia. I had lived in Rome for more than a dozen years, mixing with journalists, academics and intellectuals, and I had never heard a single word about Italy's savagery in Libya. Between the initial Italian invasion, in 1911, and World War II, a quarter of the country's population had been eradicated. As the Italians retreated along with the Germans, Libya was left one of the poorest nations in the world, with a per capita income of $25 a year and an economy based on the export of scrap metal discarded by the Axis and Allied armies.

Now buoyed by petrodollars, Libyans earned on average almost $12,000 a year, the highest per capita income in Africa. Whatever secret resentments they harbored toward the Leader, they couldn't dispute that they were living better. The question was how much longer Qaddafi would last. And would the oil give out before he did?

Khalil zipped along Tripoli's corniche, a sleek version of Alex's scruffy coast road. Like Christmas trees, the Corinthia Bab Africa Hotel and several soaring office towers lighted the seafront.

"This all used to be water," Khalil said. "The Mediterranean reached right up to the medina. We filled it in to build the new city."

The old city, however, looked shabby and unchanged. Guidebooks called Tripoli "the Havana of North Africa," as if that were high praise. Maybe it was a reference to the vibrant Havana of fifty years ago, a burlesque queen tricked out with tassels and sequins. But if Tripoli's medina resembled anything, it was Havana as it existed today, after decades of isolation and economic anemia. For all the oil money sloshing around in rich Libyans' pockets, very little of it appeared to trickle down.

Khalil turned onto a dirt road that was under repair. As he maneuvered past piled sand and giant earthmoving equipment, he kept up his constant patter. "Marcus Aurelius arch," he said, "built in AD 164. Mussolini, can you believe it, wanted to tear down the city walls and the Sidi Abdel Wahab Mosque to show better these Roman ruins."

I found Khalil lively and likable. But if he was this manic after midnight, what would he have been like on a four-day drive the length of the Libyan coast?

"Where did you learn English?" I asked.

"From Americans at Wheelus Air Force Base." He didn't look old enough to have worked there. Wheelus had closed in the early '70s. But he stunned me by saying he was fifty-four years old. In addition to a full head of dark hair, he had an unlined face and a lean, bantamweight physique.

Khalil parked next to a ditch. Beyond it stood the Zumit Hotel, a boutique establishment, beautifully restored in an historic setting. Or so Khalil said. He made no move to hop out and take me inside. "About tomorrow."

"I'd like to sleep late," I told him.

"Yes, rest yourself." He fretted with the car keys as if with worry beads. He had hands as small as a child's. "Mr. Mike, I'm sorry about the border. But it wasn't my fault."

"I understand."

"The problem now is, my wife's in the hospital. She's pregnant. The baby may be born early. Of course, my duty is to you."

"No, it's to your wife. I'll look after myself."

"Just tomorrow I'll leave you alone," he said. "We'll talk later and replan your trip."

"I'll have to think about that."

"Of course, Mr. Mike. Think. Rest. Call me if there's trouble. But in Tripoli there's no trouble. You'll see. It's safe. If you leave the hotel, just stay on the main streets."

I was too wired to sleep, and the room's décor demanded fevered attention. The walls were hectic with handicrafts that might have been genuine but suggested gaudy, mass-produced kitsch. The bed, raised on a platform, lay behind a latticework screen, painted blue to ward off the Evil Eye. The mattress was covered by orange sheets threaded with silver. Just looking at the metallic thread made my skin itch, and I had a premonition of tripping on the stairs to the bed during one of my nightly jaunts to the bathroom.

But I couldn't blame my restlessness wholly on the room or on the day's roiling events. What kept me awake was also worry about tomorrow. Though I counted it a stroke of good fortune to get a day on my own, I questioned—everything I had read and heard about Libya forced me to question—the wisdom of wandering around alone.

A friend, a former State Department terrorism expert, had cautioned me that "Libya is complex and interesting, but dangerous." He characterized one of Qaddafi's sons, Hannibal, as a gangster, and sent news clippings describing the thirty-year-old's violent run-ins with police in Rome, Paris and Geneva. More than playboy pranks, these incidents involved guns, broken bottles and high-speed car chases down the Champs-Elysées.

There had been international repercussions when Hannibal and his wife, Aline, were arrested in Geneva for assaulting their own domestic staff. Libya exacted "eye for an eye and tooth for a tooth retribution." Qaddafi cut off flights between Tripoli and Switzerland; withdrew more than $8 billion from Swiss banks; shut down Swiss companies in Libya; expelled and, in some cases, arrested Swiss nationals; and halted the export of crude oil to Switzerland, which depended upon Libya for 50 percent of its energy. In the Leader's mind, my friend warned, the personal often became political. But even Qaddafi didn't go as far as Hannibal, who proclaimed at a reception for Arab diplomats, "If I had an atomic bomb I would wipe Switzerland off the map."

The U.S. Travel Advisory on Libya reported: "Recent worldwide terrorist alerts have stated that extremist groups continue to plan terrorist attacks against U.S. interests. Therefore, any American citizen who decides to travel to Libya should maintain a strong security posture by being aware of surroundings, avoiding crowds and demonstrations, keeping a low profile, and varying times and routes for all required travel. [Libyan] security personnel may at times place foreign visitors under observation. Hotel rooms, telephones and fax machines may be monitored, and personal possessions in hotel rooms may be inspected."

But much of this sounded to me like a holdover from the last century, when Libya more than deserved its reputation as a rogue state. Since then, Qaddafi had paid millions of dollars in reparations for the Lockerbie bombing and a settlement with the French for the loss of their airliner. He had stopped funding subversion and quit executing his enemies, at least on TV. Crucially for Americans, Qaddafi had condemned the 9/11 attacks, declaring himself an ally in the war against terror, and he advocated regime change in Iraq and pledged to relinquish his arsenal of nuclear and chemical weapons. After Saddam Hussein's capture, he reportedly confided to Italy's prime minister, Silvio Berlusconi, "I will do whatever the Americans want, because I saw what happened in Iraq, and I was afraid."

Still, Qaddafi sometimes behaved like a tinhorn tyrant and seemed to be the same crackpot who had ordered all Libyans, even city-dwellers, to start raising chickens; the zany Leader who had called for the burning of Western musical instruments and welcomed the itinerant PLO chairman Yasser Arafat to Tripoli with the gift of a set of Samsonite luggage; the teetotaler who hired beer-swilling Billy Carter as a Libyan lobbyist; the clown who flew to Paris for a state visit and slept outside the Elysée Palace in a tent; the Arab traditionalist who had backtracked on his ban on western music and invited Lionel Richie to commemorate with a rock concert the twentieth anniversary of Reagan's missile attack on Tripoli.

But my State Department friend argued that Qaddafi's erratic actions weren't always funny. Despite the temptation to laugh off the Leader as though he were a comic character in an Evelyn Waugh novel, his jokes had lethal punch lines. Six Bulgarian nurses and a Palestinian doctor had been in jail for years awaiting execution on trumped-up charges of murdering Libyan babies with HIV-infected syringes. (They were released during the summer of 2008.) In 2003 Qaddafi exchanged insults at an Arab League summit with Saudi Crown Prince Abdullah and later made plans to kill him. Then documents captured in Iraq revealed that 20 percent of the foreign *jihadis* there came from Libya. An article on this subject ran in *Newsweek* during my stay in Libya, and was summarily banned from the country. It contended that fifty-two Libyan *jihadis* had grown up in the small coastal town of Darnah.

As I dithered over what to do tomorrow—Stay in the room? Stick to the main streets, as Khalil advised? Seize a rare opportunity to roam the city and see things for myself?—I turned on the television, expecting the usual limited late-night fare of bearded imams railing against infidels. Instead, more than a thousand channels spanned the entertainment spectrum, from South American soccer to Thai sex shows. While Libya had managed to interdict the flow of alcohol and foreign magazines and newspapers, it had apparently despaired of shutting down satellite transmission.

This surprised me. I had read that TV used to be interrupted on a regular basis, and the screen would fill up with flowers. Legend had it that Qaddafi kept a switch in his office and whenever he didn't approve of a program, he cut the connection for the country.

For a while I watched a harrowing BBC documentary about the young man, Seung-Hui Cho, who had shot and killed thirty-three fellow students in the United States, at Virginia Tech University. Presented by the narrator as another in the endless line of insane American assassins, Seung-Hui Cho reminded me of the Egyptian cab driver's diatribe about the false distinction between Islamic terrorism and America's home-grown mass murder. What difference did it make whether you got gunned down by a religious or political fanatic or by a deranged college boy? Statistically, I decided, I had no more to fear in North Africa than I did in Key West. So why hole up in the hotel and miss a chance to explore Tripoli without a government-imposed guide?

The next morning, not far from the Zumit, I ducked into the Gurgi Mosque, deserted at that hour of day. A caretaker unlocked the front gate and stored my shoes on a shelf. It was a small mosque, financed in the nineteenth century by a Libyan naval officer who had imported Italian marble pillars, Tunisian tiles and Moroccan stucco for the dome. I strolled around, ostensibly admiring the craftsmanship, in fact convincing myself that it was safe to go deeper into the medina.

A block away, the Old British Consulate had an admonitory plaque on its facade that read, "The so-called European geographical and explorative scientific expeditions to Africa, which were in essence and as a matter of fact intended to be colonial ones to occupy and colonize vital and strategic parts of Africa, embarked from this same building."

With that warning shot fired across his bow, a visitor might reasonably feel unwelcome. But the guard at the consulate was the soul of friendliness and refused to charge me admission. He urged me to climb to the roof terrace and enjoy a view of the sea, the arch of Marcus Aurelius and the minaret of the Gurgi Mosque, capped by a gold crescent. In nearby courtyards carpets had been hung out to air, and their dazzling arabesques patterned the whitewashed walls.

Farther on, a plaque at the restored Banco d'Italia also didn't mince words. It accused this branch of the central bank of Italy of "aiming to find an excuse to colonize Libya." For balance, the plaque might have mentioned the incompetence of Italy's colonial expansion. As German Chancellor Bismarck observed, Italians have "a large appetite and very poor teeth."

Not far from the bank, the Catholic cathedral was open, and I stepped inside to check the Mass schedule. Some sort of sacristan—he wore a grey wool sweater and a crucifix on a string around his neck—pounced on me, eager to speak English. But he had a harelip that made him hard to understand. He responded to my question about Sunday services by nudging me toward a bulletin board. If I read it correctly, the cathedral was now an Episcopal church.

He jostled me toward the altar. I said no thanks; I didn't care for a guided tour. Face glistening with sickness or desperation, he yanked out a fistful of dollars and shoved them at me. He wanted to change money.

Lisping, he muttered about a poor family, perhaps here or in Cairo. They needed food and he needed local currency. He pulled me down onto a hard bench and kept haggling. Didn't this violate Biblical precedent? Trading money in the temple?

I feared I was being bamboozled. Still, the man was so determined that I took what he offered and handed over what he asked. Then I hurried out of the church, past a shop where severed camels' heads, their nostrils stuffed with parsley, gazed down from shelves at the ground where their hooves were planted in pools of blood. Next door a money changer had chalked numbers on a board; the harelipped sacristan had given me precisely the right amount.

On and on I walked, my wariness fading. Nobody took any special notice of me. No one asked if I were American or showed animosity toward an outsider. I was just another browser on a street of market stalls, a lone swimmer in an ocean of Arabs. The shopkeepers paid me no attention. They catered to natives, not foreigners, and they didn't bargain. They stated their price, take it or leave it.

Free to poke my nose here and there, I noted how many buildings incorporated Roman columns into their facades; the Ionic and Corinthian capitals smartened up the seedy neighborhood the same way a blazer adds a touch of elegance to jeans and sneakers.

Laborers, many of them black Sub-Saharans, slouched against a wall, hoping to be hired for the day. Each held an object that indicated his trade—a hammer for a carpenter, a wrench for a plumber, a trowel for a bricklayer, a light bulb for an electrician. One man brandished what looked to be a weapon for splitting skulls. What was he, an executioner?

From the medina, I crossed former Martyrs' Square, now Green Square, green being the color of the revolution that brought Qaddafi to power. Squads of policemen prevented walking here from becoming the life-or-death gambit it was in Alexandria. Newly married couples gathered to have their photos snapped, and a fellow with a baby gazelle argued that no wedding album was complete without a shot of the bride and groom with his cute horned pet.

Then, abruptly, I entered Italy—a neighborhood of wrought iron balconies and stucco facades with Art Deco motifs. Colonnades shaded the sidewalk, and ficus trees, their trunks painted lime white, formed a tunnel for the traffic. Without a map or any idea of my whereabouts, I detoured from Sharia 1st September Street and stumbled into . . . what? A derelict palazzo? An abandoned opera set?

While I sidestepped greasy bags, pistachio shells and cigarette butts, above me soared arches and architraves, fluted columns and volutes, pillars and floating pilasters. The immense ensemble was peeling paint and crumbling. Pigeons zoomed in and out of broken windows and roosted on the lion's head that presided over the sublime scene.

A handsome, silver-haired man of about seventy stopped beside me, and I took the chance of greeting him in Italian. He told me we were in Galleria de Bono. He didn't know whether it was being repaired or razed.

Continuing in Italian, I asked if he had lived in Tripoli during the occupation, and he nodded. When I prompted him for memories, he said, "I was small. I remember studying Italian in school. Nothing more."

"During the war life must have been hard," I said.

"I don't know. We left town and moved to the countryside. Anyone who could, they left the city." Then so I wouldn't think him lacking in manners, he wished me *"Tant de belles choses"* ("Many beautiful things") and walked away.

M aidan al-Jezayir, formerly Piazza Algeria, was as pleasing to the eye as any modern plaza in Europe. A Swedish architect in Libya with an NGO swore to me that Tripoli, as an example of city planning, was far superior to anything Mussolini achieved at home. For the centerpiece of the square, the Italians had constructed a neo-Romanesque cathedral. But soon after Qaddafi seized power, the Catholic church was converted into the Jamal Abdel Nasser Mosque, one of the few in Tripoli off-limits to non-Muslims.

I ordered a cappuccino in a café across the street, the tastiest coffee I had on my entire trip. In a dry fountain near my table, a tree hammered out of extruded metal attracted live birds to its dead limbs. From where I sat I could see a column that proved Khalil hadn't exaggerated when he told me, "Libyans don't forget."

A grainy poster pictured the 1911 invasion, with armed Italian troops abusing Libyan civilians. Another poster was of Omar Al-Mukhtar, the leader of Libyan resistance from 1911 until 1931. He had been captured and executed at the age of seventy-three, after a farcical trial that ended with the imprisonment of his Italian attorney, accused of being too staunch in Al-Mukhtar's defense.

In Tripoli these weren't ancient grievances. The wounds were fresh and Al-Mukhtar's legend lived on in Technicolor. A 1981 movie of his life, *The Lion of the Desert*, starring Anthony Quinn, still circulated on DVD and was reputed to be popular viewing for Libyan *jihadis*. The film had never been released in Italy.[3]

I roamed until dark, then ate dinner at Mat'am al-Saraya Restaurant, looking over Green Square. The excellent food couldn't be ruined even by the saccharine Lebanese keyboard player or the awful nonalcoholic beer. On my hike back to the hotel, I had a choice of the brightly lit corniche or the dim warren of the medina. I followed the alleys through the medina, lost my way a time or two and had to ask directions, but sensed no danger. Indeed, I felt as I often had in Alexandria, as though I didn't exist. Before the trip, I had expected to be upbraided for being an American—when, that is, I wasn't being accosted by beggars or menaced by fundamentalists. But this was almost more troubling—to be ignored. Was it, I wondered, because I had reached the age of invisibility, the point where I represented nothing of interest to anyone except myself?

At the Zumit, I rounded off the day like a lonely bachelor by watching TV. To my surprise and delight, a satellite channel was showing Bernardo Bertolucci's 1990 film of Paul Bowles's *The Sheltering Sky*. As novelist Walker Percy wrote in *The Moviegoer*, nothing offers greater validation to our existence, nothing infuses experience with more meaning, than seeing it on film. After my days in the desert, after exploring North African streets for hours, I was delighted to watch John Malkovich and Debra Winger doing the same. Then, at the end, Bowles

---

3 In June 2009, Moamar Qaddafi flew to Rome for a state visit, wearing a military uniform worthy of a Gilbert and Sullivan operetta. His shoulders were fringed with gold-braid epaulets and the visor of his cap glinted with gold tracery as thick as scrambled eggs. The left side of his chest was weighted down by campaign ribbons from unknown wars. On his right breast was pinned a large photograph of Omar Al-Mukhtar in chains, flanked by Italian troops. Taking sharp exception to what they regarded as the Leader's violation of protocol, some Italians started wearing pictures of the Pan Am Flight 103 crash site.

himself, an old friend now dead, came on camera and asked a haunting question: "How many more full moons will we witness in our lifetime?" Eager as I was to reach Tangier, Bowles's home base for forty years, I was also determined to enjoy everything in between.

The next morning, Khalil was waiting in the lobby. He looked drawn and exhausted, but was still his ebullient self. "Did you hear about the bus crash in Benghazi?" he asked. "It fell off a cliff and killed many people."

This was to become a trope for the rest of the week. He started off each day with news of another disaster, usually a car wreck, as if to remind me how lucky I was to have him as my driver.

I asked about his wife, and he opened his cell phone, flashing pictures of a premature baby in a bassinet. "My son was born last night," Khalil said. "He needs help breathing. That's why there are tubes in his nose. But he's going to be okay, *inshallah*."

"And your wife, how's she?"

"Very good. Tired but good. *Inshallah*. They're both in the hospital."

"Congratulations. Look, you should be with them. I'm fine on my own."

But he said we needed to see the boss today, to revise my itinerary and discuss a refund for the portion of the trip I had missed. I asked him to stop on the way at Egyptair so I could cash in my return ticket to Cairo. With Khalil as translator, I figured there'd be less trouble collecting the money.

It turned out to be no trouble at all. It was simply impossible. The Egyptair manager maintained that it was illegal in Libya to reimburse money that had been paid in a foreign country in a different currency. "You'll have to collect it when you return to Cairo."

"I'm not going back. I'm going to Tunisia."

"Perfect," the manager said. "Pick up your refund at the EgyptAir office in Tunis."

"But how can I be sure they won't palm me off on the office in Algiers or Tangier?"

"I'll write our manager in Tunis. He's a personal friend. I'll instruct him to pay you what you're owed." As good as his word, he inscribed in spidery Arabic script a message that, Khalil promised, called for prompt attention and full respect. The manager urged me to deliver it to his colleague with his full esteem.

"See, we are not savages," Khalil said as we climbed into his SUV. "Count on getting your money in Tunis. The question is how to make things right in Libya. If you'd like to go to Benghazi, we have to arrange permission."

"How much time would I have there and in the Cyrenaica region?"

"Maybe two days." He gunned into the traffic. "Benghazi is a twelve-hour drive to the east. After we see the Greek and Roman ruins, it's twelve hours back to Tripoli. Then after a layover, we need a day driving to the Tunisian border and up to the island of Djerba."

That was a lot of time on the road—and a lot of time with Khalil. After spending yesterday on my own, I yearned for the freedom to walk where I pleased and speak to anyone I liked without having him peer over my shoulder. Then, too, after wasting days in Egypt, there was no slack in my schedule for a leisurely circuit of Libya. I had interviews and appointments in countries down the road, and I couldn't cancel them.

"Traveling to Benghazi will take you away from your wife and baby," I said.

"Don't worry about them. This is my job. You are my job."

"No, I'll stay in Tripoli. We'll make day trips out of the city. The rest of the time you can be with your family."

We were at a stoplight. It turned green, but Khalil didn't go. "Oh, Mr. Mike," he exclaimed. For a moment I thought he might kiss me, but he contented himself with squeezing my arm. Horns blared as the light cycled to orange, to red, then to green again. "Thank you, thank you."

"Let's go talk to the boss," I said.

I anticipated trouble and less prospect of a refund than from EgyptAir. Yet because much more money was at stake, I couldn't just write it off. I had paid in advance for hotels, meals and Khalil's services from the Egyptian border to Tripoli, and then from here to Tunisia. Since I wouldn't be getting half of what I had counted on, I wanted something back. But I had little leverage.

The boss, Mansour, when he had spoken to me by telephone in the States, had sounded brusque. Trouble with the language and long-distance lines, I hoped. But as soon as I stepped into his office, my heart sank. Mansour was mustachioed, enormous and intimidating. He didn't deign to stand up. He crouched like a linebacker and stuck out a paw as rough as a ham hock wrapped in burlap.

"I assume no responsibility for your problem with the visa," he got us off to a rollicking start.

"I'm not concerned about who's to blame." I sat across from him, conscious that Khalil had skedaddled. "I'm interested in what we do now."

"Good, good."

"Khalil and I talked it over. There's not enough time for me to backtrack along the coast. We'll make a few day trips out of Tripoli."

"Good, good."

"But that leaves the four days I lost."

His jaw jutted out in a massive overbite as he chewed at his mustache. "I'll pay you $750. Best offer. Last offer."

I countered, "A thousand dollars. That's less than I deserve, but I'll settle for it."

He flexed his fists like a pugilist, rolled his shirtsleeves and unlocked the top drawer of the desk. He produced a bundle of U.S. bills, counted out a thousand in fifties and twenties and slid them across the desktop. I wore a kind of money belt around my calf, and I folded the refund into it, along with a couple of thousand dollars' worth of different currencies.

"Do you like Libya?" Mansour asked, signaling his satisfaction with the settlement. "For an American, it must be interesting."

"Yes, but hard for a man in your job," I said. "The rules and bureaucracy, the visa trouble. . ."

"You cannot know how hard." He was chewing his mustache again, biting at the Brillo Pad. "Last year I lost twenty groups. Hundreds of clients. The country lost thousands of tourists."

"Why not change the regulations?"

He smirked. "Please tell that to the Leader when you meet him. And when you see Mr. Bush, tell him he's stupid for making Libyans have their passports translated into English. If he fixes that, Americans will get into Libya, no problem."

This was a variation on a theme I'd frequently hear. Most North Africans agreed that their governments were idiotic and corrupt. But they expected better of the United States and were suspicious when it disappointed them. Since they didn't believe that America was dumb and were convinced it was too rich to be corrupt, they assumed that its policies must be motivated by a hatred of Islam or prejudice against Arabs.

Mansour complained that although his country was supposed to be back in America's good graces, a brother in arms in the war against terror, the States still hadn't dispatched an ambassador to Tripoli. And the city's U.S. consular office didn't deal with visa applications. Libyans hoping to travel into the United States had to fly to Tunisia or Malta for visas. So it wasn't surprising that Libya made things difficult for Americans.

I asked whether he thought there could ever be mass tourism in Libya given the conditions the government imposed.

"The conditions aren't the problem," Mansour declared. "We need better infrastructure. More hotels with five stars. Once we have that, and once Libya learns about discounts, everything is okay. Now whether I bring two tourists or a thousand, the hotels charge the same. They don't understand tourism lives on discounts."

"What about the ban on alcohol?" I said. "Doesn't that hurt tourism?"

He shook his head emphatically. "People understand."

"Understand what?"

"Tourists to Libya are cultural. They come for the Roman and Greek ruins and maybe a trip to the desert. Not for nightclubs or dancing or drinking."

"But they can't travel alone here like they do in other North African countries."

The smirk returned to Mansour's face. "You plan to travel alone in Algeria? You expect to be free there from danger? Good luck, my friend. Anyway, do you not like Khalil? You want a different guide?"

"No, Khalil's fine." I feared I'd get him fired and find myself saddled with a more intrusive minder. "He's taking me to a museum today."

"Good, good." Mansour assumed his linebacker's crouch and extended a bone-crushing hand. "Enjoy."

As we entered the Jamahiriya Museum, Khalil said, "You need an expert guide," and introduced me to a man in a skullcap and grimy striped tunic, cooling his face with a fly whisk.

From previous trips to Africa, the Middle East and Central Asia, I immediately sized up the "expert" as the kind of chatterbox who'd insist that I admire every exhibit while he ran on about it in Esperanto.

"Please get rid of him," I whispered to Khalil.

"He'll be insulted."

"Explain that I'm deaf. I'm dumb."

"Okay, but you must pay five dinars, to save his pride."

"Gladly."

In the first gallery, maps and mosaics presented an overview of the nation's historical and artistic heritage, and I glided by without a second glance. But then a display caught my eye, and I paused at it so long that Khalil grew restive and finally exasperated. Why, he asked, would I linger at a green 1967 Volkswagen Beetle, the very one in which Qaddafi had tooled around during the '69 revolution? Was I mocking the Leader?

I might have mentioned that the VW reminded me of the first car I ever owned, the one that Linda and I had driven during our first trip to North Africa. But what transfixed me was the screed in English that accompanied the Bug. It reduced the Libyan revolution to a conflict between German automobile brands. According to this text, Qaddafi's VW symbolized "simplicity in confronting the Mercedes-Benz car which has incarnated clamor, haughtiness and false arrogance. There were great differences between both cars. While the VW was rolling up time and distances to bring closer the salvation day, the Mercedes was moving between night clubs, gambling halls and military bases driven by agents of the Italians, the Americans and the British in the defunct regime. All paid from Libyan people's wealth. The people are suffering from poverty, oppression, sleeping on the ground and protecting themselves from heat and cold by zinc panels under the yoke of an agent regime that had lost sovereignty, will and legitimacy, whereas it infiltrated to the country from abroad in the darkness under the cover of charlatanism and heresy."

Who wrote this stuff? Was it the same guy responsible for the plaques on the Old British Consulate and the Banco d'Italia?

The Jamahiriya Museum contained forty-six further galleries. There were scale models of Sabratha and of Cyrene's Temple of Zeus. There were tomb reliefs from Slonta and relics of the Saharan empire of the Garamantes who introduced horses, camels and wheeled vehicles to the desert. I examined samovars, incense cellars and kitchen equipment from the Ottoman era, and I accorded due reverence to the Libyan Resistance and dozens of likenesses of the Leader. I soldiered on through Galleria 41 and its collection of deformed animals and camel fetuses in jars. But I'm afraid that for me everything after the '67 Beetle smacked of anticlimax.

K halil had set aside the next day for the Roman ruins at Leptis Magna. He proposed leaving at daybreak. A notorious late riser, I argued for a 9:30 AM departure. The buffet in the hotel courtyard was a dog's breakfast of instant coffee and stale crackers that became palatable only when the waitress produced a jar of Skippy peanut butter.

The waitress was the same woman, I recognized, who cleaned my room, and I attempted to convince her that whatever I tossed into the trash basket, I meant to throw away. She had been fishing out newspapers and business cards and stray pages of notes. Thinking them too valuable to discard, she smoothed them with her hand and left them on the night table. Since she spoke no English and I no Arabic, I resorted to pantomime until it dawned on me that she had referred to the peanut butter as *crème de cacahuètes*. Then we conversed in French.

It turned out she was Algerian. The other chambermaids came from Morocco, as did the bellboy. Libya was home to two million guest workers and refugees from all over Africa. Since it had money, and the Leader had grandiose notions about Pan Arabism and Pan Africanism, Libya had become another oil-rich, underpopulated nation that no longer needed to do its dirty work and farmed it out to the less fortunate. As the bellboy lamented, "Libyans just lounge around all day and talk on their cell phones." Meanwhile, the refugees flocked the roadsides and traffic circles, scrambling for dollar-a-day jobs.

While most North Africans intended to return to their native countries once they had accumulated a nest egg, sub-Saharans viewed Tripoli as a transfer station. As soon as they saved enough money, they paid a smuggler to ferry them across the treacherous waters to Italy or Greece, any place in the European Union where they might be granted political asylum.

K halil started off the drive to Leptis Magna by asking in exhilaration, "Do you know what today is?"

I conceded that I didn't.

"The day Mussolini died. They hung him upside down." Khalil couldn't have sounded happier had he himself slipped the rope around the tyrant's heels.

As we cleared the outskirts of Tripoli and passed the Philadelphia Fast Food Restaurant, he asked, "You know what Philadelphia is?"

I wanted to growl at him to give it a rest. But that seemed as cruel as crushing a puppy. "Philadelphia's in Pennsylvania," I said. "The City of Brotherly Love."

"No. The *Philadelphia* was a warship that the U.S.A. sent to attack us in 1805. We captured it and threw your sailors in jail. We still have the ship's mast at the Red Fortress."

Though Khalil didn't mention it, these events had transpired during the era of the Barbary Pirates, when the Mediterranean coast churned with Arab corsairs that preyed upon passing ships. The U.S. attack on Tripoli had been a punitive expedition after Americans had been seized for ransom. In the nineteenth century North Africa was synonymous with piracy as Somalia is today.

"This shows how far back our fights with America go," Khalil said. "But we are friends now."

"Yes, friends."

"I'd like you to learn our history. I must buy you the movie *The Lion of the Desert*. It will teach you about Libya."

Beyond Tripoli's frowsy suburbs the desert commenced and any impression of modernity and prosperity evaporated. The highway shriveled to a snail track. Cultivated fields were burnt brown at the edges, and stalks of wild vegetation bristled in the sand. Thorny trees had been blown cockeyed by a constant wind that kicked up dust and hazed over the sun.

Only 1.4 percent of Libyan land was arable, and the country had to import about 80 percent of its food. But Khalil assured me that the Leader had the issue of desertification under control. At unimaginable cost and with unpredictable ecological consequences, Qaddafi was building the Great Man Made River, the Eighth Wonder of the World. Draining water from aquifers in the Sahara, he meant to pipe it hundreds of miles north to the cities of Benghazi, Sert and Tripoli at a rate of more than seven million cubic meters a day. As with so many of the Leader's projects, there was debate about whether this one was evidence of lunacy or genius. His defenders claimed he had no choice but to risk destroying the Sahara's water table and dozens of oases. Critics complained that the Great Man Made River was likely to run dry in fifty years, and it would have been more economical to construct desalination plants on the coast.

Through the blowing grit, we ripped past roadside vendors selling something in plastic bottles. "Olive oil and honey," Khalil said. "The best olives in the world. Leptis Magna grew rich exporting them to Rome."

I had read about this. Indeed, I had read a great many books about Leptis, including Aubrey Menen's estimable and beautifully illustrated *Cities in the Sand*. So I was familiar with the story of Septimius Severus, the Phoenician boy born in Leptis Magna, who through sheer will, raw courage and cunning became emperor of Rome and decreed that his home town should be transformed into the most magnificent city on the Mediterranean. Now it was the most magnificent Roman ruin, "a river of stone," as Menen hailed it.

But Khalil protested, "Reading is nothing. You must see it. You'll walk there for miles. For hours! I have the best guide. He's a student with good English."

"I don't want a guide. Let's do like we did yesterday—just the two of us."

"That's not possible, Mr. Mike. You have to have a guide. It's the law."

Shame prevented me from telling him to turn back to Tripoli. I was afraid he would take me for a vulgarian.

For the past thirty years, I've enjoyed an affectionate relationship with the American Academy in Rome, one of the world's foremost centers for the study of classical history and archeology. Among my friends, I number many prominent Roman scholars, one of whom, when she heard I was headed to Libya, reminisced that she had been to Leptis Magna long ago and had wept at its marvels.

I felt like weeping now. For the sad truth is I have limited interest in Roman antiquities and far less in guided tours.

Or perhaps it would be truer to say that after years of clambering over historical sites in Italy, Spain, France, Greece, Turkey, Lebanon, Israel, Egypt, Tunisia and Morocco, I have had my interest almost exhausted. I wouldn't pigeonhole myself in the same jaundiced category as Septimius Severus who, according to Aubrey Menen, remarked that he had "seen everything and done everything and it was all worth nothing much." But I confess to being more intrigued now by living culture than by potshards and splintered rocks. If I could have visited Leptis Magna alone, I'd have done it more than justice, but . . .

My guide, a young lad in a Stanford sweatshirt, might have passed for an undergrad in Palo Alto—with a major in English as a fourth language. He demanded strict obedience and absolute attention. He was in my face and in my space and brooked no deviation from his regimen.

When he declared that we should start in the museum, I explained that I had visited the Jamahiriya yesterday and didn't need a refresher course. He ignored me and kept walking and talking. "Here is picture of game in olden times," he said of one exhibit. "Children have such game today. You do such game in America. Jump in chalk box."

"Jump in what?"

"Chalk box." Annoyed at my obtuseness, he hopped on one foot, then two, then one again. I thought he had gone mad. If there was anything I disliked more than tour guides, it was charades. "Hopscotch," I guessed.

"Yes. Jump in chalk box."

The next exhibit was a thirty-foot-tall cutout of Qaddafi in a creamy white suit and blue shirt open at the collar. He looked like an Italian gigolo hugging two tiny cardboard people. This demonstrated, as nothing else could, how huge the Leader was and how insignificant his subjects.

"You don't listen," the guide scolded me. "You write in your little book."

"I hear you," I said.

"But you don't look."

The museum had twenty-five rooms and I did my best to breeze through them at the rate of one every two minutes. I could have made better time had we not bumped into a few displays that struck my funny bone. Among them was a letter written in blood to the Leader by an Iraqi admirer. But the *pièce de résistance* was a nest of twigs and wood shavings that an impertinent bird had woven in a window frame, tucked between the pane of glass and its protective grillwork. As I admired it, the guide became apoplectic. "Do you criticize?"

"Just looking," I said.

"You should not criticize. You should listen."

Outside, the ancient streets of the city had been buried for a millennium before being partially excavated by the Italians. Much of Leptis Magna remained underground. Except for muttering the odd date or name, the guide now kept his mouth shut. He also kept his distance, as if my indifference to his spiel caused him personal pain. Sympathetic to this, I asked an occasional question and tried to be patient with his garbled answers. But my attention wandered to what interested me.

At the Arch of Septimius Severus, wildflowers and coarse grasses miraculously sprouted in cracks between the crushing weight of limestone blocks. Oleanders had sprung up in the wheel ruts of an ancient Roman road, and the wall that ran alongside it was tufted with purple succulents that a helpful English lady swore to me were called Hottentot figs. The rear of the red granite Nymphaeum had collapsed to reveal a lovely copse of olive and eucalyptus trees; their tangled roots gripped the time-worn rocks in a green vise.

It felt good to be walking, to take in the sites at my own pace, with the sullen guide a few yards to my stern. At the Old Forum, wind had scoured pillars into the fantastic shapes of melting candles. Near the seafront, leaning into a gale-force blow, I gazed down at some columns laid out on the shore. In the seventeenth century, the French consul to Tripoli had plundered Leptis Magna for marble and shipped it to Paris where it was used as building material for the church of St. Germain des Prés and the chateau at Versailles. The columns on the beach, discarded because of their great size, had weathered and acquired a patina of grey lichen.

For centuries Leptis Magna had served as a port for African wild-life bound for Rome. As classical scholar Ingrid Rowland has written, "the Romans didn't just pillage the continent for slaves, gold, incense, and ostrich feathers. They sacrificed the North African ecosystem in the quest to provide exotic animals for their arenas." Now in the absence of lions and elephants, nothing larger than a lizard survived, and as

Tacitus summed up Imperial Rome's annihilating power, "Where they make a desert, they call it peace."

The guide waited for me out of the wind, whispering into his cell phone. When I told him I had seen enough, his contempt might have combusted into flames had I not tipped him handsomely. It would have been futile to explain that I meant no disrespect to him or to the past. I simply agreed with the German artist Anselm Kiefer, who said, "Ruins are moments when things show themselves. A ruin is not a catastrophe. It is the moment when things can start again." And now, after pausing briefly at Leptis Magna, it was the moment for me to start my trip again.

Because so few Americans visited Libya and because so few Libyans were willing to speak openly to a foreigner, I often felt I was skating over the surface of the place. Even long-time, Arab-speaking residents of Tripoli complained of the isolation and of the superficiality of their experience. As a State Department employee put it, "Libyans are the most self-censoring people on earth. Fear keeps them in line."

But I had one local contact, the friend of a friend, a man well connected with the top levels of the government. He agreed to talk. His only caveat was that I not quote him by name. I'll call him Said. "Otherwise," he explained, "I'll go to Guantanamo." He chuckled mirthlessly. "I don't mean the real Guantanamo. There are others. Each of these countries has its own Guantanamo and you can disappear for no reason."

He insisted that we meet at a coffee shop. Not at my hotel, not at his office. Thickset and burr-headed, Said wore a green knit shirt with a Ralph Lauren logo. The crocheted polo player on his chest wielded a mallet like a sledgehammer. He balanced his briefcase on his knees and kept his cell phone close at hand. He appeared to be pressed for time, and while he knew I was a writer, he expressed no curiosity about my point of view or my project.

In Libya outspokenness was dangerous, even fatal. But Said had no patience for small talk. "This country, this whole part of the world, is a disaster," he said. "The primary problem is that wherever you turn, whatever you try to accomplish, you bump into a bureaucracy that prevents anything good from happening. There's always the wrong man in the wrong position."

His bluntness gave me pause. I didn't regard it as paranoid to wonder whether he was trying to entrap me. But since our mutual friend was a former CIA agent, I plunged on. "Is it a question of inefficiency or corruption?" I asked.

"Both." He broke off when the waiter came; he ordered coffee for me and tea for himself. His cell phone rang and he dismissed the caller with a curt word of Arabic. "There's a lot of money floating around loose, but there's no logic, no system to accomplish things."

He offered a complex explanation of the financial bind that oil-rich countries such as Libya face. It was difficult for me to follow, especially since he spoke at headlong speed. I asked him to slow down, and he referred me to a quote from the economist Robert Skidelsky that summed up a monetary paradox:

"Resource exploitation is the quickest way for a country to grow provided the resources aren't stolen. However, natural resources are exhaustible, so unless an economy expands beyond its natural resource base, its capital runs down even as its income grows. Governments can mitigate this outcome by various technical devices such as the establishment of sovereign wealth funds that save part of the resources for future generations. But such remedies are made more difficult because multinational companies combine with corrupt domestic dictators to rob the populations of resource-rich countries of the wealth that could be theirs."

To Said it was incontrovertible that Libya's wealth was being siphoned off. But he stressed that stupid choices complicated the corruption, and as one factor compounded the other, it was impossible to distinguish personal from institutional malfeasance. In the end, what mattered was that the country was becoming impoverished even as its financial statistics made it appear to be growing richer.

"You have foreign oil companies here making billions of dollars," he went on. "They realize that to improve public relations, they need to ensure that the people appear to benefit. So they donate millions of dollars to what they see as good works. But let's say they give twenty million. Half or more of that will be wasted; it'll simply disappear. And the rest will go for something that does no good and isn't what we need."

I pressed Said for an example.

"We have problems in medicine," he said, "with diabetes. We have to educate the population about the disease. We need to have prevention programs. We need to identify patients at risk and treat them. But the government never implements managed care, and anyway the oil companies are only interested in making a big splash. They'll ignore diabetes and donate an expensive MRI machine. That's always the way. Important problems go untreated and as conditions worsen, the oil money is thrown away on splashy projects."

I reminded Said that according to the UN's Human Development Index, healthcare in Libya was better than in other North African nations. Based on access to medicine and hospitals (both are free), on infant mortality, and doctors per capita, Libya compared favorably with Europe and America.

But he laughed and said, "The statistics are total fiction. You read figures about longevity in Libya and they say the average man and woman lives almost eighty years. But go around Tripoli and tell me how many old people, how many people more than sixty, you see. Then go into the countryside. It's worse there. People don't live so long. Don't believe the figures."

What I had to keep in mind, he said, was day-to-day reality. "For the average Libyan, the quality has gone down. Thirty years ago there were medical procedures, quite sophisticated ones, that we could deal with locally. Now we have to send patients, the lucky ones with powerful connections, overseas. We fly them to the States and pay $80,000 for an operation when we supposedly have all these good doctors here. Libyans travel to Tunisia even for minor operations."[4]

When I mentioned that I had visited Leptis Magna, Said called it "a shambles, a shame. It's an International Heritage Site, a great national landmark. Yet it hasn't made any improvements in thirty years. The embargo and the UN sanctions didn't help. That's where our bad logic and lack of a system collide with America's bad logic and lack of a system. Congress declares an embargo here, an embargo there. But this achieves nothing. It hurts nobody except the poor people. The rich at the top are untouched. They *are* out of touch."

---

4. In June 2009, *The New York Times* reported that Fathi al-Jahmi, Libya's best-known dissident, who had been imprisoned for years for calling for democracy and mocking Qaddafi, had died in the Arab Medical Center in Amman, Jordan. Jahmi's family accused Libya of cruelty for not providing medical care in a timely fashion. A researcher at the Human Rights Watch said al-Jahmi was moved out of the country to a cardiac unit in Amman to "absolve the Libyan government of responsibility for his well-being." It's worth wondering whether the move and al-Jahmi's death weren't an indication of the inadequacies in Libya's medical services.

I understood that Libya resented the suffering it had endured during the colonial period, but hadn't it also inflicted pain on itself? I asked about the televised executions during the '70s and '80s, and Said conceded "the country made mistakes then like the U.S. is making now. It thought it could torture and kill people and make progress."

"Doesn't a segment of Libyan society still think that?"

"There's much less torture and fewer people in prison."

"But there are Libyans who believe they can make progress by killing and dying." I cited the *Newsweek* article about the large number of Libyan *jihadis* in Iraq.

"That's a different matter," he said. "We don't view it as you do. We see the Americans as occupiers. If somebody invaded your country and occupied a couple of your states, I'm sure many Americans would go there and fight. The divisions in the Arab world are arbitrary and invented by colonizers. We are all one people, all Muslims. So when we see what's happening in Iraq, men go there to help.

"Some of them have nothing better to hope for in this life. So they bet on the next life. If they die in a boat to Europe or from a bomb in battle, that doesn't seem worse to them than no job, no chance here."

There was nothing for me to say except the truth. "That's sad."

"It is sad," he agreed. "I feel sorry for the people. I feel sorry for their misery. I worry what would happen to us without oil. It would be bad like in Egypt. People are starving there. Even with $12,000 per person we have problems, but at least we're not starving."

With that, Said pocketed his cell phone and picked up his briefcase. "I'll leave first," he said. "Please stay until I'm gone."

I regretted not asking Said about Libya's status as the Arab world's most advanced nation for women. According to most accounts, this was an area where Qaddafi had implemented significant reforms. In a stunning *coup de théatre*, he had even instituted the Revolutionary Nuns, a cadre of female police officers and personal bodyguards.

On paper, Libyan law protected a woman's right to schooling, to equal pay, to professional equality. More females than males earned college degrees, and they were no longer coerced into arranged marriages. Nor could they be discarded in divorce. They could own and dispose of property, and they were theoretically at liberty to dress as they liked. After the revolution Qaddafi had abolished the *furushiya*, the shroudlike white robe that Libyan women had traditionally worn.

But what I saw in the streets of Tripoli and surrounding towns caused me to question these alleged improvements. Almost every female from adolescence to doddering old age wore the *hijab*. Cafés catered exclusively to men, and the commercial life of the medina was segregated into female shoppers and male shop owners. I had spent a week in Libya before it occurred to me that apart from the Moroccan and Algerian chambermaids at the Zumit, I hadn't spoken to a woman, and certainly none had initiated any contact with me.

When I arranged to interview a female State Department employee, she, too, asked that I not use her real name. Whether "Helen" was afraid of offending her bosses in Foggy Bottom or local sensibilities, I couldn't say.

From my hotel, I could have cut diagonally through the medina to the Corinthia Bab Africa Hotel. But it was a beautiful day, and I followed the corniche. There were few other pedestrians, perhaps because thunderous traffic separated the city from the sea-front. Tripoli's snarl of roundabouts and overpasses, its determination to squander money on grandiose projects, replicated the urban planning errors made decades ago in other countries.

The Corinthia Bab Africa's polished glass and steel panels winked a shiny welcome to travelers, but its entrance was an obstacle course. For half a mile, I circled a high wall to a tunnel that slanted down to a garage. Security guards waved me off. This was strictly for cars, each of which underwent bumper-to-bumper scrutiny. While one guard popped the trunk and another lifted the hood, a third wielded a mirror on a pole, checking under the chassis for explosives.

At a different guard post, I flashed my photo ID and walked past a concrete barrier to a revolving door. Inside, a metal detector screened people and an X-ray machine screened valises. As the temporary quarters of the U.S. Consulate and the home away from home for oil executives and corporate carpetbaggers, the Corinthia was a mini–Green Zone. You could register here and never have to rub up against the reality of Libya.

There was a futuristic bar in the lobby, with a flat screen TV that broadcast ESPN'S *SportsCenter.* There were pretzels and potato chips and salted nuts, and boisterous customers drinking their lunch. All the bar lacked was alcohol. Instead it had a menu of mocktails.

I asked the concierge about room prices, and he quoted me a walk-in rate of $600 for a single. When I asked about access to the sea, he said a room with a view cost more.

"No. How do I get to the sea?"

He handed me off to a young lady with limited English, who walked me down to a buffet laid out on a horseshoe table sparkling with ice sculptures. We advanced through the fitness center, past a heavily chlorinated indoor pool, then a patio café where no one sat, then an outdoor pool where no one swam.

"The sea?" I asked.

She pointed to a porthole in the surrounding wall. "Sea." Or maybe she said, "See!" Sure enough, there was an oval of the Med, divided into azure squares by iron grillwork.

Back in the lobby, I met Helen, and we went to an Italian restaurant on the hotel mezzanine. She was in her mid-thirties, married and a mother, a strawberry blond in a beige twin set. Despite the demureness of her dress, her opinions were anything but neutral. She had done stints in Syria, Jordan, Tunisia and Turkmenistan, and when I asked about Libyan women, she said, "This is the most sex-segregated place I've ever been. Libyan women work with men, but socially and religiously they're separate. The country has financing to send girls overseas to study, but a lot of them won't go for fear of ruining their reputations and their marriage prospects."

She stressed that it wasn't government policies that discouraged women: "It's social pressure. This is a conservative society and very difficult to penetrate. In other Islamic countries where I've served, it's common to get invited to private houses. Especially during Ramadan, they'll invite you for *iftar*, when they break their fast. In Libya that doesn't happen."

She felt that Libya deserved its designation as "a hardship post." But at least she didn't experience the prejudice that she said embassy females of Hispanic descent encountered. They were sometimes mistaken for Libyans and harassed in the streets for not covering their hair. "It's not men who do it," she said. "It's the women who get angry, and they're even harder on African-American personnel. They accuse them of being illegal immigrants and call them dirty blacks and criminals."

A waiter brought our pizza and Cokes, and after a lull in the conversation, Helen took pains to make sure that I understood she bore no antipathy toward Muslims. An Arabic speaker, she expected to work in Islamic societies for the rest of her career. She admired the Libyans, described them as smart, curious, and eager to over-come their pariah status. "But once you're here on the ground," she said, "you find out how hard it is to get anything done. It's ten times harder than I anticipated."

"Give me an example."

"Libyans are subsidized in ways they don't realize and don't like to admit. Because of the oil money, they expect life to be easy. When things don't go right, they blame the government or the United States. If you graduate from high school, you automatically qualify for college here. There's no competition. After college, they're hired by the government, which has set-asides for certain families and ethnic and geographical groups. You've got to admire the Libyans for their egalitarianism, but it leads to a lot of incompetence and a sense of entitlement."

As she described them, Libyans sounded like lottery winners who couldn't handle sudden wealth, who suffered from what psy-chologists called affluenza. "Libya's going through a debate like a rich family with children," Helen said. "Do you will the money to the next generation and risk spoiling the kids? Or do you improve current services and infrastructure? The situation gets complicated when the family is ill-prepared and uneducated. They need to hire experts. But to do that they need to know who to hire, who to trust, and they need to provide the experts with resources and freedom."

She told me the Libyan government wanted to send four thousand medical students to English-speaking universities overseas. The trouble was that the country didn't have that many graduates qualified to study in the States, the U.K. and Canada. They lacked basic language and computer skills.

"Most American universities don't accept paper applications," Helen said. "They expect students to apply online, and when Libyans won't do that, universities view this as evidence that they aren't going to do well in America."

"Can't you explain this to the government?" I asked.

"We've had difficulty identifying the appropriate government officials. Supposedly, the country is ruled by committees. But in fact, the regime hands down mandates from the top and demands to be obeyed. Qaddafi just announced he's firing all his ministers and letting the people work out their own solutions. But he's still the boss. Meanwhile, the education department is caught between these unrealistic quotas and students who believe they should be exempted from the Graduate Record Exam and the MCATS."

The answer, Helen said, was to improve educational standards, especially in English. "Right now, the country has the capacity for just seven hundred TOEFL [Test of English as a Foreign Language] takers a year. The U.S. Embassy offered to bring in teachers to increase the number of test takers. But the Libyans wouldn't give them visas. They don't seem to understand the connection between A and

B. And we're trying to determine whether the problem is bureaucratic inefficiency or policy resistance."

I repeated what Said had told me: "There's always the wrong man in the wrong position."

"That's part of it. But there's also this penchant for punishing what they consider to be unfairness and prejudice against them. They have no sense of proportion. We had a small musical program scheduled as part of a U.S. cultural exchange. But then a court case in the States went against the Libyans, and they cancelled the musical program." Helen couldn't help laughing. "They cancelled a ukulele player. That's their idea of quid pro quo."

On my last full day in Tripoli, Khalil asked "Do you know what yesterday was?"

"Don't have a clue."

"The day the police in Los Angeles beat the black man, Rodney King."

"How do you know these dates?"

"They're in the newspapers." Then Khalil hinged open his cell phone to show the latest pictures of his son—a movie clip of a squalling pink infant furiously shaking his fists. "He will grow up to be a boxer. Another Muhammad Ali. 'Children are the ornament of this life,'" Khalil said, quoting the Koran. "Now, Mr. Mike, where do we go today?"

South of Tripoli was the troglodytic town of Gharyan, and I wanted to see its underground houses. Also an Englishwoman who taught school there had invited me to meet her students. But Khalil said such a trip was impossible. First, we didn't have permission to visit Gharyan and the police would turn us back at a roadblock. Second, school visits required extra permission and that would entail days of wrangling.

"I think the woman wanted me to meet her students at her house."

"Worse yet," Khalil said. "The government doesn't like foreigners talking privately with students. This would make trouble for everybody."

"Okay, I leave it up to you where we go. Surprise me."

For an hour Khalil threaded his Hyundai through Tripoli's back streets, searching for a DVD of *The Lion of the Desert*. When he couldn't find one, he suggested I see the Libyan Studies Center and its collection of one hundred thousand photographs of the suffering Italy had inflicted on the country.

With Khalil in the lead we climbed from the bowels of the building to its upper stories, stopping at four different offices to wheedle and cajole information from the comatose staff. Anybody less indefatigable than Khalil and, more pertinently, anyone who didn't speak Arabic, couldn't have coped with the Libyan Studies Center.

Finally, a woman in Western clothes thrust an application at Khalil and instructed him to fill it out in triplicate and supply a photocopy of my passport and his guide's license. Then we perched in front of a computer along with a girl in a tan robe, rimless spectacles and a Burberry-patterned headscarf. She maintained a firm finger on the mouse, scrolling through files at a speed that suited her and providing captions in Arabic. Another instance of bureaucratic overkill, this undercut the presumed goal of the Studies Center and denied the public meaningful access to Libyan history.

The photos should have been available—no, obligatory—for anybody interested in the origins of Arab rage. If in fact they hated the West (and I had witnessed no firsthand evidence that they actually did), it was because of the mass graves full of corpses, cadavers stacked like cordwood, row upon row of hanged men, walls blood-spattered and pockmarked by firing squads.

Afterward Khalil hurried off to the hospital to his wife and son, and I roamed around on my own one last time. On Sharia 1st September Street, I dropped by Fergiani's Bookshop, browsed through its English-language stock and bought a copy of Qaddafi's *Green Book*, an eccentric discourse on politics, religion and high finance. As I was paying the cashier, an older customer, obviously Libyan but with an American accent, told me he had lived in San Antonio, Texas, and Biloxi, Mississippi. Did I know these towns?

"Yes," I said. My older brother had served in the Air Force and done his basic training in San Antonio, then was stationed with the Strategic Air Command in Biloxi.

"Randolph Airbase and Lackland!" the man exclaimed. "I was there, too, training with Libyan pilots. I like America." From his wallet he extracted a photograph of himself as a young man in uniform. "I still have a girlfriend in Texas."

He showed a black-and-white snapshot, now sepia-toned, of a cute blond sitting at a bar in front of a beer glass with a frothy head.

"Ever been back?" I asked.

"Never. I have a wife and family, and I have no money. But we write letters. We stay connected, just like America and Libya are connected."

The next morning I was my laggardly self, and Khalil fumed about our late start. He planned to drive me to Tunisia and return to Tripoli tonight. Since he was in a hurry, I volunteered—as if it were a great sacrifice on my part—to skip the ruins at Sabratha. But to Khalil this was sacrilege.

"Okay, I'll have a quick look," I said. "I don't want you driving back in the dark."

"Dark or light doesn't matter, Mr. Mike. What matters is you have a tour with a good guide. The best."

"The best" proved to be a frail, elderly gentleman with wretched English. I feared he'd never find another paying customer, so I couldn't possibly send him away. And out of respect for his aged dignity, I didn't dare beg him to be quiet.

From guidebooks I knew the basics. Sabratha had been a Phoenician settlement, populated by emigrants from Carthage. Then, in the second century BC, Greeks started to dilute the community's Punic character. In fact, "Libya" was the Greek word for all of Africa. Eventually, after an earthquake leveled the city in the first century AD, the Romans arrived and rebuilt it into an architectural splendor that was second in grandeur only to Leptis Magna. This halcyon period lasted until a more devastating earthquake struck in AD 365.

Sabratha never recovered and remained buried in drifting sand until the Italians dug out about 30 percent of its total area. Now weeds and thistles and dunes had reasserted themselves, and lethargic lizards lazed on the scorched stones. Greenish grey, the lizards were difficult to distinguish from the lichen that grew around them. But if you stared hard enough, you noticed their minuscule hearts pulsing at about three beats a minute.

"To know," my guide asked, "how do Italians find treasure under mound?" His question had the ring of a dirty joke—like how does a Frenchwoman hold her liquor?

I didn't wait for the punch line. I moved to a slice of shade in the ancient public latrines. The guide joined me there. "Olden times," he said, "people make sweat, then bath, then talk here and things."

An uncouth tourist demonstrated those "things," squatting on a marble slab punctuated by the holes of a communal toilet.

We proceeded to the theater, the crown jewel of Sabratha. The largest Roman theater in Africa, it boasted a proscenium that opened in the rear onto the sea. I paused to marvel at four distinct bands of blue—the sky, the horizon, the deep channels of the Med, then the lighter shallows. But the guide had eyes only for the chipped bas-reliefs around the stage. Seizing me by the arm, he said, "Look! This is Oedipus complex. Kill father, marry mother."

He maneuvered me to the next block of marble. "Wife, slave, husband. Husband gone long time. Slave loving wife."

We hiked through fields of heather and Scotch broom to the beach, and up close, the water looked less enticing. Hundreds of plastic bottles had washed ashore. Several fully dressed adults—they appeared to be teachers with their grade school pupils—waded knee deep in the water and splashed the kids, also fully clothed.

At a museum of mosaics, the guide fired off questions that he answered himself. "What fruit this is? Fig fruit." But about the mural of a swan raping Leda in a rush of feathers, he said nothing. Nor did he comment on the pubic bush somebody had penciled onto a statue of Venus.

Like those angels of mercy who dispense cold drinks to marathon runners, Khalil waited at the finish line with a bottle of water. I drained it in one long slug. Then, relieved to put another Roman ruin behind me, I paid the guide and we hit the road.

Through a waste of scrub brush and trash, we hugged the coast. It could hardly be said to have hugged us back. Supposedly Libya possessed the last undeveloped beaches on the Mediterranean. By some blunt measurement this might be true, but that didn't make these miles of torrid shore any less inhospitable. Wild dogs nosed around the burnt-out shells of cars while raptors circled overhead.

The post-apocalyptic desolation deepened as crude wooden boats replaced the wrecked cars, and black men sheltered miserably beside them like desert island survivors. "They're waiting for night to cross to Italy," Khalil said. "The boats have no numbers, no names, no papers. If anything goes wrong, the smugglers and the boat owners can't be traced."

According to an estimate in the Italian news magazine *L'Espresso*, thousands of refugees embarked every year from Libya, and 13 percent died at sea. Their bodies washed up on Sicily and Malta. I had trouble believing that anybody made it alive. Clunky and unpainted, the boats appeared to have been hewn from logs and were powered by rusty outboard engines. It should have been simple for a police state to control immigration, especially since the human trafficking was so blatant.

But the question was whether anybody in Libya cared as long as the sub-Saharans left the country.

While the Mediterranean and its glare were fixed on our right, mirages receded on our left into dry riverbeds full of silt, glittering salt crystals and tree stumps that had washed down in flash floods from distant oases. Peeled of bark and bleached by sun, the wood had vaguely human shapes, like the broken statues at Sabratha. Then mud huts emerged from the heat ripples and Khalil parked at a mosque to pray. The temperature gauge on the dashboard registered ninety-eight degrees.

As we neared the Tunisian border, I had flashbacks to the nightmare at Sallum. Khalil promised there'd be no problem, and he spoke brightly of a VIP fast lane. Where a tailback of cars ended, he didn't fall into line. He barreled west to a barricade manned by officials in white shirts and ties.

"Let me have your passport," he said. "You stay here and I'll handle everything."

Like the men huddling for shade beside their boats, I hunched next to the Hyundai. With the ignition and AC off, it was too hot to sit inside. The temperature had risen to one hundred.

People teetered past me with cartons piled on their heads and harnessed to their shoulders. They carried shoes and cigarettes, canned food and baby formula. They weren't in business for themselves. They were small-time mules for smugglers who paid the customs guards to look the other way. Nobody bothered them so long as they kept in line and kept moving. They stumbled back and forth all day, an appalling conveyor belt of commerce and suffering. Sometimes one fell to his knees or tipped over onto his back, but the others quickly set him on his pins, and the foot traffic never ceased.

Vehicular traffic was a different matter, and as usual, I was in a category all my own. After an hour Khalil reported, "They're suspicious that you didn't fly from Tripoli. What do I tell them?"

"I'm traveling overland to enjoy the country."

"That won't work. There's nothing to enjoy."

"Is it the Libyans who won't let me out? Or the Tunisians who won't let me in?"

"It's the Tunisians."

I realized that although I had entered Libya on my Irish passport, it might be wiser to cross into Tunisia on my American passport. Khalil agreed, and scurried off again. I offered to speak French with the Tunisians. But he insisted it was his job.

As another hour burned away, I remembered reading about politicians calling for North African unity, proposing international initiatives to preserve the Mediterranean coast and control pollution. These struck me as a quixotic aspirations when countries couldn't even deal with the cluster-fuck at their borders.

In two weeks, I was scheduled to meet a driver at the Algerian frontier. That figured to be a difficult and dangerous crossing. But what if I never managed to get that far?

Khalil came back bedraggled, slumped behind the wheel and switched on the air conditioning. "I got it. Your visa for Tunisia. Now we just need to wait." He drummed his hands on the steering wheel, quietly chanting, "Open the gate, open the fucking gate."

A man in sunglasses, white shirt and tie signaled for him to lower the window. Khalil quit chanting and cursing and spoke politely to the officer in Arabic. Then, after a four-hour purgatory, we were allowed to cross the border.

With the AC on maxi-cool and the vent tilted to his face, Khalil said, "It's because of two Austrian tourists that Al Qaeda kidnapped near Matmata. That's what took so long. The Tunisians are nervous."

In ten miles we ran into six roadblocks manned by rifle-toting soldiers. While they checked our passports, time ticked by and Khalil resumed drumming his palms on the wheel. To distract him I asked questions. Were the roadside vendors here selling olive oil and honey? No, Khalil said, it was gasoline smuggled in from Libya.

And the men shaking fistfuls of cash like cheerleaders shaking pompoms—what were they?

"Money changers," he said.

With each answer he recovered a quantum of energy, and soon we were cruising along at full speed over salt flats. The sea was still beside us, a darker blue in the evening light and darker yet compared to the blinding white salt. On one of these *chotts*, a visionary landscape artist had arranged an installation of tires—circles of black on a blank canvas.

The causeway to Djerba reminded me of the road from Miami to Key West, spanning emerald stretches of ocean. In legend this was the island of the Lotus Eaters, which led me to expect lush vegetation and sybaritic living. But much of Djerba was agricultural—hard-worked fields and tidy villages of sugar-cube houses trimmed in green and domed with barrel vaults.

When we reached the main town of Houmt Souk, Khalil assumed I planned to stay in the *Zone Touristique*. But I had no interest in a luxury seaside resort. I asked him to drop me at the Hotel Machrek.

"The Sunrise," he translated the name for me.

"Why don't you spend the night?" I said. "We'll eat dinner and you can drive back tomorrow."

"No, Mr. Mike. I'll smoke *sheesha*. Then I'll get out of Tunisia and back to my son as quick as possible."

In an exuberance of affection, I said I'd miss him and his reminders of each day's historical disaster. I was tempted to give him a hug, a manly *abrazo*. But I was afraid he'd take it wrong and consider me a big condescending American. So I settled for a handshake and a touch of the heart.

TUNISIA

Before I left the States, men invariably asked how I meant to protect myself. Some suggested that I carry a gun—as if North Africa were the Wild West and I could gallivant around packing a sidearm.

Women, more practical, wondered how I'd do my laundry. While I sometimes washed my socks and underwear in the sink and hung them out to dry—in this climate, cotton hardened to cardboard in an hour—the Hotel Machrek, like every other place I stayed, had prompt laundry service. My shirts and trousers came back crisply ironed and smelling of sweet soap. If the dependable women who ran these hotel laundries governed North Africa, I mused as I changed into clean clothes, they'd have soon had these countries humming with efficiency.

I stretched out in bed. On the ceiling of my room, a blue arrow jutted east toward Mecca, the direction I'd just come from. But I was too wound up to nap. So I decided to take a jaunt out to the *Zone*

Touristique after all. It had been ten days since I read a newspaper, and I figured I'd find back issues at the hotels that hogged the prime real estate on the beach.

First, however, I called home. Linda sounded frazzled. She was shutting the house in Key West and would join me in Tunis. But it wasn't the ordeal of packing that upset her. Our friend, the novelist George Garrett, who had taught me at the University of Virginia, had gone into hospice care. Having fought ill health for years, he didn't have long to live.

The *Zone Touristique, a* gated, security-mad section of the island, did little to lift my spirits. Harlequin-colored golf pro haberdashery, loud bars, a brassy soundtrack, poolside cosseting—these had become universal signifiers for a sort of anti-travel in which people stayed comfortable while taking their prejudices out for a spin. But how was I any different?

The yearning for an authentic undiscovered destination and unspoiled people—as long as the water's safe and the food's palatable and the poor are kept at arm's length—was a commonplace of tourism. Although I wasn't traveling in five-star luxe, I wasn't bunking in a tent in the palm grove, either. When it suited my purposes I ditched my high-minded ideals and skulked into the *Zone Touristique,* for English-language newspapers.

As it happened, these hotels had little truck with walk-in trade. Geared for tour groups, they reserved their tennis courts, raked beaches and gift shops for prepaid customers. They made it clear that I was lucky to be allowed to buy three-day-old copies of British tabloids. Djerba depended on tourists yet despised them, and people in the service sector depended on tips and despised themselves for doing so.

Glad to get away, I caught a cab to what had been a fishing village. Now it was a marina, a solid mass of yachts and speedboats. The octopus trappers and shrimp trawlers who once worked from here had moved elsewhere, and condos and cafés lined the port. Because Saudi cash had financed this replica of Saint-Tropez, wine—one of Tunisia's principal exports—was forbidden.

I pushed on to Restaurant Haroun, outside the harbor. It had alcohol. Tired, lonely and depressed about George Garrett's looming death, I drained a glass of wine and ordered another, then another. I had expected to find French-speaking Tunisia enjoyable after Libya. But suddenly everything seemed alien and unwelcoming. This was the worst time for a traveler, a low moment in a strange town. I hurried back to the hotel, half drunk and deeply unhappy.

The next day I prowled the byways of Houmt Souk, which bustled with salesmen who commandeered the sidewalks and laid out straw hats and sand roses, antiques of dubious provenance and fossils that looked mass-produced. Droves of browsers stepped gingerly among the knickknacks.

Decades ago Djerba had been a winter destination for backpackers, aspiring artists and writers eager to live on the cheap in an exotic locale. Now it attracted retirees, folks my age and older, who arrived on charter flights from Europe and who abandoned the *Zone Touristique* only to buy souvenirs. At an outdoor table, over café au lait and a croissant, I looked at home in this grizzled crowd as I swallowed my daily ration of pills and vitamins.

Tunisia's success at attracting senior citizens depended on more than its benevolent climate and long coastline, its history, celebrated desert stations and franchise hotels. Its North African neighbors had as much or better. No, its success came down to its image as a politically moderate Muslim state, an ally of the United States, a safe and enlightened democracy.

Soon after gaining independence from the French, in 1956, Habib Bourguiba, the nation's first president, banned the veil for women, outlawed polygamy and instituted educational reforms and progressive social policies. Not many Tunisians objected—not out loud at any rate—when, in 1975, a compliant National Assembly declared Bourguiba president for life.

But behind the scenes of what Bourguiba cheerfully referred to as this "mere postage stamp on the vast package of Africa," the country's opposition parties and Islamic groups began to spread their tendrils. In 1978 the army had to be called in to crush a national strike, and dozens of demonstrators were killed. By the '80s, under international pressure, Bourguiba permitted elections but only after excluding Islamic parties. In 1984, when seventy people died during bread riots, even Bourguiba's most fervent supporters questioned his mental competence. By 1987, he was declared senile and was deposed in a bloodless coup led by Prime Minister Zine al-Abidine *Ben Ali*.

Ben Ali has been Tunisia's president ever since. Having rewritten the constitution, he was due to run for an unprecedented fourth five-year term in 2009. The result was a foregone conclusion. He had won the 2004 election with 99.9 percent of the vote and gained a nickname, *Ben à vie*—Ben for life. Now seventy-one and rumored to be suffering from prostate cancer, he had a three-year-old son by his second wife, and people quipped, only half joking, that the boy was destined to be the next president—for life, of course.

Yet Tunisia continued to be hailed as the "Arab country that works." Even a journalist as astute and astringent as Christopher Hitchens dubbed it "one of Africa's most outstanding success stories." Writing in *Vanity Fair*, Hitchens praised its economic competitiveness, high rate of home ownership, low rate of poverty, and surplus of clean water and electricity.

For dissidents, this confirmed a suspicion that Tunisia had discovered a magic formula for having it both ways—for repressing its own citizens while burnishing its reputation among foreigners. But Max Rodenbeck, *The Economist*'s Cairo-based correspondent, characterized "Tunisia's dictatorship" as "quietly vicious." The London *Guardian* described it as "one of the most unfree states in the region, where the media is strictly controlled and democratic politics are little more than a façade." Human Rights Watch charged that, despite official denials, "there are still dozens held in Tunisian prisons just because they opposed the government." Reporters Without Borders claimed that Ben Ali's interference with the Internet was "among the most repressive in the world . . . Journalists and media are actively discouraged from being more independent by means of bureaucratic harassment, advertising boycotts and police violence."

Yet regardless of how many alarms were raised, Tunisia managed to remain in the West's good graces. Ben Ali's regime somehow preserved its status as a faithful American ally even after opposing the Gulf War in 1991 and the ouster of Saddam Hussein in 2003, and it was praised for its moderation even as public sentiment in the streets vociferously rejected the occupation of Iraq and Afghanistan and other keystones of U.S. foreign policy.

Critics complained that Tunisia curried Washington's favor with a classic strategy—by exaggerating the threat of terrorism. But in truth, the country had good reason to worry about a spillover of violence from Libya and Algeria. In December 2006 and January 2007, militant Islamists associated with Al Qaeda had fought skirmishes with Tunisian security forces. Fourteen terrorists and two soldiers died in shootouts. Fifteen terrorists were arrested, tried and convicted, and several had been sentenced to death. Now the nation waited to see whether Ben Ali would go ahead with the executions. It was feared that if he did, the terrorists would be viewed as martyrs and urban areas would erupt in riots.

Tunisia's most devastating episode of terrorism occurred here on the island of the Lotus Eaters. In April 2002, a suicide bomber drove a gas tank truck close to the El-Ghriba synagogue, the oldest in North Africa, and detonated it. The blast killed twenty-one people—fourteen Germans, a Frenchman and six Tunisians. Al Qaeda in the Islamic Maghreb (AQIM) claimed responsibility.

After breakfast, I traveled out to the village of Erriadh to visit the renovated synagogue. It was closed, and I had trouble understanding when it would reopen. The security guards spoke neither English nor French, and I needed an interpreter. Back in Carthaginian days, according to Flaubert's historical novel, *Salammbô*, there had been legions of translators easily recognized by the parrots tattooed on their chests. But I had to hike into the center of Erriadh for information.

It was a mile away, and as the sun beat down on my skull, I felt I had staggered into a De Chirico cityscape of distorted distances and dream perspectives. At the Dar Diafa Hotel, I found shade and water and a waiter who told me that the synagogue reopened at 3 PM. So I sat in the courtyard for a few hours and read about Jews—those in Djerba and elsewhere in North Africa.

By most historical accounts Jews had migrated from Jerusalem to North Africa, settling first in Cyrenaica, in present-day Libya. Then after a rebellion against the Romans, they retreated into the desert. Later, Arab chronicles recorded that the stiffest resistance to the spread of Islam came from Jews commanded by Queen Kahenna. As Islam continued to advance, a sizeable Jewish community withdrew westward to the Algerian Sahara.

Although it's often claimed that Jews, as people of the Book, lived free of persecution in Muslim countries, American author Robert Satloff pointed out in *Among the Righteous: Lost Stories from the Holocaust's Long Reach into Arab Lands*: "It is a mistake to exaggerate the amity and friendship that characterized relations between rulers and ruled in Muslim lands. For centuries, Jews in North Africa . . . lived as *dhimmis*, a legal status defined by Muslim law in which Jews . . . paid for the privilege of protection from arbitrary attack. In practice, *dhimmi* status left Jews heavily taxed, physically quarantined and socially reviled."

They were restricted to certain trades and forced to dress in outfits that made them instantly identifiable. The Jews of Djerba, for instance, used to wear black pantaloons and black skullcaps, and worked as blacksmiths and jewelers.

Muslims weren't alone in their mistreatment of North African Jews. Nor was anti-Semitism limited to ill-educated masses. The English author Norman Douglas, celebrated for his books about Italy, notably *South Wind*, spent the winter of 1912 in Tunisia, and while he had something nasty to say about everybody, he saved his worst venom for the Jews. "So far as I can see, their dirt does not detract from their astuteness—perhaps it aids it by removing one source of mental preoccupation—cleanliness."

During World War II, the Germans, French and Italians sentenced thousands of North African Jews to slave labor camps. Anyone who resisted was tortured or killed. Hundreds were shipped to Europe for extermination, and 1,200 North African Jews who had the misfortune to be living in Europe during the Nazi occupation died at Auschwitz and Dachau.

The French and Italians confiscated Jewish property in Tunisia, excluded them from schools and professions and exploited them as slave labor. But the Germans operated at an altogether different pitch of cruelty. In Gabès and Sousse they systematically pillaged banks, targeting Jewish deposits, and they extorted tribute in gold from Djerba's Jews. In Tunis, they unleashed SS Colonel Walter Rauff, the maniac who invented the mobile gas chamber for expeditious killing. Although the Germans never had a chance to implement all their plans, they did round up thousands of Jews and force them to clear rubble from airfields while Allied bombers strafed them. All told, 2,575 Tunisian Jews died, most during air raids, and the casualties would have been far higher had the Germans had a free hand.

The Americans did have a free hand after they drove the Axis army back to the Italian mainland. But they showed little interest in righting the flagrant wrongs done to the Jews. As American Rick Atkinson wrote in *An Army at Dawn*, his magisterial account of the war in North Africa, 1942–1943: "When [French General] Noguès complained that Jews in Morocco and Algeria were demanding restored suffrage, [President] Roosevelt jauntily replied, 'The answer to that is very simple, namely, that there just aren't going to *be* any elections, so the Jews need not worry about the privilege of voting.' " President Roosevelt also proposed restricting Jewish participation in law, medicine and other professions to reflect their percentage in "the whole of the North African population." This, he confided to General Noguès, should "eliminate the specific and understandable complaints which the Germans bore toward the Jews in Germany."

A s I set out again for El-Ghriba Synagogue, the school day ended, and shoals of kids in blue smocks swarmed along with me, singsonging, "*Bonjour, bonjour.*" Their older sisters shied to the far side of the street, cloaked in *hijabs* and modestly averting their eyes. As we approached the synagogue, the kids peeled away, and I hotfooted it over a parking lot to a flimsy modular structure that housed a metal detector. A new shift of security guards was on duty, and one of them spoke French and asked why I had walked here instead of taking a bus or cab.

"*Je prépare pour les Olympiques,*" I told him.

He laughed and said, "*Oui, pour les vétérans.*"

Out the far end of the prefab, I headed for a gate with an armed guard and a rifleman in a tower to back him up. But the security struck me as laughable compared with the bunker mentality at the average Manhattan office building. Maybe it was the heat that had left the guards so languid. Or perhaps it was the casual dress of visitors that lulled everybody into complacency. They looked like they were headed to the sea, not the scene of a terrorist atrocity. Most didn't wear enough to conceal a fifty-cent piece much less a bomb.

One striking blond with luminescent pale skin sported black short shorts and a black camisole, and she walked arm in arm with a black man in camouflage fatigues. Behind them ambled a contingent of Eastern Europeans in swimsuits and flip-flops. I fully expected them to be turned back. I had seen girls expelled from St. Peter's Basilica for wearing sleeveless dresses, and I had once been scolded at the Dome of the Rock in Jerusalem for holding hands with my wife.

Not wanting to witness their rejection, I ducked into a courtyard across from the synagogue. Pilgrims slept here in rooms no bigger than cells during a yearly tribute to the seventeenth-century Talmudic scholar Shimon Bar Yashai. The rooms had stone shelves for beds. I touched a door and drew back my hand with blue on my fingertips. That's how hot it was—hot enough to melt paint.

When I went to the synagogue, I discovered that the guards hadn't, after all, rejected anybody. Many were called and everybody was chosen. This made for a tight fit and sweaty jostling. There was, however, a dry, cool spot in an alcove where old men prayed aloud in antiphonal chorus, oblivious to the mass of gawkers.

The synagogue's second room was smaller, stifling, and the crowd milled about on tiptoes, attempting to catch a glimpse of the world's oldest Torah. Oil lamps suspended from the ceiling swayed in the commotion. Then two new arrivals squeezed in—a plump French couple dressed in yellow Lycra racing gear with MARLY CYCLO stenciled on front. They looked like a pair of goofy bumblebees from an old John Belushi skit.

No commemorative plaque mentioned the 2002 bombing. No part of the synagogue showed any sign of damage or gave any indication that people had died here. Terror forgotten, tourism reigned.

The next day a female Avis agent in a black pantsuit and matching headscarf delivered a rental car to my hotel. She frittered away two hours filling in the contract, confirming my creditworthiness, then establishing via a call to headquarters in Tunis that I could leave the Renault Clio anywhere in the country without a drop charge. After that, it was smooth sailing on a ferry to the mainland, an interlude that allowed me to take stock. On the plus side, I had still not been pestered by hotel touts, guides pretending to be students, or students pretending to be pimps. Some might say that it was also a plus that except for traffic, I hadn't encountered anything that could be construed as terror. But I intended to keep looking for trouble. I headed for Matmata, where the two Austrians had been kidnapped by Al Qaeda.

For eons this corridor leading inland had been bandit territory, and Berber highwaymen used to force-feed captives hot water to flush out swallowed gold nuggets. Now the road sizzled with four-wheel-drive vehicles in convoys to the mountains, the desert or to

Matmata's subterranean houses, the site of memorable scenes from *Star Wars*. The Greek historian Herodotus wrote that these underground dwellings were inhabited by molelike humans who spoke a language that he compared to the cry of a bat.

After the flatness of the Egyptian coast, then Libya, then Djerba, the craggy hills and escarpments here had the majesty of the Himalayas, and as a world of long horizontals tilted into abrupt verticals, I felt dizzy. Or perhaps this vertigo was induced by the sight of Tunisian families who had parked under acacia trees for a picnic. The men in burnooses and the women in *hijabs* lounged full length on the gravel. A variation on Manet's painting *Déjeuner sur l'herbe*—call it *Déjeuner sur les roches*.

At Matmata, signs and souvenir shanties cluttered the countryside, and long lines snaked into the sunken houses. Nobody appeared to be on the alert for Al Qaeda kidnappers. Some listened to lecturing guides. Others kibitzed at the rim of what resembled a volcanic crater, staring down into a sunken living room. On a parking lot I counted two tour buses, two minivans and six SUVs and decided to give Matmata a pass.

Lucky I did. Otherwise I might have missed the thrill of a rocket ship roaring past me on the road, breathing jets of flame from its exhaust pipes. I doubted that anybody would believe what I had seen, no more than they believed those loons who claim to have spotted a flying saucer. But half an hour later, I caught up to the podlike vehicle where it was parked beside a steeple of rock. A couple clad in leather hopped out of it through gullwing doors, and as I pulled in behind them I read the FORMULA RAID TEAM decal on the rear window.

Gerard Bonielli and his wife were French, middle-aged and affable. They had just completed a transnational race from Marseilles to Tunis and then south to the Libyan town of Nalut. Now, minus their support-team trucks, they were bound for Douz "to relax in the sun."

They regretted not having been able to participate in the Paris–Dakar Race, which was cancelled in 2008 after terrorists killed four French tourists in Mauritania. But there'd be other years, Mr. Bonielli said. Terrorism was a short-term problem; desert racing would be around for the long haul. Despite the soaring price of gas, the economic slump and the protests of African villagers who'd had relatives mowed down by speeding cars and motorcycles, the game would go on, and Bonielli and his wife intended to compete in it as long as their health permitted.

He invited me to check out his car and explained that it was a Chevrolet with a Corvette engine capable of traveling 120 mph. It looked like no Chevy I'd ever seen—like no other car on the road. It had fat tires that wouldn't have been out of place on a tractor, and its chassis was raised high off the ground so it could clear deep ruts and washboard pistes. The cockpit had more dials and buttons and levers than a 747. But the rest of the interior was spartan, with no insulation and two thinly padded seats. As Bonielli and his wife yanked on their helmets and strapped themselves in, I asked, "How comfortable is it in there?"

"Very uncomfortable," he screamed over the ear-splitting engine. Then he slammed the gullwings shut and vanished like Hans Solo and Chewbacca into hyperspace.

Toward Douz, the true desert set in: dunes, miles of singed pebbles, crushed rock and blowing sand. Braided palm fronds fenced the road to prevent dust from drifting over the asphalt, and there was something touching and pathetic about these barriers whose delicate embroidery was pitted against the implacable advance of the desert. Sand went wherever it wanted. It coiled and uncoiled in the wake of passing cars and piled up in jarring speed bumps. Then it crusted over with salt, and snow-white flats nearly blinded me. Even with the windows shut, grit sifted in and ground between my teeth and peppered my nostrils.

In one of his brainless tirades, Norman Douglas wrote in *Fountains in the Sand* that historians were mistaken to believe that the desert had formed the Arabs. Just the reverse, Douglas argued, the Arabs had destroyed everything in their path and made the desert: "The evils which now afflict North Africa, its physical abandonment, its social and economic decay, are the work of the ideal Arab, the man of Mecca. Mahomet is the desert-maker."

Today even the most rabid anti-Islamic crusader would laugh off such guff, for in fact Arabs managed to survive in the desert only through ingenuity and ceaseless diligence. A sparse, nomadic population had cultivated a lifeline of oases that would have died off without them. The palm groves of North Africa didn't spring up naturally. They had been planted and irrigated by a system of tunnels (*foggaras*) and channels (*sequias*) that required Herculean effort to dig and constant maintenance.

Of late, the main street in almost every Tunisian town had changed its name to avenue de l'Environment, and the mascot of the Green Movement, an eight-foot statue of a blue rabbit-eared rodent, occupied a place of prominence. But when I passed through the village of Kebili, the big blue rat, called *Labibe*, kept a lonely vigil. The population was indoors watching soccer on TV, their loud cheering the lone sign of life. Here, as elsewhere in Tunisia, the desert was encroaching during a prolonged drought. At the edge of town a derelict Parc des Loisirs, with dry fountains and a sand-filled swimming pool, looked less like a leisure park than a cemetery.

For a month, my trip had been a journey of discovery. Now it took on the trappings of a return and a reappraisal. Thirty-two years ago, I had traveled through this area doing research for a novel about a film crew shooting a movie in the Sahara. A friend of mine, the publicist on the TV miniseries *Jesus of Nazareth*, fixed it for me to watch Franco Zeffirelli direct an international cast that included Laurence Olivier, James Mason, Rod Steiger, Anthony Quinn, Anne Bancroft, Claudia Cardinale, Christopher Plummer and Ian McShane. In a sweetheart deal with Habib Bourguiba, the production company had set up shop in the president's ancestral village, Monastir.

I lived with the crew in a beachfront hotel where the meals were commissary style and nighttime entertainment consisted of gossip and high jinks over too much wine. In that pre-CNN, pre-Internet, pre-BlackBerry era, news was hit or miss. Nobody could believe it when we learned that a peanut farmer from Georgia named Jimmy Carter was running for president. Since phone calls to the States cost a fortune and took hours to connect, Rod Steiger's wife agreed to carry a message back to Linda, saying I was leaving Monastir for the

Sahara. In seven years of marriage, this was our first separation, and it had been painful. I begged Linda to write me a letter care of Poste Restante, Nefta, near the Algerian border.

Vincenzo Labella, the producer of *Jesus of Nazareth*, told me that an American company was shooting a sci-fi film in Tozeur, right on my route. He urged me to include that set in my research. He also promised to arrange for me to stay at the Sahara Palace in Nefta, the finest hotel in the country.

In a rental car, I drove south, not at all certain I cared to drop in on the sci-fi film. Called *Star Wars*, it sounded like a low-budget dud and was directed by a newcomer named George Lucas. I was more interested in reaching Algeria and exploring the Grand Erg Oriental, a vast domain of sand dunes sculpted into crests hundreds of feet high. There I'd stay in the legendary oasis of El Oued, once home to the equally legendary Isabelle Eberhardt. The illegitimate daughter of a Russian anarchist, Eberhardt had pitched up in the Sahara in 1899 at the age of twenty-two and promptly scandalized the natives and the French *colons* alike. Born Jewish, she converted to Islam, married a Muslim, then cross-dressed as an Arab man and joined a camel caravan. Falling in with the Foreign Legion, she entertained the troops by playing the piano and "sleeping her way through the Armée d'Afrique," as one historian expressed it. Predictably, given her melodramatic personality, she met a bizarre end. She died in a flash flood in the globe's greatest desert.

On top of its other attractions, El Oued featured the Souf Museum. Everyone encouraged me not to miss it.

Meanwhile, I had plenty to see on the drive to Tozeur. In each town, the principal boulevard, usually named after a dead holy man or revolutionary hero, drowsed in heat-drugged torpor. But back on side streets, camels frisked in courtyards, blacksmiths hammered brass trays, men lugged goatskin water bags over their shoulders and walked hand in hand with their male friends.

I arrived just after darkness, when the flies that pestered Tozeur during the day were being supplanted by moths. Nothing appeared to be open except the Grand Hôtel de l'Oasis, where *Star Wars* had its production headquarters. The lobby teemed with dwarfs. Labella hadn't prepared me for this: Dozens of little people had been imported to play Ewoks and Androids. Labella also hadn't warned me about George Lucas, a bearded martinet, who informed me, "It's a closed set."

"I thought you were shooting in the desert."

"Right. And it's off-limits to the press."

"The whole Sahara?" I asked. "Look, I'm not a reporter. I'm writing a novel."

"Whatever you're writing, don't do it here."

With that, he stalked off, and as it turned out, I wasn't just banned from the set. I was persona non grata at the Grand Hôtel de l'Oasis. The restaurant wouldn't seat me, and when I took a table anyway, no one would serve me. I wasn't ordered to leave. The waiters simply ignored me. After half an hour of being eyeballed and whispered about by dwarfs, I retreated to the road for Nefta.

Now men in pale robes joined the moths that flapped around my headlights. Directly behind me and bearing down hard was a bus labeled SPIES in big red letters. Spies—pronounced "speece"—was a Danish tour company, but I couldn't help feeling I was under surveillance and being pursued.

My nerves frayed further when I found no signs for the Sahara Palace, and nobody I asked seemed to have heard of it. Nefta was darker than Tozeur, more folded in on itself. Yet its labyrinth of alleys was large enough to swallow me and spit me out on the far side of town. Finally, a teenage boy swore he knew the hotel and agreed to lead me there in exchange for a Bic pen. I motioned for him to hop aboard.

We swerved uphill, around the lip of a sunken garden that the boy called La Corbeille ("the basket"). When he heard that I was headed to El Oued tomorrow, he confessed his jealousy. "Be sure to see the Souf Museum."

The boy climbed out of the car and lifted a barrier that blocked our path. It was the sort of striped gate that you'd find at a pay parking lot. At the end of a pea-gravel lane there was a luxury hotel. But the windows were dark, the grounds deserted, the silence absolute. I glanced at the kid for an explanation, any clue. He offered none. He turned and trudged off, my Bic pen in his hand.

I rapped my knuckles on the lobby's glass door. I knocked long and hard and roused a man in undershorts, undershirt and a turban who'd been sleeping behind the reception desk. Scratching and yawning, he unlocked the door, and when I mentioned that I was from the film in Monastir, he perked up. "Soyez le bienvenu," he salaamed. "Welcome."

The Sahara Palace was closed, for reasons he didn't care to discuss. It had no electricity, no water, no food and no heat, but he said I was welcome to stay as long as I liked. By lantern, he led me to a suite with a private swimming pool on its terrace and a view over La Corbeille. The pool had been drained; the delights of La Corbeille were invisible in the dark.

Placing the lantern on an end table, he leaned back against the bolster on the double bed and said, "Tell me now, please, about Claudia Cardinale."

I apologized that I hadn't made the acquaintance of Miss Cardinale, and that all things considered, I preferred to sleep elsewhere.

"There's only the Marhala Touring Club," he cautioned me.

The Marhala didn't look as bad as he'd made it sound. The Spies bus was parked out front, which seemed an encouraging sign. In the dining room the Danes drank and sang beerhouse songs. I sat with them, said nothing and ate whatever was plunked in front of me. Then the group trooped out to the bus, and as the driver hauled giant drawers from its undercarriage, I assumed they were fetching their luggage. But no, the drawers contained mattresses and pillows, and it was in these crypt-like quarters that the Danes curled up for the night. Like a morgue attendant, the driver slammed them shut.

Though more spacious, my room at the Marhala had as little charm as a bus-borne crypt. Above the bed, the reed ceiling rattled with insects and lizards intent on making a meal of them. Unsettled by their life-and-death combat, I dozed fitfully until dawn, then tottered outside to watch the sunrise, which in the desert was a spectacular overture to the day, just as sunset was the day's aria. In between lay a blankness of heat, dust and discomfort. But at the start and finish there were polychrome crescendos of cloud castles and shafts of light like cannon fire.

As I set off to explore Nefta's palm grove, I picked up a bamboo pole, an absent-minded move that soon proved lucky. I hadn't gone fifty yards when a fierce pack of dogs attacked me. It was all I could do to hold them off with the bamboo club. I whacked their skulls and jabbed their ribs, but they kept circling and snarling and lunging at my shanks. It took ten minutes to fight my way back to the Marhala.

A hotel gardener who had witnessed my narrow escape maintained I had never been in any real danger. They were guard dogs, not mad dogs, trained to keep thieves from stealing dates. "We have the most delicious ones in Africa," he said. "Except, of course, for the dates in El Oued."

When I told him that that was my destination, he exhorted me not to miss the Souf Museum.

At the border, Algerian customs officials decreed that I could enter but that my rental car had to stay in Tunisia. Something was wrong with the insurance. Finding it intolerable to fall short of the fabled city, I parked the car and caught a *louage* stuffed with passengers sharing this long-distance taxi. The beat-up Renault had grease smeared over its front end to prevent sand from scouring off the enamel, and a Hand of Fatma dangled from the rearview mirror as an amulet against the Evil Eye. We needed every bit of luck we could get.

Zigzagging into the dunes, the road to El Oued was overwhelmed with sand. Deep drifts squeezed us into a tight defile, and whenever we met onrushing traffic, the driver had to brake with a fishtail slide. More than once we scraped side mirrors with madmen speeding in the opposite direction.

Brigades of workers cleared the road with shovels and buckets. But it was hopeless. The sand they dumped in the dunes soon slithered back where it had been, and the process started over again, ceaseless as the wind, inexorable as the sun.

Kids swooped and danced in front of the car, flashing sand roses and amethysts for sale. Like a cargo cult, they believed that everything good in life—money, water, food, miracles—arrived in these hurtling machines, and they were willing to chance death for a few coins or pieces of candy. The driver plowed past them, one hand on the horn and the other on the radio dial. He steered with his knees.

An archipelago of oases lay scattered across the sand, calling to mind cartoon desert islands. Wavelike dunes flooded them every day, and farmers bailed them out with wheelbarrows. Palms flourished in deep hollows, their roots straining for buried moisture, their fronds spreading carpets of green studded with orange dates.

The architecture of El Oued was as extraordinary as the landscape. Even the town's meanest hut had a barrel-vaulted ceiling that protected the interior from the worst of the heat. But in this "city of a thousand cupolas" so many buildings looked interchangeable, it was difficult to locate the Souf Museum, and once I found it, I was stunned to see a building no bigger than a suburban garage.

The first display resembled the business end of a feather duster. A sign described it as the last ostrich killed in the Sahara. A French Legionnaire shot it in 1937.

In addition to aerial photographs of El Oued, the museum contained local handicrafts, tribal jewelry and a miscellany of creatures that crawled and scuttled, crept and oozed. There were venomous snakes the size of earthworms; intestinal worms the size of boa constrictors; scorpions the size of lobsters; horned beetles as big as

Princess telephones; hairy spiders, poisonous lizards and centipedes like lit fuses.

The prizewinning exhibit floated in a jar of formaldehyde. At first, the fat grey blobs looked to be marinating grapes. But a label in three languages thoughtfully identified them as "Blood Engorged Camel Ticks."

Some travelers, I suppose, might have been disappointed after such an extended buildup and exhausting pilgrimage. But I left El Oued in a state of euphoria, convinced, as always, that the "awful" and the "awesome" are alternating currents that fuel the most memorable journeys.

Returning to Tunisia, I stopped at the post office in Nefta to collect Linda's letter. But the building was padlocked. A passerby explained that today was a holiday. He knew where the postmaster lived, and in my eagerness to hear from my wife, I tracked the man down. He took mercy and opened the office. Then he spent an hour rifling through baskets of mail for the one envelope emblazoned with American stamps. The postmaster wouldn't accept a tip, but he let me buy him mint tea, and as we settled in a café he insisted I go ahead and read Linda's letter.

For thirty-two years I've fondly remembered that day and have longed to revisit Tozeur and the post office in Nefta. But both had metastasized—the post office into a modern, anonymous structure, and Tozeur into a goiter on the palm grove. A divided highway, heavy with traffic, ran from one side of the city to the other, past a gauntlet of souvenir shops. The Grand Hôtel de l'Oasis, scene of my ostracism three decades ago, appeared too small and inconsequential for high drama. Bigger, glitzier establishments had cropped up.

Tozeur now boasted a theme park. Depicting historical events from the Big Bang to the birth of Islam, Chak-Wak displayed plastic dinosaurs and papier-mâché Neanderthals dressed in what looked like smartly cut fur coats. Everything was off-kilter, out of scale and over the top. While the statues of Adam and Eve were ten feet tall, replicas of giant Greek and Roman sculptures had been downsized to knee-high miniatures.

Heading west, the highway passed a statue of Hannibal posed between two elephants no higher than his waist. A couple of sphinx-es monitored the entrance to the *Zone Touristique*, a Vegas-style strip of hotels. Billboards advertised Planet Oasis Tozeur (a sound-and-light show) and agencies that leased mountain bikes, motor scooters and off-track vehicles.

Opposite the *Zone Touristique*, a feeder road to the airport paral-leled the Parcours de Santé—a path for joggers with stretching posts, chin-up frames and incline boards. Not a single person used this facility—not surprising, I guess, in ninety-five-degree heat.

At the new terminal, two 747s lolled on the runway like white whales. Daily flights and charters connected Tozeur with Tunis and numerous European cities. Tour groups landed, checked into hotels, flopped into hot tubs and never bothered with the rest of the town. I thought back to Siwa and Mounir Neamatallah's battle to keep the Egyptians from building a commercial airport in that oasis. This was what he feared would happen to Siwa, and seeing what had befallen Tozeur, I sympathized.

I confess, though, that I stayed in the *Zone Touristique*, at the Sofitel Palm Beach for $218 a night, a price absurdly beyond my budget. But I had an appointment with a couple here on holiday. A mutual friend had arranged this rendezvous with Tunisians on the proviso that I not disclose their identities.

Karim, as I'll call him, was big and beefy but had a gentle, forgiving nature. "Rachida," a loquacious academic, had vehement opinions that were a source of discomfort to her partner. He suggested it would be wiser not to talk in the hotel. So we ate dinner at Le Petit Prince, a restaurant named for Antoine de St. Exupéry's cloying French fable. At an outdoor table, under strands of faerie lights, Karim and Rachida ordered wine—the first Muslim drinkers I'd met in North Africa.

I wanted to discuss Tozeur and how radically it had changed. But the topic didn't gain much traction with them. They liked the oasis well enough for a vacation. They were too young to remember how it used to be, and too smart to be shocked by the political trade-offs behind its evolution from an outpost on a caravan route to an international resort. They regarded Tozeur's growth as just another aspect of President Ben Ali's push to decentralize the country and develop the south. There was, Rachida said, now a university in town. This would have been unimaginable under Bourguiba, who had favored the north.

Karim and Rachida were keener to talk about my trip. They had both traveled widely in Europe, spoke excellent English and had lived for years in Paris. But neither had visited any other North African country, and the image they had of their neighbors was unflattering.

"In Egypt," Karim asked, "did you see people living in cemeteries? I hear it's nothing but beggars and poverty."

As for Libya, Rachida regarded it as primitive, uneducated and uncultured. "Libyans come to Tunisia to drink and hunt for women. They think Tunisian girls are easy."

"People tell me there's nothing to do in Tripoli," Karim said. "The rich boys wear their best clothes and gel their hair and sit in front of their big houses in their fancy cars."

They said they wouldn't dream of traveling in Algeria and discouraged me from doing so. They spoke of suicide bombings, throat-slittings, and blood and body parts in the streets.

They knew little about the two Austrians who'd been kidnapped near Matmata. "I really think it didn't happen here," Karim said. "I think it happened in Mali."

"No, Mali is where they're being held for ransom," I said.

The two of them shrugged.

Despite their isolation—or because of it—they were worried, even if ill-informed, about terrorism and the instability of the regimes on both sides of their country. They wanted no part of Qaddafi's Jamahiriya or Algeria's Islamic fundamentalism. They conceded that Tunisia wasn't perfect, far from it, and they discussed Ben Ali with the same joking contempt as U.S. blue-state voters did of George W. Bush. But for all Ben Ali's faults, they believed he had what it took to deal with troublemakers.

"He started in the Interior Ministry," Karim explained, "and has a very strong background in intelligence. He knows everything about every potential terrorist in Tunisia."

"They say he sometimes dresses in a djellaba," Rachida added, "and goes alone into the medina to see for himself where the trouble spots are and who's planning attacks. So we don't have to worry so much—except when there are mistakes."

Karim made a gesture, signaling that she should stay mum about Ben Ali's mistakes. But Rachida said a sad thing had happened to a friend of theirs who somehow fell afoul of the state security apparatus. "I don't believe he was political. He was never very religious. Not like a fundamentalist. But they took him into custody."

"His name must have matched somebody's on a watch list," Karim said. "No system is perfect."

"They tortured him," Rachida said.

"I wouldn't call it torture," Karim whispered. "They questioned him for awhile."

"For a year!" Rachida said. "He was mentally and physically wrecked."

Karim moved his hand over hers and squeezed tight. In solace? Or to shut her up?

I made sympathetic murmurs about how awful it must have been for their friend.

"It was bad luck," Karim said.

"Yes, but it shows how security policies can injure innocent people," I said. "We've had that problem in the States."

"If we want Tunisia to stay safe and prosperous, Ben Ali doesn't have a choice," Karim maintained. "Otherwise the country could end up like Algeria." He argued that Tunisia couldn't risk real democracy. "The fundamentalists would win and destroy everything we've built."

"You believe the majority of Tunisians are fundamentalists?" I asked.

"I'm not sure what they are or what they might become under the influence of outsiders. Already they've arrested agents of AQIM. We can't take chances."

Set in cold type, his words might seem to indict Karim as a right-wing zealot, a defender of the status quo, which disenfranchised less fortunate people. But in person he sounded scared, not selfish. A modern, educated man, an enlightened technocrat, sophisticated enough to drink wine in public—that was how he viewed himself. He simply feared the nation might slide into chaos and bloodshed. But he hadn't considered the possibility that his fears had to some extent been manufactured and manipulated by self-serving politicians.

Rachida saw things differently and said so. That in itself was some credit to Karim; Rachida felt free to speak her mind to him. As a university professor, she had a perspective on the country that differed from a businessman's. Tunisia had more than four hundred thousand college students, she said. While that sounded impressive, the problem was finding them meaningful work so that they wouldn't become fundamentalists.

"Officially, university graduates have a 15 percent unemployment rate. Actually it's closer to 40 percent. To get jobs, many have to leave the country and go to the Gulf. They come back with crazy Wahhabi ideas about women and Islam. Those who stay here don't find work, and that means they can't afford to marry. Some of them get frustrated and turn to terrorism."

I said I'd like to meet her students. Again I was thinking that some of them might have radical leanings and contacts with terrorists.

Rachida said, "That's a problem. I can't bring you to the campus without permission." It was the same situation as in Libya.

"It's enough to describe things," Karim told her. "You don't need to involve other people."

So Rachida described higher education in Tunisia as part of a larger corruption. "To become a teacher, you have to pass a qualifying exam. Then you're assigned to a university. It could be anywhere in the country. Naturally everybody prefers to be in Tunis. So people pay bribes to get good positions. Some of them pay to get a passing grade on the test. Of course, if you have a powerful family or friends, that's as good as money."

"What kinds of people teach in Tozeur?"

"Either they have no money or no influence. Or they got really, really low grades. I would guess most of the professors don't live here. They fly in or drive in for their classes, then return to their homes."

"Why wouldn't they live in Tozeur?"

Rachida thought I was kidding.

"I'm serious," I said.

"It's okay for a holiday, but there's no culture, nothing to do. And southern towns are very conservative. If you're a woman, it's no place to be."

She recounted what had befallen another female professor, an acquaintance of hers. Assigned to Medenine, south of Matmata, the woman had rented an apartment and relocated there full time. Almost immediately local men began to harass her. They presumed that any young unmarried woman living alone was fair game. They stalked her in the street, shouting obscenities. They banged on her door at night and demanded to be let in.

"She complained to the police," Rachida said. "She could identify the men. But the police did nothing. When she found out the
names of the men and reported them, the police told her nobody
with those names lived in Medenine. Finally she had to resign. She
quit teaching altogether and moved home. I wouldn't claim it's a
common story, but it's an example of how without power or influence you're not free in Tunisia."

The next day, a dense brown cloud closed like a clamshell over
the oasis. It was *brume sèche*, a fog of dust particles suspended
in the bone-dry air. Setting out for Nefta, I had trouble seeing the road
and was tempted to return to Tozeur.

Stranded in the mist, pedestrians signaled from the desert,
begging for water. With one hand they pantomimed swigging from a
bottle, with the other they pressed cell phones to their ears. The cell
phones convinced me that this wasn't an emergency. In any case,
I had no water. Then, too, something that happened years ago in
Morocco—an incident I didn't like to remember—doubled my reluctance to stop and offer help.

At the entrance to Nefta, a grandiloquent arch bridged the road,
and three soldiers stepped from behind it to check my papers. Grit
seamed the crow's-feet at the corners of their eyes. I asked about the
Sahara Palace, but they either didn't speak French or were too eager
to escape the dust to bother answering.

In town, school was letting out for lunch, and kids gamboled
about, as if the *brume sèche* were a spring shower. I located the Marhala Touring Club, much expanded since my stay in '76. The trees

and grain fields in the palm grove were powdered grey with sand. I didn't notice any guard dogs.

Although it hadn't changed as drastically as Tozeur, Nefta wasn't the village I remembered. Nor, of course, was I the man I had been at thirty-three, the romantic who had reveled in such spots and was prone to confuse seediness with exoticism, every idiosyncratic experience with adventure. Still, even if not shivering with bliss, I was glad to be back and happy to find a sign to La Corbeille and the Sahara Palace.

The road swept uphill past a soccer pitch that might have been fired in a kiln. Over ceramic-hard dirt, boys sprinted after a ball of rags while a few camels gnawed on cactus. Then, at a café that sold djellabas and burnooses—they fluttered from a trellis like flags—I glanced over La Corbeille. The name referred not just to the ravine's oval shape but to the wickerwork of palm fronds that surrounded it. La Corbeille's spring brimmed with water the color of pesto sauce, and the drought had browned the palms to a crisp.

A boy stepped out of the café and snapped my long string of good luck. He nagged me to come to his house for tea, or into the desert for a camel ride, or out onto the *chott* to the ruins of a *Star Wars* set, or to the location where *The English Patient* was shot. "Cheap," he promised. "I am student. Not guide. I do this for friendship."

I thanked him, but said I'd rather see things on my own.

"Alone is dangerous," he warned.

"Alone is best," I said, and climbed back into the car.

Lonely Planet describes the Sahara Palace as the "best hotel in town . . . panoramic views directly over the *Corbeille* . . . a wonderful place for a sunset drink." So I expected at long last to savor the hotel's amenities. But in the sort of dreadful repetition common to bad dreams, I rolled up to it and found my way barred again. Beyond the locked gate lay a scene of stark devastation. The garden had been bombed or burned. Was it terrorism? A natural disaster? The trees and shrubs were blackened sticks, and every window in the building was an empty eye socket.

I drove on to what appeared to be a town older than the pyramids and sadder than the Sahara Palace. A hundred or so barrel-vaulted hovels squatted in the sand, guarded by feral dogs that bared their teeth and bit at my tires. Another nightmare repetition, I thought, as the howling pack chased me up one bleak street and down another.

Then a man materialized out of a dust devil. He had a shovel over one shoulder and a little girl over the other. He dropped the shovel and waved for me to stop. The dogs kept yelping and snapping, but they didn't bother him.

I lowered the window an inch.

"Do you make a film?" he asked in French.

"No. What is this place?" I shouted over the barking dogs.

"Chabbat. They film *Star Wars* nearby and *Indiana Jones* and *The English Patient*."

"Where do you live?"

"Here. I dig sand from my house. You can make a movie in it."

"How old is the town?" I asked.

"The government built Chabbat in 1988 as *maisons populaires* (public housing). Most people left because the houses are too hot. But mine is good."

I gave him a few coins. "For your pretty daughter," I said, quick to yank my hand in before the dogs locked their fangs on it. They chased me for blocks, loping alongside until I picked up speed and outdistanced them.

Back on the main road, signs cautioned: ATTENTION, KAMEL'S CROSS-ING. Then, more accurately, in French: PASSAGE DROMADAIRES. Around one signpost, yellow orbs the size of cantaloupes had sprouted from green vines.

I stopped and picked one of the fruits—or was it a vegetable?—and hoped I wasn't pilfering some poor Tunisian's garden. I cradled it in my lap on the return to Nefta and tried to fathom how it had survived the desert. It felt plump and lush, and I was tempted to bite into it.

In town I searched on foot for someone who could tell me what it was. Streets tunneled into the medina, as mysterious as a cham-bered nautilus. In the dimness, men sat on stone benches sheltered from the *brume sèche*. I showed them what I had, and they hefted it and smelled it, muttered among themselves and spoke a word in Arabic that I couldn't understand.

I walked on into an area of Nefta that had dissolved during a downpour in 1990. The normal brick pattern of the houses was as in-tricate as a basket weave. In dry weather the weave lasted forever. But in rare wet weather it unraveled. Like desert dwellers everywhere in North Africa, the populace of Nefta prayed for rain—and sometimes, in cruel irony, their prayers were answered with a deluge.

At the far end of the medina, I entered the palm grove and fol-lowed a path to a cinder block bungalow that had tables and chairs out front on the bare pounded earth. A few locals were drinking mint tea.

The interior of the Restau Bar El Ferdaous smelled of stale beer. At the bar three glassy-eyed gents hunched over empty bottles. Their overalls were mud-spattered after a day spent mucking out irrigation ditches. Tired and drunk, they took a sloppy, friendly interest in me.

One of them noticed what I had in my hand and warned that it was poison: "*Ne mangez pas.*"

"What is it?" I asked.

He palmed the strange fruit and said in French, "It's a colocynth."

For me the word possessed an almost talismanic shimmer. It recalled college, and the first book I had ever read about North Africa, a novel I had reread before leaving the States. André Gide's *The Immoralist* opened with a narrator's invocation: "I present this book for what it is worth—a fruit filled with bitter ashes, like those colocynths of the desert that grow in a parched and burning soil. All they can offer to your thirst is a still more cruel fierceness— yet lying on the golden sand they are not without a beauty of their own."

"Poison," the man warned again. "Do you want a beer?"

I said I'd have a Coke, and he laughed. "Ah, like a good Muslim. I am a bad one. I drink a little. First time in Nefta?"

"No, I was here thirty-two years ago."

"Everybody comes back. *C'est la crème du miel; une seule nuit et l'étranger s'y sent chez lui.*"

I was astonished to hear him describe his town as "the cream of the honey," a place where after a single night a stranger felt at home. But then he pointed to two placards on the wall. One was inscribed with his flowery tribute to Nefta.

The other—to my greater astonishment—quoted Gide: IF I HAD KNOWN NEFTA SOONER, IT'S NEFTA RATHER THAN BISKRA THAT I WOULD HAVE RETURNED TO MANY TIMES.

"The town has changed," I said.

"It's grown," the man said, "but it hasn't changed. Not the people and how we live. The problem is water. We don't have enough. The tourists come and go. But we stay and we need rain."

As I left Restau Bar El Ferdaous, he called me back. I had forgotten my colocynth.

L ate that afternoon, the *brume sèche* burned off, and the blue bowl of sky took on a glazed sheen. A spring day in the Sahara, the temperature one hundred. A convention of French executives from the Xerox Corporation had checked into the Sofitel Palm Beach along with their wives and girlfriends, who sunbathed in bikinis around the lake-size swimming pool. The hotel was profligate with water, just as it was with air conditioning and floral air freshener. It was the sort of sybaritic Third World tourism that made Djerba seem modest and tasteful by comparison—the kind I often skewered. But today, despite twinges of guilt, I took delight in swimming, then basting in the sun, with the Frenchwomen and their lovely buttery brown skin.

Somebody sagged onto the chaise longue beside me. Not one of the beauties. Punishment, divine retribution, in the form of a teak-colored Tunisian man wearing a cache-sexe swimsuit. Worse yet, he was a talker: "What is your profession?" "Where do you live?" "Do you find Tozeur expensive?"

I couldn't very well object. After all, what had I done during my trip except cross-examine strangers? Maybe my questions annoyed people as much as his did me. Then as I lied to Mr. Cache-Sexe—I told him I was a retired schoolteacher—I wondered how often I had been hoodwinked in my travels. Could I trust this guy's story that he was a cosmetic surgeon? Doctor, cure thyself of sun damage, I was tempted to tell him.

"Business is very good," he volunteered. "I have a specialty that's in demand."

I didn't need to ask. Nothing short of a bullet could have stopped him from telling me, "I do hymenoplasties."

I had read about the procedure and its increasing popularity in the Arab world. As more and more Muslim women gained the education, money and independence to travel abroad, they adopted European mores. Or, as the cosmetic surgeon put it, they "lose their most valuable possession before marriage. Then they meet a good Muslim man and want him for a husband, but are afraid of their wedding night. Unless they bleed, he will know the truth. So . . ."

"So what?" I said.

"So I make them a new hymen." He offered to diagram the operation on a cocktail napkin.

"No, thanks. I'd better get out of the sun," I said. "I'm beginning to burn."

In the room, my colocynth was on the nightstand where I'd left it, but it had shriveled and blackened. Having flourished in the Sahara, it had been killed by an hour of air conditioning.

The road north to Tunis passed through Gafsa, an ill-favored town that had for millennia been conquered, razed and rebuilt by marauding armies. In 107 BC, the Romans leveled it during their scorched-earth campaign against the Numidian king Jugurtha, and it had since suffered constant misfortune. During World War II, the Allied and Axis armies traded Gafsa back and forth, capturing and relinquishing it four times in three months. The fly-bitten phosphate town's reputation had then been maligned in a popular Arab song:

> *Gafsa is miserable,*
> *Its water is blood,*
> *Its air is poison.*
> *You may live there a hundred years.*
> *Without making a friend.*

Its tourist attractions comprised two pools from the Roman era where youngsters would dive into the soupy water if you tossed them a coin. It wasn't an edifying spectacle, but not nearly as bad as Norman Douglas made it seem. "I am all for keeping up local color," he wrote, "even when it entails as it generally does, a certain percentage of local smells; yet it seems a pity that such glorious hot springs, a gift of the gods in a climate like this, should be converted into a *cloaca maxima*, especially in Gafsa which already boasts a superfluidity of open drains."

As in other North African cities, sidewalk markets competed for customers on the main thoroughfare. But Gafsa was unique in one respect: It had a wide range of safes for sale, from strongboxes as big as walk-in closets to flimsy tin containers with combination locks. Maybe this craving for security reflected the town's history of invasions.

As the road climbed onto a high plateau, cultivated fields of cactus recalled Mexico and its tequila factories. But in each village there was a mosque, not a church, and storks fed hatchlings in huge twig nests atop the minarets. Flatbed trucks transported bales of esparto grass to Kasserine and its factories, which manufactured paper and a dreadful stink.

The rolling, arid countryside had been the background to countless World War II histories, films and even computer games. At a mountain pass northwest of Kasserine, American troops famously collided with Rommel's German Afrika Korps in February 1943, and the U.S. Army II Corps sustained heavy casualties and a loss of fifty miles of territory. The Americans regrouped in Algeria, then bounced back three months later and, along with the British, drove the Axis powers out of North Africa.

While this story had been told and retold by Europeans and Americans, the campaign's disastrous consequences for the local population have gone largely unreported. One of the great virtues of Rick Atkinson's *An Army at Dawn* is its candor about the cruelties inflicted on civilians out of cultural ignorance, casual racism and callous disregard for military ethics. At best, Allied troops viewed the Tunisians as enemies, at worst, as no better than animals. In anticipation of traffic fatalities during their sweep north, the Allies established a sliding scale of reparations, to be paid in French currency, "25,000 francs ($500) for a dead camel; 15,000 for a dead boy; 10,000 for a donkey; 5,000 for a dead girl."

To prevent the desperately poor Tunisians from stealing gasoline, the Americans smeared bacon grease on their fuel cans, figuring that Muslims wouldn't touch pork products. When peasants pilfered battlefields of food and clothing, the GIs took potshots at them. Some soldiers confessed to gunning down Tunisians like gophers. Atkinson quotes from letters and oral histories that characterized the natives as "useless, worthless, illiterate, dishonest and diseased." They were often summarily executed on the slightest suspicion of espionage, and in a distressing foreshadowing of Vietnam, Allied troops imposed collective punishment, torching whole villages. "It is not pleasant to stand round blazing huts while women and children scream inside," one American witness said.

The French protested through official channels to General Dwight D. Eisenhower that GIs were raping, assaulting and killing civilians. But the French had little claim to the moral high ground. After the Axis defeat, France switched its allegiance to the Allies and reasserted its colonial rule with a vengeance, launching a ruthless campaign of reprisals against Tunisians suspected of collaboration with the Germans. A secret report from the OSS (the U.S. intelligence agency that preceded the CIA) revealed that "a general reign of terror was instituted in which arbitrary arrests and torture of Muslims became frequent occurrences." The French set up detention camps on Djerba, imprisoning 3,000 Arabs "with beatings, killings and mass executions reported."

For the Allies, the campaign in North Africa ended in triumph, but its aftershocks have endured until this day. "Sixty years later," Atkinson writes, "Tunisian authorities were still digging up an average of fifty unexploded bombs, shells and mines every month."

From Kasserine, I veered east toward the coast, pausing to visit El Djem and the third largest Roman coliseum ever constructed. Its immensity interested me less than its location, smack in the middle of the medina. While tourists clustered at a ticket booth, kids skittered in and out of the Coliseum as if it were their private playground. Teenagers on bikes did wheelies on the handicap ramp, and vendors hawked everything from cold Cokes to scorpions preserved in bottles of formaldehyde.

North of Mahdia, a *Zone Touristique* clamped hold of the coast all the way to Tunis. The towns of Monastir, Sousse and Hammamet had gentrified and homogenized into a blur of condos, cabanas, cafés and casinos. Not bad places. Not really. One could appreciate why hordes jetted in from Amsterdam and Munich for the sun and the sea. Yet I had no interest in stopping longer than an hour to re-explore the *ribat* in Monastir, an outstanding example of Islamic military architecture.

I had watched Franco Zeffirelli film scenes here for *Jesus of Nazareth* in 1976. One day the Tunisian extras took his direction literally, and when he told them to rough up a troupe of British actors playing Roman centurions, several costumed thespians needed medical treatment. Shooting was cut short while the extras were calmed down and taught to pull their punches. The *ribat* later served as the setting for *The Life of Jesus Christ* and later still for Monty Python's *Life of Brian*. It was hard to guess what, except a payday, the Tunisians made of this progression of Biblical tales from the classic to the parodic.

Linda joined me in Tunis with our younger son, Marc. The plan was to spend a week showing them the city that I had seen several times before. Then the three of us would drive west to Ain Draham, and they'd drop me at the Algerian border. But what I had envisioned as a vacation threatened to turn into a family intervention. From the moment they arrived, Linda and Marc implored me not to go to Algeria. Everything they had heard and read convinced them that I should skip the country and fly to Morocco.

To me there was no debate, no reason not to proceed as planned. I had come safely this far, and to celebrate I booked us a table at Dar El Jeld, the best restaurant in Tunis. Dinner there, I told them, would have the elegance of the banquet in Flaubert's *Salammbô*, where slaves served "flamingoes' tongues with honied poppy seeds on a spread ox hide," followed by "a few of those plump little dogs with pink silky hair and fattened on olive lees—a Carthaginian dish held in abhorrence among other nations."

But Linda and Marc weren't listening to me. Course after course, they drummed it in: Don't go to Algeria. Didn't it matter that they loved me? Didn't I care how they'd feel if something happened to me?

"Like what?" I asked.

"Like getting kidnapped and chained to a radiator for the next five years memorizing the Koran," Marc said.

"Like dying," Linda laid it out straight.

This was Dido's city, ripe and soft. While it was tempting to sink into it, I couldn't let myself do that. Just as Aeneas had abandoned the Phoenician queen of Carthage and traveled on to found Rome, I felt obliged to stay the course I had set for myself.

Not that I didn't enjoy Tunis. I rambled up and down avenue Bourguiba, where all the French hallmarks were still evident—*grandes places*, flower-banked roundabouts, a baroque opera house, the Cathedral of St. Vincent de Paul, plashing fountains and sidewalk cafés. The aroma of fresh baked croissants and Gauloises Bleues laced the air. Only the most recent addition, a clock tower like Big Ben's little brother, would have looked out of place in Paris.

But some of the folkloric touches that I used to love about Tunis had vanished. The bookstalls, newspaper kiosks and flower markets had moved away from avenue Bourguiba, and men in *jebbas* and red fezzes no longer sold sprigs of jasmine. Someone had silenced the music and the Koranic chanting, and fewer Berber women with tattooed faces sashayed around in *sefsaris* and *haiks*. Even the starlings that once roosted in the trees on the esplanade had flown away, and I noticed nobody on the benches puffing a water pipe.

I doubted I'd ever again witness street life like I had in 1994 on the eve of Eid el Kebir. To commemorate Abraham's readiness to sacrifice his son Isaac, every Islamic family of means was supposed to slaughter a sheep, and preparations for the feast convulsed the city as clerical workers, ladies-who-lunch and bargain-hunting housewives had one thing in mind—bringing home a lamb. Some of them dragged the next day's dinner on a leash. Others carried the critters like babes in arms. Still others slung them across the handlebars of their motorcycles or stuffed them into the backseats of cars. The lambs bleated and thrashed. A few escaped and hightailed it through traffic, clattering on nimble hooves over the hoods of stalled cars and across café tables with pedestrians in hot pursuit.

Tunis today seemed more subdued, more content with its European patina. The medina had shrunk and had a population of just fifteen thousand. The souks sold computers and iPods along with traditional spices and perfumes, and kids sported T-shirts with Nike swooshes and obscenities that I trusted they didn't understand. One read SUCK DICK.

Only the Grand Mosque Zitouna hadn't changed; it remained an architectural ensemble of elements from every epoch of Tunisian history—Carthaginian pediments, Roman columns, Ottoman Turkish arcades, Byzantine brickwork and Venetian glass chandeliers.

"Noble trades" held privileged positions near the mosque, and it pleased me that booksellers were numbered among them. One cubbyhole shop had an inventory of gold-embossed, leatherbound copies of the Koran. Even illiterate Muslims bought the Book, the shopkeeper told me, because leafing through its pages was believed to be as spiritually rewarding as reading them.

One afternoon, the three of us caught a taxi to Sidi Bou Said, a hilltop village on the outskirts of Tunis. Along the way, the cabbie uttered a refrain that had become the Muzak of my trip. I barely listened as he exclaimed, "America good. Bush no, no, no!" But Linda and Marc were new to this and asked what the man thought about the war in Iraq.

"Let the people live," he said. "That's all they want here or in Iraq."

"What do you think caused the war?" Marc said.

"Oil. Just oil." Then he asked us, "Why don't you see terrorists in Tunis?"

"Because there's no oil," Marc guessed.

"No. Because one out of every four men is a policeman in plainclothes." But he warned us not to take the train back to Tunis. "Dirty passengers, bad people, they put a knife on you and steal your money."

Sidi Bou Said was the type of tourist trap about which visitors lamented, "It must have been heaven before it was 'discovered.'" But I suspected there was never a moment in its history when it hadn't been "discovered," and it was as beautiful now as it had been three decades ago, when I first saw it. The trouble was you had to share this heaven with heaving masses of people.

Purple scrolls of bougainvillea, potted pink geraniums, white-washed walls, blue grillwork, views of the Mediterranean that gave you a head rush—Linda, Marc and I left the taxi and admired Sidi Bou Said's stock footage. Then we fled on foot downhill to La Marsa. Once the site of the Ottoman Bey's, the provincial governor's, summer residence, it was now a suburb spangled with espalier roses.

Because we couldn't find a taxi, we wound up taking the train to Tunis despite the cabbie's warning. It was filthy, and raucous with kids pounding bongo rhythms on the coach walls. But nobody pulled a knife and demanded money. And the greatest danger, I thought, was to the teenagers themselves. They pried open the doors and egged each other on, pushing and shoving, pretending to jump out onto the tracks.

I couldn't bear to watch; I couldn't quit looking. It seemed certain one of them would trip and be shredded under the train. Or else, as we stormed into a station, that somebody would lean out and smash his skull on a pillar. Where were the plainclothesmen in this crowd?

By the time we got to Tunis, Linda was distraught and transferred her worry about the reckless kids to me. "Please," she begged, "don't go to Algeria."

The next day I packed Marc and Linda off to the ruins at Carthage. After Leptis Magna and Sabratha, I had no stomach for another archeological site. And I had a worthy excuse: I had been to Carthage before and I needed to collect the refund for my return plane ticket to Alexandria. At EgyptAir's office on the ground floor of the Hotel Abou Nawas, I asked for Abdel Mouty, the manager. An officious young lady broke off chatting with a friend long enough to flick a blood-red fingernail at his door.

By contrast, Mouty was all charm. He spoke excellent English and listened attentively. Then he read the letter in Arabic from his colleague in Tripoli. He never quit smiling as he informed me, "My friend is wrong." He reached for the phone. "I must call and correct him."

"Call your friend later," I said. "Tell me first."

"What he proposes is impossible. It's illegal to refund a ticket in Tunis that was purchased in a different country. I could write you a check, but no bank would cash it."

"I don't want a check." I was conscious of my voice rising. "I paid in cash and I expect a cash refund. One thousand Egyptian pounds or $200."

"It's not a question of cash. It's not whether I wish to help or not. The problem is the law."

"I'm sure there's a law that you can't deny a passenger the refund you owe him."

"Of course, you'll get your money back."

"When?"

"When you return to New York."

"I don't live in New York. I'm not going to New York. I bought the ticket in good faith and was guaranteed a refund."

"You're right. This in unjust." Mouty stood up. The underarms of his shirt were grape-purple with sweat. "We should discuss this with Mohsen Khalil, the *directeur général* for Egyptair in North Africa."

We stepped around the corner to a large suite, where Khalil, dressed in a sharkskin suit, manned a desk papered over with Post-it notes. Every bit as gracious as Mouty, he wished he could help, but the law had him shackled. He crossed his wrists as if they were manacled.

"I understand that in this part of the world"—I slathered on the sarcasm—"we'd all agree that nothing is more important than respect for the law." I meant to flash in their mind's eye a panorama of North African anarchy, a Technicolor kaleidoscope of bribe-taking cops, renegade cab drivers, smugglers at international frontiers and vehicles careening the wrong way down divided highways.

"Quite apart from the law," Khalil conceded, "there are taxes and fees that need to be deducted."

"Deducted from what?"

"From a possible refund." The bargaining had begun.

"Taxes and departure fees for a flight I never took?"

"Yes. The government collects them the instant you board the plane, and we can't recover the cost."

"Let me get this straight. The Egyptian government deducts taxes and departure fees for a return flight from Tripoli?"

"Exactly."

"So what are you offering?"

Khalil reacted badly to my bluntness. I had violated the bargaining protocol, betraying a lack of subtlety and civility. He stiffened in his chair and spoke with icy politeness. "I am prepared to break the law and accept responsibility. Out of friendship and in the spirit of international accord and good customer relations, I am offering you fifty Tunisian dinars."

That amounted to a measly $45. "Why should I accept a quarter of what I'm owed?"

"Best offer, last offer," Khalil said.

"Okay," I caved in. "When do I get the money?"

"Now."

The three of us went to the reception area, where I completed some forms in triplicate. Then we moved over to a man in a cage who objected to giving me a cent. But Mouty and Khalil browbeat him into compliance, and he grudgingly counted out fifty dinars as rumpled and stained as used tissue.

I was on the street when I realized that I didn't have my original ticket, the sole record for tax purposes of my flight from Cairo. So I returned to the office, opened the door . . . and was stopped dead by Khalil's bloodcurdling screams. The veins in his neck were as engorged as the camel ticks in the Souf Museum as he delivered a blistering tirade to Mouty, berating him for not getting rid of me himself.

I closed the door quietly and tiptoed away without a receipt.

laubert described Carthage as "a galley anchored in the Libyan sands, it was with toil that she maintained her position. The nations roared like a bellows around her, and the slightest storm shook this formidable machine."

Ultimately, as every high school student learned, Rome became the roaring "bellows" that brought Carthage down. During the Third Punic War in 146 BC, the city was razed, its survivors were sold into slavery and the ground was sown with salt to render it barren.

In view of its history, its bellicose neighbors and its proximity to the Middle East, one might expect contemporary Tunisia to feel similarly storm-tossed and vulnerable. But the country gave every evidence of bending to whatever winds blew. One example of its flexibility was its attitude toward the Palestinian Liberation Organisation (PLO). Despite Tunisia's declared opposition to terrorism, its warm relations with the United States and its moderate policy toward Israel, the country had welcomed Yasser Arafat when the Israeli army expelled the PLO from Lebanon, in 1982. For a dozen years the PLO maintained its headquarters outside Tunis, at Borj Cedria. Although the PLO continued to launch terrorist attacks, and the Israelis struck back, bombing the PLO's base, Tunisia permitted the PLO to remain.

After the 1994 Oslo peace accords, when Arafat switched his operations to Gaza, a rump party of PLO hard-liners rejected the settlement and stayed on in Tunis. Farah Kaddoumi, a PLO founding father and the head of its militant wing, Al Fatah, was said to live here still. Likewise, Arafat's widow Suha divided her time between Tunis and Paris, enjoyed a warm relationship with Leila Ben Ali, the president's wife, and was rumored to have secretly married Leila Ben Ali's brother. (Suha denied this.)

President Ben Ali might have paraphrased Benjamin Disraeli to the effect that Tunisia had no permanent allies, only permanent interests. Consider Berge du Lac, a Saudi-financed development on the shores of Lake Tunis. In exchange for cleaning up the water, which had become a cesspool, the Saudis insisted that the supposedly liberal and enlightened Tunisian government ban alcohol everywhere except at the Berge du Lac Hotel and the U.S. Embassy.

When I went to the embassy, I understood why the Americans needed liquor. Who'd care to be sober in such a setting? Berge du Lac resembled a California strip mall—or rather a Saudi Arabian fantasy of a California strip mall on steroids. Sterile, lunatic, laughable—no adjective adequately conveyed how depressing it was, and how funny. Amid the McMansions and condos, there was a bowling alley, a nightclub called My Way and a wedding reception center, Top Happiness. On avenue de l'Environnement, an eight-foot statue of the rabbit-eared rat, *Labibe*, stood sentinel over an ecological disaster. Sure, the lake was clean, but miles of earth had been sealed under asphalt.

Why the U.S. Embassy had moved from the city to this dead zone wasn't difficult to guess: more space, modern conveniences, an international school and, above all, security. With high walls and barbed wire, Mylar and bulletproof metal, the building was a fortress with clear lines of fire in all directions. Buffeted by gusts off the lake, an American flag the size of a jib sail fluttered and snapped.

I came there to discuss Algeria with Pat Kabra, the U.S. public affairs officer, who had sent me concerned e-mails via Linda. I hoped that if I spoke to her in person she might have a nugget or two of inside knowledge that would calm my family.

An Arab speaker married to a Middle Easterner, Kabra was the mother of a teenage daughter. Like other U.S. Embassy personnel in North Africa, Kabra—whatever her own views—never said anything that might be construed as an official U.S. position or that accepted responsibility for my safety. Much as she might like to be helpful, she knew little about me except that I was committed to a project that could cause trouble.

When I asked about the kidnapped Austrians, she repeated what I had read in newspapers. Tunisia still denied that they had been captured on its territory. Meanwhile, Austrian authorities, Algerian sources and the kidnappers themselves maintained that the Austrians *had* been taken hostage in Tunisia and transported to Mali. There were demands for ransom money and a prisoner exchange, but no agreement had been reached.[5]

At one point, Kabra's daughter came into the office carrying an after-school snack of French fries and a milkshake. Her mother asked her to leave. This prompted a conversation about kids and colleges and the difficulties of family life in the Foreign Service. Trying to keep things friendly and informal, I spoke a bit about Linda and her fears. "I don't think it's as dangerous in Algeria as she does," I said. "But if you have different information, I'd be grateful to hear it."

"I don't speak about security issues. But I sent you the State Department's travel warning, didn't I?"

"There's nothing else you can tell me?" I asked.

---

5. Six months later, in the fall of 2008, the two Austrian tourists were released deep in the Sahara, presumably after ransom was paid. But within weeks, in the same desert region, kidnappers snatched two more Europeans, one of them an Englishman named Edwin Dyer, sixty-one, who had traveled there for a Tuareg festival of nomadic culture. When the U.K. refused to free Abu Qatada, an ally of Osama bin Laden's wanted on Algerian charges of terrorism, Dyer was decapitated on May 31, 2009. AQIM (Al Queda in the Islamic Maghreb) took credit for the killing and renewed its threats against foreigners.

"There've been reports of increased chatter about threats of violence in Algeria," she said. "This really isn't my area. I could ask Embassy intelligence, but they'll just say you should play it safe. Why don't you speak to somebody outside of Embassy channels?"

She recommended Larry Michalak, the American director of the local branch of the NGO that was sponsoring my lectures in Algeria. Then Kabra escorted me to the lobby, and I retraced my steps outside under the snapping Stars and Stripes, through the blockhouse of guards and metal sensors, and onto the street where workers were propping up newly planted palm trees with two-by-fours.

A t dinner that night with me, Linda and Marc, Michalak was of the opinion that the U.S. Embassy often exaggerated the dangers in North Africa. He knew for a fact that buses and long-distance taxis shuttled back and forth every day from downtown Tunis to Annaba, the first city of any size in Algeria.

"Great," I said. "So you've done it?"

"Not personally," he admitted.

"But you know somebody who's done it."

He shook his head.

"What about Bob Parks, the CEMA guy in Oran?" I asked. Linda and Marc, I noticed, hung on his answer. "Has he traveled overland from Algeria to Tunisia?"

"No, he flies. But he does drive from Oran to Algiers. That road's safer than it used to be."

"That's good news," I agreed. But it still left the border and hundreds of miles of mountains in northeastern Algeria.

That night Linda received an e-mail from Kabra, who had, after all, checked with security officials at the U.S. Embassy. They strongly advised against overland travel in Algeria. What's more, she had contacted the public affairs officer in Algiers who said that I shouldn't cross the border at Ain Draham.

We departed from Tunis on an overcast day. Linda and Marc wanted to spend the night with me in Ain Draham before I met my Algerian fixer tomorrow. In the coastal town of Raf Raf it started raining, and cats took refuge in the recesses of the seawall, staring out at passersby with hungry eyes. I had passed a memorable time in Raf Raf years ago, when I was brought to a hotel by a man on horseback. That had seemed a stroke of good fortune. But my room had been mosquito-infested, forcing me to check out before daybreak.

Back then, I had detoured from the main road and followed an unpaved track toward Cap Negro, where the guidebook promised an unspoiled beach on the Coral Coast. Start to finish, the drive had been a boulder-strewn disaster. For fifteen miles, I told myself I was crazy to keep on going. For fifteen more miles, at a speed of five miles an hour, I drove on, jouncing and clanging through an uninhabited countryside of cork oak and oleander, a wild place as beautiful as it was forbidding.

At the very least, I expected that when I got to the sea I'd have the beach to myself. But I was wrong about that, too. Four gun-toting teenage French boys had arrived before me by motorcycle and were shooting at tin cans scattered on the sand. Because of an oil spill, the water was unswimmable.

On my return a rock ripped a hole in the car's fuel line, and I had the choice of waiting and hoping the French boys would pass by, or of driving on in fear that a spark would ignite the leaking gasoline. I pressed on to a village where the only garage was closed but a stranger rescued me, wrapping the fuel line in plastic bags and allowing me to limp back to Tunis.

"Hurry on along and don't take no cut-offs"—such was the advice from a survivor of the Donner Party, the nineteenth-century pioneers who'd been trapped in the snowy Sierra Nevada and turned to cannibalism. These words of warning echoed in my ears as Linda, Marc and I cut inland at Tabarka through heavily forested hills. Low clouds snagged like carded lamb's wool in the trees, and Ain Draham, at an altitude of almost three thousand feet, exuded the cool, sharp air of an alpine station. Its slate roofs were steeply pitched to shed winter snow, and shops advertised excursions into the mountains on bikes and horseback.

We took a trial run to the border and had the road to ourselves. On both sides, bundles of cork oak waited to be collected. Within minutes we came to an abandoned customs shed. Indifferent to the drizzle, three dogs slept on the asphalt, and we drove by without waking them. Up ahead, a soldier stood guard in the rain beside a rusty gate. Beyond it sloped a field of red mud, and beyond that was a concrete building with a drenched Algerian flag hanging motionless. The sound of birdsong, the smell of crushed grass, wood smoke and manure—it was a pastoral scene that might have been conjured by Grandma Moses.

Back at Ain Draham, we checked into the Royal Rihana Hotel, a nearly deserted hunting lodge. A damp chill clung to the dining room walls, along with trophies of deer, mountain goats and fiercely tusked boars. We ordered wild boar in wine sauce and discussed plans for later that summer. Then Marc, a committed bodybuilder, joked about the gym where he had worked out in Tunis. The place had female clients who came in baggy robes and *hijabs* and lifted weights in an isolated corner.

Neither he nor Linda asked me again not to go. Still, Algeria was on our minds. It lay a few short miles to the west, and in the morning they'd drive me there and wait to see whether I got in or got turned back. Meanwhile we did our best to ignore the hotel elevator, which had wiring problems that repeatedly set off an emergency alarm.

ALGERIA

Morning mist shrouded the hills and glazed the road. Dogs still slept in front of the shuttered customs house, and we had to thread our way through them. Linda and Marc dropped me at the rusty gate, and we said hurried goodbyes. It had started to rain, cutting off any chance of emotional last-minute pleas. I shouldered my two carry-ons and squelched across the field of wet clay.

Tunisian passport control was a formality. But on the Algerian side things slowed down. A soldier instructed me to leave my bags on the porch and proceed into the concrete-block building. The border at Ain Draham, unlike the Egyptian, Libyan and Tunisian frontiers, had no smugglers carrying fat plastic bags full of contraband.

The six customs officers had nothing to do, yet they shunted me down the line to the last man.

"Can I bring in my bags?" I asked.

He shook his head.

I handed over my passport, and he tossed it onto a shelf and motioned for me to wait elsewhere while he and the others fell into spirited conversation in Arabic.

I studied faded posters peeling off the walls. These weren't the standard rosy pictures aimed at tourists—they were health warnings. There was an anti-smoking advisory and one for a campaign called Let Us Protect the Family Against AIDS. I paid rapt attention to an alert about bird flu. Don't mix with chickens, turkeys or their excrement, it read. And don't eat raw meat.

The customs officers had stopped talking yet studiously avoided eye contact with me. When I asked whether there was a problem, one of them said, *"Nous faisons le nécessaire"* ("We're doing what's necessary").

"What's that? My passport's in order. So is my visa."

Things were *compliqué*, he told me. They had to verify matters with a superior.

A burly man in a khaki vest, one of those multipocket outfits favored by photographers and game wardens, muscled in beside me. He spoke so brusquely to the customs officials, I assumed he must be their boss. He had buzz-cut hair, and despite the distracting constellation of moles on his face, he bridled with authority.

"Fucking bureaucracy," he whispered to me in English. He introduced himself as Ahmed, the driver/fixer I had been communicating with for months. "They say you need a military escort."

"For what?"

"For the ride to Algiers. They claim those are their orders—any white skin who crosses the frontier has to have an escort. That's bullshit. They're scared. They've probably never seen an American, and they're afraid to take responsibility."

If there was no way around it, I told Ahmed, I'd rather have an escort than get turned back. But he said, "No. It'll waste all day. The military will take you to the first town, and we'll have to wait there for an escort to the next town. At that rate, the trip to Algiers will last a week. Let me deal with this."

He switched to Arabic, which even during exchanges of pleasantries sounded to me like an argument, and the customs officers sagged under the sheer weight of Ahmed's personality. Like a door-to-door encyclopedia salesman, he had a reply for every objection and refused to accept no for an answer. After browbeating them, he announced in English, "We go." And we went. We went so fast we almost forgot my bags. Ahmed dashed back to fetch them.

At the wheel of his car, he continued talking, saying that he had told them I was an important guest of Algeria. The hard part was explaining why such an important person wouldn't fly to Algiers.

"I want to see the country," I said.

"Exactly. How could they protest that you shouldn't see it? How could they admit it's too dangerous?"

"How dangerous is it?"

"Not much. A little."

It didn't look dangerous at all. We descended from the mountains through pine forests, more a Scandinavian than a Mediterranean landscape. At lower elevations, in the marshes of the El Kala Nature Reserve, birds roosted during their seasonal migration from Europe.

Ahmed had no interest in ornithology except to the extent that it reminded him of other bruising run-ins with Algerian bureaucracy. He had once picked up some elderly birdwatchers at the Algiers airport and fought a futile battle at customs over their binoculars. Soldiers seized them as military equipment, declaring that they had to be sequestered at the airport and collected when the birders departed the country. "How can we attract tourists when we are so stupid?" Ahmed demanded.

He didn't expect an answer. He didn't expect anything from me except total attention. I had the impression that he would have grabbed my shirt collar and shaken me—if he had dared to remove his hands from the wheel. A terrifying thought on these narrow roads. When I interrupted to ask him to text-message Linda that I had crossed the border safely, he drove one-handed for a few kilometers, almost causing me a heart clot.

While Ahmed was a manic talker, he seemed to know what he was saying. More than a driver/fixer, he claimed to be a journalist and flashed a press card. He bragged about his past employment by an A-list of European and American reporters and paparazzi, including Michael Palin for one of his lighthearted BBC travelogues, and Don McCallum, the legendary British combat photographer.

His proudest triumph, he told me, occurred in 2003 when, shortly after the Bush administration announced that the Algerian regime "was the most democratic in the Arab world," Secretary of State Colin Powell jetted in for a press conference. While Powell would praise the country's "exceptional cooperation in the war on terrorism," he would fail to mention the water-boarding and blowtorches that Algeria inflicted on its own citizens.

In preparation for the press conference, the crucial question, Ahmed said, was where it should be held. "The logical place, the Press Club, was impossible."

"Security problems?"

"No, the toilets are disgusting. The U.S. Embassy asked me to help. They knew and I knew that if Powell spoke at the Press Club every American journalist would write that Algeria has billions of dollars of oil money and the shittiest bathrooms in the world. So I organized Powell's speech at the Hilton Hotel."

There was no chance to ask why he hadn't just had the Press Club clean its toilets. Fulminating, he went on to complain that 25 percent of the Algerian population lived below the poverty line, defined as one U.S. dollar a day. "This is so stupid. We are the closest gas station to America and Europe. We have oil reserves. We are the world's fourth leading exporter of natural gas. We have a $150 billion economic surplus. But very little reaches the people. We have a saying—the powerful *veulent manger seuls*. They wish to eat alone."

Tense and tentative—okay, frightened—at being in northeastern Algeria, I would have preferred a more gradual and certainly a calmer introduction to the country. But since there was no way of quieting Ahmed without giving offense, I accepted that an abrupt immersion might be best.

When he tired of talking, Ahmed played CDs of BBC programs that he had helped produce. Features about Berber hamlets that harbored armed insurrectionists. About Islamic fundamentalists blowing up police barracks and military checkpoints. About innocent civilians having their throats slit at roadblocks.

Much of this I already knew. Much of it was contained in the CIA *World Factbook*, which described Algeria as a nation racked by "large-scale unemployment, a shortage of housing, unreliable electrical and water supplies, [and] government inefficiency and corruption." And much of this accounted for, even if it could never excuse, the ferocity aimed at *le pouvoir*, the shadowy cadre of men behind the president who throttled every attempt at reform.

Some political analysts argued that the current situation had its roots in the unresolved contradictions of the war for independence. They contended that the National Liberation Front (FLN) had kicked out the French only to exploit the country and its resources for itself. Maintaining a stranglehold on power after almost fifty years, the FLN had devolved into a repressive, self-perpetuating kleptocracy.

Fed up with being disenfranchised, a loose coalition of students, teachers, women and Islamic groups had taken to the streets in 1988 demanding free elections. As the marches and demonstrations grew more disruptive, the government cracked down, and during the riots that ensued, the security forces opened fire.

Low-grade violence simmered for several years until 1992 when, under internal and international pressure, the regime allowed a wide spectrum of candidates, including those from religious parties, to run for office. But many in positions of power feared that the Islamists intended to accept the principle of one man/one vote—just one time. Their suspicion was that if the Islamists won, they'd impose Sharia law and never permit another election.

The army wasn't willing to wait and find out. After the Islamic Salvation Front (FIS) posted surprising wins in the preliminary rounds of voting, the military staged a coup and cancelled the elections. The

FIS fought back, as did other dissident groups, and in great spasms of protest that spiraled out of control, any hope of compromise died a bloody death. The statistics were staggering. In a decade, more than two hundred thousand Algerians were annihilated in what was less a civil war than a savage cycle of provocations and reprisals; battles between government troops and radical armies; mass executions, the liquidation of collaborators and traitors; the extermination of entire villages for motives unknown by attackers never identified or punished.

Small wonder that Algeria was now a nation in profound shock, its population traumatized. For the "black years" constituted just the latest chapter in nearly two centuries of horror that had shaped—or skewed—the national psyche. According to *A World History of Genocide and Extermination from Sparta to Darfur*, by Ben Kiernan, the French conquest and pacification of Algeria from 1830 until the early twentieth century slaughtered 825,000 people. And since then the killing had never stopped.

In 1953, Frantz Fanon, a psychiatrist from the Caribbean island of Martinique, called attention to the extraordinary number of Algerians who suffered mental problems caused by French racism and cruelty. But Fanon prescribed a cure as provocative as his diagnosis. He theorized that the proper response to colonial violence was more violence, worse violence, cathartic violence—which would purge the victims of their inferiority complex by inflicting sadistic torment on their oppressors. During the war for independence, from 1954 until 1962, more than a million Algerians died.

It would be hard to exaggerate the impact that Fanon's book, *The Wretched of the Earth*, had on the National Liberation Front. And it continues to have influence today. Armed Islamic groups currently regarded terror both as a military tactic and a global strategy for exorcising rage, exacting revenge and liberating people from humiliation.

The French had referred to Annaba as *Bône la Coquette* ("the Elegant"). Ahmed called it a "very Frenchy town," and it retained touches of Gallic charm along Cours de la Révolution, where cafés were shaded by palms and gigantic fig trees. But nobody sat at the outdoor tables today. The trees dripped moisture, and a leaden sky threatened more rain. "There used to be a sign here," Ahmed said. "No dogs and no Algerians."

In the '90s, Annaba had had a reputation as a safe city. So safe that the president then, Mohammed Boudiaf, one of the historic figures of the FLN, came here in 1992 to speak to a youth group. A member of his own security team shot him dead during the speech. Suspicion persisted that the assassin hadn't acted alone. *Le pouvoir* was rumored to have resented Boudiaf's anti-corruption campaign and to have eliminated him.

Annaba, known much earlier as Hippo Regius, had been the home of St. Augustine, a fifth-century church father and author of *Confessions* and *City of God*. Recently Algeria had embraced this reformed sinner and Christian convert as a central figure in the country's supposedly multicultured, multifaith society. In 1999, soon after being installed by the army, President Abdelaziz Bouteflika praised Augustine as "a saint as much for Christianity as for Islam."

But there had been no acknowledgment of how few Christians remained in Algeria or how resolutely the government discouraged the practice and spread of Christianity. Missionaries in the region of Tizi Ouzou had been arrested, and one had been imprisoned for the possession of Bibles.

Bouteflika also avoided any reference to Augustine's ethnicity. He was a Berber. Although 99 percent of the population had some Berber blood, most Algerians identified themselves as Arabs and disparaged Berbers, their language and culture. The mountainous region of the Kabylia, with its high concentration of Berbers, was feared as a hotbed of political opposition and armed resistance.

A man of enormous appetite, Ahmed knew where to eat in Annaba, as he did in every town, and the restaurants he chose were invariably cheap, smoky and difficult to access. A deaf parking lot attendant directed him in sign language to a spot in an alley choked by cars and cooking braziers. It looked to me like a perfect target for suicide bombers.

Ahmed ordered potatoes, salad and two types of grilled meat, and he ate it all with his hands. *Both* hands. None of this business about eating right-handed and reserving the left for sanitary purposes. He stared at me askance when I settled for a bowl of *chorba* soup.

After fifteen minutes of nonstop gobbling, he proclaimed *"Alhamdu lillah"* ("Thanks be to God") and hustled off with the deaf man to retrieve his car. He was intent on reaching Setif before dark.

I didn't understand his rush. Setif was barely two hundred miles away. And I wanted to explore the waterfront in Annaba, a launching pad for illegal immigrants bound for Europe. Known in Arabic as *harraga*, a term that implied the burning of bridges, these boat people risked their lives to reach the Italian island of Sardinia, 150 miles north. But Ahmed insisted we'd see nothing at this time of day. And we really needed to get back on the road.

The countryside flattened into fields of wheat as tawny as a lion's mane, and the colors, the play of light, the sky and the immensity of scale differed from anything I had seen thus far. For comparison I had to recall distant parts of Africa—the Masai Mara, the Serengeti Plains.

Yet the scope and beauty of the land highlighted the shabbiness of the strip of asphalt that crossed it east to west. The lone road linking major cities in Algeria, it was packed with traffic, particularly trucks, and pocked with holes and ditches. And there were frequent military checkpoints preceded by jawbreaking speed bumps.

"They search for terrorists out here," Ahmed said, "before they get to the big towns."

He gunned the engine between checkpoints, going eighty and ninety miles an hour, overtaking slower cars and trucks, then stomping on the brakes when he noticed the traffic backed up at the next roadblock. For hours the trip unfurled in this stomach-churning, stop-and-start fashion.

"This used to be the breadbasket of Rome; now we have to import food and subsidize bread and milk," Ahmed was saying when he spotted something ahead.

A horrendous accident had happened moments ago. Twisted metal lay smoking amid dead bodies. Survivors and farmers from the fields staggered through the wreckage. A minivan had been ripped inside out like a pocket. Its upholstered interior was on the surface, the seats on the roof, the engine rammed back into the passenger compartment.

"A brand-new car," Ahmed lamented.

How could he tell? I didn't recognize the make or model.

"Car crashes kill more people in Algeria than terrorism," Ahmed said. But that didn't slow him down.

Constantine soared on its promontory above the khaki plains. Webbed by spectacular bridges, the place had been a natural fortress since Neolithic times. The Numidians, the Romans, the Ottoman Turks and the French had taken possession of it for periods, but no one had managed to gain a permanent grip on what the Arabs called the City of the Air.

We climbed higher and higher on suspension bridges that wobbled under the weight of traffic. From the town, at an elevation of two thousand feet, sheer cliffs dropped away to deep gorges. A chasm split Constantine down the center, and since every street ended at an abyss, pedestrians seemed in danger of plunging to their deaths.

This wouldn't have been without historical precedent. At the southernmost corner of the casbah, at a rampart called Sidi Rached, criminals and adulterous wives had been flung over the edge—a form of capital punishment both swift and brutal.

As he had in Annaba, Ahmed described the city as "very Frenchy." It was difficult to tell what he meant. With its minarets and ceramic domes, the skyline had a distinctly Levantine flair, and the sidewalks bustled with women in *hijabs* and bearded men in skull-caps. Banners announcing a visit by President Bouteflika fluttered from lampposts.

Ahmed crossed the Sidi M'Cid Bridge to the Monument to the Dead, a copy of Trajan's arch at Timgad, with the addition of a statue of Winged Victory and the incised names of those who had died "Pro Patria," meaning for France, not Algeria. The monument offered spectacular views and, I gathered as Ahmed spoke on his cell phone, good reception.

As we recrossed Sidi M'Cid Bridge, he lowered a window, and we listened to the racket of waterfalls. "This is a favorite spot for suicides," he said.

In the casbah he parked in front of a pungent cheese shop and suggested that we walk. He was tired and wanted coffee; I was wide awake and jumpy. Sensing my reluctance, Ahmed said, "It's safe. Don't speak English and stay close to me."

As we explored a cat's cradle of alleys, he whispered in French, "With your mustache and the way you're dressed"—I wore blue jeans and a denim work-shirt—"you could be a Berber, an old grandfather down from the mountains for the day. Nobody believes you're American."

We stopped at a café and stood at the crowded bar. Other customers watched the TV, not me. Ahmed ordered a café au lait for me and a noisette for himself, and instead of feeling wired as I sipped the strong coffee, I felt myself relax. Leaving aside the beards and skullcaps and burnooses, and the absence of women, the café could have been in Athens or Rome or Barcelona. A bomb seemed no more likely here than there.

Back on the road, checkpoints came at quicker intervals— perhaps because Ahmed had picked up speed. He repeated that he didn't care to drive after dark. The cops didn't like to work after dark, either. Brusque and surly, they demanded our papers; sometimes they searched the trunk. Ahmed did what they told him, but he didn't kowtow as Khalil had to the authorities in Libya. "I give respect," he said, "and expect it in return."

We reached Setif at 7:30 PM, nine hours after leaving the Tunisian frontier. The *muezzin* was calling the faithful to evening prayers, and stray cats caterwauled in response. "This is a town of crazy drivers," Ahmed said, as if the traffic so far had been sane. "Their motto is that it's better to be in the hospital than to be late."

Decorative lights glittered in the branches of plane trees and arched over intersections in crescents and crowns. Three days earlier, Setif had celebrated the events for which its main street was named—May 8, 1945. For the French, this was VE Day, the victorious conclusion of World War II in Europe. For Algerians the date marked an altogether different occasion.

North Africans had constituted 90 percent of the Free French Army, and they had fought for the Allies, among other reasons, to win equality for Muslims. After the armistice, they assumed that

Algeria would become a separate republic federated with France. But when the French refused to grant the country autonomy, protests erupted in many towns, including Setif. Police cracked down on the demonstrators, and Muslims retaliated with clubs, knives and axes, killing 103 Europeans.

Fearing a general rebellion and hell-bent on revenge, the French unleashed a rampage of their own. They declared martial law, arrested opposition leaders and called in the army—which, abetted by civilian vigilantes, killed thousands of Muslims. The French conceded that as many as thirteen hundred Algerians had died. But Algerians claimed that the death toll was much higher, close to forty-five thousand. Whatever the figure, these events were a rupture that made the war for independence unavoidable.

Ahmed parked next to a muddy trench, and we leaped over it to a hotel that could have benefited from the lights that sparkled in the trees. My room was dim and dirty, with splintered wooden furniture and a spavined bed. It seemed pointless to unpack, pointless to shower and put on clean clothes. Ahmed wanted to eat at once. As always he knew a restaurant and as always it was in an obscure corner of the city—so obscure that he couldn't find it and had to hire a taxi to lead us there.

The Lisboa's owner, an Algerian married to a Portuguese wife, promised excellent fish, and Ahmed ordered a plate full of it, deep fat fried. I nibbled at a kebab and rice, and drank too much wine and watched him dismantle the fish with both hands, reducing it to a delicate trellis of bones. Still garrulous after the day's drive, he asked where I had been on my trip. Then he told me what each country was really like.

"I hate Libya and the Libyans," he said. "They believe they can shit on everybody because they're rich. Just like the Saudis, they shit on the rest of us. Lots of Algerians go there to work and wind up in jail for nothing.

"And Qaddafi is a madman. He came to Algiers but wouldn't stay in a hotel. He put up his tent and demanded phone service and a camel he could milk for breakfast. He's crazy and everyone knows it."

In his opinion, Tunisia and Morocco were no better than Libya. In many ways, he thought them worse. Americans, including government officials, acted as if all Muslims were the same and united in their hatred of the US. But this ignored the differences and ancestral enmities between Muslims. For better or worse, I realized North Africans were wedded by geography and religion yet estranged by politics, psychology and language. Although they all spoke Arabic, the dialects differed so radically, citizens of one nation often had no idea what their neighbors were saying.

"Tunisia is a dictatorship," Ahmed declared. "I hate our government, but at least we are free to express criticism. In Tunisia you say something against the regime, you make fun of Ben Ali, and you go to jail. The Tunisians tell everybody it's too dangerous in Algeria, don't travel there. They don't want us to have tourism. Millions of Algerians vacation in Tunisia each year. But the Tunisians don't admit it. They claim they get more Germans. That's bullshit. They don't want people to know how many Algerians go there. They're afraid tourists will quit coming."

He ordered dessert, a crème caramel. He didn't pick this up with his fingers; he used a fork. Between bites, he jabbed it in the air to punctuate his sentiments about Morocco: "They have a king. Say he's gay and you go to jail. We are against the Moroccans not just because of him but because of the Western Sahara. They grabbed that land during their famous Green March. It's good they kicked out the Spanish, but then they stole from the people. We don't care about the phosphates there. We side with the Polisario in the fight to get their country back. We want peace, but we also want justice."

I wanted to go back to the hotel and sleep. When I said so, Ahmed agreed that we needed to rest. "Tomorrow is the hardest part," he said. "The most dangerous. There are terrorists and Al Qaeda in the Kabylia."

The door to my room had a lock that a child could have broken. I dragged over a chair and wedged it under the doorknob. I felt silly for doing so. *Stooopid!* as Ahmed would have said. Still, I didn't move the chair. And as I tried to sleep on a foam rubber mattress that bore the imprint of previous guests, it came to me that North Africa was a shatter-zone in more than the geological sense. It crackled with enough tribal conflicts, political instability, personal quarrels and prejudices to cause nightmares.

Morning rain drenched the mountains and the foul-tempered troops and the miserable market stalls beside the road. Some Berbers huddled under lean-tos slapped together with reeds. Most squatted next to their baskets of eggs or fruit, and swaddled themselves in black plastic bags. They looked like trash set out to be collected, and often the soldiers treated them no better than that.

It was cold and it got colder as we climbed. Slick with mud and water, the road veered around sharp bends and along ravines without guardrails. Trucks lumbered past at an elephantine pace, belching smoke and farting exhaust fumes at cars piled up behind them. At this speed, we wouldn't reach Algiers before nightfall. Meanwhile we were sitting ducks for snipers.

The idea made me queasy. So did the dizzying drive and the carbon monoxide from trucks. I rolled down a window for air, but that brought in stronger fumes and gusts of rain. Even for Ahmed, normally full of bravado, passing was impossible now. The opposite lane was a linked chain of downhill traffic.

As we stuttered and stopped and started again, Ahmed kept up his chatter. He told me about a woman whose husband, a journalist, had been kidnapped. She never saw him again. She presumed the government was responsible. "Whether he's alive or dead she believes he's lost," Ahmed said. "Even if he survived, he has to have gone mad from torture. If you like, I'll introduce you to her."

The mountain villages looked raw and unfinished and, at the same time, centuries old. Constructed of hollow red bricks, the lower floors of houses were intact. But on every flat roof, steel rods, wooden framework and plastic pipes jutted into the sky, suggesting do-it-yourself projects that had been forsaken.

Ahmed stopped in a town that he swore had the best butcher in Algeria. He had promised to bring his wife a couple of kilos of fresh meat. He waited a long time for a break in the traffic, then darted across the street. Moments later, he trotted back empty-handed. "Do you know meat a little bit?" he asked. "I want to buy this. . ." He touched his shoulder. "But I can't judge what's good."

I confessed that I'm hopeless at shopping, especially at butcher stalls where gutted carcasses rotate on hooks like macabre mobiles. So he sprinted across the street again, taking his chances that he'd choose a good cut, just as he took his chances at getting sideswiped.

We pushed on with the meat wrapped in butcher paper on the backseat; an iron smell of blood mixed with the diesel fumes. Gagging and ready to vomit, I asked Ahmed to pull in at a gas station. The toilet was unspeakable, so I tossed my cookies outside on the parking lot. Then I drank a Coke to calm my belly as we forged back into the flow of cars.

We passed through a village that appeared to be polka-dotted. Every house had a satellite dish. Hundreds of dishes were for sale on the sidewalk. "*Parabolique diabolique*," Ahmed said. "During the black years the Islamicists declared that satellite dishes were the devil's work, and they attacked anybody who owned one. These days they don't bother. They'd have to kill too many people."

The road straightened for a while, and we made better time—better, that is, than ten mph. But then ragged cliff faces rose on both sides, funneling us into a defile barely wide enough to accommodate two cars. And there were roadblocks, one after another, each worse than the last. Soldiers in sandbagged gun emplacements and in upright concrete pipes aimed rifles at us through gun slots. Higher in the hills, troops manned guard towers and drew a bead on the stalled traffic.

"The French called this Gorge de Palestro," Ahmed said. "It was a bad place during the war for independence. We call it Lakhdaria. It's a bad place now."

According to the State Department Travel Warning, three suicide bombers had struck here in the past year, and there was an ongoing threat of "false roadblocks, kidnappings, ambushes and assassinations."

At the entrance to a tunnel, heavily armed men in helmets and flak jackets worked with dogs that sniffed for explosives. Behind them, an armored personnel carrier leveled its machine gun on the intersection.

Nearby, a train bed had been hewn out of rock, and the blackened shells of a locomotive and six passenger compartments were welded to the tracks. This was a major connection between Algiers and Constantine. It had been cut four months ago, and no one knew when it would reopen. The train had exploded, Ahmed explained, but he couldn't say whether it was an accident or an act of terrorism.

As drivers waited for their cars to be searched, enterprising merchants set up beside the road. They lighted braziers and laid out wicker cages packed with rabbits and quail. Business was brisk. People ordered a live bird or rabbit for the road; others had a meal cooked on the spot. The patience of Algerians struck me as admirable, incredible. Or after a decade and a half of horror, perhaps it was fatalism and fatigue rather than patience. While the Berbers wrung the quails' necks and skinned the rabbits, everybody stood stoically in the rain.

Beyond the tunnel, the land tapered toward Algiers, yet we never picked up much speed. We had eighty miles and more than three hours to go. I shut my eyes and tried to sleep, but that made me seasick.

We now had to contend with delays caused by construction crews. "They're building a highway from Tunis to Morocco," Ahmed said. "When it's finished, we won't have all this fucking traffic."

I feared my eyes were deceiving me. The crews appeared to be Asian. They hunkered in the mud, eating rice with chopsticks. Ahmed told me that the highway was a Chinese project.

"Why aren't Algerians building it?" I asked.

"Chinamen are cheaper and faster and more efficient."

"With so much unemployment, local people should have these jobs."

"They won't do this work," Ahmed said. "Not for what Chinamen get paid."

A nineteenth-century traveler, George Augustus Sala, wrote that "the houses of old El Djazair [Algiers] are as white as brand-new dice, and the little peep-holes of windows in them stand for the pips. I question if there ever lived such a nation of inveterate white-washers as the modern Moors, who have been incited, perhaps, to a profusion in the use of the double-tie brush by their French masters."

But today the fabled "White City" was grey under scudding storm clouds, and its architecture was a hodgepodge of styles. Beside the dice-shaped hovels in the casbah and the grand French villas, brutal apartment blocks called to mind Moscow and corporate oil headquarters in Houston. With more than three million people, Algiers was a drowsy port falling to pieces under the pressure of rampant overpopulation.

Ahmed headed uphill to Mustapha Supérieur, a residential neighborhood of palatial mansions, embassies and subtropical parks where the air was said to be more salubrious, the streets safer. But five months ago suicide bombers had attacked the U.N. office, killing dozens. Nearby, the U.S. Embassy was barricaded behind heavy-gauge steel gates and concrete bollards.

I had reserved a room at the El Djazair, formerly the St. George Hotel. Six hundred feet above the sea, it boasted a pool, a fitness center and a tennis court; I would use none of these during my stay, but I hoped the place would let me unwind after the nerve-jangling drive. I hoped this right up until we slowed down at the hotel drive-way—and a taxi plowed into our rear end, whipping me like a bob-blehead doll.

I sat there numb. For an instant Ahmed didn't move. Then he bellowed and jumped out of the car. He ran back almost immediately to reassure me the damage was minor. As if my greatest worry were his car! I wanted to get into my room and book a plane to Paris.

"Are you okay?" he asked.

I wish I'd had the presence of mind to quote Marsellus— Marsellus Wallace, that is, from Quentin Tarantino's *Pulp Fiction*: "I'm pretty fucking far from okay." But I said nothing.

Ahmed couldn't have been kinder. He couldn't have been more solicitous. He could have been quieter. But that wasn't his way. At the El Djazair, he knew everybody, and the staff greeted him by name. He got me a discount on the standard rate, demanded I have a room with a view and signaled to the bellboy to grab my bags. Ahmed did everything except sign my name on the register and slip my Amex card back into my wallet. Walking me to the elevator and pressing the button for my floor, he said, "See you tomorrow."

Deeply ashamed to be so unstrung, I stretched out on the bed and puzzled things through. Okay, we'd had a fender bender. I had spent hours bumping over bad roads. I had vomited. I had passed through a hundred army roadblocks and police barricades. I had inhaled thousands of cubic feet of exhaust fumes, and I had seen dozens of wretched towns and thousands of poverty-stricken people. Now I was in a comfortable room and they were still out there.

That was a disquieting realization. Nothing had happened to me. It had happened and was happening to them. They endured this and worse every day. For me, the trip was a process of discovery and clarification. Or was it obfuscation? I was traveling to prove something about myself. Or hide it. But what I experienced as culture shock Algerians suffered as constant toxic shock. I had the luxury of leaving. They had their noses shoved in the muck and had to go on living here. The least I could do was stick around for a while and witness what they went through.

D own in the bar, I sipped iced tea, soothed by American easy listening. Substitute pastis and Edith Piaf and this had probably been the afternoon routine of many a *colon*. There were still surprising numbers of French in Algiers. And as befitted their status as the country's most important trading partners, they maintained an immense embassy with eight hundred staff members, acres of gardens, a swimming pool and a golf course.

Americans, by contrast, were thin on the ground. I noticed none at the hotel. But it hadn't always been thus. During World War II, with Operation Torch in 1942, thousands of U.S. troops invaded the city, and after beating back strenuous Vichy French resistance, they settled in for the duration. The French then did an abrupt about-face and joined the fight against Germany. This prompted Churchill to quip that he wished the Vichy had fought the Germans as hard as they had the Allies.

American General Eisenhower established his headquarters at the Hotel St. George, and In *An Army at Dawn*, Rick Atkinson captures the atmosphere of those days when Arabs with worry beads frequented the lobby and barefooted women swept up mud ground into the carpets by combat boots. Ike tried to hold the headquarters company down to 150 officers. But within weeks, twice that many moved with their retinues into "400 offices scattered through eleven buildings. Three hundred officers now devoured as much meat as rationing allocated to 15,000 French citizens." Eventually Algiers became home to what Atkinson calls a "huge, chairborne force" of more than eleven thousand officers and fifteen thousand enlisted men occupying two thousand pieces of real estate. A popular gripe circulated among front-line GIs: "Never were so few commanded by so many from so far."

I had trouble picturing the El Djazair as it had been when "American coding and teletype operators worked among the scattered ottomans and brass tables in the hotel lounge." Now nobody lingered at those tables and ottomans, maybe because a metal detector at the entrance set off such an irritating beep.

In the garden, the drizzle had stopped and a single ray of sun slanted through the clouds, bathing the palm trees in bold light so that they looked like Fourth of July fireworks, their fronds a green explosion, their unripe dates an orange spray. Past splurges of purple bougainvillea, pink oleander and blue plumbago, I went down the driveway, through security, and out into the off-white city. I was conscious of testing myself, taking the temperature of the streets. It was cool, and I was glad I wore a windbreaker. Passersby nodded and said, "*Bonsoir.*" No one seemed curious, much less menacing.

I detoured on a lane and climbed steeply. Walls hemmed me in, and eucalyptus trees touched overhead, showering down a medicinal scent. At the end of the workday, gardeners, pool men and servants lumbered downhill. Given the grade, it was an effort for them not to break into a trot. They greeted me in French and Arabic and kept on going.

I made it as far as the British Embassy where armed guards patrolling the perimeter of the compound paid little attention to me. I could have continued uphill, or I could have branched off on a footpath through the eucalyptus forest. But I thought I had proved my point.

Which was what? That I was fearless to walk around Algiers alone? No, it wasn't fearlessness I felt. It was a confusion that I remembered from living in Rome during the Red Brigades era. There had been terror then in Italy, sporadic bombings, kidnappings, kneecappings and killings. Yet you could walk the streets day after day and see no signs of trouble. That didn't mean it didn't exist. That meant you were lucky. In April 1978, in front of the American Studies

Center, I was one of the first people on the scene when Aldo Moro, the former prime minister, was discovered in the trunk of a car, assassinated by terrorists.

Back at the El Djazair, I asked for the *Herald Tribune*. The man at the *tabac* said he had no newspapers in English: *"Je suis désolé."* Sorry to disappoint me, he glanced around to make sure no one was watching, then dug a five-week-old copy of the *Economist* from under the counter. "Take it for free," he said. "Just to pass the time."

Annette Fuller, an American journalist, sounded young, lively and bright over the phone. She readily accepted an invitation to meet me for dinner. In person she looked young, too, and had a pert manner. But she was forty-nine, divorced and the mother of two college-age daughters.

The hotel had several restaurants. One was moodily lit and romantic, with a pianist playing a medley of American standards— "Autumn Leaves," "Moonglow," "Stardust." The brightly lit brasserie down the hall seemed more appropriate for an interview.

Despite her nervous laugh, Fuller was a professional, with an impressive résumé and an enviable spirit of adventure. After beginning her career as a reporter for the *Indianapolis Star*, she had worked for more than a decade at the *Dallas Morning News*. Eager for a change, she signed a thirteen-month contract with the Journalism Development Group, a U.S.–funded NGO, to introduce American standards to Algerian newspapers.

It was the first time she had lived outside of the States. She spoke no Arabic and next to no French. She had difficulty reading the menu. Yet she had an expertise that was valued, "almost worshipped here," she said. "Which is pretty ironic. In the States these days, journalism sucks. There's no respect for reporters, and lately we've had cutbacks and layoffs and budget problems. That's why American newspapers welcome reader participation. We're glad to get what people send in because it's free. We publish a lot of snapshots by mothers of their kids jumping on trampolines. But in Algeria, people—the young ones, anyway—want to use journalism to change their lives, change the country."

Older Algerian journalists, Annette conceded, were considerably less enthusiastic. "They feel they laid their lives on the line during the '90s and they're content to kick back. They think they deserve an easier time as their reward. They're happy to publish government news releases. You know, prepackaged stuff about tourism and finance and development."

"Is there much government interference?" I asked.

"Except for a couple of private newspapers, they're all dependent on government ad revenue. And the government runs the printing presses. Whenever there's an anti-government story, there's a crackdown. So publishers have to suck up to the regime."

Still, Annette stressed that she taught "standard reporting procedures, getting them to give both sides and to get sources for what they write. At first they were shy with me about writing anything critical of the U.S. But I told them as long as they can support their assertions, I'm not offended. Really, they worship America. They know the popular culture better than I do. They hate Bush and his policies, but otherwise they're pro-American."

"Which policies do they hate?"

"The war in Iraq and our unqualified support for Israel. After all they've gone through, the Algerians are touchy. They don't like to be pushed around. But then the funny thing is they're pushed around by the government and the police and even by the French and their influence. Why do they still eat baguettes? Why do they show such deference to France?"

But she liked the Algerians and was enthusiastic about her experience, which she said was "better than I could have imagined. I'm hopeful about Algeria's future. If I had money, I'd invest it here. The young people are so eager to improve things."

After her contract ended, she was considering a similar journalism project in Afghanistan. But she added, "Maybe that's too much. I don't want to die." She delivered this like a punch line and laughed.

"Do you feel you're in danger in Algiers?"

"No. But I did wonder"—another laugh—"after the UN bombing last December." She poked fun at U.S. Embassy personnel who never left their compound and were flabbergasted when they learned that she lived unprotected in the city, mixing with the locals. She acknowledged, though, that she hadn't been outside of Algiers and she knew the situation was much tenser in the mountains.

As we finished dinner and waited for dessert she brought up the one discomfiting, and to her incomprehensible, experience of her stay. The NGO had assigned her a translator, a thirty-six-year-old man who smoothed the rough spots that any non–Arabic, non–French speaker figured to run into. She and he had become friends, and he confided in Annette about his personal and professional frustrations. He felt blocked because he didn't have a job that paid much money. And because he didn't have money, he couldn't get married. He confessed that he was a virgin and feared he would remain one. Even if he met an Algerian woman who was willing to have sex, he was afraid his family would find out, and if they did, they'd punish the woman. They'd beat her a hundred times on the soles of her feet, he told Annette.

She said she had listened to him and expressed sympathy but felt uncomfortable. "What was I supposed to do?" she asked me.

I assumed the poor guy probably had fantasies of sleeping with her, perhaps even marrying her and moving to America. Despite her misgivings, Annette kept him on her staff and let him use her laptop computer. Then she discovered that he had hacked into her files.

"And stole your financial records and money," I guessed.

"No, it was worse," she said. "He downloaded family photographs, pictures of me and my daughters, and showed them to his friends. I felt violated. I felt I was being stalked. It really creeped me out."

"Did you talk to him? Did you tell him to stop?"

"No, I told people at the office and they fired him."

The anecdote killed my appetite for dessert. There was nothing more to say. The story was as shapely and complete as any classical tale of cultural misunderstanding. In the sort of setback that might breed a suicide bomber, the translator had lost his job, his identity and what he probably viewed as his last, best chance.

When Ahmed came for me in the morning, I reminded him of the woman he had mentioned whose husband had been kidnapped. I said I'd like to interview her. "I'd also like to talk to a terrorist."

"Very difficult." He brushed a hand over his buzz-cut hair, testing the bristles with his palm. "Very dangerous."

"Do you have any contacts?"

We were in the hotel bar, in plush leather chairs, finishing our coffee. Ahmed slapped at the pockets of his photographer's vest as if searching for something he couldn't find. "If you do this," he said, "they'll never let you into Algeria again."

"I can live with that. But what about the risk to you?"

He sighed. Despite the earliness of the hour, he sounded weary. "What I'd rather do, I'd rather introduce you to a repentant terrorist, an important one. He and his men—he had more than five thousand of them—accepted a government amnesty."

"Do you think he's worth talking to?"

"This man I have in mind is responsible for killing more people than died on 9/11."

I asked him to line up the interview. Then we set out for the Catholic basilica, Notre Dame d'Afrique. Since the city was draped over hills and steep valleys like a fishnet hung out to dry, the shortest commute in Algiers could become an ordeal. And while there were lovely views and hidden marvels along the way, there were also monuments to grim events, recent and long past.

At the Maison de Presse, a car bomb had exploded in 1994, killing six journalists; a plaque on the wall listed their names. A total of fifty-seven reporters had been murdered during the "black years," Ahmed said, and eight hundred fled into exile.

Then we came to a prison where the French had tortured and executed Algerians during the long course of the occupation. "The French called it Prison Barberosa," Ahmed said. "Everybody who was guillotined has his name on a plaque. A different plaque names the martyrs the French executed during the war for independence."

I remembered my horror at learning, during college in the early '60s, that the French tortured suspected FLN members and sympathizers as a matter of policy. It had struck me in my naiveté as unthinkable that the civilized world would permit such atrocities. I couldn't conceive of living in a nation that practiced torture with government approval. Yet here I was in 2008, a citizen of the United States, living in what Nobel Prize–winning South African author J.M. Coetzee has called "shameful times." At Guantanamo, at Abu Ghraib and Bagram Air Base, at black sites around the globe and in "extraordinary renditions" to countries that care nothing about human rights, America had dumped thousands of detainees and subjected them to the same unspeakable treatment that we once condemned the French for inflicting on Algerians. "In shameful times," Coetzee has written, "shame descends upon you, shame descends upon everyone, and you simply have to bear it, it is your lot and your punishment."

The lanes of Bab El-Oued boiled with pushcarts, trucks, cars and women with bundled laundry on their heads. This lower-class district had long been a cauldron of anarchy and insurrection. In 1988, gangs had paraded captured policemen in front of jeering mobs, forcing them to confess, "I am a braggart; I am a betrayer."

In 2001 flash floods killed more than six hundred. Four years earlier the government had plugged the drains in Bab El-Oued with cement to prevent armed Islamists from hiding there. After the "black years" ended, nobody had thought to reopen the sewers, and whole neighborhoods had been swept away. The survivors rioted for days.

Albert Camus had been born and raised in Bab El-Oued. I wanted to visit his home, but Ahmed warned me there might be problems. His family's apartment was now privately owned. The government had no interest in making it into a museum. While some Algerians regarded Camus, a Nobel Prize–winning author, as a source of national pride, most dismissed him as another dead white male colonialist whose books offered nothing of value in the current context.

"You're the first person in eight years to ask me to see Camus' house," Ahmed said. "Michael Palin was the last one I took there, and I had trouble convincing the owner to let him in. Palin traveled with a big BBC crew and a bodyguard, and the government sent many policemen and they blocked the street out front. It was a crazy scene and it screwed up traffic for hours. After all that, Palin never used the film of Camus' house, and the owner was angry. I'll try, but I promise nothing."

Notre Dame d'Afrique commanded a thorny promontory with an unparalleled view of the port. For travelers arriving by boat, the church was the most conspicuous landmark in the city, a Romano-Byzantine structure capped by a gold dome. Once a shining symbol of Catholicism and the French occupation, the basilica now had the melancholy appearance of a marooned ship. Though Mass was said there every day, the congregation was dying off and the church was often the site of funerals.

Impressive from the outside, Notre Dame d'Afrique was less distinguished inside. Ex-votos cluttered the walls. An amateurish statue of a Black Madonna bore an inscription in French, Arabic and Berber that translated to "Pray for us and the Muslims." A plaque commemorated the 1970 visit of astronaut Frank Borman. Another named the clerics—a total of twenty—killed during the '90s. "There's no greater love than to give one's life for those one loves," read a tribute to Bishop Claverie, who had been assassinated in Oran, and to seven monks from the monastery at Tibhirine who had been beheaded in 1996.

"There used to be photos of the monks," Ahmed said. "But after the amnesty and reconciliation, the police ordered the church to take them down. The government feared the pictures were an incitement."

"An incitement to what?"

"To anger and revenge. Officially, it's against the law to call someone a terrorist or to say somebody was killed by terrorists in the '90s. The press is supposed to describe them as 'victims of national tragedy.'"

On the drive back to Bab El-Oued, I wondered what Camus would have made of these equivocations and euphemisms. A man of his intellect—the author of *The Rebel*, a treatise on the deadly paradoxes of revolutionary violence—would surely have had something significant to add to the debate. The question was whether he would have chosen to speak out.

During Algeria's war for independence, Camus had never openly rejected the French right to rule. In Stockholm to receive the 1957 Nobel Prize for Literature, he had been rebuked by an Algerian student for not supporting the FLN, and Camus replied: "It is with a certain repugnance that I give my views in public. I have always condemned terror. I must also condemn terrorism which operates blindly in the streets of Algiers, and which one day could strike my mother or my family. I believe in justice, but I will defend my mother before justice."

Critics seized on this as evidence of ethical obtuseness, as if he prized his mother's safety more than a country's freedom. Others accused Camus of stereotyping Arabs as irrational and of erasing Muslims from his fiction. In *Albert Camus: Of Europe and Africa*, the noted Irish intellectual Conor Cruise O'Brien argued that while Camus' novel *The Plague* had been viewed as an allegory of French resistance to Nazism, the French actually treated the Algerians not much better than the Germans had the Jews. In O'Brien's opinion, by eliminating virtually all traces of the Arab population from *The Plague*, Camus had created "an artistic final solution."

This struck me as unduly harsh. While Camus may have had a blind spot about Arabs and a sentimental attachment to the idea that the French would gradually grant the Muslims equality, he shouldn't be held to a higher standard than other European authors in North Africa. Cavafy, for example, wrote poems about his lovers but never mentioned that they were Arabs or Egyptians or Muslims. Forster's book about Alexandria described a city immaculately cleansed of living humans. To single out Camus and equate his flaws with Nazism was, to cite his signature word, absurd.

As Professor David Carroll pointed out in *Albert Camus the Algerian*, Camus declined to choose between unacceptable alternatives. He wouldn't support an *Algérie française* based on terror and repression, "nor a formally free and nominally independent Algeria whose population would in reality be ruled by a ruthless revolutionary-nationalist bureaucracy controlled by the FLN."

Rue de Lyon couldn't have changed much since Camus' day. Once a street of poor *pieds-noirs*, it was now an Arab neighborhood of market stalls, rusted-out cars and unemployed men slumped on curbs. Until his college years, Camus had lived here in a cramped three-room apartment with his mother and grandmother, his brother and an uncle. They had no running water and no electricity. The family fetched water from a communal faucet and bathed in the kitchen sink, and they shared a Turkish toilet in the hallway.

His grandmother slept in her own room. Albert and his brother Lucien slept in a double bed in the same room where their mother had a single bed. Uncle Etienne made do with a mattress on the kitchen floor. Camus' father had been killed in World War I, and his mother was illiterate, partially deaf, mostly mute and perhaps brain-damaged by typhoid fever or traumatized by her husband's early death. She worked as a charwoman, cleaning offices and houses, and Camus attended *lycée* on a scholarship as "an orphan of the French state."

Ahmed gestured to the window of Camus' apartment and said there used to be a barbershop and a wine merchant below it. Now there was a shoe store and a cell phone shop. In a city emblazoned with plaques commemorating hundreds of dates and personages, Camus didn't rate a mention on the building.

Ahmed repeated, "I make no promises," and we crossed to the cell phone shop. He and the shopkeeper exchanged greetings in Arabic. The man remembered him. Or claimed to.

"He'll check with the owner of the apartment," Ahmed whispered to me. "He warned that lots of groups try to get in, whole busloads of Japanese and Europeans, and the owner is fed up."

"Shall we offer him money?" I asked, "As a courtesy?"

"Not at first. Slip him something afterward."

A shrunken, leathery old man entered through the rear door of the cell phone shop, which served as the foyer of the building. His chilly formality, the chocolate brown suit coat he wore, the sag of his mustache . . . everything suggested a funeral director with no tolerance for frivolity. "I'm seventy-seven years old," he said in French. "I've worked all my life. I have women in my house. I'm tired of strangers violating my privacy."

I was ready to leave him in peace. A crowd had gathered in the shop, the kind that clusters at car wrecks and arguments hoping to see blood.

"I have Chinese, I have Japanese pounding at my door. I had the wife of the president of Spain," he rumbled on. "If they all love it so much, why don't they buy my house and turn it into a museum? I'll make them a good price. I told this to French TV."

I apologized and told Ahmed in English that we should go. But Ahmed ignored me and spoke to the man, Hadj Amar, as if they were in a bazaar bargaining over a carpet. Dismissing a first, second and third refusal, Ahmed pleaded with Hadj Amar that I was a pilgrim, *un pèlerin.* "He flew all the way from America to visit your house. He respects you and understands your position. But he begs you and I beg you, don't send a pilgrim away."

Hadj Amar told us to return at five this evening. That would give his women time to tidy up the apartment and conceal themselves.

Ahmed couldn't believe our good luck. He couldn't believe—he trusted I appreciated—his powers of persuasion. Nobody but he could have talked his way into Camus' house. Now, since we were on a literary pilgrimage, he offered to show me La Grotte de Cervantes.

"The what?"

"Cervantes, the Spanish writer of *Don Quixote.*"

"I know who he is. What does he have to do with Algiers?"

"He lived here for five years as a slave. He escaped and hid in a grotto." Ahmed spoke animatedly as he drove, exultant that he knew more about Cervantes than I did. In this mood it mattered not at all that when we got to the grotto, the gate was locked. For him it sufficed that we could spy the mouth of the dank cave through the fence and read a sign attesting that Cervantes had been a prisoner in Algeria from 1575 until 1580. After his liberation, the sign said, he returned to Spain and consecrated himself to literature until his death, in 1616.

Although exceptional in literary talent, Cervantes's life, for all its drama and pain—his left hand had been maimed in 1571 during the Battle of Lepanto—hadn't differed much from that of tens of thousands of Europeans who had been shipped to North Africa as slaves. For centuries before white men began capturing black Africans and dispatching them in chains to the Americas, Islamic Africans had been systematically kidnapping Christians. The Ottoman Turks who ruled the Mediterranean during Cervantes's day depended on a civil service and military cadre, the *janissaries*, comprised of Christians who had been captured and converted into the Sultan's most loyal subjects. According to historians, after the Turkish defeat at Lepanto killed forty thousand men, leaving the sea so thick with corpses that the flotilla had trouble navigating, twelve thousand Christian galley slaves were rescued.

"Now the Casbah," Ahmed announced. He was on a roll and undeterred by a traffic accident. Grinding his gears into reverse, he sped around the wreck on an alternate route. "A brand-new car," he lamented, as he always did.

For foreigners, no place in Algiers, perhaps no place in the whole of North Africa, possessed greater iconic status than the Casbah. Mention of the word made the travel writer's prose run purple. It embodied mystery, intrigue, romance, licentiousness and danger. The setting of novels, the location of famous films—*Pépé le Moko; Algiers*, with Charles Boyer; *The Battle of Algiers*, director Gillo Pontecorvo's masterpiece—the Casbah had metamorphosed in the popular imagination from a squalid native quarter into an Oriental state of mind, a condition more than a destination, in which outsiders saw whatever they wanted to believe.

During the war for independence it had been a guerrilla staging ground. During the "black years" it frothed with Islamic fundamentalism. But for the most part it was then and remained now a slum of eighty thousand residents competing for space and air in a neighborhood that fifty years ago had less than half that many people. Since earthquakes and floods had destroyed a thousand homes, the crowding had increased. According to anecdotal evidence, so had the crime. The State Department's Travel Warning made it sound like Baghdad's Sadr City: "The Government of Algeria requires U.S. Embassy personnel traveling . . . to the Casbah within Algiers to seek permission and to have a security escort."

Despite its dicey reputation, the Casbah had been declared a UNESCO World Heritage landmark in 1991 and hailed as "one of the finest coastal sites on the Mediterranean." This struck me as a cruel tease—proclaim the Casbah's beauty and cultural richness, then caution visitors to stay away; solicit contributions for its renovation, then send out SOS signals.

Ahmed parked near the citadel, and on foot we plunged downhill through a tangle of alleys toward the sea. Except for its precarious setting, barnacled to cliffs and ravines, the Casbah was indistinguishable from dozens of other souks and medinas. Where it did differ from those in Alexandria, Tripoli and Tunis was its relative lack of color and liveliness. Maybe the warnings had scared off even Algerians.

Still, the Casbah had its charms—massive wooden doors with brass hinges and Hands of Fatma as knockers; streets, or *ruelles*, that narrowed to needles' eyes; latticework screens, or *mashrabiyas*, that separated public space from private, the world of men from that of women.

At a house where a cage hung from a window ledge, a man was feeding lettuce leaves to baby squirrels. "Are you raising them for food?" I asked in French.

He shot me a look of complete horror. "We are not cannibals."

"En Amérique, on mange les écureils," I explained.

This appalled him. He demanded to know whether I ever ate them. I lied and swore to the gentle animal lover that I hadn't.

The Casbah's most celebrated spot was the house where the French army had blown up Ali La Pointe and his fellow insurgents in 1956. Now reconstructed and aflutter with Algerian flags, it was a shrine to the war for independence. But like a lot of other shrines in the city, it was shut, and Ahmed said that when it was open women used it for cooking and sewing classes. I found it difficult to believe that in two generations it had gone from a rebel stronghold to a home economics schoolroom.

Still, the original house lived on in *The Battle of Algiers*, a 1966 docudrama that immortalized—some say, romanticized and oversimplified—the struggle for independence and the insurgents who died here. During the '60s and '70s, Pontecorvo's film was broadcast on U.S. university campuses as a sort of user's guide to revolution, and its poster of freedom fighters refusing to surrender gained a vogue with radicals that briefly rivaled the bearded picture of Che Guevara.

In 2003 as the occupation of Iraq went belly-up, the movie enjoyed a comeback when the American State Department and Pentagon studied *The Battle of Algiers* for lessons in defending against urban warfare and asymmetrical combat. Like Ali La Pointe's hideout that had been converted to domestic purposes, this fictionalization of the Algerian War had flipped from a revolutionary Bible to a neo-con textbook.

To be sure, there were troubling parallels between our misadventures in Iraq and those of the French army in Algeria. When Paris first sent troops, in 1830, it was on a pretext as flimsy as the Bush administration's blather about weapons of mass destruction. Allegedly the Bey of Algiers had slapped the French consul's face with a fan. To redeem national honor, Paris launched a punitive expedition that amounted to a turkey-shoot. Not satisfied with a quick surgical victory, the French decided to seize the whole country.

The Algerians, while roundly beaten on the battlefield, continued to resist with hit-and-run guerrilla tactics. Pacification of the cities required sixteen years of bloody street combat. The mountains and desert remained beyond France's control, except for isolated enclaves and forts. When the French drew down their troops in 1871 to suppress a rebellion in Paris, the Berbers in the Kabylia reclaimed their land. Decades passed before the area was repacified, and there never came a time when the occupation was less than a drain on the economy, a political liability and a mortal danger to European settlers.

Determined to complete their "civilizing mission"—the French purported to be spreading culture along with their hegemony—they wouldn't compromise. Instead, Paris kept raising the stakes and expanding the conflict. As American historian Douglas Porch shows in *The Conquest of the Sahara*, the military never had a coherent plan or a counterweight to the hard-line philosophy of "more boots on the ground." The farther the army advanced, the more viciously the Algerians fought back. And each act of resistance was punished by deeper incursions and savage reprisals.

Eventually, France annexed Algeria as a *département*, no different from Brittany or Provence. No different, that is, unless a man wanted to vote or find a job. Forced into ghettos or restricted to rural areas where starvation wasn't uncommon, Muslims had all the obligations of citizenship, such as taxes and military service, but none of the rights and privileges. Most of the land and the economy passed from the *indigènes* into the hands of the *pieds-noirs*, who constituted a mere 10 percent of the population.

Called "black feet," because they, unlike the Algerians, wore shoes, the *pieds-noirs* were French by virtue of residency, but the majority of them were immigrants from Spain, Italy and Malta. Gradually they became a class unto themselves, a bloc of generally poor voters whom politicians courted and manipulated, then callously discarded.

When open rebellion first broke out in the 1950s, even the Communist and Socialist parties in Paris refused to negotiate. They labeled the FLN as bandits and terrorists. As Washington would do in Vietnam and later in Baghdad, France responded in Algeria with shock-and-awe operations, forced migrations, internment camps and killing zones. But as the body count climbed, there was no break in the political impasse.

Contrary to myths in France and Algeria, the army effectively crushed the FLN in the Battle of Algiers. But victory was prohibitively expensive, politically disastrous and utterly Pyrrhic. France lost its standing in the international community and was at risk of losing access to the oil and natural gas in the Sahara. So with a nudge from Charles de Gaulle, the French—after eight years of vowing there would be no compromise, no betrayal of the *pieds-noirs* and those Algerians who had stayed loyal—started to negotiate.

This didn't stop the brutality. The FLN continued fighting during the peace talks, and it didn't limit its targets to the French army. It systematically executed moderates, Francophile Arabs, suspected traitors and collaborators, political opponents and anyone who happened to be in the wrong place when the FLN decided the moment was right to heighten the climate of terror.

Not to be outdone, the *pieds-noirs* formed the Organization of the Secret Army (OAS), which more than matched the FLN's ferocity. Both in Algeria and metropolitan France it murdered Arabs at random and attempted to assassinate French politicians, including de Gaulle. In one infamous episode, the OAS drove an oil tanker to the top of the Casbah, set it on fire and let the lighted fuel flow down into the tightly packed streets.

Then, finally, it was over. Except for the flight of a million *pieds-noirs* to France. Except for the murder of thousands of Algerians, the *harkis*, who had served in the French army. Except for years of score-settling, coups and countercoups, and purges within the FLN. Except for the current conflict over inequities that began during the war for independence and raged today.

When we reached the bottom of the ramped streets of the Casbah, Ahmed announced that he was hungry. After washing his hands and face at a fountain, he tucked into a hole-in-the-wall and ordered sardines and an omelet. I asked where to find a bathroom.

"Try the mosque," he said. "Just don't talk. Nobody'll guess you're not a Muslim."

I went alone to Place des Martyrs, formerly Place du Gouvernement, which retained its grand scale and graceful arcades. But boys on bicycles dervished through the crowd, cutting fierce figure eights, and men lugging buckets sold soft drinks and fruit juices. Glancing back at the Casbah, I noticed hundreds of rooftop satellite dishes cocked like sunflowers toward Europe.

Djemaa el Djedid, known as the New Mosque, was almost four hundred years old, and according to legend its architect was a Christian who sneakily laid out the foundation in a cross shape. Feeling like a sneaky Christian myself, I removed my shoes and climbed the steps to the porch where crowded lavatory cubicles lined one wall. I joined the queue and when my turn came, I found that an inch of urine covered the floor. If I backed out now, I feared I'd expose myself as a nonbeliever. So I yanked off my socks, stepped inside and contributed my share to the puddle.

Afterward, I washed my feet at the courtyard fountain, lost in a crowd of worshippers. Once I put my shoes on and made it back onto Place des Martyrs, I felt less like an imposter, more like I had passed over and knew a little better how things stood on either side.

I gave Ahmed the thumbs-up, and he grinned: "I told you you look like a Berber."

Since we had time to kill, he proposed that we visit the Musée des Beaux Arts. The improbability of the idea appealed to me. In a city scarred by Islamic fundamentalism, in a country coruscated by sectarian conflict, in a culture opposed to representational art, why not tour North Africa's foremost museum of European art?

Of course it was closed. But Ahmed banged the door until a guard opened up, and after a tiresome give-and-take, the man let us in.

"What bullshit," Ahmed griped. "He claimed they keep it shut for security. But security from what?"

"Maybe they're afraid of art thieves."

"No, they're afraid of fundamentalists. The imams don't like people to look at pictures. Since you're a Christian and already damned, they don't care."

Gallery after gallery, I had a world-class museum to myself. No crowds, no guides, no numbskulls nattering that their kids could paint better than Picasso. This was a feast, and I savored every morsel of it. Renoir, Degas, Gauguin, Matisse, Vuillard, Bonnard, Monet, Utrillo, Dufy, Delaunay, Sisley, Pisarro—all my favorites were represented, often with canvases I had never seen before, even in reproduction.

The paintings stirred a powerful nostalgia. They must have had the same effect on homesick *colons* who ducked in from the dusty swirl of Algiers to enjoy Paris under snow, Provence in mimosa season, the Houses of Parliament through mist, the ruins of Trajan's Forum in golden sunlight. A fierce yearning, a craving for cultural familiarity, took hold of me. Half an hour ago in a mosque I wanted to pass for a Muslim. Now I wanted to be in Montparnasse sipping a glass of burgundy.

On the drive back to rue de Lyon, I was sunk deep in myself.

"What's wrong?" Ahmed asked "Didn't you like it?"

"I liked it a lot," I said and kept the rest to myself.

After his initial reluctance to let us into Camus' childhood home, after complaining that he had to protect the privacy of his women, Hadj Amar welcomed us warmly and showed everything, including his wife, a henna-handed woman in a green rayon housedress, and two pretty teenage granddaughters in blue jeans and *hijabs*.

"I have had many European and Asian visitors," he told me. "You are my first American." From the cell phone shop, we climbed deeply scalloped steps to a hall that ran along an airshaft caged with wire to keep out thieves. "I bought the apartment in 1962 from a widow, a *pied-noir*. This was five months after independence, and she was leaving for France. I had no idea about Camus. I'm living in his house, but I know nothing. When people started wanting to see the place, a Frenchman gave me a book of Camus'. "

"*By* him? Or *about* him?"

"I don't remember. I never read it. I lost it."

We entered single file. "It's two different apartments connected together," he explained. "The original apartment is this way."

We proceeded down a corridor to what had been the bedroom of Camus' grandmother. A refrigerator hulked beside a double bed. The tiny kitchen where Uncle Etienne slept on a mattress had undergone repairs and modernization—it now had running water and electricity.

"How does it feel to live in a famous man's house?" Ahmed asked Hadj Amar.

"I don't care. People ask me, but I don't care about the fame. I get nothing out of it."

But one of his granddaughters was thrilled. "If you look on the Internet," she said, "you can see these rooms."

Amar was more interested in displaying a photo of the Portuguese soccer star Cristiano Ronaldo that he had clipped from a magazine and thumbtacked to the wall. "He looks like my grandson," he said.

"How many children do you have?" I asked.

"Ten: six sons and four daughters." Squaring his shoulders, he gave a little speech about his life—how he was a simple man, now retired and looking forward to peace and quiet as he got older. "From fourteen years of age, I was working. I worked in an *infirmerie* as a sort of nurse. I also worked as a stonemason."

He had me feel the hard palms of his hands. Then he opened the last door with a flourish. Like the other rooms, this one had minimal furniture—a cane bottom chair, a single bed and a table. It reminded me of the severe beauty of Van Gogh's room in the asylum at Saint-Remy.

Hadj Amar crossed to a window. "This is the view that inspired him," he repeated what he must have heard a previous visitor say.

From the railing of a balcony fluttered a pair of men's underpants. Next to them was a satellite dish. Down in the street, cars and pedestrians set off a racket that must have been as clamorous in Camus' day. Yes, I thought, this was the view that had inspired him to finish school, master his craft, find his voice and escape. Yet even as he moved to Paris and won a place in the world, his childhood remained, as he wrote, "a glue that has stuck to the soul."

At the El Djazair that evening, I ate alone in the restaurant where a pianist ran through his playlist of American standards. To my embarrassment, I responded to the schmaltz as I had to the paintings at the Musée des Beaux Arts. I couldn't guess what an Algerian might make of Gershwin or Cole Porter, but to me they signified home and my parents, now dead.

From the moment I arrived in Algeria, I had had the impression of being trapped in a film projected at the wrong speed, twice as fast as it was supposed to be. Part of that was Ahmed and his frantic pace. Part was the quickened pulse of the country, the higher stakes, the life-or-death issues. Egypt and Libya and Tunisia had also been chaotic, but in a desultory fashion, like a terminal patient falling to pieces on an operating table. But in Algeria the patient was more like Frankenstein, with his disparate parts stitched together and bolts of electricity crackling through his body. The monster was coming alive.

At 4 AM, my bed shook and heaved, and my first thought was a bomb. When I got to my feet, the floor shuddered. Then I realized there was a rhythm, a beat. Not Gershwin or Cole Porter, but rap. I called down to the front desk and learned it was disco night at El Djazair. Despite the dangers in Algiers, the *jeunesse dorée* danced till dawn. The management made no apology, but switched me to a room on a higher floor in a different wing.

The next day, Ahmed was pacing the lobby, whacking a rolled newspaper like a riding crop against his thigh. "Problem," he said. "Big problem." We had planned to drive to the monastery at Tibhirine. But six municipal guards had been killed yesterday in the mountains outside Médéa. "Somebody slit their throats," Ahmed said. "It's dangerous to go to Tibhirine today."

"How dangerous?"

"I don't know. The area will be full of police and soldiers."

"Won't that make it safer?"

"The problem is whoever murdered the municipal guards stole their uniforms. They could set up a roadblock and kill more people."

"Is there a way to Tibhirine that doesn't go near Médéa?"

"It's not just the town. It's the countryside around it. Right where the monastery is."

"What do you suggest?"

"The decision is yours. I leave it up to you."

"How can we get more information?"

Ahmed agreed to stop at *El Khabar*, an independent newspaper with the largest circulation in Algeria. It had published a front-page story about the killings. None of the newspapers or TV stations controlled by the government had reported the incident. "Maybe *El Khabar* knows whether the roads are open," he said.

In a neighborhood of cobbled streets and dilapidated houses, one modern building glinted like a gold tooth. A secretary at *El Khabar* photocopied the most recent clips on Médéa. But neither they nor a journalist Ahmed reached by cell phone could provide details about the safety of the roads.

"Do we go? Or don't we?" Ahmed asked.

From the planning stages of the trip, I had been aware of the dangers. I had come to Algeria despite the warnings because I wanted to see it for myself. And here I was. Though afraid, I told Ahmed, "Let's go."

We bore south into the Mitidja. Known in the '90s as the Triangle of Death, the region between Algiers, Blida and Médéa had suffered incomprehensible horrors. Both sides—or since there were multiple warring factions, all sides—seemed to have subscribed to Frantz Fanon's pathological notion that violence was cathartic, cruelty was empowering and blood was cleansing. Dissident groups zeroed in on the police, soldiers, teachers, journalists and politicians, and subjected them to ritual humiliation before murdering them. Throat-cutting, disembowelment and castration were favorite methods of execution.

To pacify the triangle, the government formed an antiterrorist squad of fifteen thousand men. Dubbed the "ninjas," they sought to restore the rule of law by unleashing a lawless campaign of their own. As recounted in *Algeria: Anger of the Dispossessed,* by Martin Evans and John Phillips, the "ninjas became infamous for a whole host of torture techniques including electric shocks, sexual abuse with bottles, beatings with sticks, especially on the genitals, and an Algerian specialty, the *chiffon* (cloth), in which prisoners were tied down and partially suffocated with a cloth soaked in dirty water."

In short order, the Mitidja mutated from an agricultural area into a battlefield of armed camps and barricaded villages. Anybody caught in the crossfire was considered fair game; anybody out at night became a target. Towns of three and four hundred people were wiped off the map by unidentified attackers while soldiers in nearby bases turned a deaf ear to the gunfire and screams for help. Dead bodies rotted in the street. Corpses polluted wells. Eyewitnesses claimed that government agents, not terrorists, did most of the killing.

Opposite the monastery at Tibhirine, the army had erected what seemed a caricature of a religious cloister with barbed wire, cinder blocks and searchlights. Whether the soldiers were there to protect or to intimidate the Cistercian Trappists remained a matter of debate. One night in 1996, during a strict curfew, the military, safe in its fortified hill position, somehow failed to notice twenty men speed up the road, smash through a window, ransack the monastery and kidnap seven monks. Fifty-four days later, after the Algerian and French governments refused to negotiate for their release, seven decapitated heads were discovered in a tree. Where the monks had been killed, how they had been killed and, crucially, who had killed them were closely held state secrets.

Beyond the harrowed plains of the Mitidja, Ahmed and I entered the Gorge de la Chiffa. The air freshened and cooled, and in the lush vegetation clinging to vertical cliffs, there was a gurgle of streams and the shrieks of Barbary apes. Signs warned motorists to steer clear of the apes, but plenty of them stopped to feed them and snap photographs. A boy with two preening peacocks charged a dinar for a picture of the birds spreading their iridescent fans.

On a bright spring day, with rainbows flashing from waterfalls, the gorge might have been a splendid picnic spot had it not been for the roadblocks and the burnt out buildings; the sandbagged gun emplacements and army barracks; and the cries of the peacocks which were as disconcerting as the shrieks of the apes. A few restaurants had optimistically reopened within eyesight of the charred foundations of defunct businesses. Somebody with a black sense of humor, or no sense at all, had set up a checkpoint next to a monument dedicated to drivers who had been murdered at false roadblocks.

That was the thought that clung like a nettle, the thought that six municipal guards had been killed and stripped of their uniforms. There was no way of knowing whether the men who signaled for us to stop were assassins or policemen.

When we reached Médéa—a name out of Greek tragedy—
Ahmed said, "This is the worst time. The guard shifts are changing.
That's when the fundamentalists strike, when one shift is tired, and
the new one isn't prepared.

"My wife is a doctor," he said. "Sometimes she operates on
patients who've had their throats slit. They don't all die. Some survive. They can't talk again, but they live."

From the town, Ahmed pressed on into the countryside. The
hills reminded me of rural Tuscany, dotted by cypress trees, farm
houses with red tile roofs and fields of poppies. "It's beautiful,"
Ahmed agreed, "but I wouldn't care to drive here at night. This place
has always been hell for Christians. Three years before the monks
were killed, a team of twenty Europeans was working on the dam at
Tamesguida. The GIA [Groupe Islamique Armé] ordered all foreigners to leave or be executed. A man named Saya Attiya—he called
himself Emir—captured twelve Catholic Croatians at the dam and
slit their throats. There were eight Bosnians, but since they were
Muslims, Emir let them go."

At Tamesguida, Ahmed took a wrong turn. He hadn't been at
the monastery since the monks' burial and had forgotten the way.
We blundered along, asking directions of the only people on the
road—police. Intentionally or not, they led us further astray, and as
we circled for an hour I had that tense, half-sick feeling of sitting on
an airplane that's locked in an endless landing pattern.

When we finally arrived at Tibhirine, there was an intoxicating
scent of pine. But any sense that we had achieved a peaceful sanctuary was dispelled when a soldier with an AK-47 loped down from the
military compound and demanded our IDs. I produced an American

passport that inflamed his suspicion and confusion in equal measure. Again Ahmed claimed that I was a pilgrim, an honored guest in Algeria, here to pay his respects to the dead monks.

As the soldier trudged back up the hill with our papers, a gardener admitted us to the monastery grounds. The Cistercians had established the community in 1934, devoted to caring for the population, not converting it. During the war for independence, they had provided refuge and medical treatment and food for orphaned Muslim children. When the Armée de Libération Nationale had mistakenly kidnapped a monk, they released him immediately once they realized he was a doctor who treated seventy Muslim patients a day.

After independence, the monks stayed on, bearing witness, trying to convince people that not all Christians came as conquerors or colonizers. They wanted the monastery to be a place of Christian-Muslim dialogue. The very night the monks were kidnapped, there had been a meeting of the Lien de la Paix, an organization committed to interfaith understanding.

The gardener worked here with the help of a second man. Clearly the job was beyond their capabilities. From what Ahmed said, it was a miracle the monastery stayed open at all. Algerian authorities wanted to shut it down. But the Cistercians insisted that it be maintained for when new monks arrived—whenever that might be.

The footpaths, once neatly spread with gravel, hadn't been raked or weeded. The gardener showed us a cistern, constructed in 1875, and an orchard that still bore fruit. He offered fig and apple jam, and Ahmed bought a couple of jars that the gardener fetched from a dungeonlike room that had a painting of the Crucifixion on the wall.

Only the cemetery was well tended. Of the fifteen graves, eight had worn-down stones. Seven were new, with mounds of fresh earth on top and white stones stenciled with the first names of the monks— Christian, Luc, Christophe, Michel, Bruno, Célestin and Paul—and the presumed date of their deaths, 21/05/1996.

You didn't need to be Catholic or a believer in any definition of the divine to be touched by the cemetery at Tibhirine, its aroma of lavender, the tessellated pattern of shade and light, the trickle of water in the cistern. What moved me most was the simplicity of the seven graves, the mounded earth, the men's names. They had known they were in danger. They had been warned by the government and threatened many times by terrorists. But the monks refused to leave. As Brother Michel wrote in a letter to his family, "If something happens to us, I wish to be in solidarity with the people here."

At the gardener's urging, we climbed a flight of steps covered with straw to a chapel used now as a storeroom. Plaster flaked off the ceiling. Splotches of green mold grew on the walls like the maps of imaginary continents. There was a rusty scale for weighing grain, a rusty oil drum that once held heating fuel, and a rusty stove with a rusty flue that no longer reached the roof. The locked-in air of twelve winters created a mortuary chill.

We went on to what the gardener called *la bibliothèque*—a room with shelves, a few books and a small soapstone bust of Pope John Paul II, a trinket from the Vatican. On the bulletin board, a sign in French said, THE ONLY VIOLENCE THAT CAN SAVE THE WORLD IS THE VIOLENCE OF FRATERNAL LOVE.

A second chapel, in much better condition, appeared to be prepared for Mass. Or for one of the Cistercians' interfaith gatherings.

Damask covered the altar. The room had a reed ceiling, like an Algerian hut, and stained glass windows on one wall and arabesque tiles on the opposite wall.

At the monastery gate, the soldier handed back our IDs and quizzed Ahmed in Arabic. I assumed he was asking about me. But as we drove away, Ahmed explained that the soldier wanted a favor. "He'd like to get married, but he can't until he finds an apartment to live in. He thought I might have influence with someone important. Or you might."

"What did you tell him?"

"I said he's in the same sad fix as millions of others. I'm sorry, but there's nothing to do."

In Médéa Ahmed stopped for lunch. I wasn't hungry, but I encouraged him to eat while I caught up on my notes. Maybe he didn't know an out-of-the-way restaurant in this town. Maybe he didn't care to leave the main street on a day when the back alleys were crawling with police. Or with men masquerading as police. At a grill on the busiest boulevard he ordered a whole roasted chicken. The smoke and grease were so thick my pen skipped on the notebook pages.

I stepped outside. I didn't notice the soldier until he jabbed me with his rifle. "What are you doing?" he demanded in French.

"Writing."

"Writing what? Are you a journalist?"

"A journalist" was always the wrong answer. "I've been to the monastery at Tibhirine. I'm writing my impressions."

"What's your mission?" Then with a harder jab of the rifle, "Show me your orders of mission."

"I don't have a mission. I'm just—" Claiming to be a tourist in Médéa seemed like admitting either insanity or guilt. So I identified myself as Ahmed did, *"Je suis pèlerin."*

"Come with me." He grabbed my arm.

"Where?"

"To the police station."

I screamed for Ahmed, and he burst out of the chicken shack with a drumstick in one hand, a wad of paper towels in the other and a mustache of grease. I don't know what he said to the soldier. It didn't work at first. The guy insisted that both of us follow him to the station. Ahmed tossed the paper towels and seized my free arm, and I bobbed between them like a flag on a tug-of-war rope. Ahmed won the contest and convinced the guy to let me go.

After settling his account in the chicken shack, he drove out of Médéa toward Algiers yelling, "This is so so stoopid!"

That evening, after I showered and changed clothes and calmed down, Ahmed dropped me at the U.S. Embassy, where I had an appointment with Thomas Daughton, the deputy chief of mission (DCM). He had invited me to come in to discuss the security situation. Ahmed offered to wait for me, but I told him I'd walk back to the El Djazair. He made me promise to catch a taxi if I left the embassy after nightfall.

Set back from the street, the American compound was behind a broad esplanade, a high wall and fence, then another esplanade that ended at concrete bollards along the curb. By now the security drill was second nature, and I forked over my passport, clipped a badge to my shirt pocket and stepped through the metal detector. There were fifty U.S. citizens on assignment at the embassy, thirty of them Marine guards.

Daughton bore a striking resemblance to the men who protected him. Tall, lean and tanned, he looked to be in his late thirties and had his dark hair cut short and combed to the side. The part in his hair might have been made with the same razor that had shaved his face to a high gloss. His trousers had a military crease, his shoes a bright shine and his tie a firm knot. While this might suggest an uptight, by-the-book Foreign Service drone, he had a wry, wisecracking style that I liked and fell right in with. It was tonic to meet somebody at a U.S. Embassy who didn't speak in bromides and wasn't reluctant to laugh.

When I mentioned my impression that in Algeria life was incredibly hectic and stressful, he quipped, "You should try dealing with the Algerian government."

"What do you do to relax?"

"I play golf when I can get away. The embassy has a pool and a tennis court. I'm afraid a childhood of tennis lessons put me off that game. I try to exercise. But there are days, whole weeks, when I don't leave the compound."

"Do you think it's that dangerous?" I asked.

"For you or for me?"

"Let's talk about you and people at the embassy. Are they allowed to bring their families with them?"

"Yeah, we have married couples, and three kids here now. By summer we'll have ten kids, mostly infants. When they get to be four years old, their parents have to rotate out. The assumption is kids under four don't need to go into the city and don't need to go to school yet."

When I asked if the security situation reduced the embassy's effectiveness, he itemized a long agenda of successful U.S. projects and American-financed NGOs that trained journalists and healthcare professionals, and sponsored conferences and seminars to upgrade the Algerian legal system. In the field of education, the embassy set up virtual classrooms and virtual universities and interactive Skype sessions between American and Algerian students.

But when I inquired whether these were adequate to keep the country from falling apart, Daughton answered without hesitation: "No." He added, "Algeria was France; it was the West for 130 years. So it's excellently positioned to be a bridge between the East and West. That's the hope. But that's hardly the reality. If Algeria didn't have oil, this would be Zimbabwe.

"The need for regime and leadership change is similar in both Algeria and Zimbabwe," he said. "But there's no national identity here except 'We fought the French and made them go away.' As for the friction between the Arabs and Berbers, essentially they're all Berbers. The conflict, false as it is, is used for political advantage."

"No hope for new leadership?"

Daughton shook his head. "All the contenders are creatures of the FLN system. Bouteflika's successor, assuming the law doesn't change and he doesn't run for a third term in '09, will come from a handpicked group. There are no dark horses, no knights in shining armor."[6]

He reminded me that many of the men running Algeria, either officially or behind the scenes, had been in power since the

---

6. The law did change. Bouteflika ran for a third term and in April 2009 he won with 90 percent of the vote.

revolution ended, forty-seven years ago: "The government is scle-rotic and self-serving." What's more, he explained, it had never entirely let go of its post-independence, Soviet socialist mentality. "They dig in their heels at the idea of relinquishing control not just on human rights issues and personal freedom but on central plan-ning and the economy. We've been trying in some respects to drag them into the twentieth century. Forget about the twenty-first. But they're afraid of deficit spending. They're reluctant to take on debt to finance projects and improve infrastructure."

I mentioned my amazement that Algeria imported Chinese la-bor. Daughton agreed: "It's a mistake. Sure, they do a quick cheap job, but they send the money home, and the locals don't get jobs or learn skills. Then some Chinese stay on and create a different kind of problem. You know, this newfound interest of China's in Africa isn't simply about emerging markets and cornering natural resourc-es. It's about locating countries for their excess population."[7]

As the discussion turned to Islamic terrorism, Daughton ob-served that despite the bloodshed of the '90s, many Algerians continued to sympathize with the fundamentalist groups that had caused so much havoc. "Some people still feel the answer lies within an Islamic framework."

Equally puzzling to him, President Bouteflika remained more popular than one might have expected. "Even though he hasn't delivered economically, he plays the Ronald Reagan role and blames his underlings for not implementing his reforms and ideas. His allies say, 'Let Bouteflika be Bouteflika. He understands the problem.' He knows that young people now have two choices—

---

7. *The Nuclear Express: A Political History of the Bomb and Its Proliferation*, a book by Thomas C. Reed and Danny B. Stillman, revealed that China had exported more than labor and excess population to Algeria. It secretly passed on nuclear technology that the Algerians used at a desert base to produce enough plutonium to build one bomb per year.

become *mujahaddin* or *harragas*, join the terrorists or take a boat to Europe. But he hasn't proposed any solutions."

"What about his program of amnesty and reconciliation?" I asked. "Isn't that a step in the right direction?"

"You'd think so. But some of the recent suicide bombers, it turns out, were repentant terrorists." Daughton laughed ruefully. "How awkward is that? Bouteflika declared victory after the amnesty, but now he has repentant terrorists switching back to the other side and blowing themselves up."

I thought it best not to mention Ahmed's efforts to introduce me to a repentant terrorist.

"Algeria's a strange place," Daughton went on. "The people seem inured to violence. But then the rest of the world pretty much ignores it too. The ETA kills three in Spain and it makes headlines in the States. But here you have fifty to a hundred killed each month and you don't hear about it. Civilian deaths have gone down. But there are ongoing guerrilla attacks on the police, and police killing terrorists."

I confessed I was of two minds about the alleged dangers in Algeria. I described my trip to Médéa today and admitted it had been tense and at times scary. But except for the soldier who grabbed me, nothing had really happened.

"You're lucky," he said, "that your driver talked him out of arresting you. Probably the driver's reporting on you and he convinced the soldier he had everything under control."

"I don't think so. Ahmed's been willing to take me anyplace I want to go. I've never had the feeling I was under surveillance."

"You'd never know. Like I said, you've been lucky."

"That's not how it seems to me. Yesterday I walked from the top to the bottom of the Casbah with no problems."

Daughton grinned and shook his head. "I'm glad you didn't tell me until after the fact. The Casbah is out of bounds for Americans. Because of crime, if nothing else."

"I'm no expert," I said. "I can only say what I saw and did and how it felt to me. I've read the State Department Travel Warning and heard from your public affairs officer. Frankly, I figure there's a large element of bureaucratic ass-covering in these warnings."

Daughton quit smiling. He was seated on a sofa, elbows on his knees. His voice lost its ironic lilt. "You're in real danger. You wouldn't know a thing until it's too late. You represent a very juicy target."

"For whom?"

"Any number of groups." He mentioned one: AQIM. "There's evidence of contacts between them and Ayman Al Zawahiri, Bin Laden's second in command. The Algerians have adopted Al Qaeda tactics—suicide car bombs, multiple timed events. Suicide bombs are the most troubling. That's new to Algeria.

"We also know from communications intercepts that AQIM would like to get an American or a Frenchman. False roadblocks are the biggest danger. You don't want to be the guy they kidnap."

I decided I preferred the DCM in his joking mode. "I've told my wife to cash in my IRAs and ransom me."

Daughton wasn't laughing. "You don't want to have your head cut off. We truly believe Americans should not travel overland, especially not in the northeast."

I still had difficulty sorting out his description of the country from my own experience. Or was it less my experience than my contrariness and reluctance to cancel the rest of the trip across Algeria?

"You mention the danger in the northeast," I said. "I've heard it's safer in Oran and Tlemcen. That's where I'm headed."

"They killed a terrorist in Tlemcen yesterday. Since a lot of security resources have been relocated to Algiers, and it's gotten hot for fundamentalists here. They've moved their operations elsewhere."

"And the train to Oran, what's your advice about it?"

"Well, it's safer than driving. Almost anything is."

The DCM stood up. His creased trousers didn't have a single wrinkle, his shirttail was neatly tucked in. He had told me what he had to say. There was no more to add. Daughton returned to his joshing self. "You've been brave enough. Now behave." With that he ushered me out his office's bulletproof door.

The sun had gone down, but it wasn't dark, so I walked back from the embassy. At every street corner there was a view of the bay and, beyond it, the Mediterranean, with the night ferry steaming toward Marseilles. Jasmine scented the air, and purple jacaranda trees had bloomed, their flowers a pointillist fog, like the delicate brush strokes on a painting in the Musée des Beaux Arts.

Not interested in another meal at the hotel, I caught a taxi to Le Dauphin, a fish restaurant with Greek décor and a clientele that consisted that night of Chinese businessmen. I wished I had invited Daughton to dinner. He was good company—smart, articulate, funny.

Of course, he couldn't have come, not without a military escort. I understood his predicament. He was a high-profile target. If he got kidnapped or killed, there would be international repercussions. Considering the potential downside, he couldn't take the risk.

I wondered, though, how much his inability to move around and meet people without Marines or Algerian minders prevented him from forming an accurate picture of the country. I didn't delude myself that I had a clearer idea of things or that my short time here trumped his expertise and intelligence sources. But it struck me that there needed to be some way for U.S. Embassy personnel, in Algiers and elsewhere, to escape their bubble.

On the return trip from the restaurant, my taxi collided with a car on an unlit side street. No great harm done. Still, it jolted me into sobriety, and as the cabbie and the other driver argued who was at fault, a crowd gathered, and I realized that this was precisely the kind of incident Thomas Daughton was anxious to avoid. As for myself, I took notes.

At Ahmed's instigation, I spoke by telephone to Safia Farhassi, the Algerian woman whose husband had been kidnapped and was never seen again. I hadn't expected her to agree so easily to speak with a strange man, especially an American, but she said she'd meet me at the El Djazair. Ahmed explained that she was fearless and accustomed to dealing with foreigners. Since her husband's disappearance, thirteen years ago, she had supplemented her teacher's salary by serving as a tour guide. In her spare time she worked for a national movement that supported the families of missing persons.

So I expected Safia Farhassi to be a Europeanized bluestocking in Western clothes. Instead, she wore a *hijab* and a black burnoose with floral panels on the front. In a corner of the bar, she ordered a cappuccino and told me she saw no contradiction in a female dissident's wearing a headscarf. "It's a choice," she said. "If I was forced by a father or brother or husband, that would be different. To me it's a symbol of freedom of religious practice. Some women regard the *hijab* as a restriction of freedom, but it doesn't have to be that way."

She had done her graduate thesis on feminism as a world movement after the Industrial Revolution, with emphasis on the position of females in Islam. "Women here have more freedom than they realize," Safia insisted. "The Koran says men and women are equal—equal in duties and rights. That's the theory, but not the current reality."

As for her current reality, she was a forty-three-year-old single mother with a thirteen-year-old daughter who had been an infant when the kidnapping occurred. The girl had no memory of her father. Yet in his absence he remained the dominant influence in their lives.

"Djamel was a journalist working in French for Algerian Radio," Safia said. "He was not political as far as I know. He reported people's opinions, not his own. His family was a revolutionary family. His father was FLN, one of the founders of the trade unionist movement. The French threw him in prison and sentenced him to death. But he was saved and released after independence. I'm glad he was not alive when the FLN kidnapped his son.

"Djamel started by supporting the FLN," she told me. "But in 1988, people were asking for democratic change. He was among those people. He believed in democracy. To the FLN this meant you were rejecting them. It was an offense, like a betrayal, treason. But before he died even Djamel's father no longer believed the FLN reflected the people's wishes."

Safia emphasized that "Djamel reported accurately and objectively" and that's what had put him in danger. "He was warned. He got anonymous calls, no different from many journalists back then. He didn't take special precautions. He didn't stay in protected areas for journalists. He told me, 'I didn't do anything wrong. So I don't need to hide.'"

Safia paused, as if she'd like to delete what came next. "He was a good man. He was one of fourteen children. Most of them were blue-collar workers. Djamel was the only one who went to university, and he used his university grant to help his family."

Then she had nowhere to go except back to the day it happened. "He was walking near our house. Witnesses say he was forced into a car. There's no news since that time. Nothing from the government. No demands from any group. At first I had hope. I thought he would come back soon. Then ten days after his disappearance I got a call saying he was kidnapped by the government. But I have no evidence. I have no proof either way and no knowledge of who called me.

"I write complaints to the government. They said they are investigating but have no information. My life became no life. It was like a nightmare. It's still a nightmare. You wake up each morning with hope, but I ended every day very bitter, feeling I have no help, no power, no moral support. The authorities didn't care. Many people were disappearing. So it was a time of frustration and disappointment for years and years.

"When Bouteflika came to power, I had hope that he could be a savior and give us answers and tell us the fate of our loved ones. I was upset when he couldn't do anything. He could just bring reconciliation. But the truth is also important. I am in favor of reconciliation, but everybody needs to know what happened. The big thing for the future is for this not to happen again.

"By '95 the families had started a movement for the disappeared. The government says six thousand are missing. We believe the true number is between ten and fifteen thousand. And the majority of them were kidnapped by the authorities, by the army."

"How do you know that?" I asked.

"Because when Islamic groups kidnap people, their bodies are left where they can be found. It's part of the terror, to frighten the population. But when the government took people they were never found."

"What's the government's reaction to your movement?"

"I've been warned many times. Especially in the '90s, I got anonymous phone calls telling me to stop. And I said I won't stop until you release my husband. Whenever our movement spoke with journalists or with Human Rights Watch or Amnesty International, we were followed. It's not as dangerous now, but we still don't have the mechanism for stopping and punishing kidnapping. I can be kidnapped at any time."

But fear for her own safety was secondary to worry about her daughter and the damage this was doing to the young girl. "With a baby at home and a husband missing, I couldn't be as good a mother as I wanted to be. I regret I was too busy, too upset trying to find my husband. I still avoid her questions. She only knows her father disappeared and he could reappear. She knows also that he's probably dead and will never come back. When my own father died . . ."

Safia lost her composure and started crying. I offered to stop the interview, but she insisted we go on. "When my father died, I didn't take my daughter to his tomb because I didn't want her to ask 'Where is my father's tomb?' This is the hardest part—not being able to explain to a child where her father is or whether he's dead or alive."

"Where does your strength come from?" I asked.

"I don't know." She dried her eyes on a cocktail napkin decorated with hearts and swizzle sticks. "From religion, I suppose. Also, it's my education, and I'm from a family that participated in the revolution. I have two uncles who were martyred by the French. They add strength. And my job and my independence helped me get over the hardship. I have seen many women in my situation, but with no education, no families to help them."

She was on the verge of sobbing again but became furious instead. "Even if our husbands or sons did something wrong, why are we women being punished? If our men are criminals, at least tell us what they did and where they are. As it is, they are torturing us and our children. And it's not finished yet. We don't have any rights or any justice. The reconciliation, the moral regeneration, is incomplete. We still don't know who are the criminals and who are the victims.

"There also has to be a recognition of how this has affected families in practical terms. This is a rich country, but they pay compensation of one hundred and sixty euros a month. You can't find a place to live or support a family on that. We suggested they build a counseling center to deal with the psychological impact. There has to be a program for children in particular. The kids are bitter and angry. The government has to settle this problem at the roots, so there aren't future terrorists. The kids are young now, but we have to avoid horrible things ahead. In the countryside I hear boys saying they will join the fighters in the mountains, not just to avenge their dead fathers, but to avenge the suffering of their mothers."

Sorrow surged through me along with guilt for upsetting her with questions. But she thanked me for my interest and hoped that I would write about "the disappeared." Despite all that she had gone through, she said, "it's not too late for the government to make things right. But it has to regain the people's trust and confidence."

On a blustery, overcast afternoon, Ahmed drove me out to the university, a bleak compound on the fringes of the city. The dorms and classroom buildings had all the hallmarks of Stalinist architecture, of the former Soviet Union's unerring instinct for constructing edifices of unimaginable ugliness. They reminded me of the interchangeable *paneláks* in Eastern Europe, Central Asia and Africa—wherever Russia had imposed its right-angled mind-set. In Algeria, it was as if some bitter educational czar had determined to make conditions in these tenements unbearable so that students would finish their courses quickly and clear out.

Ahmed stopped on a dirt lot strewn with trash and tumbleweeds of esparto grass. Wind buffeted the car. "Now we wait," he said. "He'll come after he finishes praying at the mosque. He doesn't want to be seen talking to a foreign journalist at a hotel."

I didn't understand this need for secrecy. If the man had accepted an amnesty and repented of terrorism, why this rigmarole of a rendezvous on a vacant lot and an interview in a parked car? What was he afraid of? Or should I be scared?

Ahmed explained that the man—I didn't yet know his name—maintained his contacts in the mountains and the loyalty of certain people who might still be active insurgents. He had to protect them and take care what he said. He harbored political aspirations, but had to proceed cautiously. His talking to a writer was a way of testing the waters, Ahmed said, and of keeping his name, whatever it was, alive.

As bearded students in djellabas streamed back to the campus from the mosque, a red car swung onto the lot, circled Ahmed's car, checked us out, and sped off. I was acutely aware of how simple it would be to set me up. As Daughton warned, repentant terrorists could change their minds. For years the news had been full of stories about reporters taken hostage by men they had come to interview. Daniel Pearl's kidnapping was the best-known and most tragic case. But there had been others. David Rohde of the New York Times held the distinction of being kidnapped twice—once in Bosnia, then again when he went to meet a Taliban official.[8] If it could happen to prominent reporters with powerful corporations behind them, I couldn't kid myself that I was bulletproof.

Although the air felt combustibly dry, it began to rain, and the drops were speckled with dust. Having brewed up in the Sahara, the storm brought as much sand as water, and the windshield quickly crusted over. *Pioggia del sangue* was the Italian term for it—blood rain.

---

8. Rohde escaped from the Taliban in the spring of 2009.

A metallic grey van pulled onto the lot and parked parallel to us, about five yards away. "It's him," Ahmed said.

"Before we start," I said, "let's get this straight. I'll speak English and you translate my questions into French."

"Your French is fine."

"No, do it my way. It'll give me time to take notes, and while you're talking to him in French, I can follow it and decide what to ask next. Don't use Arabic."

We ran to the van through the gritty drizzle. I got into the backseat. I didn't want anybody behind me and I wanted to watch them both.

The man at the wheel was big, overweight and in his late forties. He had a trimmed mustache, an unruly beard and a prayer bump on his forehead, the first I had seen in Algiers. He wore a khaki skullcap, or *chachia*, and a striped burnoose with a grey sport coat over it. He shook hands ceremoniously and had no hesitation about supplying his name, which Ahmed spelled out for me as Madani Mezerrag. His former position was leader of the Armée Islamique de Salut (AIS), the military wing of the FIS.

When I asked how active he had been, he grinned. His expression was disarming, as long as you didn't look too deeply into his eyes. "I was always ready. I never said no."

He came from Kaous, a village about two hundred miles east of Algiers, and he was the father of six children. He had been "political" since the age of eighteen and had started fighting in the mountains at thirty-two. He stayed there eight years. "I didn't hide from the army. I fought it. I've never denied that. It was a war. I can't estimate how many battles there were. Airplanes, helicopters, everything was after us. We lived among the people. They had the same convictions as us, and the terrain helped. It wasn't easy for the government to pursue us."

The serenity of his voice, the placidity of his face, the banality of the leaf-shaped deodorizer dangling from the rear view mirror all contributed to the incongruity of the scene. Madani gave off no menace, only a sleepy boredom. Perhaps it was because he was speaking French. Maybe in Arabic he would have sounded sinister. The substance of what he said was out of sync with the lazy way he said it. He might have been dreamily recalling adolescent pranks, not events in a merciless war that had resulted in a million casualties and two hundred thousand deaths.

To break the amiable flow of his monologue, I asked how he had gotten started as a terrorist.

"The Boy Scouts," he said. "It began with the Boy Scouts."

"Are you serious?"

"Very serious. The Boy Scouts taught us how to form cadres. It gave us tools and values. The Scouts are a military organization. You learn to tie knots and build fires and feed yourself in the woods—all the things we needed to survive in the mountains. The Boy Scouts taught us about honor and duty and obedience. During the war for independence, the PPA [Parti du Peuple Algérien] and the FLN also profited from the Scouts. So it's not unusual that the AIS benefited *beaucoup*."

I glanced at Ahmed. It crossed my mind that he and Madani might have concocted a practical joke. The Boy Scouts! What was to prevent Ahmed from hiring some fat, bearded imposter to tell tall tales about his years as a terrorist?

Madani went on to discuss his involvement in the re-Arabization of Algeria, weaning it from French influence. At the university, he had worked for a movement to have courses taught in Arabic and passports and IDs translated into Arabic. "The regime was contrary to us," he said. "After liberation the country was supposed to be founded on religious principles, but it stayed secular and still part of colonial France. We favored pure Islam. We wanted a war against drugs and prostitution and bad behavior."

"What turned you to violence? What about the kidnapping and killing, the throat-slitting and bombing?"

"It wasn't my decision to take action and arm myself." Madani sounded unruffled. "It was the course of events. The government forced these events. The FIS agreed to go along with the law and with elections in 1988. But when the FLN realized that the majority of Algerians preferred national sovereignty, welfare and democracy under Islamic principles, they annulled the election."

Even then, he claimed, the FIS didn't resort to violence. "We weren't convinced that it would do any good to use the iron arm [le bras de fer] against le pouvoir. We didn't act until the government pushed the situation to the next phase with its coup d'état."

In early 1992, Madani was arrested on charges of inciting unrest. "They sent me to a concentration camp in the Sahara."

"Were you tortured?" I asked.

Again he smiled. "When you are in your enemy's house, anything can happen. Let's say I became sick, and they transferred me from the desert to a hospital in Jijel. I escaped on May 19. The government offered a reward of 4,500,000 dinars [about $100,000] for my capture. They searched for me everywhere. They printed my picture with a beard and a computer image of what I was supposed to look like shaved."

"Who helped you escape?" I asked.

He refused to acknowledge that he had needed accomplices. But he conceded that once he was out of prison, on "my native ground, my family and faithful followers helped me. I had brothers who shared my convictions. Some dissidents left Algeria. Some hid their beliefs. Some fought back. My group believed only by arms could we find a solution."

Outside, the drizzle kept falling, and the crust of sand on the windshield liquified into a bloodshot eye. I asked about the amnesty. How had it come about and why had he accepted it?

"The people we lived among in the mountains became tired of the pressure and that made it more difficult for us," he said. "In the woods my group and others like it weren't just isolated in Algeria. We were cut off from support from Tunisia, Morocco, Libya and in the Arab world. So we decided to take what the government offered."

"What did you get apart from a guarantee that you wouldn't be punished?"

Ahmed appeared reluctant to translate. Perhaps he considered the question an insult. The amnesty was a sensitive topic. The Salafi'ist Group for Preaching and Combat (GSPC) had declined to reconcile with the government and had allied themselves with Al Qaeda. Those who did abandon armed struggle and supposedly repented often acted like conquerors and expressed no contrition. They paraded around the country in camouflage uniforms as if they were active guerrillas. One ex-AIS leader drove an armored Mercedes.

I gestured for Ahmed to go ahead and ask Madani. For the first time, Ahmed spoke in Arabic. "Speak French," I said, but he ignored me.

Bristling, Madani replied, "People believe that the FIS and the AIS rejected dialogue. That's wrong. We always accepted negotiations. From the start it was in our literature that we sought negotiations. We began to *dialoguer* with the government in 1994. It went on for years. Bouteflika had direct contact with us. By 2000 everybody agreed that if Algeria continued like it was going it would be the end of the country. You ask what I gained from the amnesty. I gained Algeria, my country, my land, my people, its history and religion."

Ahmed, speaking Arabic again, asked a question of his own, and Madani said to me in French, "You want to know what I lost. I lost my position, my brothers who died, many years of my life. But now we have a true accord based on Algerian sovereignty, democracy and independence under Islamic principles."

I doubted the government would agree that its principles matched Madani's. I mentioned the six dead municipal guards in Médéa. Whoever killed them surely didn't believe that "a true accord" existed.

"That's a different matter," he said. "An aberration. The government hasn't moved things forward fast enough, and that provides an excuse to those who still fight in the woods." He thought that elements of *le pouvoir*, the government within the government, indirectly financed a low-level, ongoing insurgency. Because they feared that a complete cessation of conflict would be bad for their interests, they turned a blind eye to the arms and explosives that flowed to the former GSPC.

Shifting his weight behind the steering wheel, he said, "Let me show you how much the situation has changed in Algeria. We can sit in my car and talk. We can walk in the streets together. We can drink tea. But before the amnesty, even if you brought NATO troops with you, we couldn't do that. We'd have to meet in the mountains and maybe I'd kill you. People still get killed, but the process is moving. *Le pouvoir* has to keep it going. I never regret accepting the amnesty. I will carry on and struggle within the constitution. I was never against the law. I was forced to defend myself. When the other side accepted a solution, we accepted it too. Now we'll see where things go."

Ahmed and I hurried to his car. The drizzle had turned into a downpour, washing the red sand from the windshield. As we drove back to the El Djazair, I wanted to believe what Madani Mezerrag had told me, I wanted to believe that Algeria had changed. But Ahmed must have intuited my doubts. "Tomorrow I'll bring you something to read on the train to Oran. It'll answer all your questions, even those you didn't ask."

The next day we settled our accounts—always an awkward moment fraught with the possibility of misunderstanding. Arabs have a reputation as sharp traders, hard bargainers, and all too often in tourists anecdotes as blatant cheats. But during my trip, not a single one stiffed me except for the good folks at Egyptair. Ahmed accepted the envelope I handed him without bothering to count the cash. He gave me a bottle of water for the train—"a souvenir," he said—and a photocopy of an article from *Jeune Afrique*, a French magazine.

As we headed downhill into central Algiers for the last time together, he warned me to watch my luggage on the train. But he swore
there was little danger. Not like the old days when fanatics yanked
the emergency cord, stopped the train and poured through the compartments robbing and killing passengers. Back then the Algiers-
to-Oran railroad had been the most dangerous in the world.

"It's better now," Ahmed said, "because they removed the
emergency cord. When I worked for Michael Palin, he had a whole
compartment to himself. We cleared out the other passengers, questioned them, then let them back on. There were twenty men with
machine guns guarding Michael."

He swung onto a side alley, a shortcut to the station. As he accelerated, a man with a briefcase stepped from between parked cars,
straight into our path. The front fender smacked him hard, and he
went down. I feared he was dead, at the very least badly hurt. But he
bounced to his feet, swinging the briefcase for balance, then sagged
to the asphalt again.

Ahmed burst from the car, spluttering. Miraculously the man
bounced to his feet a second time. He was more apologetic than
Ahmed. He swore he was fine and shook off our help. There was no
chance to say more. We were blocking the street, and drivers behind
us hollered and leaned on their horns.

I arrived at the station badly shaken, almost as if I had been
sideswiped.

"It was so stupid," Ahmed said. "He stepped right in front of
me." He stowed my bags on the rack above my seat. Then he embraced me. We had been through a lot together, maybe too much,

and while I said I'd miss him, I was relieved not to be traveling to Oran with him or anyone else by car.

I asked what he'd like as a gift from the States, and he said, "That book about World War II in North Africa." He meant Rick Atkinson's *An Army at Dawn*. I promised to send him a copy.

My seat was next to a window. Marred by minute bubbles and scratches, the glass magnified the sun's heat and made the outside world look like medicine dissolving in water. On the *quai* waving goodbye, Ahmed slowly vanished from view, and a woman in a *hijab* and a burnoose settled next to me. Her cell phone rang with a Koranic ringtone. She answered in a low whisper and concealed her mouth with a cupped palm as though afraid I'd read her lips. No doubt she thought she was taking a huge risk sitting beside me.

Among the hundred men in the compartments were three other women. Two huddled together. A blond in a T-shirt sat alone, looking as out of place as I felt. A Puma logo was stitched across her breasts. It fit her fierce, feline appearance, which attracted attention but held men at bay.

Labeled *rapide*, the train chugged along in slow motion and stopped at every *bidonville*. In these shantytowns, constructed of scrap lumber and tin cans, passengers clambered off and on, carrying cardboard boxes and plastic bags that looked like the makings of more *bidonvilles* down the line.

When I felt up to it, I read the article from *Jeune Afrique*. Madani's picture accompanied the piece, but his last name was spelled differently from Ahmed's rendering—Mezraq rather than Mezerrag. A pull quote on the first page described him as having "as many deaths on his conscience as he has hairs in his beard."

In the interview, Mezraq said many of the same things he had told me about his arrest and escape, his years in the mountains, the amnesty, his renunciation of terrorism. There was also a bit of the bravado that had made me question whether he might be a poseur. In 1994, a BBC correspondent had asked, "If I meet you, what am I risking?"

"In the best case, an easy death," Mezraq told him. But he gave the guy an interview.

Jeune Afrique speculated about the wealth he had accumulated through robbery and extortion. Mezraq denied he was rich but conceded he had some cars and cash left over from his days as an insurgent. He declined to say more about the money except that it wasn't in African banks and that he depended on it for the well-being of his old troops.

In contrast to his evasiveness with me, Mezraq admitted, "I have killed with my own hands." His first murder "was in 1993, in the region of Jijel, during an ambush of a military convoy. The young soldier was dying when I pulled the Kalashnikov out of his hands. I kept the rifle for years, but I hated it because it always reminded me of the death rattle of the soldier at the moment he gave up his soul."

While he claimed he never harmed innocent civilians, he confessed that he had killed government officials, soldiers, police and gendarmes. Then drawing a Jesuitical distinction between innocent and guilty civilians, he said he had set up false roadblocks and liquidated people suspected of collaboration or of being thieves, racketeers and looters. Almost as an afterthought he added, "Prisoners were systematically killed. Of course this touches me on a human level, but as the leader of a war I couldn't be weighed down by the state of my soul. It was kill or be killed."

Jeune Afrique quoted a grotesque eyewitness account of Mezraq's digging the eyes out of a soldier's face before cutting his body to pieces. Then the article concluded by asking, "Does he symbolize the return of peace or the price of impunity?"

I folded the pages, laid them carefully in my lap and tried to decide how I felt. Frightened after the fact? Foolish for suspecting he was a fraud? The question that nagged me most deeply was whether I had finally met a terrorist or a monster, a rebel soldier or a sadist, a political leader or a psychopath?

Halfway on the four-hour train ride, the hills and farms and grain fields disappeared and were replaced by a flat pebble-filled plain. From the railroad tracks to the washed-out horizon, plastic bags supplied the only color and animation. Sailing along on invisible currents, they resembled sea nettles trailing stingers in their wake. Then, for no discernible reason, the train stopped, the plastic bags subsided and the air conditioning died with a strangle. Almost immediately the compartment became an oven. Sunlight burned through the window like molten lead, and I shifted to the far side of the aisle to escape the heat.

When a boy came through with a cart selling soft drinks, I tried to buy a Coke, but he couldn't break a twenty-dinar bill. A bearded man paid for me and asked if I spoke Arabic. I told him no and asked if he spoke French. He shook his head, and there was nothing more to say. The train resumed, and we trundled along in silence until we arrived in Oran and he handed me a stick of gum and smiled.

ob Parks, the director of Centre d'Etudes Maghrebines en Algérie (CEMA) met me at the station and apologized that he and
his fiancée had plans that evening. I was just as glad to be alone as I
acclimated.

CEMA had booked me a room at the Hotel Résidence le Timgad, an establishment that made no great claims for itself yet maintained that despite the lack of frills, it was functional and friendly
and centrally located. Well, the bellboys were friendly, and the lobby
was brightened by cages of trilling canaries. But the Timgad fell short
on every other score.

The shower dribbled cold spray or none at all. The bedside
phone, on the rare occasions when it had a dial tone, couldn't connect
me with local, much less international, numbers. The toilet, even when
I hadn't used it—especially when I hadn't used it—filled with turds
during the night. And the flat-screen TV was frequently on the fritz.
While the management had no interest in repairing other appliances, it
promptly summoned an engineer for the television.

Via satellite, the set provided the consoling illusion that Oran
was *au courant* with the rest of the world. It had twelve hundred channels of news, stock reports, sports, history, science, weather, science
fiction, real estate, porn, and religion in countless languages and
complexions and costumes. Watching it, I entertained the notion that
a narrative genius—a reborn James Joyce or a contemporary Proust—
might, through judicious cutting and pasting, produce a monumental
pastiche, an epic novel, from this jumble.

As for Timgad's location at the hub of five streets, it was con-
venient during daylight hours, but at night it turned into a scrum
of teenagers, pugnacious drunks and purse-snatchers. To borrow a

term favored by Algerians, it was an area of *hittists*. Derived from the Arab word *hit*, or wall, *hittists* literally meant "those who hold up the wall," and that described a large segment of Algerian male society. More than a quarter of the men couldn't find jobs. So they loitered against walls, shouted at passersby, slap-fought, then scooted when the cops showed up.

My first day dawned overcast and unseasonably cool. I hiked uphill, to rue Larbi ben M'Hidi, a boulevard named after a revolutionary martyr. In a recent French documentary, *Intimate Enemy*, Ben M'Hidi's French captors, now in ripe old age, remembered him as a man of exceptional intelligence, courage and aplomb. This hadn't, however, dissuaded them from torturing then executing him.

In the sixteenth century, long before the French occupation, Oran had been a Spanish garrison town—according to a contemporary account, "one of the most jovial, most rollicking, and wickedest places it is possible to imagine. It gained the sobriquet of *La Corte Chica*, 'the Little Court.' Night and day there was nothing but balls, collations, and festivities, wine-quaffing, cigarette-smoking, guitar-strumming, bull-fighting, love-making and gondoling. It was a *presidario* of pleasure, but every now and then the Arabs or the Turks would come thundering at the gates."

By the mid–twentieth century, citizens of Spanish ancestry still constituted a major part of the population. But the collations, bull-fights and gondoling had died off, and Oran was thoroughly French-ified. Arabs and Turks no longer thundered at the gates, and less than 10 percent of the city was Muslim.

This had been the demographic when Albert Camus lived here and wrote his novel *The Plague*. In the European town, isolated from Oran's small casbah, he had rented an apartment at 65, rue Larbi ben M'Hidi. I found the address, but the concierge had never heard of Camus. At shops and boutiques along the arcaded street, I spoke with a policeman, a few young people and several old people, but nobody recognized the name. Then an Algerian man about my age offered to help. I suspect that he just wanted to chat with an American and recollect the years when he had worked on a U.S. air base in Morocco. I returned three days in a row, and this fellow, nicknamed Bixi, never had any luck at getting me into Camus' apartment.

Parallel to rue Larbi ben M'Hidi, a rambunctious street market ran past blocks of residential housing. Right at their doorsteps people had a supermarket thirty feet wide, a mile long, bustling with customers. I bought fruit and yoghurt and salted peanuts and ate on the move.

I'd have done better to watch where I was going. A passing car grazed my leg and sent me reeling like that fellow with the briefcase in Algiers. The driver didn't bother slowing down. Since I hadn't fallen, maybe that meant no foul.

Bruised but unbloodied, I limped downhill to the rail on Promenade Ibn Badis, gazing out over the port, north toward France. In *The Plague*, as a fatal epidemic grips Oran, the city is quarantined, and characters congregate here, recalling the freedom and space and opportunities that they've lost, and struggling against the fear that they no longer matter to those who once loved them.

The curve of the bay, ships bobbing in the harbor, the heights of Djebel Murdjadjo—none of these could have altered essentially.

More than a thousand feet above the town, the Church of Santa Cruz commemorated an earlier plague, a cholera epidemic that had decimated Oran in 1849. Separated from my wife and family, doubly cut off by the undependable phones, I was suffering one of those dips that seize travelers, an estrangement that verges on the existential if you let yourself ask unanswerable questions: What am I doing here? Where am I going?

Camus had firsthand familiarity with these feelings. World War II had trapped him in France while his wife was stuck in Algiers, unable to cross the Mediterranean and join him. The separation lasted years, and their marriage never recovered.

I walked west toward Mers el Kebir, the best anchorage along the coast. Having slipped like quicksilver through Phoenician, Roman, Turkish, Spanish, French and American hands, this naval base had witnessed human tragedy on a catastrophic scale. Wiped out by an earthquake and tsunami in 1790, it had been rebuilt as a port for French battleships. In 1940, after Paris surrendered to the Germans, the British navy demanded that Vichy France hand over its fleet for fear that it would fall under German control. When the French tarried with their response, the English opened fire on Mers el Kebir, killing 1,300 sailors in a five-minute salvo.

Still battling the blues on this grey day, I circled back to Oran's main square. Originally named Place Napoleon, then Place d'Armes, then Place Maréchal Foch, it had been rechristened Place du 1 Novembre, and adorned with a bust of Moulay Abdelkader. Though there were reminders of French rule—a pompous town hall (bombed by the OAS in '62) and a baroque theater—Algerians sipped mint tea, not wine or cognac, at the outdoor cafés. To ease my aching leg, I sat among them until a wind gusted up and tumbled a few empty chairs into the street.

The military had commandeered most of the land on a promontory near the *place*, but a twenty-five-story abandoned building hovered behind the army installation. A skeleton as stark as any bomb site in Kabul or Baghdad, this skyscraper had started off as a hotel designed by the French architect Fernand Pouillon. But the project had generated controversy and protests that became politicized. Some objected that a resort had no business in this historic district, on the same headland as the Bey's Palace and the Pasha's Mosque.

Then, too, the approach road to the hotel burrowed through the ancient gate of the Château Neuf, which wasn't big enough to accommodate tour buses. To widen it would have required a massive reconstruction project. So the hotel, intended as a symbol of Oran's recovery, had never been finished.

It was hard not to see this as another example of Algeria wasting its oil billions. Why hadn't the hotel been turned into public housing? Why had its grounds been allowed to degrade into a graveyard for wrecked cars? If the Château Neuf was such a national treasure, why had squatters taken over its empty rooms? And having fought to save the Bey's Palace from desecration, how did Algerians excuse its current state of collapse?

Constructed for Sultan Abou Hassan in the fourteenth century, the palace had a royal view of the sea and the city—which was, no doubt, why the Spaniards, the Ottoman Turks and the French occupied it during their periods of dominance. Easily defended and utterly private, its gardens had served as elegant stages for the Bey's self-indulgence and the colonialists' self-importance. But time and indifference had inflicted more damage than any invader had.

A man in uniform let me in and stayed with me every step of the way, as if to guard the palace against vandalism. But only dynamite could have reduced it to a state of greater disrepair. The Salle du Diwan, where the enthroned sultan welcomed visitors, had window frames fanged with broken glass, and the fireplace was as black as a coal furnace. The ceiling sagged and peeled off, exposing bony lathing. The parquet floors had been left to rot.

Le Pavillon de la Favorite, recently renovated, had fallen apart again. Olive trees rooted in the walls and pried the masonry apart. In the courtyard, a dry fountain was bordered by dying flowers and unpruned trees. A birdcage, empty except for dead leaves, rusted in an alcove.

At the harem rooms, wooden struts buttressed each keyhole arch, and the effect was that of seeing a once lovely lady on crutches. In this precinct of pleasure only ashes remained, drifting about like the restless souls of dead concubines.

On a terrace, a printing press, an old-fashioned machine as big as a steam locomotive, had cracked the tiles. "Soldiers left it here long ago," the guard explained.

"How long?"

"Since independence."

"Why don't you haul it away?"

"*Ce n'est pas mon métier*" ("That's not my job").

I couldn't argue with that. I offered him a tip, but he wouldn't accept it. His *métier* was admitting people to the palace. He didn't expect charity for doing his duty.

That evening I attended Mass at St. Eugene's. Santa Cruz used to house the bishop when Oran was a diocese of eighteen parishes. But after only a handful of Catholics didn't join the exodus to France, St. Eugene became the last active church, with a small congregation of aging *pieds-noirs*, Eastern Europeans married to Algerians and refugees from sub-Saharan Africa. They milled around the courtyard before Mass, catching up on gossip and welcoming newcomers. A nun from Burkina Faso introduced herself as *"une Soeur Blanche"* ("a white sister"), then giggled and said, "But I am black." Two other nuns had come to town from the Sahara, where they worked with the nomadic Tuareg tribe, and there were laywomen who provided free medical care and education for the poor.

Brother Michael Sexton, an Australian, gave me a tour of the Centre Pierre Claverie, which was named for the bishop assassinated in 1996, months after the monks at Tibhirine were killed. A fourth-generation settler, Claverie condemned all violence, drawing no distinction between radical fundamentalists and fanatical elements of the Algerian security forces. Infuriated by the bishop's outspokenness and his refusal to take sides, unknown agents parked a car full of explosives next to the rectory. The bomb blew a metal door off its hinges, crushing Claverie.

The wall had been repainted and the doorway bricked up. Its rectangular shape suggested a coffin. Nobody had been charged with the murder. The regime blamed the FIS, which in turn blamed the Département des Renseignements et d'Investigation (DRS or Department of Information and Investigation). *Algeria: Anger of the Dispossessed* claimed that potentially "Claverie's death served a triple purpose for the DRS: not only had it got rid of a notoriously turbulent presence, it had also won over public opinion by discrediting the Islamists and had tied France to the Algerian regime."

To Brother Michael none of this mattered. Claverie was dead, and with him had died an influential voice for moderation. In the rear of the church we paid our respects at his grave. He was buried under the floor. A single flickering candle, a few vases of flowers and a photograph marked the spot.

Boulevard de la Soummam resembled avenue Foch in Paris, with palms rather than plane trees shading the sidewalk. On whitewashed buildings glyphs and black wrought-iron balconies described ornate arabesques. At Restaurant Cintra, where Albert Camus had reputedly written *The Plague*, I joined Bob Parks and his fiancée, Marianne, for dinner, and we spent hours discussing the future. Theirs seemed uncertain; Marianne had to depart soon for a project in Nicaragua. I thought that my short-term path was surer; I would cross into Morocco. But Bob disabused me of that idea.

The border had been closed for more than a decade. Long-standing political differences between a country defined by revolution and one ruled by a monarch had now been complicated by terrorism. While Morocco feared that fundamentalists would invade its territory, Algeria was anxious to keep them from setting up safe havens across the frontier.

After dinner Parks and I went to Meloman. Marianne begged off, and I understood why. The nightclub was deafeningly loud, muscled up with men, and roistering with prostitutes of all sizes and, I'd suppose, sexual specialties.

I had hoped to hear *Raï*, the subversive music of the Algerian streets. A fusion of French and Spanish influences, it had originated in Oran in the 1930s, but as the political climate festered during the '90s, it became an affront to the regime and to Islamic radicals alike. With its raw sexual yearning and scathing opinions, *Raï* had cost some of the most popular performers their lives. Singers were still in danger from government agents and sectarian assassins.

Unfortunately, the Meloman wasn't featuring *Raï* tonight. A band covered American and British hits, and when it broke into "I Will Survive," Parks explained that this disco number had caught on as a defiant anthem during the "black years." "The owner's brother was killed back then," he said.

"Why?"

"Because he was a poet and he refused to be shut up."

As women slithered around us like Apache dancers in an old black-and-white French film, we resumed discussing the future. After hours of drinking, I declared that Parks should marry Marianne. As for my future, he said I should catch a ferry to Spain, then a boat to Morocco. Or I could fly by way of France. At the moment both ideas made me seasick.

I slept hard that night, and woke early to be driven out to CEMA's headquarters where I delivered the same lecture as I had in Alexandria. Among the students in the audience I noticed a nattily dressed old man with a goatee and an ascot. It took a minute to recognize Father Thierry Becker, the priest who had said Mass at St. Eugene's.

Parks invited him to join us for lunch at an Indian restaurant in a pagoda plunked down on a vacant lot. After the late night at Meloman I didn't have much appetite, but the Tandoori chicken strangely settled my stomach.

Father Thierry volunteered to chauffeur me back to the hotel in his ancient Renault whose gearshift jutted out of the dashboard. Despite the flamboyant ascot, he seemed to have sworn a vow of modesty that forbade him from speaking about himself unless directly asked. And when he did talk, he depended on a mélange of French and English that alternated within the same sentence.

Born in France, he was seventy-four and had lived in Algeria for almost fifty years. As a young priest, he had studied Arabic in Lebanon, then hitchhiked across Iran, learning Farsi along the road to Afghanistan. In '62 he came to Algeria to minister to a shrinking congregation of Catholics and "to build bridges with the Muslims. I'm not interested in converting them," he said. "I emphasize our common ground. Have you heard of Father Foucauld?"

Charles Foucauld was a famous French priest who lived for decades among the Tuaregs, never proselytizing, simply bearing witness to his faith. In the end, the Tuaregs had killed him.

"I want to live like him," Father Thierry said. "Not die like him. But I came close at Tibhirine. I was there the night the monks were kidnapped."

"Do you mind talking about it?" I asked, never expecting I'd meet a witness.

"*Pas du tout*. I went to the monastery for a conference. There were twelve of us, all members of an ecumenical group that got together to discuss the interfaith movement. We slept in a separate house from the monks, and one night we heard noise—arguing and screaming and a car motor. We realized something was wrong, but we were helpless. They had cut the phone lines and they had weapons."

"It must have been terrifying," I said, although nothing in Father Thierry's calm voice conveyed that.

"Yes, I was scared. I thought it might be the end for me and I tried to compose myself. I had some dossiers on our work in the Oran diocese, and I prayed that I'd live to finish them. I was afraid they'd be lost and that no one else could deal with them if I died."

"How did you survive? Why didn't they kidnap you too?"

"The terrorists had stolen a minivan, with space for seven hostages. So that's how many they took. They didn't look for more. That's what saved me. When the kidnappers left, I got my flashlight and went to alert people. I didn't dare go to the army post or into town for fear they would mistake me for a terrorist and shoot me. I knocked on doors in the countryside, but no one answered. They were afraid that the terrorists were right behind me.

"I walked back to the monastery, aiming the flashlight at my feet, making as little sound as possible. At dawn when the curfew lifted, I hurried to the army post. The captain was asleep and wouldn't wake up, so I went to the gendarmerie in town and told them. They didn't ask any questions. They didn't appear to be interested."

"Do you think they knew what was going to happen to the monks?"

"Nobody knows to this day what happened," Father Thierry said. "Nobody knows who kidnapped them or where they hid them or what was done to them. We can only speculate." Then he did just that, speculating that "the monks were probably killed with their captors."

"By their captors?" I asked.

"No. *With* them. I believe the government found the kidnappers in the mountains and killed everybody indiscriminately. I think they cut off the heads of the corpses and brought them to a base for identification and that's when they learned they had killed the monks too. So they put those seven heads in a tree and blamed the terrorists."[9]

When I mentioned how moved I had been by the monks' graves, Father Thierry said, "Yes, it's a beautiful spot. But only their heads are buried there. They never found the bodies. That's best. Their bodies are mixed somewhere with dead Algerians, perhaps with the very ones who kidnapped them. The monks were always here for the people, and now they will always be with the people."

As we arrived at Hotel Residence Le Timgad, the *hittists* swung their eyes in our direction, like birds of prey on a fence, scanning a field for rabbits. I asked Thierry if he missed France. Was he ever homesick?

"No. I'm glad I grew up there. I like to visit my family once a year and I enjoy eating foods I remember from childhood. But as for the rest of it, wherever I am, that's where I am."

9. In July 2009 *Le Figaro* in France and *Time* magazine in the United States broke a story that confirmed Father Thierry's speculation. Retired general François Buchwalter, an army intelligence officer who served at the French Embassy in Algeria, told investigators that his sources had informed him that the monks had been mistakenly killed by a helicopter during an attack on a jihadist camp. When the Algerians learned the truth, they blamed the Armed Islamic Group (GIA), and the French, who knew better, stood by that story to protect relations between the two nations. Independent terrorism experts theorized that GIA leader Djamel Zitouni, now dead, had claimed responsibility for the killings when he was in fact a double agent working for the government to foment violence and swing public support behind the campaign against Islamic extremists. According to published reports, it is unlikely that either the French or the Algerians will corroborate Buchwalter's accusations, especially since the two countries have become more dependent on one another as they confront new jihadist threats and permutations of terrorism.

That night at dinner, I thought how much Father Thierry resembled one of Graham Greene's good priests. The sinners and bad priests and damned souls were often Greene's most fascinating characters. The good ones tended to be a little dry and boring, not free spirits or visionaries. Like Father Thierry they kept their feet on the ground, and at the brink of death they worried about their files and who would finish them. There was something to be said about solid, salt-of-the-earth folks in life, if not in literature.

I ate alone at Restaurant le Comète and ordered *salade aux tomates*, lamb shish kebab, rice and half a bottle of wine. I can't claim that this was food I remembered from my childhood. And I can't say that the clientele—nineteen Algerian men and not a single woman— reminded me of people I grew up with. But that was fine by me. After almost two months on the road, I felt wherever I am, that's where I am. And tomorrow, I would be in Sidi bel Abbes and then Tlemcen.

In the car, the sullen driver said little and had no patience with the other passenger, an Algerian linguistics professor. The professor, the pedantic type, switched his attention to me, and as we pressed on into outlying agricultural areas, he identified the vegetation in each field. "Palm tree, olive tree, cypress, almond," he exclaimed in French, like a kid playing a naming game.

I felt under the weather and feared I was coming down with a cold. But I tried to perk myself up and commented that it was a beautiful day. The professor said, "Weather is contextual. In Sidi bel Abbes we have many hot bright days. So for us a beautiful day is one that brings rain."

I zoned out for the rest of the trip and felt guilty for doing so. The point of travel wasn't simply to move through space. It was to be open, to engage with people and enter the life of a place, revel in experience no matter how capricious or maddening. But sometimes I couldn't do it. I wanted to be alone and to be quiet.

At the university in Sidi bel Abbes, the driver parked and started polishing his car while the professor escorted me to the English Department. Bare earth alternated with asphalt and cement. Although not as bleak as the campus in Algiers, this one had the look of army barracks. The students stared at me and giggled. I guessed my days of passing for a Berber were over.

The English Department director, a youngish woman in tailored Western clothes and horn-rimmed glasses, greeted me with a tray of pastries, coffee and tea. Once I had a cup of espresso in hand, she and her staff dug into the honey-dripping sweets.

"You are very famous," the director said.

I regarded this as a question. "Not at all." Her name, if she ever mentioned it, had escaped me.

"You are very modest," she said.

"No, I'm not that either."

"You have done many books. I noticed this on Google."

"Everything's on Google."

"I am not on Google. My colleagues are not. But I am the one person who has been to America."

With that she jumped from my alleged fame to her trip to Minnesota. Her colleagues, who had obviously heard the story before, continued their assault on the sweets. I had time to eat a second pastry and pour more espresso before she interrupted herself, saying, "You must have a tour of our town."

She, the pedantic professor and I piled into another professor's car. "We'll visit our natural lake," the director said, "and then Petit Paris."

We bounced for miles through corn and wheat stubble. The rolling hills, the dry husks and airborne chaff reminded me of the Oklahoma panhandle in winter. But the temperature hovered near one hundred, and a wind out of the Sahara lashed us with sand.

The "natural lake" coalesced as a brown stain at the end of the road. Weeds and willows fringed the shore where fishermen were attached by lines to their reflections in the water. I almost blurted how sad it was that drought had diminished the lake to a puddle. But the director saved me from that faux pas. "It began as a little spring and grew into this. Do you like it?"

I said that I did: "A nice place for a swim on a hot day."

"It's too dangerous to swim. The current is bad."

The pedant corrected her: "The danger is the muddy bottom."

The director ignored him, adding, "I'm glad you see the lake in its natural state. We fear it will be turned into a resort and ruined."

On the trip back to town, the professors texted messages on their cell phones, completing preparations for my lecture. But first I needed to see Petit Paris. "The French gathered here in the evening to remember home," the director explained. "There was a Café Chantant with songs and dances more wicked than in Paris. The Foreign Legion trained in Sidi bel Abbes and they liked to believe they were in France." To me, it looked neither petite nor Parisian.

The Foreign Legion's former base would have interested me far more. I presumed it had a museum commemorating their exploits. But I presumed wrong. Now a school for gendarmes, it was off-limits to outsiders. "Anyway," she said, "we have no time."

In a last fusillade of text messages, we drew up in front of a hall to find a crowd in the courtyard and a janitor jimmying the door. It was locked tight, and he had to rush off and fetch a key. Once inside, he discovered that the PA system was on the blink and wasted twenty minutes monkeying with switches and wires.

In the end, I spoke without a microphone, and when people started leaving, I didn't know whether they couldn't hear me or were bored. Some of them came back, stayed for a spell, then bolted a second time. Late arrivals, early departures and loud returnees punctuated my talk throughout. Losing heart, I leaped ahead to parts of the lecture that I hoped might keep them quiet. But the hubbub didn't cease until it was their turn to talk. Then the room fell respectfully silent.

During the tragicomic Q&A session, I had trouble understanding their English and they could barely follow mine. The pedant posed a question that coiled like a snake eating its tail, an uroborus of dependent clauses and parenthetical phrases that had no beginning and no end.

A female student with an anxious face noosed in a *hijab* asked in a quavering voice, "Why have human values disappeared from the earth? Why does materialism rule the world?"

A young man took vehement exception to America's ignorance of Islam. He said there was no excuse, since Muhammad Ali, Mike Tyson, and Barack Obama were Muslims.

I suffered an eviscerating sense that I had failed to present an accurate picture of the States and failed to acquit myself as anything except a buffoon. But afterward a professor confided in French that he didn't understand English at all; he had attended the lecture "for the experience." For many of them, I was the first foreigner, the first writer of any nationality, the first native English speaker, they had ever met. This day was a cause for celebration. It had nothing to do with me. What counted was the brief contact with the outside world.

The director had organized lunch, and although I was stuffed with pastry, I couldn't beg off—not when I would be denying her staff my company and a free meal. While I forced down a little food, she said, "I have information for your book about North Africa. The men differ from country to country. In Algeria we call Tunisian men *'femmelette'*—weak like little women. Men in Morocco we call *'sidi'* because they carry themselves like princes. But men in Algeria are *rjala*, which means macho."

"And sexist," I suggested.

"*Bien sûr*," she agreed.

Tlemcen lay less than two hours southwest of Sidi bel Abbes. Exhausted, emotionally drained and scratchy-throated, I was definitely coming down with a cold and planned to check into the Hotel les Zianides and collapse. But the desk clerk handed me a message to call someone named Adnan at the university. Adnan said it was his assignment—and his pleasure, he hastened to add—to give me a tour of the town. When I demurred, he sounded hurt. So I said I'd meet him in twenty minutes.

"What would you like to see?" Adnan asked. "I assume you know Tlemcen has the best examples of Moorish architecture outside of Morocco and Andalucia."

I confessed I was bone weary and needed a strong coffee before I saw anything.

The café on place Mohamed Khemisti was crowded, all its outdoor tables occupied by boisterous young men. So we crossed rue de l'Indépendence to a café so quiet we could hear the murmur of afternoon prayers at the nearby Grand Mosque. I ordered a double espresso; Adnan drank fruit juice. He was an excellent English speaker, a trim, flat-bellied, sporty-looking fellow in a Lacoste knit shirt, tan slacks and polished loafers. But he had a melancholic air and spoke wistfully of his sabbatical in London years ago. Now he was married and had children and doubted he would ever get back to Europe. He was forty-something and acted as if his life were over.

Adnan seemed to embody something Jean Paul Sartre had written about colonialism: "The European elite undertook to manufacture a native elite. They picked out promising adolescents; they branded them as with a red hot iron, with principles of western culture, they stuffed their mouths with high-sounding phrases, grand glutinous words that stuck to the teeth. Then after a short stay in the mother country they were sent home whitewashed." Now a lot of those "whitewashed" intellectuals were trapped. After the "black years" and especially after 9/11, no one wanted academic exchanges with Arabs in general and Algerians in particular.

Conscious of cheering him up, and myself at the same time, I told Adnan that Tlemcen struck me as prosperous and peaceful compared to Algiers and Oran. He reverted to French for his reply. *"Ici, on a souffert beaucoup."*

"You personally have suffered a lot?" I asked.

"Everybody did." He indicated a hotel down the street that had been bombed during the '90s.

"Thank God those days are over," I said.

"They're not. This week the police got a tip that a terrorist had returned to Tlemcen. They surrounded his house and shot him dead. It's not as dangerous as it was, but sometimes things remind you of how it used to be.

"Jihadis targeted professors and teachers," he went on. "The greatest danger was in villages where teachers had no protection. They never knew whether the people they worked with during the day, or their own students, were insurgents at night. In one rural town, nineteen teachers were killed. No one knew who was responsible. That's why we all asked, 'Who's killing who?'"

In Tlemcen during those years, he said, "the streets emptied after dark and people stayed indoors out of fear. The mosque shut down and didn't open for the night prayer. People prayed at home. We couldn't travel. The border with Morocco where we always went— it's just fifty kilometers away—closed down. Then we couldn't even walk around in our own town."

"How was it at the university?"

"Very tense. The Groupe Islamique Armé ordered female students to cover their hair. They sent letters to professors warning us to announce in class that the women should wear headscarves. I turned the letter over to the rector. It wasn't up to me to enforce such a rule. But some professors were frightened and read the letter in class, and the government arrested them. People didn't know what to do. Either way they risked punishment."

He quoted a poem from that period by Tahar Djaout. "'You'll die if you don't wear the veil / You'll die if you do wear the veil / So shut up and die.'" Adnan added, "Djaout himself was killed in 1993."

I finished my espresso and followed Adnan to the Grand Mosque. We removed our shoes and padded into the courtyard, where men washed their feet at a fountain. I had once lived in Spain, in Granada, and the tiles here, the great waterfalls of faience, reminded me of the Alhambra.

Suddenly a man started screaming and brandishing a Koran.

"We'd better go," Adnan whispered.

"Why? What's he saying?"

"I don't know. I think he may be foolish." It took me a moment to understand that Adnan meant he was mentally unbalanced. "He's accusing us of making fun of the mosque."

We retrieved our shoes and retreated on a side street. Adnan was embarrassed and eager to put the mosque behind us. On a meandering lane in the medina, a boy with a twig broom swept string beans into a pile, then gathered them in a basket. Spice stalls lined the crooked length of an alley, cleansing the air. Cardamom, dill, anise and coriander—I liked the colors as much as the smells. Bin after bin of saffron, cinnamon, green tea leaves, cloves and peppers.

Then the smells, the color, everything curdled. Bombed-out houses were full of shattered furniture, twisted pipes and naked wires. Some had places been pulverized; not a single brick or cinder block was intact. Bulldozers had flattened the outskirts of the neighborhood into a parking lot.

"We call it Kabul," Adnan said, "because it looks like Afghanistan. Nobody rebuilt after the bombing."

Determined not to end on a downbeat note, Adnan drove out to the ruins of Mansourah. The name meant "victorious," he said, and victory had been the goal of the Merinid invaders from Morocco who had laid siege to Tlemcen in 1299. As the campaign dragged on for eight years, their camp grew into a town of its own, with forty-foot walls and an enormous mosque.

Feverishly orthodox dynasties had repeatedly attacked out of the western desert, heaven-bent on reforming lax Muslims, punishing sinners and plundering the wealth of decadent cities. Then these devout invaders turned soft themselves and were set upon by the next band of purists. The cycle continued to this day.

Eventually Mansourah fell, and Tlemcen was victorious, growing, in the words of nineteenth-century author George Harris, into "a city of light and genius . . . its kings were lovers of the arts, science and literature. The Court was numerous and brilliant; the army was disciplined, brave and well commanded; they coined their own money, had their police, judges, etc. In one word, Tlemcen was one of the most civilized towns of the world . . . when different nations of Europe were hardly awakening from their long lethargy."

That was what Adnan wanted me to carry away from Tlemcen—an appreciation of its glorious history not a mental snapshot of mangled houses and a madman in the Grand Mosque. The minaret at Mansourah stood after seven hundred years, a tall orange flame towering over acres of silvery olive groves.

During the night, my sore throat worsened, and by morning I had a wracking cough. The university delayed my lecture an hour while Adnan drove me to a pharmacy for cough syrup and lozenges. There was never the slightest chance of a cancellation, not when a crowd had assembled and the English Department crackled with anticipation. If I weren't feeling so lousy, this might have been flattering. As it was, I wondered who the students and professors imagined they had come to see. They treated me like literary royalty, and I found this disconcerting. Quite apart from my cold, I didn't like how readily I slipped on the scepter and raiment—or cap and bells—of a public sage.

Afterward, at a lunch with faculty members, they asked me to return to the campus for an informal talk. I used my illness as an excuse. But Adnan volunteered to take me to the pharmacy for more cough syrup. I mentioned that I needed to get back to Oran; he said no driver was available until tomorrow morning. A true diva might have dug in her high heels, but I didn't have the balls of Elton John or Madonna.

Woozy and chilled, I submitted myself to a round of questions that afternoon.

"Do you write for money or fame?" a student demanded.

"You must be very rich," someone shouted.

Adnan cut off this line of inquiry: "Would you say you have a classical or a colloquial style?"

I explained that American English, unlike Arabic, didn't have a classical style distinct from the way people actually spoke.

"So you write in the demotic," a professor said, "to get more readers and more money."

The students didn't disparage writing for money. Most of them were poor and wished they were rich. But it troubled them that I had quoted Sigmund Freud to the effect that "a great part of the pleasure of travel lies in the fulfillment of these early wishes to escape the family and especially the father." To them this sounded heretical. Who would abandon his family? Who dared turn his back on his father? "Such a person," one boy said, "stinks in the nostrils of Allah."

"So none of you wants to get away?" I asked. "Nobody wants to travel?"

The response was glum, glowering silence. When Adnan pulled the plug on the afternoon session, a girl in a *hijab* lingered and handed me a gift-wrapped package. "These are from my father's shop," she said. "Eat them as thanks from me."

It wasn't until that night at the hotel that I opened the pastries and found a note. "I write in French," it read, "because my English is not good. We all want to leave. But we do not have money and we are not brave."

On the way back to Oran, I asked the driver to detour to the Moroccan border. "Only *trabendo* crosses," he said, using the Algerian expression for "contraband." "With a bribe you might reach Oujda in Morocco. After that there are roadblocks and the police would arrest you."

"Then what?"

"They'd send you back. Or if you're not lucky, you'd go to jail."

I debated whether to wing it. I had no reason to return to Oran. There, I'd just have to sail to Spain or fly to France and double back to

Morocco. Already I had a sense of things winding down—my health, my stamina. If I left North Africa, would I have the willpower to pick up my overland itinerary again? In travel, as in other enterprises, momentum is crucial. Why not sneak into Morocco and chalk up whatever happened as material?

But I didn't do it, and when I reached Oran, I didn't regret it. The Timgad had improved in one respect. The reception desk had saved a message from a friend of friends in the States. Answering an earlier call, he agreed to meet me.

Tahar was a successful businessman of forty-eight, married with three kids. He wore linen slacks and a sport shirt hanging loose at the waist. His strong jaw was matted by a beard—not a fundamentalist's mane but the five-day growth favored by trendy fellows in Paris. Sturdily built, about my height—six foot one—he told me he played basketball.

That had been my sport and I still had dreams about soaring in like Michael Jordan for thunderous dunks. The apogee of my actual, as opposed to my fantasy, career came in high school when, with the city championship already lost, future Hall of Fame coach Morgan Wootten inserted me in the lineup for forty-seven seconds to guard future Hall of Famer Dave Bing. The last time I had been on court, I told Tahar, was with the legendary Julius "Dr. J" Erving. I let him digest that for a moment before I admitted that Dr. J had been shooting hoops at one end of a public court in Amherst, Massachusetts, while I played horse at the other end with an English professor.

Then Tahar told me the high point of his career—he had played for the Algerian Olympic team—and I thought it best to change the subject.

We zoomed east in his SUV along the coast, out past the Sheraton Hotel, to one of Tahar's projects—a block of apartment buildings and offices. He swore that he didn't speak English, and although I suspected he spoke it better than I did French, he said he didn't mind my grammatical mistakes. He wasn't a linguistic or any other kind of snob.

After I had admired the unfinished buildings, we backtracked to the west side of the city, to a headland where we climbed out for a view of Oran as evening fell. "It used to be one of the most beautiful places on the Mediterranean," he said. And from this perspective, it still looked lovely.

Farther on, we got out again and strolled beside the sea. Tahar talked about 9/11, a topic that obsessed the Arab world. While Americans accepted the events at face value, many in North Africa disbelieved the basic narrative. They doubted that the World Trade Center had been destroyed by hijacked airplanes. It wasn't only fanatics and ill-informed people who felt they hadn't got the whole story. Tahar was educated, worldly, with a background in architecture and engineering, and he cited scientific evidence that he said called into question whether the towers had been brought down by airplanes.

"You are the strongest country in history," he said. "How could this happen? I'm sorry. I don't want to insult you. But this would mean America is weak."

"No nation can protect itself completely from people prepared to die," I said.

This didn't satisfy Tahar. For him, strength amounted to imperviousness. If a nation could be attacked, it was weak. And since

America was demonstrably powerful, 9/11 must have been a conspiracy, maybe of Bush and Israel, the CIA and Mossad.

The clatter of a dump truck on the beach road interrupted our conversation. Chinese workers were crammed into the truck like so many cattle. Glad to get off 9/11, I asked about the influx of Chinese into Algeria.

"For a businessman, they are a good answer," Tahar said. "I use them on my projects, and it's a dependable system. You don't pay them directly. You pay a lump sum to a middleman and he pays the workers and their transport and housing. They live in barracks like soldiers, the same as they do at work sites in China. They make about two hundred euros a month, twice what they earn at home. I'm sure it's a hard life and lonely. But after a year they go back and have money."

When he invited me to dinner, I thought he meant at his house. But Tahar called his wife by cell phone and curtly told her he was eating out. Then we went to place de la République, to Restaurant le Corsaire. Tahar bragged that it had the best fish in the country. It also had a basketball court on the parking lot, and a couple of boys were shooting hoops. "Shall we?" Tahar asked.

He called to the boys in Arabic, and one of them tossed him the ball. We each took a few shots in the dying light, and it gave me inordinate joy to sink my share of layups and jumpers, to work up a sweat and feel my heart pounding, to glance away from this familiar game to the unfamiliar geometry of the medina and marvel at my good fortune. "Now I have a new career high," I told him. "I've played with an Olympian."

"And we both have a better appetite," he said.

As we ate, I asked whether I could visit one of the Chinese labor camps. He promised to look into it and let me know. True to his word, he showed up after breakfast the next day and drove me to the outskirts of town.

An unpaved road thudded over a baked field to a compound surrounded by a barbed-wire fence. The gate was guarded, and gigantic earthmoving equipment and dump trucks parked like tanks along the perimeter of the property, adding to the impression of a military base. Not a tree, not a shrub, not a blade of grass grew on the rock-hard ground. And in the unrelenting heat, not a soul was in sight. The Chinese, Tahar said, worked in shifts around the clock, eight hours a day, seven days a week. When they weren't on the job, they rested.

Above the door to one of the identical concrete barracks, a sign in French and Chinese exhorted: LET US UNITE AS A SINGLE MAN AND WORK CONSCIENTIOUSLY.

Tahar's middleman met us, and a Chinese girl in a tight red T-shirt handled the introductions. With her short-cropped hair, porcelain features and wide, dark eyes, she resembled a *manga* figure from a Japanese cartoon. Her name was Claire, and she translated for the boss, who spoke no French. She had studied languages in China, and Algeria was the first and only foreign country she had ever visited.

In a lounge that contained the minimum of furniture and light, the four of us sat on leatherette chairs, one to each side of a plastic coffee table. Tahar told them that I was here to learn, and that they should feel free to answer my questions as if he weren't present.

I laughed and said, "You could always leave."

Tahar laughed too, but he stayed. Claire answered my first questions without consulting the boss. There were a hundred men at this base, she said, and more than fifty thousand Chinese elsewhere in the country. "They come, of course, for the money."

When I mused that it must be hard for them to live in a different culture, far from their homes and families, Claire said, "They have the habit of working like this. Americans come to Algeria, too, and live in compounds. The difference is they come individually and we come in groups. It's our culture. Here in the compound it's like they remain always in China. They eat Chinese food. They sometimes go to Chinese restaurants." (Tahar later told me they also frequented bordellos that catered to Chinese.) "This way they concentrate on the job, finishing well and quickly."

"Are they allowed to leave the compound when they're not working?" I asked.

Claire translated for the boss, and after an animated exchange in Chinese, she answered, "They don't want to leave the compound."

"Please understand that I'm trying to get an idea of the human dimension of their lives."

When she translated this, the boss held his silence. I glanced at Tahar; he didn't say anything, either.

"If they wanted to," I pressed her, "could they leave the compound on their own?"

"Always we have problems of security. The workers like to go out. But the boss prefers them not to. It's better for productivity for them to avoid trouble and not to drink." It occurred to me that Claire might have been saying this as much for Tahar's benefit as mine. "We have problems also of car accidents and accidents on the beach.

When a worker is hurt, it takes two or three months to get a visa to bring in somebody to replace him."

"Are you saying that for a year they are forbidden to leave the compound?"

This prompted a longer conversation with the boss. Then Claire told me, "I can't answer your question. It's beyond the limits of what I am free to say about our policy."

That ended the interview. Claire shook my hand and made a small bow. The boss scraped himself off the chair and presented his limp hand. Then Tahar and I left, and climbed into the oven of his SUV. We didn't speak until the AC kicked in.

"Algeria isn't alone in hiring Chinese labor," he said. "They're everywhere in Africa and in Europe. It's the reality."

"I don't question that." What I did question seemed too insulting to say. Tahar had been generous and hospitable; how could I tell him that the compound struck me as no better than the Bantustans in South Africa during apartheid?

But he wouldn't allow me the moral luxury of condemning the system in silence. "You're imposing your cultural standards," he argued. "You're not seeing things from a Chinese point of view or from mine."

"I'm curious. Tell me your point of view."

"I'm not a racist. I admire the Chinese and their willingness to travel anywhere and work. Would it be better for them to stay home and have no money and no jobs? Would it be better that houses and roads here not get built?"

"In my opinion, it'd be better for the Algerians to build things themselves."

"We don't have the skills. We don't have people willing to do this work."

"That's what we say in the States. White people won't do these jobs. Black people can't do these jobs. So we import millions of Hispanics and pay them peanuts."

"Well, that's what things are worth on the marketplace. It's a global economy. You can't afford to pay locals five times the going rate, especially when they don't work as hard or as fast. You have to outsource. That's what we're doing. The difference is, instead of sending jobs to China, we bring the Chinese here. And instead of letting Hispanics starve as illegal aliens in terrible conditions, like in the United States, we have an agreement with the Chinese that regulates everything."

"Yes, it regulates them behind barbed wire. They may accept it, but only because they're poor and desperate."

"Don't make it sound like I put them in prison."

"Tahar, you're a man of the West, with European—"

"No," he broke in, "I'm not a man of the West. I'm in the middle. The West doesn't accept me. To Europeans and Americans, Muslims are inferior. But the Chinese don't treat us like that. They respect us and we respect them and neither of us feels inferior to the other."

"You're not my inferior," I said. "I'm sorry. You've been kind to me, and I'm grateful."

Tahar bumped up onto the curb in front of the Timgad. Much as I didn't like to part company on these terms, there was no time to smooth things over. The *hittists* crowded around the SUV, rocking it.

"Be careful," Tahar told me, and as I got out, he gunned the engine and sped away.

From my room, I watched the street and the waxing and waning of the crowd. Periodically a police car stopped at the intersection, and the *hittists* dispersed down side alleys. Then, once the police left, the *hittists* crept back until the next squad car appeared.

I had invited Brother Michael and Father Thierry to dinner. Brother Michael showed up first, and we waited in front of the Timgad for the French priest, bumped and muttered at by *hittists*. Brother Michael glanced overhead. "I always check whether there are surveillance cameras. Some places are safe. Some aren't." He told me he had seen a man stabbed at a nearby square. The assailant had been tasered by police and carted away unconscious.

Brother Michael dialed Father Thierry's cell phone and learned that he had parked on a parallel street and would meet us at the restaurant. After dinner, two squad cars commanded the middle of the intersection, and the walls were clear of *hittists*. Just another night of Algerian street theater, I hoped.

Tomorrow I was scheduled to fly to France. I had discarded a lot of clothing and books along the way, and it took me no time to pack.

Yet eager as I was to join Linda in Paris, I had mixed feelings about leaving North Africa. There was a sense of unfinished business, loose ends, a fraying of the tight fabric of the trip. It seemed I had been here all my life, and I couldn't imagine what it would be like to stop traveling.

A bellboy woke me in the morning to say I had a visitor. Tahar wanted to buy me breakfast before I went to the airport. He wouldn't hear of eating at the Timgad. He insisted on the Sheraton.

In Oran, this American-style luxury hotel had inspired a popular song about a poor boy who longed to make love to his girlfriend there. For me, the Sheraton represented the world I had been away from and would be returning to—a world of climate control, deep-pile carpets, room deodorizers and breakfast buffets behind plastic sneeze shields.

"One of your projects?" I asked Tahar.

"No, Italians did it. With Chinese labor."

He said no more. He didn't need to. The splendor of the place made its own statement in defense of his position. As Adnan had at the magnificent ruins of Mansourah, Tahar wanted to show me his vision of things and what he hoped I'd remember about Algeria. The Sheraton was, as he saw it, a step in the country's reintegration, a cooperative venture based on a win-win principle, he said, not the zero-sum economics of Anglo-Saxon culture.

Over coffee and croissants we discussed the chances of his visiting our mutual friend in America and stopping by for a stay in Key West. I told him we could play basketball. There was a court two blocks from where I lived.

Tahar liked the idea. He said he liked me and hoped we'd keep in touch and have more talks. When I apologized again for my poor French, he said, "For both of us it's a second language. People in France would make fun of us equally."

The security drill at the Oran airport suggested the Islamic fundamentalist imperative that initiates should "become in the hands of their sheik like a corpse in the hands of the corpse-washer." Outside the terminal, two guards scrutinized my ticket and passport. Inside, a guard at a roped-off area reviewed the same papers. Then an airline agent compared my documents to the data on his computer. From there I proceeded to official passport control, where standards were more stringent. A soldier examined my visa and asked, "Did you have a letter of invitation?"

"Yes."

"Whose invitation?"

"*Centre d'Etudes Maghrebines en Algérie*," I said. "I lectured at universities."

He asked to see the invitation. Then he wanted the names of the universities and the hotels I had stayed at in each town. My bags and I passed through a metal detector, and this rang no alarm bells. But a soldier subjected me to a full-body frisk that included both testicles and the length—by now shriveling—of my penis.

Once in the waiting room, I assumed the worst was over. It had barely started. The flight was called, and passengers had to show their passports and boarding passes again at the gate. Then there was another pat-down and a manual search of carry-on bags before we boarded a bus to the plane.

A new platoon of security agents accosted us there, and we had to scramble through the luggage laid out on the runway, claim our bags and carry them to the baggage handler. At a folding table, an officer pawed through the contents of our carry-ons a second time, and a soldier stopped us for a third frisk at the bottom of the staircase to the plane. At the top, a man ordered us to raise our arms and spread our legs while he waved a metal wand up and down. Finally my trip to Algeria, which had started in Ain Draham with a hike across a muddy field, ended with a French stewardess asking what I wanted to drink.

Two hours later I landed in Paris, where rain thrashed the chestnut trees along the Seine. In my hotel the TV broadcast footage of riots that had broken out in Oran. *Hittists*, their faces masked, stormed under the arcades along rue Larbi ben M'Hidi, breaking shop windows and stoning police cars. I didn't know whether to feel lucky to have gotten out in time or disappointed that I had left too soon.

MOROCCO

The rampage in Oran lasted three days. Despite fears that it would spread to the rest of the country, it was slowly robbed of oxygen, and guttered out.

Looking on from France, I felt I was guttering out myself. My sore throat went from a wretched cold to a respiratory infection. For weeks I holed up shivering in the late-spring rains. Then I moved over to London for medical care, a course of antibiotics and a slow convalescence.

I wasn't up to resuming the trip, and not simply because of sickness. After the intensity of Algeria, I suffered an emotional let-down, too, and didn't care to go through the motions of traveling the last four hundred miles of North Africa. Instead I interviewed experts on Morocco, arranged contacts in the country and planned to fly there during Ramadan, the Muslim month of fasting. Meanwhile, I continued to monitor events.

The Italian government had agreed to pay five billion euros in reparations to Libya for the damage it had inflicted on the country during the colonial era. In return Libya cracked down on the boat people who set sail from its shores for Italy.

Secretary of State Condoleezza Rice paid a visit to Tripoli, the first high-ranking U.S. official to do so since Richard Nixon, then vice president, in 1957. Rice's visit thrilled Moamar Qaddafi. He told Al Jazeera television, "I support my darling black African woman. I admire and am very proud of the way she leans back and gives orders to Arab leaders. Yes, Leeza, Leeza, Leeza, I love her very much." But when there was no substantive improvement in U.S.–Libyan relations, officials in Tripoli began to question what they had gained by renewing diplomatic ties with Washington.

Stories out of Algeria turned more troubling. On August 3, 2008, a bomb exploded in Tizi Ouzou, injuring twenty-five. On August 10, a suicide bomb killed eight and wounded nineteen at a popular beach outside Algiers. This was seen as retaliation against the police who had killed a dozen people suspected of responsibility for the bomb in Tizi Ouzou. The next night, an explosion injured three more policemen.

On August 17, terrorists attacked a convoy near Skikda, north of Constantine, killing thirteen soldiers. Their uniforms were stolen and their heads cut off.

On August 19, a suicide car bomb exploded in Issera, east of Algiers, killing forty-three men who were applying to become gendarmes. The blast wounded forty others.

On August 20, two bombs struck the town of Bouira. One went off in a hotel, killing eleven guests.

In reaction to these incidents, the Algerian government announced that the battle against Islamic terrorism was in its "terminal phase." One brave Algerian journalist puckishly deconstructed the logic of this claim: "According to this political discourse . . . the increase in attacks represents undeniable proof of the defeat of terrorism. The more terrorism collapsed, the more the attacks increased." By this reasoning "the stronger terrorism becomes the fewer the attacks will be."

When the bombings stopped altogether nobody knew whether this meant that terrorism was stronger or weaker. But an Algerian friend who traveled to the country during this period wrote me: "People seemed distanced from life. I can't say they were cynical. They were completely aware of the political reality, but they went about their daily life as if untouched. What else to do? I kept thinking I was witnessing a frenzied need to live; not a Camus-like embrace of life. No, it was, rather, an unruly, lawless bravura throwing of one's self into whatever. Since there was no fear to be felt (they had experienced death from very close for a decade) they threw themselves into existence, good or bad, honest or dishonest . . . It seemed the land where 'homo homini lupus' (man is wolf to man). I do not acknowledge this place as my past city/people."

In early September, fully recovered, I went with Linda to Oujda, a Moroccan city across the border from Algeria. Although it had a population of a million, it looked like a war-torn town with a last few refugees rattling around in shell shock. The heat alone—a hundred and three degrees—was enough to unhinge anybody.

The Hotel Oujda, a high-rise on the main street, Mohammed V, promised air conditioning. It promised everything you'd expect from an establishment that once catered to businessmen when Oujda enjoyed a thriving international economy: restaurant, bar, souvenir shops, major credit cards accepted.

But the lobby was dark, the front desk deserted, the shops closed and the restaurant and bar abandoned. A teenage receptionist tottered out of a back room, his hair disheveled and his eyes rheumy from sleep. He had been fasting flat on his back, drowsing away another day of Ramadan. Since strict observance dictated that he not eat or drink between dawn and sundown, he showed scant sympathy when we begged for coffee. He said everything was shut for the month. But then he whispered that if we wanted it badly enough, he had a connection, a guy in a pastry shop, who'd help out if we told him who sent us.

Our room looked over a mosque and Eglise St. Louis, a splendid gothic church locked tight. Because the air conditioner was busted, the desk clerk switched us to a different room, where the AC functioned but the bathroom floor was under an inch of water. That was our choice—fiery heat or cold water on the floor. We chose wet feet.

Then we set off to score some coffee. The pastry-shop owner, a winking, wised-up fellow, motioned us into a back room. From the kitchen drifted the heady aroma of *shebbakia*, a sweet served at *iftar*, the evening breaking of the fast. He brewed a couple of cups of café au lait, threw in a side of pastry and left us to sin in privacy.

From past Ramadans, I remembered a more relaxed observance in Morocco. Like Tunisia, the country was supposedly secular and moderate. It had a thriving wine industry and brewed its own beer. While mountain villages and desert oases remained conservative, larger cities commonly imitated Western styles in clothing, music and, to an extent, sexual freedom. So I wondered whether I was witnessing in Oujda a regional fervor or a national shift toward orthodoxy.

I also wondered how much of Oujda's somnolence was due to Ramadan and how much to the closed border and resulting business slump. Was the city sleeping or dying? In the best of times, it would never have been mistaken for an attractive place. A frequent battleground for Roman, then Muslim, armies, Oujda had once been ruled by invaders from Tlemcen, who unhappily passed on none of its Andalusian opulence.

Bab el-Quahab, the entrance to the medina, literally meant "gate of heads"; the severed skulls of criminals used to hang here. Now drooping heads were attached to living bodies. The few shopkeepers open for business looked tired and resigned, and after a day of fasting they didn't have the spunk to cry out to customers.

Men lollygagged in cafés from sheer force of habit, hunched over tables without eating or drinking or smoking. Waiters wouldn't have anything to do until dusk, which would officially begin when in natural light a black thread could no longer be distinguished from a white one.

Because Ramadan fell this year during a brutally hot month, Morocco had gone off daylight saving time to hurry the sundown. But it couldn't come soon enough. Restaurants dressed their tables early, setting out plates and cutlery, along with the traditional *iftar* meal of *harira* soup, dates, milk, hard-boiled eggs, semolina bread and sugar pastries. In a scrupulous display of self-discipline, families sat and stared at the food but wouldn't touch it before the *muezzin* called.

On boulevard Mohammed V, the pulse quickened. Workers on the way home ducked into shops to buy bowls of *harira*. Some places sold the soup in clear plastic takeaway bags. According to the *Lonely Planet* guide, "Even Moroccan McDonald's offers [*harira*] as part of their special Ramadan Happy Meal."

At last the cry of the *muezzin* skirled across the darkening sky: "I praise the perfection of God, the Forever existing. The perfection of God, the Desired, the Existing, the Single, the Supreme; the perfection of God, the One, the Sole: The perfection of Him who taketh unto Himself no male or female partner, nor any like Him, nor any that is disobedient, nor any deputy, equal or offspring. His perfection be extolled."

As the prayer rang out from minarets around in the city and circulated through the streets, everybody started eating at once. Even curbside beggars gnawed at crusts of bread and gulped free paper cups of soup. People at sidewalk tables urged us to join them.

Cars reappeared. Having broken their fast at high speed, motorists maintained that accelerated pace, ignoring red lights. Far from dying because of the closed border, Oujda thrummed with life. Turning the clock upside down, the population slipped into narcosis during daylight hours, then roistered around most of the night. A local newspaper claimed many Believers gained weight during the month. Which raised the question—was Ramadan a fast or a feast, a penance or a party?

By the time Linda and I returned to the hotel, the air conditioner had shorted out. So the desk clerk moved us to a third room.

From the window, I peered down at the mosque where worshippers thronged the front steps and spread into the square onto vast carpets. Sandals and shoes formed a fringe around them.

By morning the crowd and the carpets had vanished, but several pairs of sandals hadn't been reclaimed. The carpet in our own room had mysteriously turned into a rice paddy, and as we packed, our feet squelched and splashed. Then the handle to the door fell off, and we had to summon the clerk to unlock it from the hall and let us out.

It was good to have Linda along to laugh with. Traveling solo had its advantages. But so did having a companion. Many travel writers brought along wives or lovers and then concealed this from readers. Bruce Chatwin and V.S. Naipaul, to name two examples, made it seem they were alone on trip after trip when in fact they had had company. Each man probably feared that candor about personal matters would undermine his pretensions to Olympian objectivity.

We drove north in a rental car through a wilderness of pebbles that the wind had raked into geometrical patterns, as if in a Japanese garden. The road followed the frontier beside *oueds* that, surprisingly in this season, oozed a trickle of water the color of dried blood. Women knelt on the banks washing clothes and spreading laundry to dry over camel-thorn bushes.

A short way from Oujda, at the town of Saïdia, the road deadended at a river lined by pink and white oleanders. On the far shore, Algerian flags snapped in the breeze and ropes beat against the poles like halyards against masts. There were no signs to mark the border, but everybody knew where it was, and any smuggler who cared to sneak across undoubtedly knew how to do that, too.

We swung around to the west and confronted a no less dramatic border between old Saïdia and the new international resort of the same name. Still under construction, still in its embryonic stages, the project had already grown to a grotesque size. Villas, golf courses and identical semi-detached townhouses sprawled to the horizon.

The development had sparked protests throughout the country and as far away as Canada. In 2007 the European Environmental Agency reported that Morocco had lost seven of its forty-seven Mediterranean beaches to erosion and pollution. A spokesman for the UN Development Program in Rabat pointed out that the Saïdia resort was "too close to the mouth of the river which has the richest ecosystem" and to the Moulouya wetland, an important habitat for two hundred species of migrating birds. Moroccan environmental campaigners complained that Fedesa, the Spanish corporation in charge of the project, had "dug up 6 kilometers of dunes and killed thousands of tortoises just so you can see the sea from the corniche." Destroying a juniper forest and despoiling one of the last pristine sections of the coast, it had also left the land vulnerable to flooding.

Fedesa and the government argued that the resort would create jobs. With a third of its population under fifteen years old, the country had an unemployment rate of 20 percent that figured to rise. But was a community of luxury vacation homes constructed in a fragile environment the answer?

At the marina, a guard smacking his meaty palm with a billy club gave us the once-over, then waved us through the gate. The harbor had berths for hundreds of yachts, but only a trimaran and a schooner registered in London were in port. Empty at the moment, restaurants and fast food outlets—Le Tuareg, Luigi's, the Oriental,

Le Voile Bleu, La Bodega, the Casse Croute, the Quick, and the Hollywood Canteen—were poised to open for *iftar*.

On the dock, a solitary worker heard the cry of the *muezzin* and dropped to his knees while a trio of jet-skiers sluiced over the water, sending up rooster tails of spray. In Morocco the jet ski had become synonomous with the youthful monarch, King Mohammed VI, who was often photographed riding a wave runner.

In a break with the autocratic and often cruel reign of his father Hassan II, the king had freed thousands of political prisoners and dissidents, and granted nine thousand of them financial reparations. Television coverage of Morocco's Truth and Reconciliation Commission hearings was watched by the largest audience in the nation's history. In 2002 a newly seated parliament passed legislation allowing for municipal elections; the teaching of Berber in state schools; and a divorced woman's right to property ownership, child custody and financial support.

Still, Mohammed VI had his critics who pointed out that he owned twenty-seven palaces and miles of mountain and waterfront property, all maintained at staggering cost by a staff of servants, administrators and security guards. In a country with half the population of the United Kingdom and only a fraction of its wealth, the king spent eighteen times more than Queen Elizabeth II on household expenses, and *The New York Review of Books* revealed that he wore $50,000 vicuna suits.

According to the 2005 UN *Human Development Report*, of 177 nations surveyed, Morocco ranked 124th (Libya ranked 59th, Tunisia 89th). To paraphrase the French adage about Morocco's being a cold country that just happened to have a warm sun, it sometimes appeared to be a poor country that just happened to have a rich king.

As for human rights, while Mohammed VI had redressed some past wrongs, there were signs of backsliding into old draconian policies. Allying himself with the American war on terrorism, he had alienated many of his subjects and driven some into extremism. There were those who believed that the deadly bombings in Casablanca in 2003, and the even more lethal bombings orchestrated by Moroccans in Madrid in 2004, showed the extent to which the king had lost touch.

Rumored to be complicit in "extraordinary renditions" for enhanced interrogation, Morocco had recently found itself accused by a U.K. citizen, Binyam Mohamed, of having imprisoned him for a year at the behest of the United States. Court papers filed by Mohamed contended that "he was routinely beaten, suffering broken bones and, on occasion, loss of consciousness. His clothes were cut off with a scalpel and the same scalpel was then used to make incisions on his body, including his penis. A hot stinging liquid was then poured into open wounds on his penis where he had been cut. He was frequently threatened with rape, electrocution and death."

And yet . . . Mohammed VI was by far the youngest and by consensus the most enlightened and forward-looking leader in North Africa. On that slender reed floated hope for the future.

W e pushed on to the fishing village of Ras el-Mar, where islands, like chunks of sea glass, lay scattered across the bay. The Jaafariya islands belonged to Spain, which maintained stringent control of these specks of land, just as it did the rest of its real estate along the coast. In 2002, when six Moroccan soldiers occupied an uninhabited rock known as Perejil, or Parsley Island, the Spanish responded by sending in troops. Only U.S. intervention prevented the opera buffa standoff from deteriorating into open warfare over territory the size of a baseball field. While Spain harrumphed about preserving its national sovereignty and worrying about drug smugglers and human traffickers, the suspicion was that Madrid feared that losing any of these islets would provoke demands that Ceuta and Melilla, the last enclaves of their African empire, be ceded to Morocco.

The *rocade*, or coast road, kept the sea in view on the right, while on the left, the Rif Mountains appeared to tilt over the pavement in a seismic wave. Another of North Africa's shatter zones, and not just in topographical terms, this dramatic countryside had been inhabited for centuries by Berber tribes who resisted pacification. Not so much a lawless region as a law unto itself, the Rif had fought in the 1920s and again in the '50s to win its independence.

In 1921, under the leadership of Abd-el Krim, an army of Berbers annihilated twenty thousand Spanish troops. It was the worst defeat that Europeans had ever suffered at the hands of an indigenous African army, and the Berbers managed to hold the Spanish at bay for the next five years. In the end, it took the combined forces of Spain and France to suppress the rebellion. And even then the tribes were never really conquered, just temporarily subdued.

After the fall of the French and Spanish colonial protectorates, in the mid-'50s, the Berbers bridled at the notion of being ruled by bureaucrats in Rabat. They mounted another in their long history of guerrilla campaigns and found Moroccans every bit as brutal and repressive as European colonizers had been. The Moroccan Royal Army attacked in 1959 with tanks, artillery, airplanes and twenty thousand troops. This ended the insurgency but not the hostility.

Today the area retained its reputation for insubordination and instability, and its fierce resentment of the government was more than matched by the government's imperiousness with the Berbers. The fact that Riffians depended on the cultivation and export of *kif*, or hashish, for a major part of their economy complicated the quarrel. Fields of *kif* flourished within sight of the road. Yet local authorities chose to ignore it and the dealers, middlemen and customers who flooded the area.

Beyond Nador, en route to Al Hoceima, Linda spotted a parked car with its hood raised. The driver frantically waved his arms. My impulse was to keep on going. The guy didn't look like a dealer or a narc, a *kif* grower or smuggler, but why take a risk?

Linda thought otherwise. She maintained that it was the law of the desert to help travelers in distress. It didn't matter to her that we were on the seacoast, not in the Sahara. She shamed me into stopping.

The driver, a nicely dressed fellow, spoke excellent French and was deeply beholden. His Peugeot had what he believed to be valve problems. The engine had conked out and he couldn't restart it. I volunteered to fetch a mechanic from the next town.

"You won't find anybody before Al Hoceima," he said.

"Good. That's where I'm going."

"Would you like a ride?" Linda asked.

Before I could break in to tell him we didn't have room, the guy said, "No, thanks. I can't leave my car. Someone will steal it. My brother owns a shop in Al Hoceima. I will write him a note, and if you'll bring it to him, he'll know what to do."

As Linda and I set off again, I felt compelled to defend my reluctance to get involved. I reminded her of what had happened on one of our earliest trips to Morocco. The incident was what had kept me from stopping in Tunisia this May for the men begging for water in the desert outside of Tozeur.

In 1972, we had driven south onto the high desolate plateau around Ouarzazate, when we spotted some women walking barefoot with bundles of thorn branches on their backs. They propped themselves up with wooden sticks and looked like crippled three-legged creatures. They were obviously in agony, at the far limits of exhaustion, and I wanted to help. But how? There wasn't room for them in the car, and offering them money seemed beside the point.

Linda suggested we give them our bag of oranges. So I stopped, and the women ran—or tried to run. The bundles on their backs kept them from going far. A few of the braver ones edged closer, eying the oranges. They looked old, with crooked spines, wind-braised skin and black teeth. But actually they were young, a couple of them no more than children.

Chattering in Berber, they begged for the oranges but were too scared to come near enough to grab them. So I tossed one to a girl, and she caught it—only to have a bigger girl snatch it from her. I threw a second orange, and the big girl stole it too. So I lobbed one straight at the bully, who dropped the two she had to catch it.

Suddenly they all started shouting and shoving and scratching for the fallen oranges. Afraid the smaller girls would be hurt and get nothing, I waded in to separate them. Most girls galloped off in terror, but one of them tumbled onto her back, pinned to the barbed branches. Her shrieks of pain stopped the rest of them, and as she squirmed and pleaded, they took advantage of the confusion to pick up the oranges.

Leaning down, I looked into the screaming girl's eyes. She was more frightened of me than of the thorns in her back. To keep me from touching her, she kicked her legs. My hands fumbled, slick with blood, to haul her upright. She yelled and spat and beat at me with bony fists. I lifted her by the arms, and the bundle clung like a burr. I shook her, and as the branches pulled away from her flesh, she sank her teeth into my arm until I let her go.

The scene had stayed with me for decades. I had had dreams about it. I had written about it as fiction. I dreaded repeating it—a naive effort at help that only caused pain. As Graham Greene has written, innocence is a blind leper without a bell spreading disease wherever he goes.

The land turned freshly plowed, each harrow as raw as a surgical incision. Then, in some bizarre micro-environment, the fields were bone white and broke into badlands of wind-tormented rock. In Al Hoceima we had no difficulty finding the stranded driver's brother.

His shop, one of the few open during Ramadan, sold djellabas, leather handbags and hassocks—standard fare for a summer beach town.

But the season had ended, the tourists had left and Abdou, the shop owner, was on a ladder, repainting his sign. Seeing us, he scurried down, and since his hands were sticky with paint, he presented an elbow for me to shake. He knew half a dozen languages, because, he told us, he had traveled the world as a circus acrobat. Now white-haired and white-bearded, he still had a robust build and a springy, pigeontoed grace.

After rinsing his hands with turpentine, he read his brother's note and passed it to a boy who left the shop while Abdou offered us tea. I thanked him and said no. But he herded us into a room behind the shop and insisted that we had been kind and generous and must let him reciprocate in the traditional manner.

We sat cross-legged on the carpeted floor as Abdou ceremoniously prepared two tea trays—one for the teapot and glasses, a smaller one for the silver boxes of mint and sugar. He washed the green tea to leach away its bitterness, then added mint and sugar and boiling water. As the tea steeped, he entertained us by talking as a *bu-ttabla*, or Master of the Tea Tray, is supposed to do.

"Moroccans believe we have been drinking tea forever," he said. "But in the beginning it was a luxury for the royal court. Common people didn't drink it until a hundred years ago." He repeated a joke I had heard before: "We came to love it so much, someone suggested we sew a teapot on our flag instead of the green star. After all, doesn't a teapot look like the typical Moroccan man—short, with a big belly and a spout curved up?"

He poured the tea, raising the pot high to add froth to our glasses. "I am fasting," he said. "But you go ahead. Travelers don't need to fast."

Linda sipped hers and said it was good. I did the same. Etiquette demanded that we drink at least two glasses, and as we started on the second, Abdou asked if we had any medicine. "Aspirin or pills for pain," he specified.

"Do you have a headache?" Linda asked.

"It is for my grandchildren, when they have fevers."

Linda took some Tylenol from her purse.

"Thank you. These are expensive and difficult to find. Let me give you a gift in exchange." Springing to his feet, he unrolled a carpet. "It's my best. An antique."

"We couldn't," Linda said. "It's much too nice."

"Yes," Abdou agreed, "but after your help for my brother and the medicine for my grandchildren, I want you to keep it. I am a poor man and cannot afford to let you have it for free. I ask only what I paid for it."

The sweet tea started to cloy. I shouldn't have been surprised and certainly not upset, but after crossing Egypt, Libya, Tunisia and Algeria, I had counted on making it to Tangier without getting conned. "We're not in the market for a carpet," I said. "We can't carry it with us."

"I'll ship it to your home."

"We won't be there for months. And we have only enough money for our trip."

"You pay what I pay. Make me an offer."

"It's a beautiful carpet." By now I was biting off my words, suspecting the entire episode had been a setup. The driver beside the road, the note to his brother—just gimmicks to get us into the shop. "We have to be going." I helped Linda to her feet.

"If not a carpet," Abdou said, "what about Berber jewelry?"

Furious, I shook his turpentine-scented hand and touched my heart, thanked him for his hospitality and left the shop feeling like a jerk. Linda, however, found the whole thing funny. "What do you suppose the note said?" she asked. "'Another sucker's born every minute?'"

We spent the night in Al Hoceima, in a hotel above Plage Quemado. There wasn't a soul on the beach. In this former Spanish garrison town, an aura of permanent siesta prevailed. Off the coast, another chunk of Spain broke the sea like a battleship at anchor. The island of Peñon de Alhucemas had been a military base and a prison, then a staging ground during the war in the Rif. The Spanish army hadn't had to advance far to engage the enemy. Abd-el Krim's camp was at Ajdir, six miles away.

In the countryside around Al Hoceima ruined houses and flattened barns suggested recent bombardment. An earthquake measuring 6.5 on the Richter scale had struck the district in 2004, doing far more damage than a seismic event of that strength should have done. Even new buildings—especially new buildings—had collapsed.

In a postmortem, scientists discovered that sand dredged from the sea had been used on construction projects, and its high salt content had weakened the foundations. Hundreds of people had died needlessly—the final toll was 564—because of lax inspections and governmental corruption. Riots erupted in the Rif, and

Berber tribes once again regarded themselves as victims of Rabat's indifference.

In the middle of the night, Linda got a message on her BlackBerry that my American Express card had been compromised by charges at a garage in Brooklyn and a tattoo parlor on Times Square. She viewed the alert as proof positive of the benefits of the cyberworld. I saw it as a pain in the ass. Linda didn't argue the point, simply cancelled my card online and said, "This makes yesterday's con man seem like an amateur. At least we got a couple of cups of tea out of him."

Before leaving Al Hoceima, I asked at the hotel about the road west. The map showed it as a green squiggle, like a garter snake kinked along the sparsely inhabited coast. Was it paved? Was it passable? Could we count on finding gas and food?

The desk clerk reacted as if I had implied that the Rif was primitive and he was a savage. He swore there was a highway to Tangier and huffily wished me bon voyage.

As promised, a dual-lane *autoroute* with guardrails and a flower-planted median strip headed out of town. At this rate we figured to reach Tangier in a few hours. And I wasn't pleased at the prospect. I hated to end the trip on a boring high-speed throughway.

But the countryside was some compensation. The sea was turquoise in the shallows, cobalt blue out in the channel. The land was rich with mineral pigments, a patchwork of green, orange, red and purple. Villages of flat-roofed huts clung to hillside ledges beside soccer pitches with fishnets as goals.

Though still straight and smooth, the highway gradually lost its grace notes. The signs vanished, then the yellow lines, then the guardrails. The median strip turned to dust, and finally the asphalt dissolved. Linda said something that I ignored. I didn't care to think about what these changes might signify. But then fate or Allah or a road crew with a rotten sense of humor dropped something into our path that couldn't be ignored—an enormous stone. There was space to pass it on the side, and that's what I did, driving on until we confronted two stones. Slowing down, I noticed there was room to squeeze between them.

"This is silly," Linda said. "We should turn back."

"I don't think so."

"What do you make of these rocks?"

"They're roadblocks."

"Right, and that means the road's closed."

"No, they're police roadblocks. But it's Ramadan, and the cops are sleeping."

We came to a bridge, an unfinished one of poured concrete pylons and metal rods. Linda whispered one word: "Mike." But I followed the well-marked detour signs down an earthen ramp, across a dry wash, and up a ramp back to the road.

"See," I said.

"I vote that we turn back," she said.

I pushed on. When we passed a few people, I depended on them to reassure Linda, even if they were on donkeys, not in cars. The women rode, the men walked beside them, everybody laden with baskets and plastic bags. It was market day, and the women wore straw sombreros with red cotton tufts on top and braided strands on the hat brims. We stopped and bought some fruit, and tried to ask about the road ahead. But nobody spoke English, French or Spanish. They didn't even speak Arabic. They were Berbers—*Imazighen*, as they call themselves, "the people"—and they spoke Tamazight.

The women had henna crosshatchings on their hands and on the soles of their feet, and their faces were tattooed with tribal markings and signs of their status. Unmarried. Married. Pregnant. Widowed. A few had blue crosses on their foreheads—a Berber, not a Christian, symbol. They subjected Linda and me to perplexed stares, just as we did them.

Farther on, the road shriveled to one lane, studded with stones and deep gullies. Climbing from the beach, it was a goat path tracing natural contours in the land. Linda, who's afraid of heights, fell silent, but I knew what she was thinking, what she was feeling. In terror, she wanted to turn back.

Still, I drove on. There wasn't room to turn around even if I had wanted to. Which I didn't. I was set on seeing this through. We soared hundreds of feet, then a thousand, above the coast. The sensation was more like flying than driving, and the flat white beaches down below might have been landing strips.

The washboard corrugations of the piste reduced our speed to a crawl, and for hours we clanked and rattled along, passing no one except for farmers precariously balanced on steep fields, tilling *kif*. This north coast of Morocco, which to my knowledge had no name and was mentioned in no tourist brochure, rivaled for sheer beauty and wildness the most spectacular drives I had taken through Big Sur, along the Amalfi Coast, around the Cape of Good Hope, over the western shore of Zanzibar, and the jungle route that in the early '60s connected Acapulco with Zihuatanejo. And we had it to ourselves—again, except for the *kif* cultivators and the occasional *kif* dealer in a four-wheel-drive SUV.

On the corkscrew descent toward Jebha, Linda's tension ebbed. Wild figs and oleanders and banana plants flourished beside white-washed houses. Fishermen sold the day's catch in baskets woven from palm fronds. A few of them spoke French and told us we had finished the worst part. They promised that *petit à petit*, the road improved to the west. Alternately we could cut inland to Ketama. Either way we wouldn't reach Tangier before sundown.

I kept to the coastline. I had fantasized that my entire overland trip across North Africa would be like this. A slow, soul-stirring journey through terrain that avalanched into the sea, past coves as white as fingernails, through villages where brightly painted boats were dragged up on the sand and men sold shrimp and limes.

Rather than that fantasy, I explained to Linda, my travels had too often taken me through tacky resorts, sprawling slums, stretches of desolation and debris. So now that I was in the place I had dreamed about, no matter how rocky the road, I intended to stay on it.

"But it doesn't make any sense," she said. "We could have an accident or a breakdown."

"The whole project doesn't make sense. That's its premise—to go wherever and do whatever and see what happens."

"What if we get stuck here overnight?"

"We won't. But if we do, it's part of the experience."

"You're crazy. You sound male menopausal." But as she had done for decades, she gave me the green light, and we continued.

Much as I liked driving, I wished I had asked her to take the wheel. Seldom in a spot to scribble notes, I had to depend on shaky memory and shaky sidelong glances. Afterward everything seemed skewed. Had the beach at Targa actually been black volcanic sand? Was there really a Spanish castle, like a child's creation, atop the town's largest rock? Was it my imagination or had men in the mountains truly cast fishing lines hundreds of feet into the Mediterranean? Had we passed haystacks that were the shape and color of *shwarma*, and had we watched farmers sidestep down the hills and slice off slabs of it to feed their sheep? Had I, in my idiocy, followed a Mercedes sedan off the main track and onto a dirt trail, thinking the driver knew a shortcut? And had that ferociously mustachioed driver stopped to say in French, "I don't know where you're headed, my friend. But I'm going to my house and this is a private driveway"?

Yes, I believe all this happened. And that by the time we got to Tangier, Linda still thought I was crazy, but she loved me and understood why I did what I did.

In 1972 , when she and I had first traveled to Tangier, we drove south from Paris through France and Spain over rural roads, behind trucks hauling oranges and lemons. Fruit tumbled to the asphalt and was pulped under our tires, so that we cruised along on the smell of citrus. To add to the intoxicating sense that we were launched on the sweet life, our car was a new, fire-engine-red BMW. Although back then a Beamer had none of the pejorative yuppie connotations that it has since acquired—it cost just $1,000 more than a VW Beetle—it was a sleek, powerful machine that drew admiring glances everywhere we went.

It didn't escape me, however, that there was something out of joint about a twenty-nine-year-old novelist and his young wife pitching up in Morocco in such a fine ride. So as soon as the ferry docked, we garaged the BMW and checked into a $2-a-night flea-bag that smelled of clogged drains and uncured animal pelts. Then we set about searching for Paul Bowles, as though he were a kind of alternate-lifestyle customs officer, the one person who could authenticate our arrival.

Bowles and the city he inhabited seemed synonymous; both existed in an ether of hash fumes, hallucinatory dreams and existential angst. By the time Linda and I landed there, Tangier had lost its status as an International Zone, loosely administered by eight nations—England, France, Spain, Italy, Belgium, Holland, Portugal and the United States—whose citizens lived tax free while the locals serviced everything including their sexual needs. After Morocco gained its independence, in 1956, most of the brothels and gay bars shut down, and the tax exiles and currency sharks swam off to more promising waters. But Tangier retained its reputation for sexual escapades, cheap living and weird vibes.

It also continued to attract artists, writers, renegade socialites and trust fund babies with an appetite for high jinks and low life. Jack Kerouac, William Burroughs, Brion Gysin, Jean Genet, Allen Ginsberg, Tennessee Williams, Truman Capote, Joe Orton, the Rolling Stones, Barbara Hutton and Malcolm Forbes all breezed through for a spell. As described by American novelist John Hopkins in *The Tangier Diaries*, it was "the white city poised atop the dark continent . . . a place where there are more shoeshine boys than shoes," an exotic microcosm that bore comparison to Alexandria during the Cosmopolitan Era.

But only Paul Bowles and his wife, Jane, put down permanent roots in this rare earth. As Bowles wrote in his autobiography, *Without Stopping*, "I had always been vaguely certain that sometime during my life I should come to a magic place which, in disclosing its secrets, would give me wisdom and ecstasy—perhaps even death." Tangier was that place, and once he settled there, Bowles never looked back. He believed "that which has finished is finished. I suppose you could say that a man can learn how to avoid making the same actions which he's discovered were errors. I would recommend not thinking about it."

To characterize Bowles as an expatriate was not so much to understate matters as to miss the larger point. He was the consummate outsider, the emblem of alienation, and his passage through life could be calibrated by the bridges he burned behind him. He defined himself by what he abandoned—America, Western culture, male and female lovers, and one successful career after another.

As a surrealistic poet, he had started publishing work in *Transition* magazine at the age of sixteen. He dropped out of the University of Virginia after a single semester and befriended Gertrude Stein and Alice B. Toklas in Paris and Christopher Isherwood in Berlin. Then he returned to the States to study musical composition under Aaron Copland and wrote the scores for half a dozen Broadway and off-Broadway plays, including *The Glass Menagerie*. Among his friends were Orson Welles, William Saroyan, W.H. Auden, Benjamin Britten and Dashiell Hammett. A polymath, he produced a libretto based on Federico Garcia Lorca's play *Yerma*, translated Jean Paul Sartre's *No Exit* into English and edited Jane Bowles's novel, *Two Serious Ladies*. Then he began writing his own fiction.

Of his marriage to a lesbian, Bowles said, "We played every-thing by ear. Each one did what he pleased." Jane lived in a separate apartment with her Moroccan maid and lover, who was later alleged to have fed Jane a poison that addled her brain.

After the publication of *The Sheltering Sky*, *Let It Come Down*, *The Spider's House* and several short story collections, Bowles shed another skin, quit working on his fiction and recorded the music of desert and mountain tribes. Then he transcribed Moroccan folk tales and the life stories of illiterate street boys, among them Mohammed Mrabet and Mohammed Choukri.

Bowles's address was in the Petit Socco, near the Grand Mosque. Lined by louche pensions frequented by prostitutes of both sexes, the area, as Bowles described it, was one of "eerie illumination and distorted distances, of covered streets like corridors with doors opening into rooms on each side, hidden terraces high above the sea, streets consisting only of steps, dark impasses, small squares built on sloping terraces so that they looked like ballet sets designed in false perspective . . . the classical dream equipment of tunnels, ramparts, ruins, dungeons and cliffs . . . a doll's metropolis."

Convinced that we'd recognize Bowles from his photograph, Linda and I spent days exploring this doll's metropolis before we discovered that he didn't live there. The Petit Socco address was a postbox. He had an apartment in the European quarter, on Chemin des Amoureux. We hurried there and boarded the elevator to the fourth floor of a modern high-rise complex. Only one thing gave me pause. Though we had hidden the BMW, it wasn't so easy to hide our identity as a guileless straight couple.

A short, slim man with the accommodating manner of a butler answered the door. Then in his sixties, Bowles had short-cropped white hair and a faraway look in his eyes. Dressed in a tweed sport coat, a V-neck sweater and a bow tie, he called to mind a character from one of his gothic short stories, a meek lamb doomed to plunge through the bland surface of the world into the delirium beneath it. He might have been the linguistics professor in *A Distant Episode* who goes to the Sahara to study a nomadic tribe, gets kidnapped by them, has his tongue cut out and is kept as a clown for their amusement. Bowles had no qualms about inviting us in; it was as if we were wayfarers in the desert whose paths had randomly intersected his.

The living room smelled of wood smoke from the fireplace and, unmistakably, of *kif*. We sat on carpets, and a Moroccan brought in a tea tray, a silver pot and four glasses. A tape played in the background. Bowles explained that it was *Jilala* music, orchestrated to induce a trance.

The Moroccan poured the tea, then joined us on the floor. He had little to say. Bowles told us that he had translated the man's stories. Some reviewers accused him of inventing or greatly embellishing these narratives, but Bowles swore that he transcribed them with the same fidelity as he recorded tribal music.

When I asked about Jane, he said she had had to be institutionalized in Spain, in Malaga, where Catholic nuns cared for her. She had gone mad, perhaps from a spell cast by her Moroccan maid, perhaps from poison. Though he spoke with the dispassion of a physician, he added nothing that might be construed as a genuine medical diagnosis.

Presently a second Moroccan arrived. While the first man wore a djellaba, this one had on blue jeans and a black T-shirt with the sleeves rolled up over his sculpted biceps. Mohammed Mrabet was the best known of Bowles's literary protégés, and his books, *Love With a Few Hairs* and *Look and Move On*, had been published to wide acclaim in the States. Mrabet talked to Bowles and us, but didn't address a word to the Moroccan.

When Bowles broke out a stash of *kif*, Mrabet said, "He smokes too much. He's always getting high. This is not good for an old man."

Bowles ignored the remark. Pinching tobacco from a cigarette, he replaced it with *kif*.

"Dope doesn't appear to affect his writing," I defended Bowles against what seemed the insolence of a dummy against its ventriloquist.

"He is no longer the writer," Mrabet. "He only translates. I am the writer."

"You mean you tell him stories."

"Yes, and he types them."

"You're lucky to have such a good typist"

Mrabet laughed. "I am very lucky in life."

It was unclear how much the second Moroccan understood. He glared at Mrabet, who remained theatrically indifferent to him. This was a rare literary rivalry between illiterates.

Bowles lit the joint and passed it to Linda. She took a toke and handed it back. Ever the considerate host, he offered it to me. A lifelong nonsmoker, I knew from humiliating experience that the shallowest puff would cause me paroxysms of coughing. When I confessed this to Bowles, he brought me a spoon and a Wilkins coffee can brimming with what looked like coagulated motor oil.

"It's *majoun*," he said. "Hash candy. Have a taste. But be careful. It's strong."

I sampled a mouthful. It had the consistency of marzipan with an overlay of herbal grittiness that stuck to my teeth. I spooned up a second dollop, recalling too late the character in *Let It Come Down* who eats too much *majoun* and hammers a nail into an Arab's ear.

Between tokes, Bowles asked about the novel I was writing, and as I tried to summarize it, my tongue felt too large for my mouth. The flutes and drums of the *Jilala* sounded louder.

"I see," Bowles said, visualizing my book. "A man goes in search of his life and discovers his death."

That sounded like one of his novels, not mine. I meant to correct him, but another spoonful of *majoun* was in my mouth. Bowles's mention of death sparked a free association about disease and disaster, and he warned of numerous dangers we faced in Morocco.

"Do you have medical insurance?" he asked.

I wanted to assure him that we did. But my face was numb, and I couldn't be certain I had spoken.

"Carry your insurance card wherever you go," he said. "When you're in a car, leave it on the dashboard, where people can see it. Otherwise, if you have an accident and are knocked unconscious, doctors won't know whether they'll be paid and they're liable to leave you to die."

While the substance of what he said was urgent, his voice, because of the *kif*, came across as mild and uninflected. Bowles droned on and on: Moroccans weren't accustomed to traffic. In the city, they walked in the street. In the country, they stretched out for warmth on the road at night and slept. If we weren't careful, we'd kill somebody, and then his family and friends would attack us. At best, we'd have to pay a hefty bribe. At worst, we'd land in jail. His advice was to flee the accident scene to the nearest airport and catch the first flight out of Morocco.

"From your books," I said, "I didn't expect this. I expected you'd tell us to push close to the edge."

"I wouldn't suggest anybody, even my worst enemy, do that. Where are you staying in Tangier?" he asked, and when I told him, he was dismayed. "That's a terrible place. You should move to the Minzah Palace."

I had lost track of time. Even as I grew ravenously hungry, I wasn't conscious that night had fallen until Bowles cut short his cautionary tales and declared that he was sorry, he had to go to dinner.

Mrabet and the other man went to fetch Bowles's car from the garage. Linda, he and I followed minutes later. Aboard the elevator my head bounced around like a helium-filled balloon. Downstairs, we waited next to a fruit stall illuminated by kerosene lanterns. Moths had crawled inside the lantern globes, and as the magnified shadows of their beating wings fluttered over Linda's and Bowles's faces, I was pierced by emotion, part fear, part giddiness.

Then a 1964 Mustang convertible rolled up at the curb, and giddiness won out. The Moroccan in the djellaba was at the wheel. Mrabet sat in back. As Bowles slid into the passenger seat, I recognized that from the moment I arrived in Tangier, I had been wrong about everything—the town, the man, the writing profession, an author's persona. I regretted that I had hidden the BMW. Paul Bowles would have loved it.

In the following years, I often traveled to Morocco, but I didn't return to Tangier until 1997, when I came back with Linda and Marc. Bowles and I had corresponded over the decades, and so I made it a point to visit him. By then he was in his mid-eighties. Housebound and bedridden, he resembled a doll, a shrunken effigy in the city he had called a doll's metropolis. He had just been to the United States for surgery and vowed never to go again. "I wouldn't have left in the first place," he said, "if I liked it."

He would die here. That fact hovered behind every feeble breath he drew. The window had a tarpaulin tacked over it, leaving the room in permanent night. A bedlam of pill bottles, medicine vials, old Band-Aids and Breathe Right strips, tissues and cotton swabs littered the floor. After a lifetime of wandering, he had seen his world shrink to the circumference of his skull.

Yet he didn't appear unhappy. A boy of about twenty, a tumbler from the town of Tiznit, where all the best acrobats are born, took care of him, cooked broth for dinner and rolled joints to help him sleep. It was as if the youthful, musclebound Mohammed Mrabet had been reincarnated.

As I left, I said I'd be back, and he replied, "You know where to find me. I'll be here." But I doubted I'd come back or that Paul would be alive if I did.

Less than a year later, however, events conspired to bring me to Tangier, and I saw him again. Although it was a struggle for him to speak, we talked a bit about Algeria, which he remembered from the '40s. "Now they've nailed up a sign in place des Chameaux," Paul said. "*Chameaux Interdits.*" He chuckled. "Imagine that—camels forbidden in the Place of the Camels."

He knew that Morocco had changed too. "Every young person in the country wants to escape to Europe or the States. There's no money, no opportunity. The country is like a jail to them."

When I left his apartment for the last time, I walked around and couldn't deny that it was a different place from the one I had visited in 1972. Hell, it was different from the year before. As Baudelaire had written, "No human heart changes half so fast as the face of a city." Apartment buildings and office towers sprouted on boulevard Pasteur. Rumor had it that drug money fueled this construction spree. If so, the cash must have slowed to a dribble. Many of the buildings were half finished, and their steel girders bled rust like pitons left by mountain climbers.

In the souk, there were fax, photocopy and Internet facilities, and on the green tile roof of every salt-white house grew a jungle of TV antennas and satellite dishes. Barbara Hutton's villa, Sidi Hosni, had been subdivided into separate dwellings, and neighborhood kids no longer romped around the front gate, regaling tourists with tales about the heiress's six husbands. Barbara Hutton was dead, and her fortune and her gigolos had vanished.

Malcolm Forbes had died, too, a year after his seventieth birthday party, for which he had lavished $2.5 million on charter planes to fly in eight hundred of his closest friends, including Elizabeth Taylor, Henry Kissinger and Barbara Walters. He entertained them with six hundred drummers and three hundred Berber horsemen. Now his mansion, Palais Mendoub, housed the Museum of Military Miniatures, the financier's collection of toy soldiers. The one oddity missing from this Xanadu was a child's sled labeled ROSEBUD.

I headed for the Continental, established in 1888, formerly the most fashionable hotel in Tangier. A nearby perfume store advertised in English, "Patronised by Film Stars and the International Jet Set." But I noticed no Beautiful People there or on the Continental's terrace overlooking the oil slicks of the new port and the massed trucks and containers waiting to be ferried across to Spain. The concierge was a gabby, good-natured guy who had memorized the area code of every American town. He had no interest in local history, however, and wouldn't speculate what had changed Sin City into a shabby jumping-off spot for emigrants desperate to get to Europe. Maybe, I decided, sin had gone global, and wicked amusement no longer required relocation to Tangier.

When Paul Bowles died, in 1999, John Hopkins, the author of *Tangier Buzzless Flies*, phoned to tell me, "The last literary light in Tangier has been snuffed out." His apartment had been sealed and the locks changed because, as John cited the adage, "Nothing attracts robbers like a corpse. Paul asked to be cremated and that's impossible in Morocco. He'll be buried in the United States."

It struck me as wrong that nothing of Bowles would remain in Morocco. But then he had described the typical character in his novels as somebody who "slips through life, if possible, without touching anything, without touching other people." He maintained that he led his own life in that manner. "If you discover you're affecting other people, you have to stop."

Now at the end of my North African trip, as I returned to Tangier, it looked less scruffy and more affluent than it had in years.

The buildings on boulevard Pasteur had been completed, and the former doll's metropolis sprawled for miles, its population having tripled to a million. No longer the *kif*-comatose town of the '60s or the dilapidated dying burg of the '90s, it had supermarkets surrounded by parking lots full of cars with European plates. On the gentrified Grand Socco, the Cinema Rif, a relic of the '30s, had re-opened as the Tangier Cinemathèque, a film society presenting classic and independent releases. Billboards blazed with ads for high-end real estate—Résidence du Parc, Santa Clara, Eden Island—and there was a golf course and a cricket club. But occasionally the new and old overlapped in ways that produced cognitive dissonance, when not downright queasiness, as with the hip restaurant Passagers de Tangier, which shared an entrance with an infirmary specializing in circumcisions.

If the town from certain angles appeared unrecognizable, I suppose Linda and I did, too, compared to the twenty-somethings in bell-bottoms who had cruised around Tangier. Our accommodations were also different from the scurvy pensions we had crashed in back then. A friend, Tessa Codrington, loaned us her family home on the Mountain, a pine- and eucalyptus-canopied neighborhood of diplomatic villas, private estates and royal palaces.

Constructed early in the last century by Tessa's grandfather, the home, Dar Sinclair, combined *mauresque* architecture with the comforts of an English country house. The whitewashed walls, keyhole arches and minaret-like towers suggested a mosque. But pillows, throw rugs and overstuffed furniture softened the austere lines and dampened the clatter of our shoes on the terra cotta floors. Watercolors and samples of Tessa's photographs alternated with picture windows that framed the reality that the paintings and photos beautifully replicated.

From the house, a lawn sloped like a fairway toward a pond where papyrus plants jutted up as stiff as quivered arrows. From there a staircase went down through semi-tropical gardens to a cabana and swimming pool. At the lip of the pool, I had crouched to test the water temperature when something huge and hairy and shrieking hurtled past my head.

It was a pet Barbary ape chained to a tree. Bungee-jumping from a high branch, the ape boomeranged back onto its perch, mugging and chattering, mocking me. For a moment my heart pumped pure adrenaline, then for the rest of the week I found myself flinching, afraid of another kamikaze attack.

After the months I had spent in cramped hotel rooms, the space at Dar Sinclair, the telescopic views from its windows, induced something like agoraphobia. North Africa's poverty and political strife seemed far away. Yet they were out there, hidden in the shadows like the Barbary ape.

Then suddenly they burst onto the front page of *Le Journal de Tanger*. Police arrested fifteen terrorists. Members of a local cell associated with Al Qaeda, they were accused of planning suicide attacks on tourists. As usual, terror, even when thwarted, terror, even when dormant, set the tone, the discordant background acoustics for my trip.

Abdellatif, the caretaker at Dar Sinclair, hailed from Erfoud, a village on the threshold of the Sahara, and he and his extended family lived in quarters behind the main house. He spoke neither French nor Spanish but had learned English from Tessa Codrington's guests. He owned a car and was a dependable driver and a pleasant companion—as long as you overlooked his eerie resemblance to O.J. Simpson. When I told him I wanted to visit the refugee camp at Ceuta, he said he had a friend there who might be of help.

Like Melilla, farther east on the Mediterranean, Ceuta was a colonial anachronism and geopolitical anomaly. If it corresponded to anything, it was to Gibraltar, a shard of Great Britain embedded in the coast of Spain.

Interestingly, Spain accused the U.K. of violating its territorial integrity and demanded that the British give up "The Rock." But it refused to forfeit its enclaves in Morocco. In addition to diplomatic difficulties, this had caused grave humanitarian problems as refugees from Africa and as far away as India swarmed in to claim asylum from the European Union. While the refugees waited, sometimes for years, for their cases to be adjudicated, they were stuck in camps.

The shortest route to Ceuta was via a highway to Tetuan, then a secondary road to the coast. But I wanted to travel the whole way along the sea, and Abdellatif indulged me. The corniche curved out of Tangier past beaches and cafés that normally bustled in September but were empty because of Ramadan. Fasting Muslims didn't have the energy to swim and play soccer and volleyball. "Plus, they can't smoke," Abdellatif explained. "So they sleep all day since without tobacco they're nervous and in a bad mood."

People who could afford it, including great numbers of the expatriate community, flew off to Europe to escape Ramadan. With so many restaurants and nightclubs shut and the servants snoozing during the day, Morocco in this month was no place for the leisure class. According to a social worker I met, even the prostitutes in Tangier closed shop.

Beyond the casino and the aqua park, the tourist gimcrackery ended on Cap Malabata, and we tunneled through a cool pine forest. The scent of lemons and lavender rifled into the car on a stiff breeze. Signs warned of strong winds and *brouillard fréquent*—frequent fog. One gust tore the cap from Abdellatif's head, and Linda caught it before it could blow out the window.

Then we rounded a bend and confronted what appeared to be a cataclysm of Biblical proportions. The ground had been skinned of vegetation, and the underlying red clay had crusted over like a scab. Enormous mountains were flattened, and the rock and soil from them formed jetties whose giant arms thrust out into the Mediterranean, making a new port for Morocco and Africa. Once the harbor was finished, ships would ferry containers and railroad cars over from Europe, transfer them to trains and send them rumbling south. That was the future. The present seethed with dust and thundered with earthmovers. Davits soared ten stories tall like the gaunt spires of Gothic cathedrals.

Away from the coast, we climbed into headlands, where clouds loomed behind the hills like a second, higher range. In the opposite direction, across the Strait of Gibraltar, hunched the brown horizon of Spain. It looked tantalizingly close, near enough to swim to. The sea seemed calm, with birds suspended above it on thermal currents. But one glance at the maritime traffic revealed a titanic struggle against the tide. It was a miracle that refugees managed to cross in rubber dinghies.

At 4 PM Spanish time, we arrived at Ceuta, where the clocks hadn't been reset earlier, as they had in Morocco for Ramadan. Rush hour was brewing, and cars, trucks and exhausted humans jammed the border—not as bad as in Libya, but awful enough to cause flashbacks. Flustered as I filled out the visa form, I stupidly printed WRITER as my occupation, and this provoked a guard to demand what kind of writer I am.

What could I say? A minor one? Midlist? Realist? Since journalists were radioactive, I stressed that I wrote novels, and the guard broke into a smile and let me through. He showed no interest at all in people headed into Morocco hauling contraband.

Forty years ago, Ceuta had been a sleepy Andalusian village, with tapas bars, an evening *paseo* and a pervasive aroma of Maja soap. Now it was a twenty-square-kilometer shopping mall, thick with tax dodgers, duty-free shoppers and smugglers.

Despite insisting on its Spanish identity, this garrison town had a Moorish flavor. Berbers from the Rif made up 30 percent of the population, and they lived on generally peaceful terms with the Catholic majority. Even in 2006, after rampaging Spanish youths protested terrorism by torching mosques in Ceuta, Muslims remained quiescent, recognizing that under the EU umbrella they enjoyed a far higher standard of living than they would in Morocco.

Osama bin Laden's second in command, Ayman al Zawahiri, had called on Believers to expel the infidels from North Africa. But far from lancing Ceuta and Melilla like pustules of Christianity, immigrants from all over the Islamic world risked their lives to get into these havens. In 2005, a thousand of them rushed the razor-wire fence around Melilla. In the melee, Moroccan soldiers shot and killed several refugees, arrested more than five hundred and trucked them to the Sahara where they were left to fend for themselves.

In Ceuta, when I asked about the refugee camp, people clammed up. Shiny-hatted Guardia Civil glowered at the mention of immigrants and claimed ignorance of the camp's existence, much less its location. Abdellatif suggested that we save ourselves trouble and find his friend.

He vaguely remembered where Mohammed lived and by Zen he navigated the labyrinth of duty-free shops and vacation villas into some scrubby hills. At a pink cinder block house he knocked on the door, drumming up an echo on the emptiness inside. "Maybe he's at his sister's place," Abdellatif said.

We drove higher, to a cluster of jerry-built homes. Teenagers on all-terrain vehicles tested their skills on the driveway, while a little kid with a trail bike did wheelies on a flat rooftop. Abdellatif fetched a tall robust fellow, who wore gold chains and a sleeveless leather vest that showed off his ropy arms. Mohammed spoke Spanish and resembled a flamenco dancer, with a pencil-thin beard, like black sutures, from his sideburns to the tip of his chin. He took the wheel from Abdellatif and roared off, scattering the ATV riders.

Mohammed had served in the Spanish army, and swore that as a "Mussleman," he had always been treated as a first-class citizen. "If you treat people with respect," he declared, "you get respect. That's what I told my son when he moved to Granada to be with his fiancée."

We free-wheeled down to a beach of grey sand where white girls in bikinis lounged under thatched umbrellas while fully clothed black men hunkered nearby, eyeballing them. "Immigrants," Mohammed said. "Hindus, Pakistanis, Somalis, not just Musslemen." His use of the Spanish term for Muslim called attention to his own physique; he was a muscleman Mussleman.

From the beach we bore uphill through a eucalyptus forest whose leaves patterned the road with paisley light. We might have been back on the mountain in Tangier. But there were no royal palaces, no swimming pools or flashy sports cars. After a mile I spotted a fence topped with razor wire and a grid of dormitories that reminded me of the Chinese labor camp in Oran.

Mohammed paused at the front gate and kept the motor running. He said he couldn't park here. He'd have to meet us at the bottom of the hill. As he and Abdellatif sped off, Linda and I approached a gatehouse that had a CITI seal, the acronym of the Temporary International Center for Immigrants.

It didn't look temporary. It looked long lived-in and hard used. But it was less desolate and restrictive than the Chinese camp. Trees helped soften the compound, and people lounged outside of the dorms fiddling with cell phones and iPods. They were free to go as they pleased. A group of black women poured through the gate as Linda and I asked to get in.

A guard told us we needed government permission. And for that, we'd have to file an application with the proper authorities. He estimated the process would take a week. "But if you want to talk to people, you can speak to them outside the camp."

A young black woman with blond streaks in her hair and tribal tattoos like arrow fletches on her cheeks walked a toddler through the gate. The guard handed a chocolate bar to the baby and fluffed her cornrows.

The woman, a Nigerian, spoke English, and when I said I'd be grateful if she'd answer a few questions, she said, "I'd be grateful for some money." I gave her $5, and she recounted her story, which was, in effect, the story of hundreds of thousands of refugees across North Africa.

Her name was Pat. Her father was dead. Her mother, back in Nigeria, was sick. Her baby's father had disappeared. Anxious to earn money, Pat had traveled north through Mali, into Algeria and finally to Tangier. She had spent years there, begging, working odd jobs and scrabbling for a way to Europe. Once she had saved three hundred euros, she paid a human trafficker to smuggle her in an inflatable boat to Ceuta. "I have been in the camp for a year," she said, "praying some country will let me in. I want to work, but there are no jobs and I'm not allowed to work in Ceuta."

Her cell phone rang, and when she answered it, her toddler wandered off. As Pat chased after her, another woman, paler, badly scarred and brassy-haired, took her place and without any prompting told her story.

She came from Somalia and was a Christian, though her grandfather had been a Muslim. She had hitchhiked for years on trucks through the Sudan, Chad, Mali, Algeria and Morocco. She couldn't afford to pay a human trafficker. She had had just enough money to buy a life jacket and swim to Ceuta.

"I have a lot of trouble," she said, "and no money. I have been hurt badly in my mouth and on my body." She gestured to the deep notches on her lips, and the puckered keloid on her chest that might have been from a bullet wound. Her left arm looked as if it had been amputated at the shoulder and crudely reattached. Yet after calling attention to her scars, she turned shy and hesitated to tell me her name. Finally she whispered, "Frances," then said, "There are three hundred refugees at this camp. They separate the blacks from the Indians and Pakistanis, and they separate the Algerians from everybody because they're troublemakers. Otherwise, it's not bad. They feed us and keep us safe. But I don't know what will happen to me."

Though she hadn't asked for it, I gave her money, too. She thanked me, put up an umbrella to protect her scars from the sun and walked down the road toward town. After a minute, Linda and I followed her and joined Mohammed and Abdellatif at the car.

"Did you get what you wanted?" Mohammed asked.

I told him I had, although at the moment I couldn't have said what that was. And except for a few bucks, what had the refugees gotten from my drop-by?

Women strolled past the car, some wearing *hijabs*, some in bright robes with swaddled children on their backs.

"It's a pity," Mohammed said. "There's nothing for them to do in Ceuta. In Europe at least they could be prostitutes. Here they can't even do that, or they get kicked out of the camp."

I asked Abdellatif to return to Tangier via Tetuan for a single reason. The previous autumn *The New York Times* had published an article about a Tetuan neighborhood named Jemaa Mezuak. The author maintained that "in the study of contemporary terrorism, there has never been a laboratory quite like [it]." In 2004, five local men had bombed commuter trains in Madrid, killing 191 and injuring 1,800. Then, in 2006, eight more young men from Jemaa Mezuak joined the *jihad* in Iraq.

In a sense, the *Times* article was a predecessor to the April 2008 *Newsweek* report about the Libyan town of Darnah, which had also produced an extraordinary number of *jihadis*. Like epidemiologists tracking the spread of a virus, political analysts were eager to discover the causes, common denominators and cures for these lethal clusters. They assumed that the lessons learned could be applied elsewhere in the Islamic world, stamping out terrorism before it started.

We had as much difficulty finding Jemaa Mezuak as we had had locating the refugee camp in Ceuta. Not that anybody denied its existence or showed suspicion at my interest. The trouble was that a constellation of Jemaa Mezuaks surrounded Tetuan, just as identical slums and *bidonvilles* surrounded cities throughout North Africa. Even with precise directions, it was hard to distinguish one poor, hardscrabble neighborhood from the next.

People must have settled here first for the water. A murky river trickled through Jemaa Mezuak. Then a mosque had been built, and tin shacks cropped up around it, followed by improvised multistoried apartments. Finally, a few shops opened and cafés that advertised coffee with the ominous brand name Carrion.

The mayor of Tetuan told the *New York Times* that Jemaa Mezuak had a population of six thousand. Others estimated forty thousand. In the end, it hardly mattered: No one intended to do anything about the overcrowding, the lack of sanitation, the unemployment and the petty crime. No one except for radical Islamic groups that distributed food and medicine and Koranic indoctrination. Inevitably a few susceptible young men became convinced that reform was futile and that violence was the answer. To quote the last will and testament of one of the Madrid train bombers who had committed suicide rather than be captured: "Many people take life as a path to death. I have chosen death as a path to life. You should hold onto Islam, through words and deeds, action and *jihad*."

As we bumped over the mud streets of Jemaa Mezuak, dodging animals and naked kids, garbage heaps and wrecked cars, I couldn't quarrel with the *Times* or with the experts who viewed the place as a laboratory and conjectured that terrorists were radicalized as much by personal disappointments and thwarted passions as by their religious beliefs. As one anthropologist put it, "Terrorists don't just die for a cause. They die for each other."

But even granting that, after so many fact-gathering missions and think-tank conferences, what was the point in studying Jemaa Mezuak unless this prompted solutions? Which policies, which sources of funding, how many international NGOs had been brought to bear on it and communities like it? Who would persuade Mohammed VI, Bouteflika, Ben Ali, Qaddafi and Mubarak, not to mention politicians in the United States and Europe, that they were not going to end terrorism any more than they were going to stop people from rushing the razor wire at Ceuta unless or until they provided these shantytown residents with more attractive alternatives.

Woebegone after the refugee camp and now Jemaa Mezuak, I felt like that character in John Cheever's short story "The Swimmer." Where he set himself the task of paddling through backyard pools all across suburban Westchester County, I seemed to have crossed North Africa from souk to souk, slum to slum. While I had seen a lot of beauty along the way, at the moment the misery weighed heavily on me.

On the return to Tangier, the wind blew, and the car shook and Abdellatif had to hold the wheel tight with two hands. The roadside was aflood with foot traffic. Men's djellabas inflated like the Michelin logo, and women's *hijabs* unfurled from their heads. Onion sellers cowered in flimsy *zeribas*, clinging to the reed huts to keep them from flying to pieces.

Hungry and eager to get home in time for *iftar*, Abdellatif wanted to speed, but couldn't. Every few miles policemen stepped out from behind palm trees and aimed speed guns at the traffic. We reached Tangier as the *muezzin* cried, and when we pulled into the driveway at Dar Sinclair, Abdellatif's wife was already carrying bowls of *harira* to the table in the courtyard.

Tessa Codrington's daughter Sarah also owned a house on the mountain, and she invited Linda and me to dinner. Christopher Gibbs, an English designer and antiques dealer, dropped by for drinks, and when he heard that we had been to the camp at Ceuta, he said we needn't have gone that far to meet refugees. He was a longtime parishioner at St. Andrew's Anglican church, which had a community of sub-Saharan migrants in its congregation, and he invited me to attend services on Sunday.

Another guest, a young South African woman in her thirties, described her traumatic marriage to a Moroccan. In a dry, neutral voice, sparing neither herself nor her in-laws, she said she had fallen in love with a man, really no more than a boy, who hired her for English lessons. An Islamic wedding was out of the question. So they married in a civil ceremony, then committed a fatal error and moved in with his family.

The man warned her that his mother objected to their relationship and might try to poison her. But he was less vigilant about himself. He ate his mother's food and gradually sickened. The poison ravaged his brain, and his mother had him institutionalized. As a non-Moroccan, his wife had no say in the matter. Now even visiting him was pointless since he no longer recognized her.

The story reminded me of Paul Bowles's macabre narratives. It was a variant on his own marriage and Jane's rumored poisoning. Gibbs, who had been friends with the Bowleses, agreed, and this prompted a discussion of the tales that street kids had told Bowles. Gibbs mentioned in passing that all of "Bowles's boys" were now dead except for Mohammed Mrabet.

"Is he still in Tangier?" I asked.

"I imagine so. Mrabet's become a successful artist. But they say he's quite bitter about Paul."

"Why?"

"You'd have to ask him."

"Do you know how to contact him?"

"Afraid not. But surely Abdellatif does."

As always, Abdellatif was ready to help. He drove us to Sawane, a *quartier* of drab shops and nondescript apartments where, by some mysterious Moroccan paradox, people had a vividness and exuberance that couldn't have been improved upon by a cinematographer. In the States and Europe, pedestrians often look like a parade of thumbs without identifying prints. But here every face possessed a striking individuality, and whether handsome or hideous, it revealed on the outside what Westerners kept hidden.

Abdellatif had been to Mrabet's apartment before, but he soon lost his way. Like a living organism, Sawane had grown and changed shape. We parked the car near a construction site and vaulted over gullies and sand pits to ask directions at a shoe shop. The cobbler's son guided us up a concrete incline to a door reinforced by tin. I knocked, and almost at once a man with a grizzled goatee and black, short-cropped hair opened up. Lost in an XXL T-shirt, his emaciated body appeared to be shrink-wrapped in crepey skin. I thought he was the concierge, a sick old man with the make-work job. But it was Mohammed Mrabet, now seventy-two and convalescing after an illness that had nearly killed him.

He was delighted to welcome us into his home. Not that he recognized Linda or me. Not that he remembered meeting us years ago. He was simply happy to have visitors—admirers, as he probably regarded us. He shuffled to the second floor, stopped on a landing to step out of his slippers and waited for us to remove our shoes. Then we entered an Oriental gazebo of wooden latticework in a corner of the living room. Abdellatif had the good sense to prop himself against the wall. Linda and I sat on the floor facing Mrabet. Immediately my lower back seized up.

Samples of Mrabet's art papered the walls and spilled out of cardboard portfolios. Sketches in India ink and drawings done with felt-tip pens showed the same obsessive motifs—the Hand of Fatma with an eye in the palm, intertwined snakes and phalluses, monstrous chimeras of mixed animal parts. Mrabet took as much pride in a monograph about his work as he did in the art. It didn't bother him that a critic characterized his palette as "ghastly greens, brash blues, outlandish oranges, putrid purples and torrid turquoises."

Mrabet passed along several catalogues, one of which listed his exhibitions and his sales to celebrity clients: Peggy Guggenheim, Tennessee Williams and Mick Jagger. A recently published album of appreciation made the case that Mrabet's stature as a literary figure was secure, but that it would eventually be rivaled by his reputation as an artist. The title of the book, *Without Bowles, the Genius of Mohammed M'Rabet*, had a tone of pugnacious self-promotion that I remembered from the cocky kid off the streets who proclaimed himself the author and Paul Bowles merely his translator. Back then I had dismissed this bragging as that of a dummy rebelling against its ventriloquist. Now I was more sympathetic, and understood his pathos as a relic of the colonial period.

Talking to Mrabet was as close as I or anyone else would ever come to an intimate eyewitness account of the power imbalance between foreigners and *indigènes*, the peculiar sexual politics that had pervaded North Africa. It was as though I was speaking to one of Cavafy's rent boys or to Forster's much beloved streetcar conductor or to Flaubert's Egyptian dancers and depilated whores.

Mrabet told us he had four children—two girls and two boys, all married and with children of their own. He was a grandfather seven times over. But he was more interested in discussing his career, past and present, and his grievances. He believed that he had never gotten the money and recognition he deserved. His resentment was deepened by a conviction that he had been exploited by people who pretended to help him.

"Paul did many bad things to me," he said. "When his friends visited Tangier, he warned them to be careful of me. 'He's very dangerous,' Paul told them. And here I cooked for him and cleaned for him and shopped for his dinner parties. I was his bodyguard. I saved his life four or five times. Americans tried to take money from him and I hit them." Mrabet smacked his skinny fist into his palm. "Hippies came into his house, and I put them out. He let everyone in."

"Yes, he even let Linda and me in," I said, trying to lighten things up. "Didn't Paul pay you for the work you did?"

"He gave me $300 a month. I was married and had kids, and I had no money, no job. So I thought $300 was *magnifique*. I also occupied myself a lot with Jane. I knew her first and told her stories, and she told Paul and he said we could make them into books."

"Tell how you went about that."

"He gave me a tape recorder, and the first day I recorded twelve stories. Then I did the translation with Paul. He claimed in interviews that he translated from Arabic or Berber. But he lived here fifty years and never learned our languages. I said my stories in Spanish. He spoke good Spanish, and each story I finished was published someplace in America. I published about thirty stories in the U.S. Then I did *Love With a Few Hairs*. Then I finished *The Lemon*, and Paul began typing and translating them.

"I was young," Mrabet went on. "I didn't understand contracts and money. I couldn't read. I got an advance, but as they published new editions, I got nothing. I had a magnificent success in the U.S. A first edition of *Love With a Few Hairs* is worth $1,000 now. But after the advance I got no more money."

"You didn't receive royalties?"

"All the royalties went to Paul. All the money went straight into his account. A big Mafia," Mrabet harrumphed. "I just saw a review of a book I did fifteen years ago. It's still in paperback. But I've gotten nothing."

He stretched a hand to one of the portfolios and pulled out a photograph of himself at the age of thirty, at the height of his physical power. In a swimsuit, knee-deep in the Mediterranean, backlit by the sun, his body gleamed.

"It was always the same with Paul. When he met someone young and strong and handsome, he fell in love and began making stories about him. That's why he told people I was dangerous. It was a story."

"What about Jane?" I asked.

"She was a fantastic person. A woman with a great heart. She asked me to take care of Paul. But she never loved him. I don't think Paul loved her. He detested women. He only loved men. He only liked to make love to men. He didn't even like himself. I saw him look in a mirror and spit at his image. He was at the top of his success. He had money and fame, and he spit at his own face."

Strident as his words were, Mrabet lounged on the carpet with no visible strain. His hands lay palms up on his lap, in a Buddha-like pose. In this attitude and at this time of his life, he looked far from menacing. But I remembered expats in Tangier who regarded him as a threatening figure, a man handy with his fists and given to brandishing a knife.

I asked about the rumor that Jane's maid had poisoned her, and Mrabet emerged from his meditative pose and exclaimed in English, "Puh-leeze, puh-leeze, please." Then he reverted to French. "This is a myth. William Burroughs, you know, shot his wife. That's one technique of killing a woman. Paul finished off his wife with lots of drugs, lots of medicine. He gave her six or seven medicines a day."

I slid over next to Abdellatif against the wall. That eased the pain in my lower back but not my distress at Mrabet's fury, his scattershot aggression, the rage of the dispossessed against real or imagined betrayals.

From an early age he had had run-ins with authority figures who left him feeling violated. He claimed he was punished on his first day of school because he couldn't read French. He knocked down the teacher and jumped out a window, putting an emphatic end to his formal education. At the age of fifteen, he beat up a soldier who was abusing a Riffian. Afraid of being arrested, he hid for months in a cave at Cap Spartel.

For many a Moroccan street kid of his generation, sex was a quick way to make money, a way of escape. As another of Bowles's protégés, Mohammed Choukri, wrote in *For Bread Alone*, foreigners "suck it for five minutes and they pay you fifty pesetas." But this

added shame to their anger, and a bitter conviction that the Moroccans were the ones being hustled and exploited.

Mrabet said, "Paul, Burroughs, Gyson and Capote, they were a
big Mafia in Tangier. They drank a lot, they did a lot of hash and ate
a lot of *majoun*. They came here because life was cheap. It cost them
nothing to live. And there were thousands of young boys."

Incessantly he circled back to his complaint that Bowles had
cheated him and misrepresented his writing, grabbing more credit
than he deserved and stealing from him: "At the end of his life, I left
a story with Paul, and he published it under his own name. Some of
my stories were published in his books and collections. Then after
he died, I was supposed to get the contents of his house. It was in
his will. But when I went to Paul's apartment, the locks had been
changed, and I got nothing. Absolutely nothing. I don't say this just
to you. I've talked on radio and TV about this."

He accused an American, a longtime expatriate in Tangier, of
having ripped out of Bowles's will those pages that benefited Mrabet.
I had known the man, now dead and unable to defend himself, and
I challenged Mrabet to explain why he believed the American would
cheat him.

"He never liked me," he said. "Why? Because he wanted to
make love to me, and I hit him hard."

Around the time Bowles died, Mrabet fell ill too. "My head was
spinning. I couldn't breathe. I couldn't see. I fell down in the street.
The doctor gave me a lot of medicine. I wasn't in a hospital. I recovered here at home with the help of God. Now I have no stomach.
I can't eat." He made as if to lift his T-shirt and show his scar but
thought better of that.

"Then I decided I could still live. I could still do my art. I could do my books without Paul. I have many European friends." He had an appointment that evening with a Frenchman who was translating a collection of his stories. He wanted me to know he had no shortage of material and inspiration.

"Now it's better here," Mrabet said. "The things that used to exist in Tangier have changed. Now there are different things. In the streets you see more women. Women are the better thing, the best thing, for a man. A beautiful woman, one for you for all your life."

As we were leaving, I apologized that I couldn't buy one of his paintings. They were too big to carry. He presented me a book instead, and I accepted it with gratitude. But he expected something more than gratitude. "Fifty dollars."

As he walked us down to the front door, he said, "I hope to see you again." He grinned, and behind the goatish, salt-and-pepper whiskers, I saw the guileful young street hustler he used to be. "Come visit me every thirty years."

"You'll be a hundred and two."

He laughed. "My mother just died. She was a hundred and three."

"It's a date then," I said. "I'll be back when I'm ninety-five."

The September weather turned cool, and the light changed. The view from Dar Sinclair went from a pastel watercolor to a vibrant Fauvist canvas. In the morning, drinking the freshly squeezed juice of oranges from the garden, we gazed thirty or forty miles, across the bay of Tangier and down the coast to Djebel

Moussa. In a few months, the highest mountain in the Rif would be snow-covered.

On Sunday we attended services at St. Andrew's, which any art lover would recognize. From his room at the Grand Hotel Villa de France, Henri Matisse had peered out the window in 1912 and painted *Paysage Vu d'une Fenêtre*, a study of the casbah with St. Andrew's and its bell tower in the foreground. Back then the church was a symbol of England's earthly power as much as a place of worship, and Moroccans resented its bulldog arrogance. According to local lore, they built the Grand Mosque to overshadow the church.

A vegetable market crowded the sidewalk around the entrance, and Linda and I had to step over piles of tomatoes and prickly pears. The Lord's Prayer was chiseled in Arabic on the chancel arch. Black Africans outnumbered the whites by three to one, and not a single white parishoner, including the priest, looked to be less than retirement age. Black men were in their Sunday best; mothers in flamboyant robes had babies strapped to their backs and they all sang in cadences that transformed familiar English hymns into African chants.

Christopher Gibbs delivered the first reading in a plummy Oxbridge accent. Then an American woman, a hippie holdover from the '60s, did the second reading. She wore a silver necklace as broad as a breastplate and a pair of slacks appliquéd with macramé.

The church custodian, a Moroccan in a pink ball cap, bustled about, making sure everybody had a songbook. During the Consecration when a cell phone tore a seam in the silence, he stared ferociously at the offender until the ring tone was strangled.

At Communion, whites processed to the altar to receive the sacrament. For an instant, I felt sick to my stomach and feared that St. Andrew's was segregated. But it turned out that the blacks weren't Anglicans: They attended Mass because it was the only Protestant service available to them. The priest invited those who hadn't received Communion to come forward for a blessing, and the blacks advanced and bowed their heads, and the priest made the sign of the cross over each of them. Sooner or later, most would risk the passage to Europe, the salvation they could see every day across the strait, and the priest urged us to pray for their safety through the miracle of God's grace.

After Mass, I wanted to speak to Gibbs, but I was intercepted by a nattily dressed Brit in a polo shirt and a yachtsman's cap. "New to town?" he asked.

"Just traveling through."

"We always hope for new parishioners."

"Actually I'm Catholic," I said. "I just came to see the church."

"You're welcome anyway. We can't afford to be choosy. First time in Morocco?"

I told him I'd been here many times, but this trip had been my first to the Rif and Saïdia.

"They say it's terrible. The ecological damage."

I agreed that it was disheartening.

"It's all so corrupt," he said. "They've made a right mess of Saïdia, I suppose, like they do most things." Now retired, he had been a businessman in Tangier. "We handed out a lot of hundred-dirham bribes to low-level officials. People said, 'You should go over their heads.' But that would have meant paying bigger bribes—a thousand dirhams—and getting no guarantee."

"I guess you've seen a lot of changes."

"Yes, it's terrible. Have you been to Marrakech? It's unconscionable what's happened. Here it's worse. They've ruined the city."

"Why do you stay?"

"Oh, one has one's routine, one's friends and hobbies. The same as anywhere. And there *is* the church."

He handed me his card and told me to call the next time I was in town. Then he shivered. "The season's changing. I'm off to Marrakech for the winter."

I caught up to Gibbs, and he offered Linda and me a lift back to the mountain. The morning market had packed up. On the sidewalk lettuce leaves and sunflower seeds crunched underfoot. Normally Sunday was a workday, but during Ramadan the stalls folded early and the streets had a Sabbath hush.

In the car, I told Gibbs about Mohammed Mrabet's angry accusations, and he cautioned me, "Remember, he's a storyteller. A fabulist." He doubted Mrabet had been defrauded of his inheritance by the American expat but added, "It isn't entirely impossible. There might have been bad blood based on sex. I wouldn't have thought he'd hold a grudge."

"Mrabet wouldn't?" I asked.

No, Gibbs meant the American.

As for Bowles's killing Jane by overmedicating her, Gibbs declared, "That's nonsense." But again he added a qualification. "On the other hand, Paul may have hastened her death by his inability to give her the love she wanted and needed. He could be cold and aloof. He wasn't the type to offer tenderness."

Gibbs stressed he had always liked Bowles and considered him a good friend. But he was candid about him, just as he was about

Jane. "Jane was a handful. She was strong meat." He described a scene she had thrown at the old Parade Bar, an establishment renowned for its tolerance of eccentricity—a tolerance that Jane at her worst had exceeded.

"Mrabet was also upset," I said, "that Bowles told friends that he was a dangerous man."

"Danger was what Paul liked," Christopher said. "It's what he tended to see around him. Morocco, by and large, is a very peaceful place. But if you mess the Moroccans over, of course they can push back. Then you get danger. But again that's what Paul liked. It was his picture of the place, and it said more about him than about Morocco."

Yes, I thought, each of us has his picture and it reveals more about us than the place.

Late that afternoon, Abdellatif drove Linda and me on a winding road between high stone walls, over the mountain toward Cape Spartel. We passed the King's Palace and lavish properties that belonged to Saudi and Kuwaiti royalty. The area roiled with armed security guards, but it wasn't off-limits, and people gathered here during Ramadan to ramble in the pine forests, killing time till the day's fast ended. Remarkably, some of them jogged, sweating and straining. It was, Abdellatif explained, an extra penance—exercise on an empty stomach in preparation for *iftar*.

We sped west, directly into the sun, as if into the fiery mouth of a cave. Then we swung east and climbed again into a forest where boys ran from the trees to sell bags of pine nuts. Ahead, a flat-topped butte, a miniature of Cape Mountain thousands of miles away in South Africa, beckoned us on.

The road ended at Cap Spartel. The Mediterranean ended here, too, as did my trip. Having started in early spring, I was finishing in the first flush of autumn. The heat and harsh sun had faded, and as Linda and I sat on the sea wall, it was Magic Time, that hour of day, TV producers will tell you, when everyone and everything appears radiant, perfect.

Behind us crouched the immensity of the continent. In front of us, the Cap Spartel lighthouse rose like an exclamation point. Beyond it, the Atlantic Ocean and the Mediterranean collided in whirlpools and white-capped currents. Across the strait, the mauve shoulders of Spain barely showed through the wave-mist around Tarifa.

I should have felt satisfied, at peace. But I was nagged by that stretch of Libyan coast between the Egyptian border and Tripoli that I had flown over. Much as I fought against regret, I couldn't help thinking that I needed to fulfill the letter of the overland project. I needed to return and cover by car or bus that final piece of North Africa. It would take time and tedious arrangements, but I could apply for another Libyan visa, go to Tripoli and backtrack to Egypt.

Then it came to me that this was nonsense. Rather than pant after some childish notion of completion, some psychobabble concept of closure, I should let it be. That part of Libya would always be there, the perfect excuse for a future trip. Now was the moment to quit moving and to reflect on what I had seen and done, and on what Linda and I would do once the light faded and we could no longer tell the difference between a white thread and a black.

INDEX

ABOUT THE AUTHOR

© Linda Mewshaw

Michael Mewshaw is the author of eleven critically acclaimed novels. In addition, hundreds of his articles and reviews have appeared in *The New York Times*, the *Los Angeles Times*, *The Washington Post*, and in newspapers and magazines around the world. His travel essays were collected in *Playing Away*. He and his wife, Linda, spend the winter in Key West, Florida, and the rest of the year traveling.